# THE BONE NEST

SHANESSA GLUHM

The Bone Nest
By Shanessa Gluhm
Published by Lost Meridian Press



ISBN HARDCOVER: 978-8-9930440-0-2

ISBN PAPERBACK: 979-8-218-75767-0



Address permissions and review inquiries to author@shanessagluhm.com

Cover Design: Aleksandra Mandic

Connect with the author at www.shanessagluhm.com

First Edition

Printed in the United States of America.

# PRAISE FOR SHANESSA GLUHM

"In *A River of Crows*, Shanessa Gluhm spins a complex web of murder and family revelation that propels the reader forward at a breakneck pace. Just when you think you know where the story is headed, she reveals another thread. If you haven't yet read Shanessa Gluhm, you need to put her on your to-be-read list."

—Allen Eskens, *USA Today* bestselling author of *The Life We Bury*

"*Enemies of Doves* is a multiple-timeline murder mystery that at its core, is a gut-wrenching love story and quest for family. Fans of suspense, mystery, and star-crossed love stories alike will not be able to put down this page-turner packed with unforeseen twists and turns."

—Rob Samborn, Author of *The Prisoner of Paradise*
and *Painter of the Damned*

"A twisted family dynamic and complex personal history combine with a touch of romance in Shanessa Gluhm's knockout second novel. *A River of Crows* grabs on with the opening pages and holds a reader tight to the very end."

—Elena Taylor/Elena Hartwell, Author of *All We Buried*
and the *Wait, Wait, Don't Query (Yet)* series

"Shanessa Gluhm delivers compelling psychological suspense propelled by complex family drama, intriguing twists, and a keen sense of place."
—Jayne Ann Krentz, *New York Times* bestselling author

"*Enemies of Doves* is a masterfully told multi-generational mystery steeped in family secrets, murder, and forbidden love."
—Sean Paul Murphy, Author of *Chapel Street*

"Like the tumultuous river flowing at the center of this gripping tale, Shanessa Gluhm has crafted a pulsating story that is just waiting to pull you into its chilling depths and slowly reveal all its darkest secrets."
—Indies Today

*To Josh, for helping me navigate every plot twist—
both in writing and in life.*

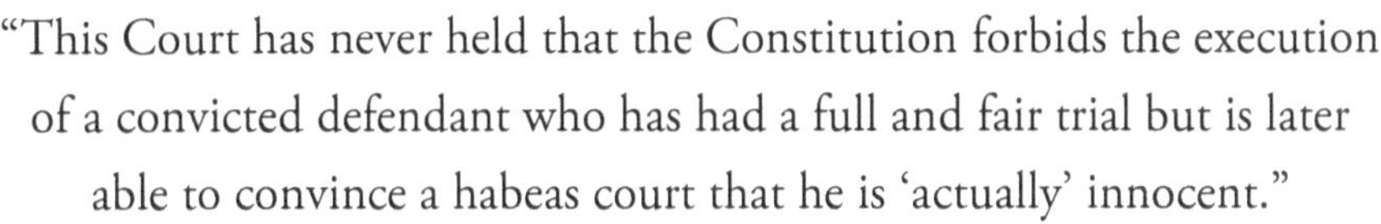

"This Court has never held that the Constitution forbids the execution of a convicted defendant who has had a full and fair trial but is later able to convince a habeas court that he is 'actually' innocent."
— Former Supreme Court Justice Antonin Scalia


"The death penalty experiment has failed."
— Former Supreme Court Justice Harry Blackmun

**To:** AdamsT@DallasMorningNews.com

**From:** Greer_Sheridan@gmail.com

**Subject**: BREAKING NEWS—Songbird Strangler Arrest

Tate,

By the time you read this, an arrest will have been made in the Songbird Strangler case.

As you know, I discovered the body of Chantilly Price, the fifth and final victim of the Strangler—and one of my closest friends—on July 4, 1986.

I also helped implicate our friend, Troy Terrell, as a suspect. Your readers know that story, but what they don't know is this: none of it is true.

I've attached the opening of my piece. If you're interested in running the rest, reach out. Trust me, Tate, this one is going to be big.

Sincerely,
Greer Sheridan
Freelance Journalist
555-263-9986

PS: Consider this story (exclusive rights and all) my apology—thirty-five years too late. Believe me, you were better off.

# CHAPTER 1

**Allan B. Polunsky Unit, 2024**

Texas was the only state with its own time zone, or so Joaquin Ramos liked to say. He'd grown up on the West Coast, where no one said "California time." In Colorado, interning for a defense attorney, he'd learned to specify "Mountain Time." But in eight years here, he'd never once heard "Central Time."

Pacific Time . . . Mountain Time . . . Texas Time.

Joaquin had found the same to be true about the death penalty. Nationwide, inmates waited an average of nineteen years on death row; in Texas, it was eleven.

So, the fact that Troy Terrell was still alive, sitting on the other side of that scratched plexiglass thirty-seven years after his sentencing, was a bona fide miracle.

"A little late for a new lawyer, isn't it?" Troy asked.

Joaquin squared his shoulders. "Let's hope not. I know they've set your execution date, but I'd like to review the case."

"They've set my date lots of times."

"And Mr. Oswald and his team always stopped it," Joaquin said.

"But now they're done trying to save me." Troy sighed. "Can't blame them. Mom's dead. My cousin Vic's all I have, and he can't take out any more loans."

"I've spoken to Mr. Oswald. He's still in contact with the governor, still willing to help, but he feels he's done all he can in court." Joaquin didn't mention that Oswald was retiring at Christmas. Joaquin couldn't fathom Oswald enjoying a cozy Christmas knowing his client's days were numbered. Some men could disassociate—separate the personal from the professional. Joaquin wasn't one of them. "Sometimes you just need fresh eyes on a case," he told him. "I've got pretty good vision."

The fluorescent light flickered above the visiting booth, casting a washed-out glow over Troy's face. He no longer resembled the fresh-faced, athletic nineteen-year-old that Americans thought of when they pictured the Songbird Strangler. "And who's paying for those twenty-twenty eyes of yours?"

"The Death Penalty Abolition Project finds attorneys to take cases pro bono. That means—"

"I know what it means."

Joaquin straightened his tie. "Right, of course. DPAP will cover the costs of another habeas corpus—if I can find grounds to file one." *Keep filing, keep them alive.* The words of Anabella Henley—Joaquin's old mentor—replayed in his head like a loop.

"You look young," Troy said.

Joaquin bristled. "I'm thirty-five. Younger than Oswald, sure, but I've got a winning record and killer instincts."

"So you believe I'm innocent?" Troy asked.

Joaquin shifted on the uncomfortable stool. "To be honest, I don't care. I oppose the death penalty."

"Why?" Troy asked.

Joaquin held up a fist, ticking off points. "It violates the Constitution, discriminates in practice, fails as a deterrent, drains taxpayer money, and sometimes executes the innocent."

Troy's lips quirked in a half-smile. "You talk fast."

Joaquin laughed. "You should hear my mom's Spanish when she's angry. If I'm going too fast, stop me. I talk fast because I think fast, and that's a plus in my profession."

"Mr. Ramos, I may talk slow, but I'm not stupid."

Joaquin opened and closed his mouth. So much for fast thinking. "I . . . um . . . I know you're smart," he said. "Smart enough to contact DPAP."

"I didn't contact anybody."

"Your cousin then?"

Troy shook his head. "My best guess is Ms. Melrose Reed."

Joaquin rubbed his chin. "Name doesn't ring a bell."

"She's a paralegal for Mr. Oswald, and she doesn't know the meaning of the word quit."

Joaquin leaned forward. "I like her already."

"Melrose came in late during my last appeal. We hit it off. She's a real firecracker and says whatever is on her mind. Reminded me of an old friend."

*Chantilly Price.* Joaquin recalled the article about her with a similar description from her father. Something about losing their firecracker on the Fourth of July.

"Melrose believes I'm innocent." Troy looked up again. "Aren't you even going to ask if I am?"

Joaquin leaned back, smoothing his tie. "Not until I represent you. Then you can share information under attorney-client privilege."

"So, you'd represent me even if I killed five girls in cold blood? Even if I *am* the Songbird Strangler?"

Joaquin nodded. "I would, but the fact that DPAP took your case suggests they believe in your innocence. They get flooded with requests and have to be careful for PR reasons."

Troy moved closer to the glass. "Do you have a wife, Mr. Ramos? Daughter? Sister?"

The phone felt heavy in Joaquin's hand. "Three sisters." He was never sure whether the one who'd died in his arms still counted, but he couldn't bear to exclude her.

"Okay, so assuming I'm this serial killer they claim, you'd want me back on the streets? Back in the world where your sisters live?"

The room was stifling. Joaquin exhaled, pushing away the image of his youngest sister, Glory, who no longer lived in this world.

"Mr. Terrell, I can't promise your release. Two juries found you guilty. A third sentenced you to death again after your original sentence was overturned. Judges and courts have upheld your conviction at every turn. But if you're innocent and we can prove it, that's the best-case scenario."

"And worst-case?" Troy asked.

"You're already in it. But we might get your sentence reduced to life." Joaquin leaned in. "Cops make mistakes. So do lawyers, judges, and juries. I'm damn good at finding them. If I do, a judge might resentence you. Maybe even overturn the conviction."

"And how many have you saved from the row?"

"One," Joaquin said, omitting the fact that he was part of a team of six lawyers, three paralegals, and two investigators. He doubted the Death Penalty Abolition Project could offer the same support.

"One," Troy repeated, shaking his head.

"One out of one," Joaquin clarified. "I've been a private defense attorney for eight years. My record speaks for itself."

"Why the change, then?" Troy asked. "Bored with getting rich boys out of DUIs?"

Joaquin wiped the sweat off his forehead. "Is it always this hot in here?"

"Better here than in my cell." Troy shrugged. "We didn't have much growing up, but Ma couldn't stand the heat. The thermostat never went above seventy. I never thought I'd get used to sleeping without AC, but the body adapts."

Joaquin shook his head. Eighty-five to a hundred degrees in a sixty-square-foot cell, twenty-three hours a day—sad what a man could get used to.

"You didn't answer my question, Mr. Ramos. Why are you moonlighting with death penalty cases?"

"Because I want to make a difference."

Troy smirked. "You mean you want to make a name for yourself?"

Joaquin sat stunned. Troy Terrell was indeed a smart man. "Yeah, that too," Joaquin admitted.

Troy nodded. "Okay, Mr. Ramos, where do I sign?"

"My administrative assistant will draw up the papers. And please—call me Joaquin."

Troy thanked him, and they said their goodbyes. As Joaquin turned to leave, Troy tapped the glass. "And in case you were wondering, Mr. Ramos, I *am* innocent."

# CHAPTER 2

**Bluesummer, TX, 1986**

Hayes Sheridan often felt caught between two worlds—his family's sprawling Southern estate and the Terrell family pig farm. Hayes's mother, Joanne, was born into money. His father, Redman, made his own fortune writing best-selling true crime novels. Old money, new money, Hayes didn't figure it mattered so long as you had some.

His life had become entangled with Troy's when they were six. The Sheridans left Tyler for the quiet of country life, the kind Hayes's father craved. Red wanted to hunt, fish, and raise his son to value hard work—a concept lost on Joanne.

They'd fallen in love during college, married, and met in the middle—a big house where they made their own bed but hired a housekeeper to scrub the toilets weekly. A life where neither had to work, but Red would teach Hayes to work anyway—teach him to make his own bed.

Hayes had been surprised the first time his family had wandered onto the Terrells' farm during a Sunday afternoon walk. The Terrell place was small, white paint peeling, roof sagging, shutters crooked. Overgrown grass hid rusted barrels and dull tools. It didn't belong on the same road as the Sheridans' home.

"Looks like the pigs live better than they do," Hayes's mother said, lowering her sunglasses to stare at the hog confinement farther back on the property.

Red Sheridan ignored his wife's pretension and stepped onto the creaky porch to ring the doorbell.

Hayes was thrilled when a boy his age appeared behind Mr. Terrell, and he was even more excited when they were invited to dinner. The afternoon flew by as Hayes and Troy played army with a real helmet that had belonged to Troy's uncle, who'd fought in Vietnam.

After dinner, Hayes and Red joined Troy and his father at the barn. Hayes had never seen so many pigs—grunting and rooting in the troughs, piglets squealing and fighting for their mother's milk. They were a raucous, smelly bunch, but Hayes was transfixed.

"These your pets?" Hayes asked, earning a laugh from both dads.

"None of them are pets," Troy said, grinning.

Hayes suddenly understood what was funny. The scent of the ham Troy's mom had baked for dinner lingered in Hayes's nose, his belly still full. "Do you eat 'em all?"

"Most of these rascals end up in the freezer section at Village Mart," Frank Terrell explained.

Hayes stared at the pigs, equal parts horrified and fascinated. Something about this farm, these pigs, these rows of corn grown to feed them, stirred a feeling that he couldn't explain.

His excitement only grew when his dad announced on the way home that they'd help the Terrells on the farm every morning.

"Oh, Red, is that necessary?" Joanne said, digging her heels out of the dirt. "They're nice people, but they're . . . they're . . ."

"They're what?" Red asked, his lip curling. "Black?"

Joanne pressed a hand to her chest. "No! I mean, yes, but that's not what I meant. They're different, that's all. And I don't see why Hayes needs to help. School's about to start."

"It's first grade, Jo. He'll have plenty of time for his ABCs."

Hayes crossed his arms. "I already know my ABCs."

Red ruffled his hair. "I know you do, son." He turned to his wife. "You heard them. Frank's brother died; his nephew left for college. It's too much work for two adults and one child. It won't hurt Hayes to wake up a little early."

Hayes silently pleaded for his mom's agreement.

"Oh, fine." Joanne sighed. "But if his teacher tells me he falls asleep in class, it's over."

"Deal." Red shook her hand.

Hayes was convinced that was why he hadn't fallen asleep in class even once in the twelve years since.

"How's the new book coming, Red?" Greer asked, squirting ketchup on her hamburger.

Hayes wished he were close enough to kick her under the table. He didn't want his dad discussing the Songbird Strangler while his friends were over. But talk of serial killers—over a burger slathered in obscene amounts of red ketchup—didn't faze Greer at all. Maybe her not knowing the first two victims allowed her to disassociate, but Erin Llewellyn had been part of their graduating class. Now Wendy Knott was missing. They all knew Wendy—Hayes best of all.

"Can you grab me another Pepsi?" Tilly asked, tucking a strand of white-blonde hair behind her ear and flashing a smile at Hayes. A smile that still made his knees weak, even while sitting. Chantilly Price had been knocking Hayes off balance since the first day of second grade. They'd dated throughout high school, but lately, something had shifted between them. He felt dangerously close to losing her. He couldn't lose her. He wouldn't.

Hayes's mom shooed flies as she set a bowl of potato salad on the smooth glass tabletop. "The flies are terrible."

"Extra protein," Hayes said, rising from the table.

"Very funny." Joanne fluffed her short hair. Both parents had the same dark hair he did, but his mom bleached hers blonde every six weeks. His dad's had gone completely gray but was still as full and thick as Hayes's.

Hayes pulled a chair out for his mom. It screeched against the concrete. "Relax, Mom. It's a nice night."

"It would be," Troy said, reaching for another hot dog. "If G would stop talking about strangulation devices and blood splatter."

"Redman!" Joanne snapped her fingers. "Hayes's friends are here to enjoy dinner, not discuss your work."

"I'm used to it, Mom." Hayes grabbed a Pepsi from the cooler, shaking off excess water. "Pretty sure Greer is only friends with me to talk true crime with Dad."

"Stop!" Greer tossed a bottle of relish at Hayes. "Not like I knew your dad was an award-winning crime writer when I met you in first grade."

"Oh, she knew," Troy said, still chewing his hot dog. "She absolutely knew."

"You're both terrible." Greer leaned back, stretching her long legs under the table as the string lights above them swayed in the evening breeze. "To become a journalist, I have to learn from the best."

Hayes heard Bryan Adams's faint voice from the boombox by the back door as he reached for the bottle Greer had thrown. He turned up the volume before he stood. Normally, his mom would scold him for playing music during dinner, but Hayes guessed that hearing Adams croon about the summer of '69 was preferable to hearing another word about the Songbird Strangler.

"Well, why don't you two discuss this later?" Joanne suggested.

"Oh, come on, Jo." Red put his arm around his wife. "How often in a crime writer's life does he have an opportunity to catch an honest-to-God serial killer?"

Joanne sipped her water. "Goodness gracious, Red, you sound almost excited about this."

Red shrugged. "I mean, if you're a storm chaser and the siren sounds, are you excited? I think so. Not that this horrible storm formed, but it's here, and now you get to chase it."

Joanne rubbed her head as if it ached. Sensing an argument coming on, Hayes avoided returning to the table and lingered by the tree in the middle of the deck. The grass was the greenest he'd ever seen; the zinnias bloomed in fiery reds, sunny yellows, and deep purples.

He'd miss this place when he left for college. He'd helped build this deck back in fifth grade. His dad still bragged about how Hayes measured and cut every board. That deck sparked his mom's push toward architecture. The next day, she showed up with blueprint paper, protractors, and drafting pencils, asking him to design flower boxes. Then came a patio bench, then a deck awning—each project building on the last, all leading to a scholarship to the University of Texas at Austin, the college where his parents had met.

Hayes had realized early on what his mom was doing—aiming his life, ensuring her only child didn't grow up to be a pig farmer. She wanted the best for him, and he had a natural talent for design. Hayes took pride in his projects. He'd enjoyed the bursts of color from the flower boxes and the awning's shade during muggy East Texas nights. And he and Tilly had shared their first kiss on that bench—still the best night of his life. He remembered Tilly resting her head on his shoulder as they sat, listening to the bug zapper and wind chimes.

Of course, all the wind chimes were long gone from their patio. Hayes bet there were no wind chimes left hanging in Bluesummer.

"Hayes, come sit." His mother's voice pulled him out of his memories. "I was asking Tilly which sorority she's planning on pledging."

Hayes returned to the table. Though not a preferred topic, sororities were better than serial killers.

"I've decided on Kappa Alpha Theta," Tilly said.

Joanne clapped. "Oh, that's wonderful. I was a Theta girl myself."

"Were you?" Tilly asked, even though Hayes knew she was only pledging that house for his mom's sake.

"I was thinking . . ." Greer said, turning toward Red. "What you were saying about storm chasers. They save lives. They can't stop the storm, but they can predict its direction and warn the public."

Red tipped the end of his beer bottle toward her. "That's right. This guy needs to be off our streets. If I happen to be the one to find him and secure a lucrative book deal in the process, so be it."

"What if you know him?" Greer slapped the glass tabletop, causing all their drinks to wobble. "Can you imagine? It would be like that Ann Rule book on Bundy."

Troy groaned. "Come on, G. No Bundy talk over burgers."

"Are there any leads at all?" Greer asked, her blue eyes growing brighter.

"All speculation." Red peeled at his beer label.

Greer shifted slightly. "Who?"

"Dad, come on," Hayes said. "You can't accuse people like that."

"I'm not accusing anyone of anything." Red raised his hands. "But there has been talk around Bluesummer about Oliver Ford peeping into windows."

Tilly shivered. "Ugh, Ollie's *such* a creep. He snuck into the high school and hid in the locker room to watch girls changing."

"That's all a bunch of rumors." Troy crossed his arms, and Hayes noticed Tilly steal a glimpse at Troy's biceps. Hayes had caught Tilly doing that a lot lately, looking at Troy. And she commented that Hayes and Troy had the same pouty lips. How did she know so much about Troy's lips? The thought made Hayes uneasy, a strange twist of curiosity and something else he couldn't name.

"*If* that happened," Troy continued, "the police would have charged him. And what could he see from inside lockers, anyway?"

"There are holes in them," Tilly said. "I believe it. I don't like the way he looks at me."

Hayes caught Greer rolling her eyes, but luckily, Tilly didn't.

"Troy is right. We shouldn't accuse that poor man of anything. He's got . . . you know, issues," Joanne said. "Bless him, but he's not smart enough to do what this killer did and leave no evidence."

"You've got a point there," Red said. "That's why I wonder if he had help."

"Someone like . . ." Greer asked.

"Red!" Joanne snapped. "This conversation is over. I want to hear more about the kids' college plans." She angled her body toward Tilly. "Now, let me give you some tips about rush week."

# CHAPTER 3

**2024**

Sunlight slanted through the blinds, slicing across Joaquin's desk strewn with case files. Bernadette Langley hovered in the doorway. "I've got the information you requested."

He kept his eyes on the file in front of him. "Information?"

"Melrose Reed." His receptionist's voice betrayed her annoyance. "You asked for her number."

Joaquin pulled off his reading glasses and rubbed his eyes. "Right, thanks." He held out his hand for the number, but Bernie's hands were empty.

"Ms. Reed doesn't work at Goldstein and Oswald," she said.

"But—"

She held up her hand, cutting Joaquin off. "They have no contact information for her—won't say why she left. There's no listing for her in the White Pages online. Zip. Zilch."

Joaquin ran a hand through his mop of curly hair. "I'll figure it out. Thanks."

Bernie peered at Joaquin over the bridge of her glasses, smeared with mascara. "Are you sleeping? Eating? Taking a multivitamin? Using hair gel? You look like shit."

"Wow, thanks."

Bernie tousled her short waves, the vibrant red accented by a striking white streak in the front. "Truth hurts."

"I'm fine. I got the Terrell files from DPAP." He gestured at the eight boxes stacked behind him. "Have my work cut out for me."

"Hate to say I told you so."

"I know. DPAP has a paralegal, but he's stretched thin. They're covering wages for me to hire a local legal assistant. That's why I'm looking for Ms. Reed. They also brought in an investigator, Luca Moretti. Best there is. So it's not our dream team from the Frazer case, but it could be worse."

Bernie straightened the nameplate on Joaquin's cluttered desk, brushing crumbs off the corner. "Well, that's reassuring. You do need help. Because you've still got your other cases. You know, the ones that pay the bills?"

"You're still gonna get paid, Bernie."

"You realize I could retire, right?" She plopped into the chair across from Joaquin. "I've worked here too damn long. Before this chair, before that fancy desk, there was Bernadette." She pointed at his bookshelf. "The only thing older than me is that potpourri."

Joaquin didn't remember any potpourri but knew Bernadette had been working here since before he was born. The lawyer he purchased the practice from had been in business for forty-five years, with Bernie by his side for most of them. Though she tried to hide her age with her leopard-printed leggings and deliberately unkempt trendy haircut, evidence of her sixty-five years showed in the deep crow's feet around her eyes and the increasing unsteadiness of her gait. But she was still savvy and smart—still invaluable to Joaquin's practice.

"You can't retire, Bernie. Not yet. I need you."

She smeared ChapStick across her lips. "Stop begging. It's embarrassing. I refuse to retire. Remember lockdown? I damn near killed Dan. No way I'm spending all day with him voluntarily." She stood. "Nice chat, but I've got work to do."

*That makes two of us*, Joaquin thought, eyeing the thick file in front of him. But before Bernie made it out the door, he lifted his head. "I'm curious. You grew up here; you get out more than I do. What's the general vibe in Bluesummer about Troy Terrell? About me representing him?"

Bernie leaned against the door frame and made a throat-slashing gesture.

Joaquin's stomach fluttered. "That's the feeling about Troy? Or about me?"

"Both," she answered, closing the door behind her.

Joaquin was starting to wonder if this case would be the big break he needed or an outright public relations nightmare. Either way, he had work to do. It was time to find Melrose Reed. He pulled out his keyboard tray and opened a browser, starting with LinkedIn before resorting to Facebook.

He hadn't checked his social media in a while, as the ninety-six notifications suggested. Curiosity got the better of him, and he clicked. "Mom," he muttered aloud, noticing most were from her, liking and commenting on every photo he'd ever posted. He cringed, remembering some of his college posts. He should have scrubbed his account before accepting her friend request.

He found Melrose Reed's profile quickly. No city was listed, but the photo—her standing in front of the Tyler courthouse—made him pause. He'd seen her there before. She was attractive, with a heart-shaped face, large brown eyes, full lips, and dark brown hair falling past the shoulders of her fitted navy-blue suit jacket.

Her bio revealed she'd earned a bachelor's in paralegal studies from Texas A&M in 2016 and had worked for Goldstein and Oswald in Tyler. He wondered why she'd left such a prestigious firm.

After sending her a message, he closed Facebook and focused on the file in front of him: the Songbird Strangler victims.

Nicole Garcia, the killer's first known victim, vanished from her bedroom during a spring-break visit home to Bluesummer in March 1986. Nothing seemed unusual except for the missing set of wind chimes outside her window. The police dismissed it—she was an adult, free to go where she pleased.

That wasn't the case three weeks later when sixteen-year-old Andrea Dalton disappeared. Under her pillow, police found a Polaroid of Nicole Garcia, dead on dewy grass with the missing bluebird wind chime wrapped around her neck. The flimsy cords weren't strong enough for strangulation, suggesting the killer had staged the photo.

Much to Andrea's parents' horror, a set of wind chimes was missing from their front porch collection. "It had a hummingbird on top, pewter flowers hanging down. Andrea bought it for me last Mother's Day," her mother told police.

Detectives kept the wind chime detail from the public—something the parents of victim number three still blamed them for. Their daughter, Erin Llewellyn, was the class of 1986 valedictorian and was killed just two weeks before graduation. If they'd known the killer targeted homes with wind chimes, they would have taken down the lone one on their porch— their nautical-themed dolphin chime vanished in the night along with their daughter. The next morning, a Polaroid of Andrea, with her parents' missing hummingbird chime around her neck, was taped to the Llewellyns' door.

By May's end, the killer had a name: the Songbird Strangler, coined by Bluesummer's newspaper. By June, no wind chimes remained in

Bluesummer, but that didn't stop eighteen-year-old Wendy Knott from disappearing. Unlike previous victims, there had been a struggle. Her parents returned from church to bloody sheets, an empty bed, and a Polaroid of Erin with the dolphin wind chime around her neck.

The last victim, Chantilly Price, was killed only two days after Wendy's disappearance. Unlike the others, Tilly was left in her bed—no Polaroid, no clues, just a phone cord wrapped around her cold, bruised neck.

The day after Tilly's death, a local search party found Wendy's body deep in Bluesummer's piney woods. Her cause of death was not strangulation but blunt force trauma. Detectives never figured out why the Strangler deviated from his modus operandi, but Wendy's head wound proved a lucky break for investigators. It was the blood trail in the woods that led searchers to the cave, where they found Wendy's body. Breadcrumbs leading to a witch's house. Because, of course, the entire world knew what else was inside that cave.

Joaquin startled at the ring of his phone. He swiveled in his chair and grabbed it from the windowsill. "Hello?"

"Mr. Ramos?" Her voice came through the receiver, raspy and tinged with a distinctly Australian accent. "Melrose Reed here."

Joaquin sat up. "Ms. Reed, thanks for calling."

"Call me Melrose. Are you with the Innocence Project?"

"No. The Death Penalty Abolition Project took on Mr. Terrell's case. Newer organization, not as much money, but willing to fight." He ran a finger along the edge of his desk. "Mr. Terrell told me you requested our services?"

"Yeah, I went down the list of anyone I thought might help."

Joaquin spun back to his desk. "Do you do this for all your clients?"

"Nah, first time, but first time I've been dead sure someone's innocent too."

"Innocent?" Joaquin glanced at the photo of Chantilly Price strangled in her bed. He shut the folder.

"Yep. Innocent. I assume that's why you took the case."

"I haven't decided yet." He leaned back in his chair, stretching one leg under the desk. "Troy signed the papers, so I'm reviewing files."

Melrose chuckled. "Sounds like you've got a bit to learn."

Joaquin pulled back a metal ball from his Newton's cradle. "Yeah, eight boxes worth."

"You're not the only lawyer on this, right?"

"Afraid so." Joaquin listened to the rhythmic clang of the metal balls. "But DPAP is assigning me an investigator."

"And a paralegal?"

"They're snowed under. So they are letting me hire one on my own."

"Perfect. When do I start?" Melrose asked.

Joaquin laughed. He wondered if this brazen attitude had cost Melrose her job with Troy's former attorney. But he'd be foolish not to leverage her expertise on this case.

"How about we meet tomorrow and discuss it?"

"Discuss what? The case or whether I got the job?"

"Both." Joaquin stood from his chair. "How about the new café on Main?"

"Time?"

"Uh, ten-ish?"

Melrose sighed into the phone. "Mate, I'm a professional. I don't do *ish*."

He let out a short, bemused laugh; she was relentless. "Okay, ten on the dot."

"See you then," Melrose said, and the line fell silent. Joaquin set down his phone, wondering what he'd gotten himself into.

Joaquin arrived at the coffeehouse early. The scent of coffee and pastries mingled in the air. He ordered his usual—espresso and a blueberry muffin—and claimed a corner table, the chair creaking softly as he sat, sunlight warming the tabletop in front of him.

He unwrapped his scarf and powered on his laptop. The place was noisy—orders shouted out, ice grinding in the blender, the steady hum of a frothing machine. He popped in his earbuds, but they barely muffled the noise. He adjusted in the iron chair and began typing, though his focus wavered. Every time the chime above the door sounded, his gaze lifted. On the third chime, Melrose Reed walked in.

She wore gray slacks and a matching wool peacoat. She was short, 5'3 at best. Unlike most people he met in the age of filters, she was even prettier in person than in her profile picture.

Joaquin stood, but she didn't notice, making a beeline for the fast-track lane to grab an order she'd clearly placed ahead.

"Ms. Reed?" he called, pulling out his earbuds.

She straightened her jacket and approached, extending her hand with a firm shake. "Melrose, remember?"

"You're early." He shifted on his feet, taking her in.

"Meant to be earlier, but got pulled over for not making a full stop before turning right on red." She let her purse slip from her shoulder onto the chair. "I swear those coppers will nick you for anything. I suppose they see working in criminal defense as being on the wrong side of law and order."

"I know how that goes." Joaquin stood until Melrose was seated.

"Looks like you're an early bird, too," she said.

"Usually, yeah." He ran a hand over the back of his neck, glancing at the papers stacked on his corner of the table. "Planned to get some work done, but I can't focus with all this noise."

"Distractions don't bother me. I can work anywhere."

"Good to know. The extra room in my office suite is small and packed with boxes I haven't gotten around to moving."

"No worries." She took a slow sip of her coffee.

"So why don't you tell me a little about yourself? Miss . . . I mean, Melrose."

"I was born in Bluesummer but grew up in Australia." She tucked a strand of hair behind her ear, eyes drifting toward the window. "Dad's from there, so we moved back when I was two and stayed until just before Year Twelve."

"What brought you back?"

"Mum's an only child, and with my grandparents' health declining, they decided it was best to return. Mum's a teacher, Dad's a nurse—they can work anywhere. They went back to Australia after my grandparents passed, but I stayed here. I like Bluesummer. I assume you do, too, since you're here."

Joaquin shrugged. "It's fine. But if I had the choice between here and Australia, I'd say—" He tried out a fake Aussie drawl: "See you down under, mate."

Melrose didn't crack a smile. "So, what brought you here then, Mr. Ramos?"

"My dad got transferred to Tyler when I was in law school—a promotion, derrick man to company man. Back then, a lawyer named William Steagell owned this firm."

"I know Willie."

"Figured you might. He taught one of my online courses at the University of Denver. He made me an offer to purchase his practice when he retired, so here I am."

"Here you are," Melrose echoed. "For Troy's sake, I'm glad."

Joaquin slid his chair closer. "What about Terrell and his case makes you so invested?"

"Troy's a good man."

"Okay. But people said the same about Bundy."

"Nothing points to Troy being the Strangler—nothing credible." Melrose leaned in. "I got hired at Goldstein straight out of college and was assigned to Wesley Oswald, Troy's attorney. The deeper I got into the appeal, the more I believed in his innocence. That's why I started reaching out for help after Oswald withdrew as counsel." She folded her hands on the table. "And for what it's worth, I'd have argued against the chair for Bundy too, monstrous as he was."

Joaquin nodded. "We have that in common, then. What makes you so passionate about your stance against the death penalty?"

"I can trace it back to living in Australia the year they passed the Crimes Legislation Amendment. They'd already outlawed capital punishment, but this locked it so it could never be reintroduced. The news coverage caught my interest. My parents are religious and believe the right to life is absolute. For me, it was more practical. What kind of example does it set when the government kills to stop killing?"

Joaquin opened his mouth to agree, but Melrose kept going.

"The US is the only Western democracy still applying the death penalty. If we're on a list with countries Americans consider backward and barbaric, shouldn't we take a hard look at what we're doing?" She traced the rim of her coffee cup with her finger. "Sorry, I'll get off my ranty soapbox."

Joaquin shifted in his seat. He wasn't sure if the flutter in his chest was from her accent—the way she added a soft "r" to words like "Australiar" and "lawr and order"—or her sharp take on capital punishment. Either way, he ordered the feeling to stop. Not the time. Not the place. Not the girl.

"Well, I'm not gonna ask the usual BS about strengths and weaknesses," Joaquin said. "But I need to clarify that this job is temporary. DPAP would pay your wages—thirty dollars an hour for forty hours a week. Bernadette, my administrative assistant, will help, too. But we both know these cases take more than forty hours a week. So, I understand if—"

"Is this an offer?" Melrose interrupted.

"Yeah," Joaquin said. He hadn't asked her about her previous job, but had a gut feeling about her. "I'm offering."

She tapped her fingers lightly on the table, eyes bright. "I'll take it. Should I start today?"

"How about Monday? It will give Bernie time to draw up your employment paperwork." *And time for me to find your desk under the mountains of boxes.*

"Monday works." Melrose chugged the rest of her coffee. "You've got my number if you need anything sooner."

Joaquin laughed. Melrose's desire for the job was obvious, but her serious face and quick exit contradicted that entirely.

"What?" she asked, slinging her purse over her shoulder. "What's so funny?"

"Just wondering if you're always this . . . intense."

Melrose slouched. "Please tell me you're not one of those insufferable blokes that tell women to smile?"

"I'm not." Joaquin stood. "But since you brought it up, it *would* be nice to see your smile at some point."

"I'll smile when our job is done—when we win. When Troy Terrell is off death row."

Joaquin held up a finger. "I'm gonna hold you to that."

"I'll hold you to it as well."

"To smiling?"

"To winning." Melrose tossed her empty cup in the trash on her way out. "See you Monday. Should be a ripper."

# CHAPTER 4

**1986**

Troy Terrell lifted the bag of pig feed and shook it into the bin. An hour in the weight room wasn't much different from an hour feeding hogs. Maybe that was why he'd never needed to train as hard as his teammates. Not that it mattered now. Thanks to a torn ACL, he'd lost the chance to break the Bluesummer High School football record for receiving yards, he'd lost a place on the podium at the State Track and Field Championship, and he'd lost a full-ride scholarship to Texas Tech. He'd lost his entire future.

And so, while Hayes, Greer, and Tilly made college plans, Troy wondered how many more fifty-pound sacks of corn he'd pour into these containers. Wondered how many more piles of pig shit he'd shovel before he died. How many pig throats he'd slash and watch bleed out.

"You always have a choice," Red had told him. "It's your life."

Easy for Red to say. He wasn't tied to this farm. Troy never understood why Red helped, but he was grateful. The farm would've struggled without him. And although Troy daydreamed about a life where the farm had failed, it was all his family had. Who would hire his dad? A sixty-year-old, one-armed man who was increasingly forgetful of the tasks he'd completed daily for his entire life? Or what about his ma? A former

Sunday school teacher who couldn't get out of bed without popping a Vicodin?

Sometimes, Troy still couldn't believe this was his life now.

Troy inspected the pigs' water, activated the sprinklers in their cornfield, and then ventured a few steps into the woods. Closing his eyes, he took in a deep breath, inhaling the scents of damp wood and pine needles. The birds were noisy this morning, yet he still caught the faint swish of grass blowing in the wind. These smells, these sounds, these woods—this was the only place Troy had ever found peace. He knew every tree, every bush, every hole in the ground. He wanted to go for a run, but he had to consider his knee. Though moving better now, he couldn't risk being sidelined again. His dad was relying on him.

So he turned away from his perfect woods back to his anything but perfect house. It needed a fresh coat of paint and a new roof. It needed a lot of things that he lacked the time or money to address. For most of his graduating class, the house of their childhood would soon be a house they visited over Christmas break and summer vacation. But the Terrell house might as well have had bars on the windows because, like it or not, Troy would be trapped there for a long time.

"Troy Michael!" He froze mid-step, heart skipping a beat, as his mother barked from the table. "The milk's spoiled! Why did you leave it out?"

"I didn't eat breakfast, Ma." Troy walked into the kitchen and touched the milk carton. Warm. "Dad probably left it out last night . . . again."

"Oh." Dottie's shoulders slumped slightly as she retied her robe. "Well, throw it out. I'll have some orange juice."

"Something to wash the pills down?" Troy asked, the milk glugging as he poured it down the drain. He felt a mix of irritation and pity—same old routine, same old Ma.

"My pills aren't your business. Two of your vertebrates didn't crack when you flew through a windshield!" Dottie snapped.

Troy stared at his mother, her hair disheveled, her eyes wild. He remembered when it had been different. The Terrells had never been rich, but they'd once been happy. That was before the accident—the one that took his father's arm and left his mother in constant pain.

"Sorry, Ma."

"What exactly are you sorry about? Those wise-ass cracks about my medication or the fact that if you had been driving, the accident wouldn't have happened at all?"

Troy tensed. "Don't blame me."

"Why the hell not? Your daddy can't see in the dark. You always drove us back from church on Sunday nights. But not that Sunday."

Troy crushed the milk carton and slammed it into the trash can.

"Because you were with *them*," she hissed. "At their church with big fancy windows and full of rich white folks. Pretending you didn't stick out like a black smudge on those stained-glass windows."

Troy squeezed his palms, digging his nails into his skin. "The Sheridans are good people. Hayes and Red are up every morning helping me and Dad with the hogs. They've fed me, gave me money, picked me up from football practice." He lifted his foot. "Who do you think bought me these new shoes? What have you done in the past three years? To help the farm? To help me?" His voice cracked.

"Son, I don't blame you for wanting to be a Sheridan." Her fingers drummed against the worn table, eyes sharp. "They've got money and status, and Hayes has all those pretty little girls following after him. But blood is blood, Troy. They ain't your blood."

Troy clenched his jaw. "Family is more than blood."

"Not really." She shifted closer; voice low but firm. "I'm your real family. Me and Daddy." She slammed her palm on the table, rattling the silverware. "One day, Red and Joanne will find a new charity project. Mark my words, you'll fall out of their good graces. They won't be there for you. But regardless of how you treat me, I will be." Her eyes bore into his. "You can bet on that, boy."

Troy considered telling her she wasn't there for him, but it would do no good. Instead, he grabbed the orange juice, rinsed a glass, and set it in front of her, his hands tight around the cup.

"Thanks," she said, her tone softening. She rubbed her back, wincing. "I'm hurting today. Would you mind getting me—"

Before she could finish, Troy pulled a bottle of her pills from the cabinet and handed her one. "Go back to bed. When Dad wakes up, tell him I fed the hogs."

"Why don't you tell him yourself?"

Troy stared at the dingy linoleum. Even as an adult, he felt guilty for doing things he wanted—fun things. "I'm heading to the lake today with the Quad," Troy said, referencing the name a teacher had given their friend group back in fifth grade—and that had stuck ever since. "I thought I told you."

Dottie chuckled. "You didn't. You never do. But it's alright." She swallowed her pill, downed the juice, and stood, pressing her hands into her lower back as she arched forward. "Happy Fourth of July."

"Thanks," Troy muttered, eyes glued to the kitchen floor.

Dottie squeezed his arm as she passed. "The grass ain't always greener, son. Keep that in mind."

Troy nodded, but watching his mom stumble back into her bedroom, smelling the rotten milk curdled in the sink, and hearing the grunts of fifty ravenous pigs through the open window, it was hard to imagine a place with grass less green than here.

# CHAPTER 5

**2024**

"So, what's your strategy?" Melrose asked, clicking her pen against a blank legal pad in her lap.

Stacks of banker's boxes crowded the office, tilting like unstable towers. The sheer volume pressed down on Joaquin, making his chest tighten.

"File, file, file," Joaquin said. He rubbed the back of his neck, trying to recall Annabelle Bailey's sharp voice. "I worked my first death penalty case with the legend herself, Annabelle Bailey. She told me that if you keep filing, you keep them alive."

Melrose set down her pen and steepled her fingers, the fluorescent light above them catching on the silver band of her watch. "What's left to file? There are almost forty years' worth of motions and only six weeks till Troy's execution."

Joaquin glanced at the boxes again. "We're filing another writ of habeas corpus, asking the Texas Court of Criminal Appeals to stay Troy's execution and vacate his conviction."

"On what grounds?"

"That's what I need to figure out. We can't repeat anything Oswald filed, so I need something fresh." He tapped his pen against the margin, a restless staccato. "Maybe prosecutorial misconduct? New evidence? Procedural errors? First, I have to catch up on what's already been done."

"Anything I can help with?" Melrose asked.

"I've got a lot of reading to do, but let me know if I miss anything major." Joaquin flipped through a thick folder, his eyes skimming over Oswald's underlined notes, most of the ink faded to a dull gray. "Okay, so they only charged Terrell with two out of the five murders."

"Right," Melrose said. "They only felt they could prove Wendy Knott and Chantilly Price. Troy didn't know the Strangler's first victim, Nicole Garcia, so there was no motive. His alibi for Andrea Dalton was solid—he'd been playing basketball at school, and a janitor could confirm it. And with Erin Llewellyn, a fingerprint lifted from her window didn't match his."

Joaquin scribbled in the margins, his cramped handwriting growing sloppier with each detail. "Yet the world believes he killed *all* of them?"

"I can't speak for the world, but they do here in Bluesummer."

Joaquin liked the name of his town better when Melrose said it, how she left off the "r," causing the word to leave her mouth open—*Bluesumma.*

His stomach emitted a loud rumble, disrupting his surely inappropriate focus on her mouth and drawing a curious glance from Melrose.

"Are you hungry?" she asked. "No time for brekkie?"

His head tilted to the side, eyes narrowing. "Brekkie?"

"Sorry, breakfast," she said, cheeks tinged pink. "Aussies shorten everything. Since moving here, I've lost a lot of my slang, but I can't let go of that."

"Well, think of all the time you save," Joaquin said with a grin.

"Exactly. More time to work. Where were we?"

She was right. Business first. Joaquin refocused. "The police think Troy fed the first three victims to his hogs?"

"Yes. Even though they found no evidence to support it."

Joaquin scratched his cheek. "I don't mean to be graphic, but wouldn't a hog eat all the . . . evidence?"

"Hogs can eat almost anything, even bones," Melrose explained. "Teeth and hair, though, are mostly indigestible. Teeth are enamel—the hardest substance in the human body—and hair's keratin doesn't break down either. That's why investigators sampled the manure pit. They found nothing, but claimed it was only because two months had passed since Erin's death and any manure containing evidence had already been spread over the Terrell cornfield."

"They should have searched the field," Joaquin said.

"They said they did a preliminary search, but short of digging up all the crops, there was nothing else to do. Since hair and some teeth from the first three victims were found with Wendy's body, police theorized the killer must have shaved them and pulled out their teeth before taking the bodies to the Terrell farm."

The theory made his stomach turn, but he forced himself to consider it logically, weighing every possibility against the scant evidence. "That's quite a theory. There could be other reasons a killer would shave his victims' heads or keep their teeth. And we can't discount an alibi—or an unknown fingerprint."

"Right, and that's why he wasn't charged with those murders. However, public opinion and online conspiracies are another story. The janitor's alibi for Troy got picked apart because of his drinking problem and close friendship with Troy's father. People said anyone could have touched Erin's window. Since no unknown fingerprints showed up at the other crime scenes, most assumed the Strangler wore gloves."

"Okay, trial one . . ." Joaquin checked his legal pad. "Hung jury. Troy's retried, found guilty, sentenced to death—then it's overturned."

"Only the sentence was overturned," Melrose clarified. "Kevin Carter, the DA, struck jurors with scruples against capital punishment, so a new jury was chosen to decide Troy's sentence. They also voted for death."

"Texas jurors don't play around when it comes to the death penalty, do they?"

"Odd, right? You can't believe the government buggers up everything it touches, but still trust it with the power to take lives."

"People are complicated."

Melrose crossed her arms. "More like contradictory."

Joaquin flipped to the next page of notes. "Direct appeals process dragged on till ninety-nine. Then Oswald filed the first habeas corpus, arguing ineffective counsel."

"Among other things, but yeah, mostly counsel. Troy's public defender fell asleep in court—more than once. Didn't put up a fight and made big mistakes. A US District Court overturned the conviction." Melrose scooted forward. "But the Fifth Circuit reversed that decision and reinstated the conviction and sentence. Gave their bulldust reasons, but Oswald always suspected it was because Troy's former public defender had become a Texas judge with connections."

"What a cluster," Joaquin said. "A hung jury, an overturned sentence, an overturned conviction, and they're still set on putting that needle in his arm."

"Not if we can help it." Melrose leaned back, crossing her legs.

Joaquin felt some weight lift at the word *we*. Liked the sound of it even more than *Bluesumma*. Unlike the last death penalty case he'd worked on, no big team was behind him this time. No big money. No Annabelle Bailey. For the first time since taking Troy's case, he didn't feel alone.

"You read about the DNA evidence, right?" Melrose asked.

"Yeah. Testing wasn't available at the time, but they determined from Tilly's sexual assault forensic exam that her rapist was a secretor with type

O blood. Troy is type O too, but so is about forty percent of the population—not exactly a smoking gun."

"Did they do a rape kit on Wendy?" Joaquin asked.

"They did, which in itself was against protocol since it had been over seventy-two hours since her death. Couldn't recover semen from her body, but there was a stain on her underwear—type O. The blood on her sheets and body was all Type AB, which was her own blood type."

The hum of the overhead fluorescent lights seemed louder as Joaquin scribbled notes, trying to keep track of every detail. "And there was a hair on Wendy's sheets, right? That appeared to be African American in origin?"

"Yeah, but her parents admitted her ex-boyfriend was black." She gave him a pointed look. "They also swore he never slept over."

Joaquin chuckled. "My parents would've said the same about my high school girlfriend. They would've been wrong."

"Exactly. Besides the hair, Wendy had a bite mark on her shoulder that the state claimed matched Troy. A former teacher testified he had a habit of chewing pencils, and the prosecution spun that into biting a human being."

Joaquin laughed. The idea was so ridiculous that it almost offended him. "You're joking."

"Oh, it gets better," Melrose said. "There was blood in Troy's truck that matched Wendy's blood type. Just a few flakes. Even without the technology available to DNA test evidence in eighty-six, the police had the good sense to preserve it. Oswald pushed to get it tested once technology caught up, but Carter fought him. By the time a judge authorized testing, the evidence was gone."

"Yeah, I saw that." Joaquin grabbed a smaller file from his desk and read. "It is with deep regret that we inform you that the evidence from

Mr. Troy Terrell's case was inadvertently destroyed during a 2002 mass destruction of several hundred boxes from closed cases."

Melrose arched one of her thick eyebrows. "Convenient, right? Oswald pivoted and filed a successive habeas to discredit the forensic dentist who testified that the bite mark on Wendy's collarbone came from Troy."

"Good old junk science," Joaquin said. "How much did the state pay the forensic odontologist to testify?"

"Twenty grand. And they took the impression of his teeth without a warrant." Melrose sighed. "We thought this was our ace in the hole. It was 2014—bite mark evidence was getting discredited left and right, freeing men on death row. But the court ruled that it wouldn't have changed the verdict even if we discredited the witness."

A phrase from Joaquin's high school physics popped into his mind. *An object in motion tends to stay in motion.* It was like those revolving doors. One step in and it owned you. It pushed you forward, no chance of going back the way you came.

"That's the short version leading to where we are now," Melrose said.

"Whew. Not sure I want to hear the long one."

Melrose tapped her foot against the floor. "So, where do we start?"

"I want to do something Oswald didn't—find an alternate suspect." He pointed his pen toward Melrose. "Think you can dig up anything on Ollie Ford? See if he's gotten himself into any legal trouble since?"

Melrose jotted a note. "I'll certainly give it a crack." She paused, twisting the pen between her fingers. "Doesn't destroying evidence violate a defendant's right to due process?"

"Only if we can prove the state acted in bad faith, and that's an uphill battle. I'm gonna focus on finding a Brady violation," Joaquin said. "Carter was retired before I started practicing, but I've heard he was crooked. If we can find evidence he withheld, that's our best shot.

Overturn the conviction, and I don't see how they can retry Troy—not with missing DNA and discredited bite mark evidence."

Melrose cocked her head. "They've still got the jailhouse confession of Titus Whitaker."

"Discrediting Three-Toed Titus shouldn't be hard."

A flicker of a smile passed over Melrose's lips before she pressed them together. "You're terrible."

"What?" Joaquin held up his hands. "Titus lost two toes on his left foot. I'm hardly the first one to call him that. He's a snake who concocted the story in exchange for a lighter sentence. I'll send our investigator over to have a chat—see if he can crack him."

"Oswald tried."

"Oswald's not Luca Moretti. I also need to contact DPAP's media liaison. Schedule some interviews and get our side out there."

"Too right. Because you can bet your arse Red Sheridan will slink out of hiding soon enough. He *solved* the crime, after all," she said, putting "solved" in air quotes. "But in reality, I reckon he just wanted a book deal."

"Never read the book, but I hear Sheridan's a decent guy. That he loved Troy like a son," Joaquin said.

Melrose cocked her head. "Would you turn your son in to the cops?"

He swallowed, weighing the question for a moment. "If I thought he killed someone? Yeah."

"He doesn't *know* he killed them, though. Yes, Troy was the last known person alone with Tilly. Yes, Red saw him driving home erratically. Sure, both Red and Troy's mom said he was acting strange and upset, but Troy explained why."

Joaquin raised his eyebrows. "I'm all ears."

"Unfulfilled expectations. What was supposed to be their final Fourth of July together all fell apart. That's hardly a motive to kill Tilly, and even if it was, that doesn't explain Nicole, Andrea, Erin, or Wendy."

"How about you call DPAP's media guy? You know more than I do."

Melrose huffed. "Shouldn't I focus on something more important than some statement?"

"The press is a weapon. Troy's former lawyers couldn't create doubt with the jury, but if we can with the public, they'll pressure the lawmakers."

"Not that it always makes a difference," Melrose said. "Missouri just went through with an execution, even though the public outcry to stop it was like nothing I've ever witnessed in the States."

Joaquin let out a heavy sigh. "Don't remind me. But maybe with that injustice still raw, a few more will stand with us this time. DPAP's got a petition up—let's promote it. And track down the former jurors. See if any regret their verdict."

"Okay." Melrose put pen to paper.

Joaquin pinched his bottom lip, brainstorming. "Troy had no priors. DPAP needs to hammer that home to the press. And how rare it is for teenagers to be serial killers."

"I'm bloody sure someone set him up," Melrose said, her brown eyes widening. "How else would Wendy's blood get into his truck?"

"That blood could have belonged to anyone with Type AB."

"Come on, Mr. Ramos." There was tension in Melrose's voice. "Then explain the class ring."

Joaquin hated that he didn't have a straightforward answer, that every explanation seemed to unravel into more questions. "If I'm going to call you Melrose, you've got to call me Joaquin." He leaned forward. "And I wish I could explain the ring. I sure as hell would like to know how Troy's class ring ended up in a cave with Wendy Knott's body, hair, and bones from the first three victims, and mementos of Bluesummer's dead girls."

"Young women," Melrose corrected. "Four out of five victims were legal adults. But anyway, Troy says he lost that ring in the woods around March. He dropped some weight after a knee injury, and it got loose. The killer must've found it and brought it to the bower. Like I said, a setup."

Joaquin's stomach turned at the thought of the bower—a shrine to the killer. He'd seen plenty of disturbing crime scene photos in his career, but nothing got to him like that nest of bones. Trinkets belonging to the Strangler's victims in the middle: a diamond earring, a tube of blood-red lipstick, a Rubik's Cube, a clear paperweight with a preserved butterfly inside, and a charm bracelet. Two decorative birds, once part of wind chimes hanging in happy homes, completed the display.

"Why did they call it the bower?" Joaquin asked.

"Bowerbirds," Melrose said. "They're native to Australia. They build elaborate nests to attract mates using sticks, bright pieces of glass, shells, and even bone fragments. Sheridan coined the term in his book, and it stuck."

"So they think the Strangler killed these girls in their beds, took their bodies into the woods, staged pictures, shaved their heads, and dismembered them?"

"Yes. Dismemberment would make it easier to get the remains to the hog pen and allow the killer to keep some of the bones as mementos."

He closed the file, willing the image of the bower away. "Let's plan to visit Troy early next week. I wanna hear his version of the events of the Fourth of July and—"

Joaquin was about to launch into another line of questioning when a sharp knock rattled the doorframe. "Five o'clock!" Bernadette announced. "Hasta mañana."

Joaquin smiled. Bernadette would do anything for him, but only between 8 a.m. and 5 p.m. "Have a nice evening, Bernie."

She peeked in. "Don't stay late, Melrose. You've got your own life, I'm sure."

"Not really," Melrose said, "but thank you."

"Bernie's right." Joaquin motioned toward the door. "You should go."

Melrose shook her head. "I'm fine. I don't mind late hours."

"I know." He closed the file. "Trust me, we'll have plenty coming. But tonight's not one of them. Go home. Rest up for the uphill climb."

Bernie grabbed Melrose's jacket from the hook. "Come on, hon. I'll walk you out. Gets dark early this time of year. We women gotta watch out for each other."

Joaquin stood. "I can walk you ladies out."

Bernie held up a hand. "Sit down. I can get to my car without a man's help."

"But you just said—"

Before he could finish, Bernie was pulling Melrose toward the door. "He's got a white-knight complex, honey. You'll get used to it."

# CHAPTER 6

**1986**

Hayes's hand shook as he held the letter he'd been waiting weeks for. He ran his fingers over the thick envelope. Was it too bulky for a rejection?

His hands were sweating now, gripping the letter. The urge to tear it open in the driveway was strong, but he couldn't face the news—whatever it was—alone.

*It doesn't matter*, he told himself as he drove to Greer's. *It's not like I can go.* But if he believed that, why had he applied? Was it hope? Curiosity? Or just stubbornness?

He pulled into Greer's driveway behind her beat-up green Ford Taurus. Thank God her mom wasn't home. Not that Ms. Collins talked much to his parents, but Bluesummer was a small town. It was only a matter of time before they ran into each other at the Winn-Dixie or Whataburger.

Greer opened the door before Hayes knocked, as if she'd known he'd be coming. They'd always had a connection like that—kindred spirits.

"What's up?" Greer mumbled, mouth full of toothpaste, brushing away at the corner of her mouth.

"I got the letter. From Cornell."

She spat the toothpaste into the flowerpot beside the door. "Where is it?"

Hayes looked at his hands, realizing he wasn't holding it. "In the truck."

Greer pushed the door open and stepped outside. "What did it say?"

He swallowed, glancing down at his hands. "I don't know."

Greer dropped her toothbrush. "You don't know?"

"I didn't open it."

"Seriously?" Greer shoved past him and sprinted to his truck, retrieving the envelope from the passenger seat.

"Don't! Not out here."

Greer bent to retrieve her toothbrush. "Let's just calm down, okay?" She handed the envelope to Hayes. "We'll go inside, and you can open it whenever you're ready."

They sat on the couch in Greer's living room. Hayes stared at the envelope, fingers drumming against his thigh. He glanced at the coffee table: a half-finished crossword sat under a ceramic ashtray. His gaze drifted to the corner, where *National Geographic* magazines were stacked.

Greer watched him, twisting the hem of her loose cotton T-shirt, legs tucked beneath her. After a few minutes, she stood. "Do you want water? Or like an Eggo or something?"

Hayes stood and held out the envelope. "Open it."

Greer blinked rapidly, a small crease forming between her brows. "You want *me* to open it?"

"Yeah." Hayes paced across the living room, his muscles twitching.

He kept his back to her and heard the envelope tear open. For what felt like forever, Greer didn't speak. The only sound was the cuckoo clock above the mantel, ticking in sync with Hayes's thudding heartbeat. He sensed Greer step closer.

*It's a no.* Greer would've said something if it had been good news. "It's okay," he muttered. "It's for the best."

"Hayes." Greer thrust the letter into his peripheral vision. "You're in!"

Hayes froze, heart hammering, mind racing. A grin wanted to burst across his face, but disbelief kept it tethered. He swallowed hard, feeling a mix of excitement and panic coiling in his stomach. He spun around, snatching the letter. He reread it, backing away. "I got in. I got into Cornell!"

Greer screamed, throwing her arms around him. "I knew it! I freaking knew it! Congratulations!"

Hayes wiped his eyes, surprised by his own emotion. "I didn't think I could pull it off."

"Come on, you were so close to being our valedictorian, and your SAT score was insane. And that expertly edited admissions essay couldn't have hurt."

"Yeah, thanks again for your help," Hayes said, still staring at the letter as if waiting for a catch.

"You've got to tell Red and Joanne!"

Hayes flopped on the couch. "About that . . ."

Greer crossed her arms. "You *still* haven't told them?"

"I didn't think I would get in, so why bother?"

"Come on, Hayes, they will be *so* excited."

Hayes looked at her, raising his eyebrows.

Greer perched on the edge of the floral-patterned couch, a faint, wry smile tugging at her lips. "Okay, excited is the wrong word, but it's lame that Joanne wants you to go to UT because she and your dad did. You realize the real reason, right? She wants you close. Cornell is a way better school, and they'll see that. Plus, Joanne can brag about it to all her scummy rich friends."

"Cornell's expensive. I've got a scholarship to UT."

Greer bumped her shoulder against his. "Oh, come on, it's not like your parents can't afford college. Stop assuming the worst and talk to them. Plus, I can help with scholarship applications."

Hayes rubbed a hand through his hair, which his mom had been nagging him to get cut. "It's not *just* selling the school but the degree program."

"Wait, you didn't apply for the architecture program?" Hayes handed the letter back to her. She scanned it again. "Agriculture?"

"See the problem?" Hayes asked, standing again to put more miles across the rose-colored carpet.

Greer bit her lip. "Yeah, but it's your life. You've always been interested in agriculture."

"Since that first day at Terrell's farm." Hayes stuck his hands into his pockets. "I like architecture, and I'm good at it. It's a practical career path, but when I envision designing buildings for the rest of my life, I feel . . . well, nothing."

Greer tilted her head. "So . . . you want to be a farmer? Do you need a degree for that?"

"I'd like to be a farm manager. Swine or poultry. I'd make decent money at some of the bigger farms."

Greer stood. "Well, this is great. You'd be great at that. Sure, it's going to suck to break it to your mom, but Red will understand. You get your love of the land from him, after all."

"But there's an even bigger problem." Hayes rubbed his face vigorously. "Tilly."

Greer let out a long, soft groan. "I should have figured."

"Come on, Greer. She's going to UT."

"Okay. And?"

"And what?" Hayes's shoulders curved forward. "If we don't go to the same college, it's over."

Maybe it was Hayes's imagination, but he swore he saw a smile flicker past Greer's lips before she pressed them tight. "Making decisions based on a girl is even dumber than basing them on your parents."

"Do you think she'd consider Cornell?"

"Hayes." Greer sighed his name. "Tilly can't get into Cornell."

Hayes hated to admit it, but Greer was right. Not that Tilly wasn't smart—she was. She'd just bombed her SAT.

Hayes dropped the letter on the coffee table. "So, it's either stay in Texas or lose my girlfriend."

"Why?" Greer asked. "If you love each other, why can't long distance work?"

Hayes knew it wasn't that easy. Not with someone as beautiful as Chantilly Price. Not to mention, things were already complicated between them. "I can't compete with frat guys," he said.

"Uh, you absolutely can," Greer raised her voice. "Not that you should have to if Tilly's serious about making it work. Just talk to her. She'll want what's best for you."

"Can you feel Tilly out about it? Get her thoughts on long-distance relationships. Say you're asking about another friend."

Greer broke eye contact. "That's not my place."

"Please? I'll owe you."

She looked back at him. "Fine. I'll ask. But you work on your parents. Get them used to the idea? Deal?"

He let out a small breath, the tension in his shoulders finally easing. "Deal. Now, go get dressed. I'll take you to breakfast."

Greer smiled. "I'm gonna miss our breakfasts. All those mornings studying over the Breakfast Barn's all-you-can-eat pancakes."

"Me too." As much as Hayes would miss Tilly if he chose Cornell, he'd maybe miss Greer even more. He loved Tilly, but his relationship with Greer was uncomplicated—he could be himself. "Hey, with your grades, you'd probably be accepted into Cornell, too."

Greer gave a two-note laugh. "Sure, no problem. Hey, by the way, do you have twelve grand I can borrow? Times four?"

Hayes stuffed his hands into his pockets. It was easy to forget that not everyone had the same advantages he did. "Sorry."

Greer slugged his shoulder. "It's fine. I'm happy with Panola College to get my basics, save money, and help my mom with tuition. Then on to UT, and as much as I hate to say this, I hope you aren't there."

"Me too," Hayes said, but as the words left his mouth, he suspected he would be.

Greer lay across Tilly's bed, watching her friend pull a different mini skirt over her purple leggings. The room was a strange mix of Tilly's childhood and teenage self: soft pink walls still peeked from behind a carefully curated display of band posters, and a frilly canopy above the bed sagged slightly, its satin ribbons catching the light. A crystal lamp sat on the nightstand, next to a neat stack of glossy fashion magazines.

"Which looks better?" Tilly asked, checking herself in the mirror.

Greer pinched the bridge of her nose and let out a short huff. "They look the same."

"The other one's shorter." Tilly glanced over her shoulder, studying the back of her outfit. "But my butt looks better in this one."

"Yeah, definitely," Greer agreed, hoping to stop her from trying on a third outfit.

"When are you gonna get ready?" Tilly asked, pulling her thick blonde hair into a high ponytail.

Greer sat up and tugged at the hem of her oversized Fleetwood Mac T-shirt, smoothing the fabric over her ripped jeans. "I am ready."

Tilly wrapped a purple scrunchie around her ponytail and sat beside Greer. "You'd be pretty if you tried. Want me to do your makeup? Cover some of those freckles?"

Greer absently wiped her cheek as if she could erase them. "I like my freckles," she lied.

"Well, boys don't," Tilly said. "And your hair." She frowned, tugging at a clump of Greer's strawberry-blonde bob. "Do you ever brush it?"

Greer ran a finger through her hair. Tilly was right; it was matted. But she *had* brushed it this morning. Sometimes, things started out nice and became a mess, kinda like Tilly.

Tilly had changed. She hadn't always cared so much about her hair, clothes, and body. When Chantilly Price arrived on the first day of second grade, Greer felt sorry for the shy, small girl with white-blonde hair and porcelain skin. She looked like a china doll, terrified she might shatter in a classroom full of rough and rowdy kids. So, Greer sat with her at lunch and introduced her to Troy and Hayes. She regretted that now. Not befriending Tilly. She'd been a genuine friend to Greer for years. And Greer could ignore Tilly's snide comments and constant lipstick touch-ups, but she couldn't handle Hayes loving her. Introducing them had been a mistake.

Before Tilly, Hayes Sheridan had belonged to Greer.

Tilly handed a hairbrush to Greer. "My family's watching the fireworks in Dallas this year. I told them I couldn't go, obviously. I have to be with the Quad on the Fourth," she said.

"You can stay the night with me," Greer suggested.

"And do what? Watch old Elvis movies with your mom? Look, me spending the night with you would be the *official* story, but we'd be at my house—unsupervised." Her eyes went wide. "I've found where Dad hides the good stuff."

Greer stopped brushing. "That's not a smart idea. If my mom ever found out—"

"She won't! Our parents don't talk. And your mom might pick up the night shift."

Tilly had a point. After Greer's dad left, her mom worked two jobs to put herself through nursing school. For years, Linda Collins picked up extra shifts to help cover college tuition for Greer's twin brothers. Now she'd be doing the same for Greer.

"Troy will come. His parents don't care." Tilly stood and stared into the mirror again, turning to the side and sucking in a nonexistent stomach. "But Joanne won't let Hayes go without a fight."

"Red might convince her," Greer said. "If he knows Troy and I will be there, too."

"So you're in?" Tilly picked up her mascara.

Greer rolled her eyes. "You already put that on."

"Three coats." Tilly brought the wand to her eye.

Greer flopped back onto the pillows. "Come on! The guys are already at Whataburger."

Tilly shrugged. "So let them wait." She turned her head toward Greer. "So you're in for the Fourth, right? My place. *All* night."

Greer hugged a pillow to her chest. "What about the Strangler?"

Tilly tilted her head back and groaned. "Ugh, the Strangler. Gag me. Are we going to let some asshole ruin our last summer together?" She waved her hands dramatically. "And I thought you were, like, obsessed with solving the case. If we meet him on the Fourth, it's solved. You and Red can write a book and become a rich and famous crime-solving duo."

Greer's shoulders stiffened. "Come on, Tilly. That isn't funny."

"Do you think some old creep will get past Hayes and Troy? Troy's two hundred forty pounds of muscle."

"Not anymore, and he's still struggling to get around after his surgery."

Tilly flopped back onto the bed, rolling onto her side. "Well, Hayes can shoot a gun. And Daddy's got an entire cabinet full." She reached out, taking Greer's hands in hers. Her eyes softened. "I don't think Troy will come if it's just Hayes and me. I want you both there." She squeezed Greer's hand the way she used to when they were little girls sharing secrets. They were all going their separate ways in August. July was all they had.

Greer exhaled, a small smile breaking through. "Okay, but only if we watch fireworks first."

"Yeah, yeah. You haven't let us miss the fireworks show in ten years, even though it *never* changes."

"Come on, Tilly. Humans have an ancient fascination with fire. And aren't we all naturally drawn to things that sparkle?"

"Guess I can't deny that." Tilly pulled a shimmering diamond necklace from beneath her shirt and let it dangle. "Now, let's get to dinner."

# CHAPTER 7



Joaquin stayed on his feet until Luca Moretti dropped into the chair across from him. "So, to what do I owe the surprise visit? I'm hoping that swagger means good news."

"That's not a swagger; that's a bad hip," Luca said, even though he couldn't be over forty-five and was in incredible shape. "But I have good news." Luca reached into his cross-body bag and pulled out a paper. "Titus Whitaker."

Joaquin grabbed it. "Is this what I think it is?"

Luca smiled, revealing his shockingly white teeth. "He wasn't hard to crack. Recanted everything. Terrell never spoke to him, much less confessed to being a serial killer."

Joaquin exhaled slowly, the tension in his shoulders easing. Finally, something concrete. "So, why'd he lie?"

"Reduced sentence. Crooked Carter agreed to drop two of the three charges against him if he testified against Troy."

Joaquin slapped the polished surface of his desk. "I knew it. This is big. A jury has to be told if an informant is offered any benefit for testifying."

Luca sighed. "The bad news is there's no written agreement."

Joaquin's hands gripped the edge of the desk. Frustration flared, but beneath it, a spark of hope. "But the charges got dropped, right?"

"Yeah, but it's not unusual for the DA's office to drop charges in exchange for a guilty plea to lesser charges."

Joaquin reclined in his worn leather chair, the cushions sighing under his weight. "Carter's retired, right? In Florida? What are the chances of getting something out of him?"

Luca leaned forward on the desk, hands clasped, a self-satisfied glint in his eye. "Zero, considering he had a fatal heart attack last winter."

Joaquin jerked upright in his chair. "Wait. Carter's dead?"

"Yep. The devil called him home."

"So you're saying it comes down to trusting the word of a well-respected district attorney versus that of a drug-dealing, wife-beating gang member?"

"Afraid that's how a judge will see it," Luca said. "When a witness recants, the question is whether they're lying now or were before."

Joaquin pulled back a metal ball from the Newton's cradle and released it. "An object in motion stays in motion."

"Huh?"

"Nothing. It's still good news, but we need more."

"Of course we do. There's no formula for getting someone off death row. We just throw spaghetti at the wall and hope something sticks."

Joaquin raised an eyebrow. "Say what?"

"Come on, you've never heard that?"

"No. Who throws spaghetti against the wall?"

"Italian moms. If it sticks, it's done."

"Well, the next thing I need you to throw against the wall is a local named Oliver Ford. He was a person of interest. I've got my paralegal looking into his record, but it may be worth paying him a visit."

Luca typed a note on his phone. "Ford. Got it. What else?"

Joaquin stood. "Have Troy sign a waiver so we can obtain his medical records. He claims he lost his class ring after losing weight from knee surgery."

"That's a rough procedure. Hard to kill five people if you can't get around," Luca said.

Joaquin propped a shoulder against his bookcase. He didn't notice Bernie standing at the door until she cleared her throat. "Need something, Bern?"

"Don't tell me you've forgotten your 10:30 hearing."

He had forgotten, and Bernie must have noticed his jeans and polo. Luckily, he had learned to keep a spare suit and pair of Bruno Maglis in his office closet for such emergencies. "We're almost finished, but thanks for the reminder."

Luca stood. "I'll let you get ready. Call if you think of anything else."

"Now that's a beautiful man," Bernie murmured, eyes following Luca as he left out the front door.

"A little young for you, don't you think?"

"Hey, I might have a few miles on the odometer, but I've still got some spark left. Has Melrose had the pleasure?"

"The pleasure of what? Meeting Luca?" Joaquin patted his stomach, silently vowing not to skip any days at the gym this week. "Not yet. Why?"

Bernie opened her compact and picked lipstick from the corners of her mouth. "They'd make a cute couple."

Joaquin's jaw tightened, just slightly. He could feel the heat in his chest, a prick of possessiveness he hadn't expected. "He's like fifteen years older than her."

Bernie snapped the compact closed. "Too young for me, too old for her. Come on."

"Isn't he married?" Joaquin asked.

"Wow, you don't get out much. They divorced at least two years ago." Bernie motioned to his worn-out Nikes. "You gonna change?"

"Yeah . . . suit's in the closet," he said, forcing a casual tone.

She flashed a knowing smile. "You forgot, didn't you?"

"No." Joaquin glanced toward the window instead of meeting her eyes. "Just here to meet with Luca and get Melrose set for the day. Where is she?"

"Guess you *also* forgot Melrose had a doctor's appointment this morning."

Joaquin smacked his forehead. "Alright, I forgot about that one. Let her know Three-Toed Titus recanted. Have her call Troy with the update, then get information ready for DPAP's media liaison."

Bernie scribbled on a Post-it note. "Three toes, Troy, media. Got it. Anything else?"

"I don't think so," he replied, though he could see from Bernie's expression that he had overlooked something. "What is it, Bernie? What did I miss?"

She snatched a check from the box by his door. "You gonna sign this? Friday was payday."

Joaquin's eyes flicked to the check. *Damn*, he thought. *I can't even keep up with this.*

"Right, sorry. We need to get you set up with direct deposit."

She pushed the check into his face. "How about you sign this, and I deposit it? Directly."

"Have it your way." He grabbed a pen off her desk and held the check against the wall to scribble his name.

She scrutinized it. "And it's not going to bounce?"

Joaquin narrowed his eyes. "Bernie."

"Kidding." She ushered him into his office. "Now get dressed and get out of here."

The windshield wipers swished away the drizzle as Joaquin and Melrose drove toward the prison the next morning. "I called to confirm I could bring an assistant, but you're already on Troy's visiting list."

"Yeah," Melrose said, adjusting her seatbelt. "I went with Mr. Oswald when he represented Troy. After that, I stayed in touch with Troy, though I haven't visited much." She stared out the window. "I've been a real bludger."

"Don't feel guilty," Joaquin said. "You contacted DPAP."

"Yeah," Melrose said, her tone flat. Something seemed off today. The usually punctual Melrose arrived ten minutes late and had been quiet during the two-hour drive despite Joaquin's attempts to engage her. The dark circles under her eyes and a drained complexion caught his attention. He remembered her doctor's appointment and hoped she wasn't sick.

"You feel okay?" Joaquin asked.

"Just a bit knackered today. I didn't sleep well." Melrose reached over and lowered the radio volume, the hum of the engine filling the brief silence. "So what do you plan to ask Troy today?"

"For the whole truth. Some lawyers may not want to hear it, but I do—the good, the bad, and the ugly. My gut says he only killed Tilly, maybe by accident, then panicked and made it look like the Strangler."

Melrose gave him a puzzled look. "What makes you think the Strangler didn't kill Tilly?"

"Timing, mostly. Since March, the Strangler had been killing one girl—I mean a young woman—a month, always within the first few days of each month. Wendy Knott was murdered on July 1. Why would he strike again three days later? When he hadn't even disposed of Wendy's body?"

Melrose tilted her head. "Opportunity? He was already deviating. Wendy wasn't strangled."

"True, but the Strangler always took pictures of his victims to leave at the next crime scene. No picture of Wendy at the Price house, and Tilly's body was not taken to the bower. Why?"

"Most likely because he was interrupted when Greer showed up. But he still took Tilly's charm bracelet to the bower." Melrose turned toward him. "And if the killer was interrupted by Greer, that eliminates Troy."

Joaquin shifted in his seat. "How so?"

"Greer didn't find Tilly till 11:55. Troy talked to Red at 11:15. So Troy was home forty minutes before she found the body. And what reason would Troy have to murder one of his best mates?"

"They were drunk," Joaquin said, loosening his shoulders. "Maybe things went too far, got too rough. That's what I've got to get out of Troy today."

"Good luck. His story hasn't changed in forty years. Yes, he was alone with Tilly, but nothing happened."

"I hope you're right," Joaquin said, cranking the heater to clear the fog from the windows.

"I finished compiling the information for DPAP's media liaison," Melrose said. "Hoping they'll have something about Titus's recant by the week's end."

"Wow, that was fast work."

She shrugged. "I don't sleep well. I also did some digging into articles about the execution date. Red hasn't spoken to the press yet, which is a miracle."

"Isn't he a bit of a recluse now?" Joaquin asked.

"Well, that's for the best. Everybody loves the bloke, the press, the public. You know his son married Greer Collins, right?"

Joaquin turned the corner to the prison. "One big happy family."

Melrose adjusted her seatbelt. "Rumor has it, Greer was green with envy over Tilly."

Joaquin blinked, incredulous. "Come on. You're not suggesting Greer Collins is the Songbird Strangler, right?" Joaquin asked.

"Of course not. I'm just saying the little love triangle ended in Greer's favor. Might be worth asking her some questions."

"Good idea. She could at least shed light on the relationship between Troy and Tilly," he said, pulling into a parking spot. "Let's get Troy's side for now."

They were processed quickly and escorted into the legal booth. Polunsky was the most depressing prison Joaquin had ever set foot in. Prison wasn't meant to be pleasant, but twenty-three hours in a concrete tomb felt inhumane, especially when you'd been here as long as Troy Terrell.

Joaquin motioned for Melrose to sit, then squeezed into the plastic chair beside her. The cramped space barely accommodated both seats on their side of the glass in the Smurf-blue room. Joaquin focused on his legal pad, scribbling the date, trying to ignore the growing tension with Melrose. A crush on an employee was unprofessional and dangerous, yet hard to push away when her hair brushed his shoulder and her perfume drifted into the cramped room—making it feel less like a prison smelling of sweat, metal, and floor disinfectant, and more like summers barefoot in his abuela's garden, the air thick with jasmine and honeysuckle.

Joaquin listened to the clopping boots and the clanking chains as the guard escorted Troy through the door on the opposite side of the plexiglass.

Melrose reached across Joaquin to grab the only phone. "How are you, Troy? You look fantastic."

Troy's lips moved, but Joaquin couldn't understand what he was saying. He edged closer, straining to listen. Melrose noticed and brought the phone between them, holding the speaker so they could both hear. "Sorry," she whispered.

"It's fine." Joaquin raised his voice. "Can you hear me okay, Troy?"

"Yes, sir," he replied. "I was just explaining to Melrose that I look better now because the last time she visited was on a hundred-and-seven-degree summer day, and my face was melting. At least I'm scheduled to die in winter. No more Texas summers for me."

Joaquin leaned closer to the receiver. "Let's focus on keeping you alive."

Troy smiled. "Even better."

Melrose handed Joaquin the phone, and he put it to his ear. "First things first, Troy. As your attorney, I need the whole truth. Unfortunately, we're limited to non-contact visits in Texas. Our conversation is privileged, but please keep your voice down."

"Okay," Troy said. "Where do I start?"

Joaquin got straight to the point. "Are you the Songbird Strangler?"

"No, sir."

"Did you kill Chantilly Price?"

"I just said—"

Joaquin raised his hand. "Answer the question."

"No," Troy repeated, eyes crinkling into angry slits.

"Even accidentally?"

Joaquin sensed Melrose's anger as she started breathing heavily, but he ignored her. Just because she trusted Troy didn't mean Joaquin was there yet.

"I said I didn't kill her." A vein bulged on Troy's forehead.

"Alright then." Joaquin placed his pen on the paper. "Let's go back in time to July 4, 1986 . . ."

# CHAPTER 8

**July 4, 1986**

Greer was the last to arrive at the lake. Troy's boombox blared Run DMC's "Tricky" while he and Hayes loaded Dr Pepper into an ice chest. She stared at Hayes; his ice-blue eyes contrasted with dark brown hair. He wore a red button-down shirt covered with large white hibiscus flowers, looking like a young Elvis straight out of *Blue Hawaii*.

She tore her gaze away, reached into the back seat, and pulled out a twenty-four pack of Bud Light. "Sometimes it pays when my big brothers are home."

Tilly rose from her lawn chair. "What are Zach and Keat doing tonight?"

*Keat.* Greer couldn't say why, but Tilly shortening her brother's name annoyed her. It suggested a familiarity—a relationship—that none of them had with her brother, least of all Greer.

"Video game marathon, what else?" Greer answered, tearing into the cardboard box.

Troy began adding the beer cans to the chest, but Tilly grabbed one before it hit the ice.

Troy looked at her. "A little early for those yet."

"Oh, loosen up." Tilly popped the top. "Hayes is driving me tonight, and my parents are on their way to Dallas," she said, pressing her body against Hayes.

Greer turned away as Tilly crammed her tongue down Hayes's throat. Even after all these years of seeing them together, seeing them kiss never got easier.

"Hey, hey, hey!" Troy scooped out a cup of ice and tossed it in their direction.

Tilly screamed and shook ice from her shirt, lifting it to flash a lacy white bra.

Troy pointed a finger at Hayes. "If y'all are gonna stay locked in the bedroom all night, I'm out."

"We won't," Hayes said, stepping away from Tilly. "We'll all sleep in the living room."

"So you're for sure going?" Greer's stomach fluttered at the thought of spending the night with Hayes. It was stupid to be excited about it, especially with Tilly, but she couldn't help it. Maybe Tilly would pass out drunk, and Hayes would fall for Greer instead. She laughed, not even buying into her own fantasies.

"Yeah, I'm going. I haven't asked my parents yet, but they'll be cool about it."

Knowing Joanne Sheridan, Greer doubted it.

"You're coming too, right?" Hayes asked her.

"For sure," Greer said. She didn't like lying to her mom, but she wasn't *technically* lying. She *was* staying the night at Tilly's.

"We are going to have *so* much fun." Tilly kissed Greer's cheek. Her breath smelled of beer and Hayes, and for a moment, Greer hated her.

The sentiment only intensified when Tilly picked up a blanket and took Hayes's hand, pulling him into the woods.

Hayes's cheeks instantly became pink-stained, matching the shade Chantilly had achieved by applying layers of Maybelline Plumberry blush on her own cheeks. But he didn't argue. Didn't hesitate to walk away from Greer into the piney woods.

Troy lowered himself onto a lawn chair. "They were careless people, Tom and Daisy," he said, quoting *The Great Gatsby* passage they'd had to memorize junior year. "Actually, let me fix that," he said, watching his friends disappear into the woods. "They were careless people, Hayes and Tilly . . ."

"They smashed up things and creatures and then retreated back into their money or their vast carelessness," Greer finished.

Troy laughed. "Mrs. Donovan would be so proud."

"Daisy was right, though." Greer plopped onto the chair beside Troy's. "Because guys seem to love the beautiful little fool thing Tilly has going for her."

Troy brushed grass from his shorts. "I know you don't want to hear this, G, but there are other guys."

"I went to prom with Ronald Moore, didn't I?"

"You did. But what about the other hundred times he asked you out?"

"Ron's a nice guy, he's just . . ." She hesitated, twisting her hands in her lap. "He's just . . ."

"He's just not Hayes Sheridan," Troy said.

*Exactly*, Greer thought, but didn't dare admit. She'd built her life on the hope that one day, Hayes would wake up from his Chantilly Price-induced stupor and realize the perfect girl was right in front of him. That his freckle-faced, red-haired, lanky "just friend" was his soul mate. It happened in the movies all the time. Now, with Tilly and Hayes possibly going to college together, Greer felt her decade-long dream slipping away.

"So what about you and Maggie?" she asked, changing the subject. "Why hasn't she been around?"

Troy's shoulders slumped as he looked away. "It wasn't gonna last. She's headed to Baylor next month."

Greer sensed the disappointment in his voice. It was sometimes easy for Greer to feel sorry for herself when she compared her life with Hayes's or Tilly's. They'd never had jobs. Greer had worked at the skating rink since she was fifteen. Their families took elaborate vacations every summer, and Greer had never been outside Texas. But unlike Troy, at least Greer was going to college. At least she had a path out of Bluesummer. "You should enroll at Panola," she suggested. "With your grades, you could get a scholarship, and it's cheap even without one."

Troy shook his head. "Come on. Dad's depending on me."

Greer's hands rested on the arms of her chair, shoulders squared as she stared him down. "No, you come on, Troy. Carthage is like half an hour away. You could manage the farm and take a few classes. You don't work *all* day."

Troy looked at the pine-littered grass. "Hayes won't be here for butchering, so that's one less hand. Dad's mind is—" He stopped and shook his head. "Can we not talk about college and just enjoy the night?"

Greer raised her hands. "Sorry I mentioned it."

Troy pulled down his cap. "Sorry."

"What's with you lately? You've been, I don't know, broody," Greer said, doing her best to put it nicely. Troy had been volatile, and his triggers were unpredictable. His temper might have served him well on the football field, but Greer didn't like walking on eggshells around him.

Troy cracked a beer despite telling Tilly it was too early. "I'm fine," he said. "Want one? Or a Coke?"

Greer shook her head. Troy was lying, but she wouldn't push. The only explosion she wanted to see tonight was the fireworks. She looked down the incline at a sunburned man struggling to inflate a child's float. "Let's go by the water and set off some fireworks."

"Don't you want to wait for Hayes and Tilly?"

"Hell no. I'm tired of waiting for Hayes."

"Atta girl," Troy set his beer on the ice chest. "Race ya to the water."

"Troy, your knee."

He pushed himself up. "It's not that far."

"Come on, don't be stupid."

"You afraid I'm still gonna beat you even with a bum knee?"

"What do you mean, *still?*" Greer asked. "I've won—"

Before she could finish, Troy took off toward the water. Greer grabbed the bag of fireworks and ran her hardest, making it to the lake right behind him.

"So close," Troy huffed.

Greer bent over to catch her breath. "You had a head start."

Of the Quad, Greer and Troy had been friends the longest. Who won that race on the first day of kindergarten remained a debated memory.

Greer grabbed a pack of Roman candles. "Are we lighting these or not?"

"I've never known anybody who likes fireworks more than you," Troy said, pulling a few punk sticks from the bag.

Greer unwrapped the plastic. "Yeah, I guess boys don't like girls who blow things up. They like girls who scream and grab onto their boyfriends for protection, like Tilly."

"You're worth ten Tillys. I mean, she used to be cool, but she's turned into a major bitch. Stop being jealous of her. That's what she wants. That's why she led Hayes off like she did, to make you jealous. What kind of friend is that?"

Greer didn't answer. He was right, but she didn't want to talk about it. She pointed her Roman candle toward the woods. "If I shoot it this way, I bet I can catch my blanket on fire."

Troy turned her toward the water instead. "Calm down, pyro. More likely, you'll catch a bush on fire and burn down the town."

Burning down Bluesummer didn't sound half bad tonight, but Greer stayed facing the water as she lit the fuse.

"Woo-hoo!" she screamed as the first orange ball flamed over the water, drawing the attention of a cluster of families barbecuing under a sprawling oak tree nearby. Each shot rocketed into the sky, shattering into sparks. It was human nature, she supposed, to be attracted to bright things, to dangerous things.

"Are you trying to yell loud enough for Hayes and Tilly to hear you?" Troy asked.

"Maybe." She passed him the trash. "I'm not going to Tilly's. No matter what they say, they won't be able to keep their hands off each other."

Troy kneeled, dousing the empty Roman candle in lake water. "Then screw them." He laughed. "Okay, terrible choice of words, but how about you and me hang?"

Greer hesitated. "But the Quad's always spent the Fourth together."

He lifted the bag. "We can all shoot the rest of these off *together* and watch Bluesummer's same old display *together*. After that, they'll go to Tilly's, and we'll go . . . wherever."

"We could hang out at my place, but the twins are there. I thought graduating from college meant you were supposed to find a job and become an adult."

"To be fair, Zach did just graduate."

"Yeah, failing classes will set you back like that," Greer said.

"And Keaton's had a rough year," Troy added.

Greer realized that. Keaton had graduated early, landed a job in Houston, and gotten engaged—all before her senior year. But when he came home for Spring Break, he revealed that Tara had broken off their engagement. Depressed, he spent two weeks in bed and lost his job. He'd been in Bluesummer since—sleeping, eating junk food, and playing video games. At least Red hired him to do some bookkeeping, giving him something to do a few hours a day. But still, Greer was tired of him being around.

Troy surveyed the woods. "We could camp out. Like freshman year. I've still got the tents."

"Are you insane? There's a serial killer on the loose."

Troy blew out a breath. "Right. Then let's get out of Bluesummer. Remember my cousin Vic? He's on vacation, but I've got a key to his apartment in Carthage. We can rent movies, eat snacks, crash out."

Greer bit her lip. "My mom would flip if she found out I left town."

"Come on, G. You're almost eighteen. She won't even know."

He was right. Greer's mom was working the ER all night, and Greer would be the last thing on her mind.

"Okay, deal."

"Alright!" Troy spat into his palm. "We gotta shake on it."

Greer wrinkled her nose, trying not to laugh. "Ugh, you're disgusting."

"Come on now. Have you forgotten our secret handshake?"

"We were kids, Troy. We didn't know all the infectious diseases that spread through saliva."

"No shake, no deal," Troy said, hand still extended.

"Oh, fine." Greer spat weakly into her hand and shook his. "But first, let's light some freaking firecrackers."

# CHAPTER 9

**Allan B. Polunsky Unit, 2024**

"What time did Hayes and Chantilly sneak away into the woods?" Joaquin asked.

Troy scratched his forehead. "Around sunset. So, eight-ish?"

"Did Hayes have protection?"

Troy raised his eyebrows. "No clue, man. You think I care that much about my friends' sex lives?"

Joaquin's lips twitched. *Smart ass.* No wonder jurors had never warmed to Troy.

Melrose took the phone. "I realize these feel like invasive questions, but the police concluded that Tilly's killer sexually assaulted her because of semen recovered from her body and a few bruises. But there's a chance that the semen may belong to a consensual sex partner, such as Hayes Sheridan."

Troy's lips moved, but Joaquin strained to listen. Melrose passed the phone back, shifting her knee away. "He thought the DNA evidence was destroyed," she relayed.

Joaquin pressed the phone to his ear, attempting to shake off the awkwardness of Melrose's sudden distancing from him. "Supposedly destroyed," Joaquin clarified, lifting a hand to his mouth to check his breath. "But that's too convenient. Our investigator's looking for it."

Troy's shoulders dropped, and he nodded, relief flickering across his face. Joaquin wondered if he was relieved someone was looking for the DNA—or that it was still missing. Either way, his reaction felt off.

"The DNA isn't the be-all and end-all of anything," he said, despite knowing there was a chance it could be. "I've got a few other avenues we can explore."

"I'm all ears."

"Titus Whitaker," Joaquin said. "He told the police you confessed to being the Strangler in prison."

Troy laughed. "I never told Three-Toed Titus shit."

"He recanted. Turns out Kevin Carter, the DA, offered him reduced charges for testifying against you. It's a good start, but I'd also like to look into other suspects. Can you tell us anything about Oliver Ford?" Joaquin lowered the phone so Melrose could listen, watching Troy carefully.

"Back to Ollie? He's a local, a few years older than us, supposedly caught peeping before the crimes."

"There was lots of talk about him being the killer. Have any thoughts on that?"

Troy shrugged. "I wouldn't want to accuse anybody without knowing. But my gut says he's harmless. Ollie's got some intellectual disabilities. Unless . . ." He paused. "Nah, forget it."

Joaquin leaned a fraction closer, eyes locked on Troy. They couldn't afford to miss anything. "Come on. We need leads."

Troy rubbed the back of his neck. "Ollie's dad," he said, jaw tight. "He liked to fight. Had a few assault and battery charges and supposedly was a pervert." He held his hands up, palms facing out. "That's all I know, and again, I don't want to accuse anyone."

A jolt of adrenaline ran through Joaquin. *This could be something.* He jotted "look into Ollie's dad" in his notebook, then flipped to the next page, eyes settling on his next question. "Okay, let's get into your relationship with Chantilly Price."

"We were all close friends. Everyone in school called us the Quad."

"I didn't ask about the Quad. I asked about Tilly."

"And I told you," Troy raised his voice. "We were friends."

Joaquin tilted his head slightly, studying Troy's expression. "With benefits?" he asked.

Troy shook his head, a crooked grin forming. "Nah, man. Nothing like that."

"So you *never* had sex with her?"

Troy's features tightened. One word came into Joaquin's mind. *Defensive.*

"Of course not!" Troy snapped. "She was my best friend's girl."

"Was she nice to you?" Joaquin asked.

"Once upon a time. But she'd changed by senior year and wasn't nice to anybody."

Joaquin watched Troy's eyes and the set of his shoulders. Had her change gotten under his skin, stirred something darker in him?

"Did that change upset you?" he asked.

"Nah. She was going through stuff—"

Joaquin rested his forearms on the ledge. "What kind of stuff?"

"I mean, she was *probably* going through stuff, like everybody is—stuff we don't talk about." Troy scooted his chair back. "Why are you interrogating me? You're supposed to be *my* lawyer, but it's like it's 1986, and I'm back in that police station."

Melrose took the phone again. "Mr. Ramos isn't accusing you." She glared at Joaquin. "Are you?"

"I'm not accusing you," Joaquin said, only to realize Troy couldn't hear him. What he wouldn't give to sit at a table with Troy and Melrose in a private conference room. "I'm not accusing you," he repeated after Melrose returned the phone. "I'm trying to do my best, but I need to understand."

Troy clenched his jaw. "Bluesummer wasn't kind to us. We were poor, Black. Daddy warned me to stay away from Chantilly. He said folks wouldn't take kindly to it. I mean, her name literally means white. I've always wondered if the wrong person saw me leaving Tilly's that night, got the wrong idea, and wanted us both to pay."

Joaquin lowered his voice. "So you're suggesting the Strangler didn't kill Tilly?"

Troy shrugged. "A part of me believes it had to be him. That he must have known the Prices left town and was watching . . . waiting, but her death was different from the rest. What I *am* sure of is that I was set up. Somebody found my ring and put it at the bower. Someone put Wendy's blood in my truck. Wendy Knott *never* rode in my truck."

Joaquin doubted every word, but if Troy had a name, it was worth hearing. "Who would set you up?"

Troy threw up his hands. "Any racist redneck son of a bitch in Bluesummer. Plenty to choose from, including in the police department."

Joaquin leaned in, voice edged. "You're sure she was never in your car? Funny, because I heard you asked her to prom and—"

"Never happened," Troy cut him off, jaw tight. "Hayes was close to Wendy, not me."

Joaquin cocked his head. "Close how?"

"They partnered for some science thing senior year." Troy let his shoulders relax. "They spent a lot of time at each other's houses, working on it."

Joaquin scribbled Hayes's name in large letters on his legal pad. Dating Tilly . . . and close to another victim? That could be more than a coincidence. He wasn't sure how long he'd been mulling it over when Melrose took the phone.

"So you weren't close with Wendy, but what about the other three victims?" she asked, then lowered the phone between them.

"No. Nicole was older. I knew *of* her. I had a few classes with Erin, but we weren't friends. Andrea went to Bluesummer High, but she was a sophomore. Didn't know her."

Joaquin removed his glasses and used his shirt to wipe away a smudge. "Speaking of Bluesummer High, tell me about your class ring. Melrose said you lost it in the woods?"

"Yeah, it was loose, and I last remembered wearing it while walking through the woods. I retraced my steps, but I never found it. Someone else must have, though—someone who had it out for me."

Joaquin didn't buy it. The stolen ring theory was a dead end, and dwelling on it would only waste time. He put his glasses back on, lifted his pen, and tried to keep his tone neutral. "Alright. Back to the night in question. Where were we?"

# CHAPTER 10

**July 4, 1986**

Troy pressed another cold beer against his neck before popping it open. He loved Bluesummer's rolling hills and rich, dark woods, but the humidity was brutal. He'd take a dry heat any day—like the kind he'd heard about in Arizona. Last summer, he stood before the map in his room and put his finger on Bluesummer, tracing his way across New Mexico until he reached Arizona. He'd traced that map for years, imagining the places he'd go. Might as well have imagined going to the moon—it was just as likely as him ever making it to Arizona.

He watched Greer wave her sparkler to the beat of "Hit Me with Your Best Shot," wishing he felt that free. Why couldn't he stop feeling sorry for himself and enjoy the night? When had he last been truly happy? Probably that final touchdown during his senior year's first playoff game. Mallowater High was up by two, with only four seconds left on the clock. Troy soared through the air to catch the pass, landed lightly, pivoted, dodged a defender, and tore down the field, legs pumping, wind whipping past his helmet as the crowd roared. In that moment, he'd felt invincible.

Then came the injury two days later. That touchdown was the last time he'd ever run across the field.

A branch snapped, pulling Troy out of the memory. Greer spun toward the woods, wielding her sparkler like a weapon.

"Not a serial killer, just us," Tilly said, tossing Greer's bunched-up blanket onto an empty lawn chair.

"Gross. Keep it," Greer muttered, tipping the chair so the blanket fell to the dirt.

"Is it yours?" Hayes asked, his shirt half-tucked, hair a mess. Troy didn't blame Hayes for liking Tilly, but he had to know Greer loved him.

"Sorry, Greer," Hayes mumbled. "I'll take it home and wash it to get all the dirt and sticks off."

Troy crushed his beer can. *Dirt and sticks. Yeah, bud, that's exactly what she's worried about.* He opened another beer and turned his gaze from Tilly, forcing himself not to notice she wasn't wearing the bra he'd glimpsed earlier. Despite his best intentions, he'd always been attracted to her—and right now, it was all he could think about.

"My necklace," Tilly said, clutching at her neck. "I left it out there."

"You weren't wearing a necklace," Hayes said, reaching into the cooler.

Troy turned down the boombox. "I think she was," he said casually, careful not to reveal he'd studied her enough to remember the delicate diamond key pendant hanging from a thin gold chain.

"See!" Tilly reached again for the invisible necklace. "Please, Hayes, it's important to me."

Hayes dropped the can back in the cooler. "Okay. Let me grab a flashlight."

As Hayes headed into the woods, Tilly picked the blanket off the ground. "Troy, can you give me a hand with this?"

Tilly's white lace bra hit the dirt as she shook out the blanket. "I wondered where that went. Can you grab it for me?" she asked.

"Get it yourself," Troy said, sitting back in his chair.

"Lighten up, Troy. I'm sure you've seen a few before," she said, a playful smile tugging at her lips.

"Lay off the beers already," Greer said, picking up the bra and stuffing it into Tilly's bag. "My brothers won't pause the Nintendo to buy more for us."

Tilly haphazardly folded the blanket, only to drop it back in the dirt. "Let's shoot off some fireworks!"

"How about we wait for Hayes?" Troy suggested.

Tilly picked up the Walmart grocery bag filled with discarded litter from the Roman candles and firecrackers Greer and Troy had set off. "Doesn't look like you two waited for us. Come on, where's the lighter?"

"You're too drunk to light any," Troy said, pushing himself up from the chair again, ignoring the pang in his knee. Greer was right; he shouldn't have run.

"I'm not drunk! Besides, I'm just getting the sparklers. Three-year-olds play with these."

"Hold it out in front of you," Troy instructed, lighting the end for her. Their eyes met, holding for a moment that stretched too long. The sparks from the sparkler felt like they were igniting something else entirely.

Tilly lit another sparkler and charged toward the water. "Come on, Greer! Come play."

Greer groaned but followed her. Troy relaxed into his chair and watched as Tilly danced wildly, flinging bright sparks, while Greer traced her name in large cursive loops with the slow-burning sparkler.

Sometimes, Troy wondered if Tilly was really in love with Hayes. He saw the way she looked at other guys, the way she'd looked at him, the way she was *still* looking at him.

Tilly held his gaze as she backed up, closer and closer to the water.

"Tilly, stop!" Greer yelled, but it was too late to stop Tilly from tumbling backward into the lake. Troy rose from his chair, then settled back down when he saw Tilly laughing.

"Come on, give me your hand," Greer commanded. But when she reached out, Tilly pulled her into the water. Troy smirked. Greer should have seen that coming.

They splashed each other like that first summer Red and Joanne brought them here for fireworks. A pang struck Troy's chest. This might be their last time here for the Fourth of July. Greer promised they'd return, but Troy knew things would change after a year apart. New lives, new friends—for everyone except Troy, stuck here in Backwater, Texas. The boy who'd always been fascinated by maps now gathered them with no place to go. He had accumulated quite an assortment over the years— maps depicting different climates, different elevations, different roads, different resources, and different political leanings. Different. He was drawn to different. Drawn to places he'd never go.

"There you are!" Tilly's voice broke his reverie.

Hayes emerged from the trees, holding Tilly's necklace. "Is this it? A key?"

"Yes!" Tilly rushed out of the water, her wet shirt clinging to her skin. "Thank you!"

"Tilly, your blouse," Hayes said, unbuttoning his own shirt. "Go change, and I'll hang yours out to dry."

Tilly strolled toward the pines, Hawaiian shirt in hand. Before disappearing, she looked back, her gaze lingering.

Troy broke eye contact, staring hard at the ground, afraid Hayes would notice. For a heartbeat, he let himself wonder what it meant—that glance, that pause. Heat crawled up his neck, the shame sharp. He should have looked away sooner. He should never have looked at all.

"Hey, Troy, wanna help me out here?" Greer yelled from the water.

"Ah. Sorry!" Troy grabbed a towel and rushed to her side.

"Thanks," Greer murmured, wrapping it around her chest. "Not like there's much to see, but—"

"Almost time for the fireworks," Hayes announced, moving chairs toward the water.

"We've gotta shoot the rest of ours off first," Greer said.

Hayes glanced at his Casio. "Let's wait till afterward. It's better that way, don't you think? A final Fourth of July send-off?"

"Don't say final," Greer said, sitting beside him. "We'll all be back next—"

"Fireworks, then back to my place!" Tilly interrupted, emerging from the trees, the top two buttons of Hayes's shirt undone. "Where the celebration really begins."

"Actually . . ." Troy looked at Greer, but she avoided meeting his eyes.

"What?" Tilly kneeled in front of Hayes and lifted her wet hair so he could fasten her necklace. "You're coming, right, guys?"

"Where did you get that necklace?" Hayes asked.

"It's from my dad."

"Why a key?" He eyed the pendant with furrowed brows.

Tilly ignored him. "Greer? I asked if you were coming."

Since Greer stayed silent, Troy guessed it fell to him to make their excuses, but Hayes spoke first.

"Greer, you *have* to come."

"I uh . . ." Greer squished the wet grass between her toes. "I don't know if—"

"Is it your mom?" Hayes asked. "We can come up with something."

When Greer didn't answer, Hayes touched her knee, nearly bare through the rip in her acid-washed jeans. A dragonfly skimmed low across the lake before vanishing into the reeds.

Troy saw Greer raise her head and stare at Hayes's hand, still resting on her knee. He kept it there briefly before moving it to his chest. "Please, Greer. I'm begging."

Troy cleared his throat, and Greer glanced at him before quickly looking away. "Okay," she said. "I'll be there."

Troy fought the urge to storm away, anger surging. He wasn't surprised by Greer's response, but the sting of disappointment cut deep.

"Then it's settled." Tilly reached into the cooler for another beer, ice clattering as she pulled the can free. "We'll *all* be there."

Troy couldn't help but notice that despite her inclusive language, she was once again looking right at him.

# CHAPTER 11

**2024**

Joaquin jogged into Melrose's office, affidavit in hand. "I may have hit the jackpot," he said, scanning the document again.

Melrose looked up from her desk, brow furrowed. "What is it?"

"I started thinking about Ollie Ford being a few years older than Troy. Troy's class ring matches the one found at the bower exactly, but did anyone check the paperwork for other students' rings? Ollie Ford's? Wendy Knott's ex?" He dropped an open file onto her desk. "Look at these pictures. It's the most generic class ring I've ever seen."

Melrose studied the pictures spread across her desk, the lamplight catching the glossy paper. "But it had to be someone born in September, based on the sapphire."

"Not necessarily. The school colors were blue and black, so maybe someone chose sapphire for that reason?"

Melrose tilted her head. "You're reaching."

"Am I?" Joaquin rotated his hand, displaying his college class ring with a ruby in the center. "My birthday is in October."

Melrose stared blankly. "That's not October's birthstone?"

"October's birthstone is tourmaline. I didn't want a pink ring, so I chose a ruby since my school colors were crimson and gold."

Melrose smirked. "Wow, I wouldn't have figured you for one of those 'I don't wear pink' guys. I mean, it's literally just a color."

"I was twenty-two," Joaquin said, adjusting the tight ring. "The thing is, most people pick their birthstone, but some don't. The ring at the bower was just a plain silver band with the school name and mascot—nothing personalized."

Melrose gestured to another photo. "And the graduation year: 1986. So it's not Ollie's."

"I know, but they can't be sure it's Troy's either. I researched it. Personalizing rings only started in the seventies and were costly. Most kids' rings weren't engraved."

Melrose hesitated. "Yes, but it's Troy's size, and his ring is unaccounted for."

Joaquin flipped through the file, pages crackling. "Look at this. The judge signed the search warrant based on the claim that the ring found at the crime scene was Troy's. That's a pretty big assumption."

Melrose's finger moved along the page as she read. "Right, but that can't be everything they listed. Troy was the last person to see Tilly alive. His mum admitted he was visibly upset after returning from Tilly's. And hadn't Red already claimed seeing blood in Troy's truck?"

"It's not in there." Joaquin straightened, hands on his hips, a smirk playing at the corner of his mouth. "None of it."

"Why wouldn't they list everything?"

"The cops knew the judge would sign the warrant, regardless. They could have written the lyrics to the 'Macarena' and gotten the same results."

"Wrong decade." Melrose stood. "But this means if we can prove the ring wasn't Troy's, then this warrant was illegally obtained."

"Bingo. Therefore, making the blood evidence found in his truck inadmissible."

"I'm impressed," Melrose said. "Good on ya."

Joaquin sank into the loveseat in front of her desk, feeling that familiar surge of confidence that often accompanied him in the courtroom.

Melrose picked up the file and leaned against her desk. "Troy might have given permission to get the mold of his teeth, but he had no idea they were searching his truck." She flipped back to the ring pictures. "You're on to something. This could belong to someone else." She closed the file and exchanged it for a pad and pen from her desk. "I'll check with the school or the ring company to see if they kept records of these orders. At the very least, I can get a list of male seniors from 1986. Troy can't be the only one with a size twelve ring finger."

"Perfect." Joaquin noticed the papers spread across her desk. "Or if you're busy, I can see if Luca has time."

Melrose pushed some loose pages out of her way and sat on her desk, facing him. "I have time. I was trying to reach the Sheridans." She pointed to her phone. "I had Red on the line for ten seconds until he told me to call his lawyer and hung up."

"Better than him telling you to go to hell. Did you try Hayes or Greer?"

"Not yet. Hayes is quite private, but I'm cautiously optimistic about Greer. Being a journalist, she's wired to uncover the truth. If I can share some truth with her, something that gets her attention, she might open up."

"Worth a shot," Joaquin said. "If she talks, ask her if Troy and Tilly were ever involved. I know Troy swears they had a friendly swim together that night, but as a former hormone-driven nineteen-year-old, I call bullshit."

"I believe him." Melrose crossed her legs. "Chantilly was his best mate's girlfriend. He was only at her house expecting Hayes and Greer to arrive. Once he realized they weren't coming, he bolted."

"And he claims it was around 10:30?" Joaquin asked.

"Ten thirty-five on the dot, according to the time on the clock in his truck."

Joaquin raised his eyebrows. "Now *I'm* impressed."

"I've got the timeline memorized. The cops didn't believe Troy, though. They needed him to be at the Price home around 10:45—Tilly's *supposed* time of death."

"Supposed?" Joaquin asked.

"They estimated Tilly's time of death from how cool her body was when Greer found her. But our forensic pathologist said alcohol, swimming, and lying nearly starkers in her air-conditioned room could have skewed that."

"Starkers, as in naked?" Joaquin deduced.

"Right, sorry, nearly *naked*," she said, attempting to mimic an American accent.

Joaquin laughed. "Okay, but if he left at 10:35, why did a fifteen-minute drive take forty?"

"He was upset, so he drove the back roads to blow off some steam. As a former hormone-driven nineteen-year-old, I assumed you'd relate."

"Touché." Joaquin checked his watch. "Client's due any minute— I'd better head to my office. Keep up the good work."

"Thanks, boss."

Joaquin grimaced. Her calling him boss just reinforced that he shouldn't be standing there, admiring how good she looked in that red pantsuit sitting on top of her desk.

"What?" Melrose asked. "Something else on your mind?"

"No, sorry. I was just noticing how different the office looks. Big improvement." His eyes swept the room: the desk neatly organized, papers stacked with purpose, binders lined up on the shelves, and a few personal touches—a lamp, a small rug—that made the space feel warmer.

Melrose looked over her shoulder. "Considering it started as a glorified storage closet, anything's an improvement."

He pointed at the painting of purple flowers behind Melrose's desk. "Did you paint that?"

"Me? No way. My nana did."

"What kind of flowers are they?"

"Morning glories," Melrose answered.

A lump formed in Joaquin's throat.

"They used to cover our fence back in Australia," Melrose said. "Bright and colorful, climbing up the wire mesh. They remind me of home, of barefoot summers in the backyard."

They reminded Joaquin of his childhood, too, but not with any fond memories. He wiped the sweat from the back of his neck.

Melrose tilted her head, seeming to notice his unease. "Everything okay?"

"Yeah." He managed a smile. "What's the story, morning glory? That's something my mom used to ask my sister Gloria every morning at breakfast. I didn't even realize they were flowers back then. That's how my sister ended up with the nickname Glory."

"Lovely story. Are you close to your family?"

"I am," Joaquin said. Although he'd never been as close to his older sisters as he'd been with sweet Glory. He wondered whether things would still be the same today. Whether he'd still enjoy playing the big brother role to her. Maybe Glory would still be here if he had played it better.

"Do you have just one sister?" Melrose asked. "Glory?"

Joaquin took in a long breath. He realized he should be glad Melrose was trying to get to know him, letting her "business-only" facade fade. But he didn't want to talk about Glory.

"Hey, boss." Bernie poked her head in. "Your 9:30 finally showed."

Joaquin exhaled. Saved by the forever-late habitual DUI offender. "Thanks for the chat. Let me know what you find out about the . . . um . . ."

"The rings," Melrose finished for him.

"Yeah, that's right—rings." Joaquin fought back tears as he walked out of the office. He hated that talking about his little sister still reduced him to the scared boy he'd been the day she died. "You have to let it go, nene," his mother had told him. "It was just an accident."

Joaquin wished that were true. Maybe if it had been just a tragic accident, the floor beneath him wouldn't still shift at the mention of her name over twenty-five years later. Maybe he wouldn't be on the verge of crying at work right before meeting with a client. Maybe he could have moved on the way everyone else in his family had seemed to.

But the reality was, Gloria's death wasn't what everyone believed. Only two people knew the truth, and one had carried it to her grave. No, it hadn't been a random accident. Her death was entirely Joaquin's fault.

# CHAPTER 12



**July 4, 1986**

Hayes dropped Tilly off at her house before daring to ask his parents about staying the night at the Prices'. Tilly had been drinking, and there was no hiding it. Convincing his parents might be tough enough without knowing they'd all had a few.

"Hayes, is that you?" Joanne emerged from the kitchen, holding a large bowl of buttery popcorn. "Your father and I were about to start a movie."

"*Jaws?*"

"Is it really the Fourth of July if we don't watch a killer shark maim unsuspecting beachgoers?" Joanne asked.

"Not to Dad, it's not," Hayes answered.

"What's this about Dad?" Red asked, coming down the hallway, wearing only a pair of plaid pajama bottoms and house shoes.

"Oh, your darling son was saying how much he'd love to stay up with you and watch a shark eat a skinny-dipping blonde so I can go to bed," Joanne said.

"Actually . . ." Hayes stuffed his hands into his pockets. "I'm just stopping by for my sleeping bag and some clothes."

"What for?" Red asked, grabbing the remote off the table.

"Yes, what for?" Joanne crossed her arms.

Hayes looked at the TV, watching the previews in fast forward. "We were all gonna stay at Tilly's tonight. Greer, Troy, and I."

"That sounds fun." Red flopped onto the glossy burgundy couch, the leather squeaking as he settled. "Guess you're stuck with me, Jo."

Hayes's mother shook her head. "Aren't the Prices in Dallas this weekend? I swear that's what Tilly's mother told us."

Hayes swallowed. This was exactly why he hadn't asked earlier. He didn't want to give his mom time to find out that the Prices were out of town.

Joanne looked at her husband. "Remember when we ran into Larry and Sharon at the Country Club? Didn't they mention they were heading to see the fireworks in Dallas?"

Red tossed a handful of popcorn into his mouth and shrugged, but Hayes realized there was no use in lying. His parents had eyes everywhere. "Greer and Troy's parents said it was okay."

Joanne squeezed her robe together. "What will you be doing?"

"Hanging out, watching movies. This could be our last Fourth of July together. We want it to be special."

"So, no late-night swimming?" Red asked. "Because that's not a good idea after you've been partying." He pointed to the screen. "Just ask Chrissy Watkins."

Hayes rubbed the back of his neck. He should have known even that second breath mint wouldn't fool his dad. "I only had one beer. But we won't be drinking *or* swimming there, I promise."

Red nodded as though satisfied, keeping his eyes on the screen, so Hayes turned his attention to his mom. Her knuckles were white from clutching her robe. She grabbed the remote and pressed pause. "Honestly, Redman—"

"Give it up, Jo. Hayes and Tilly are as good as married. I seem to remember sneaking into your dorm room a time or ten." He wrapped his legs around his wife, pulling her closer to him.

"Stop it." Joanne playfully slapped his leg.

"Yes, please stop." Hayes rubbed his eyes. "It's not like that. Greer and Troy will be there."

"It's not that." Joanne shifted her weight from one foot to the other. "Well, not *only* that. It's not wise for four teenagers to be together alone with a serial killer on our streets. Wendy Knott is missing, Hayes." Joanne's voice grew shrill with each word. "Your sweet lab partner gone in the night."

Hayes threw up his hands. "Come on, Mom. Are we back to this? People die every day in car accidents. Are you planning to take away my truck, too? You can't keep me safe from the world forever."

"Don't speak to your mother like that." Red pointed a finger at Hayes.

"Sorry, sir," Hayes mumbled.

"She does have a point," Red conceded.

Hayes clasped his hands together. "Come on, guys, please! It's our last year before everything changes."

"Do Greer and Troy's parents understand that the Prices won't be home?" Joanne asked.

"I don't know. But don't ruin it for everyone just because I can't go."

"How about a compromise?" Red looked at Joanne. "Are you okay with the kids all staying here tonight?"

Joanne tilted her head as though weighing the idea. "I don't see why not."

Hayes pressed his lips into a slight grimace. Staying here wasn't ideal, but better than nothing if his parents wouldn't budge. "Okay, can we sleep in the brig?" he asked, using Red's nickname for the detached apartment in the backyard where he wrote.

"That's more than fine," Red said. "Not like I'm doing any work tonight."

Joanne sighed, adjusting the pleated silk lampshade on the side table. "So, I guess I'm not getting out of witnessing this bloodbath?"

Red stood and set the remote on the coffee table. "Go on to bed. I'll head to Walmart. Grab the kids some snacks before I settle in for the movie." He looked at Hayes. "What sounds good?"

"Hold on." Hayes made his way to the telephone. "I've got to catch everyone before they head to Tilly's."

Hayes took the cordless phone into his room. Trophies gleamed on the shelf, and a neat stack of *Rolling Stone* magazines sat on his desk. He flipped one open, giving his restless fingers something to do while the line rang.

When Tilly finally picked up, he led with the bad news. "My parents said no."

"What? Are you serious?" Tilly's voice snapped, a sharp exhale punctuating each word.

Hayes shuffled past his bed and ran a hand over the cassette tapes stacked in a plastic holder. "Mom's worried about the Strangler, but they said we can stay here—in the brig. That way, they won't bug us, and it'll be just like being at your house."

"I've had a lot to drink, Hayes. I can't let your parents see me like this."

"Mom's going to bed; Dad is going to the grocery store. I'll pick you up and take you straight to the brig." Hayes paced back and forth across his bedroom. "They won't bother us. Dad promised."

"How are we gonna hook up in the brig? It's like one big room."

"Tonight's not about *that*, Tilly. We are all gonna hang out and spend time together. Greer and Troy aren't coming to college with us." Hayes thought again about Cornell, and a weight dropped in his stomach.

"So you're saying you don't want to be with me?" Tilly's voice was tight.

Hayes sank onto his bed, the rumpled striped comforter bunching under him. "Come on, Till. We've got our whole lives to have sex, but this is the last summer the Quad may have together."

"Well, I wouldn't say we've got our *whole* lives."

Hayes stiffened. "What does that mean?"

"Nothing. Forget it. I'm *not* going over there. I don't understand why you still let your mom call all the shots. You're an adult."

Hayes heard the thrum of his pulse in his ears. "Is that why you lied to your parents about staying with Greer tonight?"

"Don't deflect, Hayes. Be a man. Troy obviously had no problem telling his parents he was coming over."

Hayes jumped up. "Is he already there?"

"Not *yet*."

Hayes jogged into the living room.

"Did you decide what grub you want?" Red asked, but Hayes pushed past him and out of the front door.

Static filled the line as he stepped beyond the phone's range. Hayes froze—Troy's truck was gone from the Terrell driveway.

"Tilly? Are you there? Tell Troy to bring you over when he gets there. Tilly?"

The line went silent. He jabbed redial—busy. Again. Busy. "Shit," he muttered, kicking a potted plant as he stormed back into the house. Tilly must have left it off the hook. She'd figure it out soon—or Troy would. Hayes exhaled and dialed Greer's number, hoping he wasn't too late to reach her.

She answered on the first ring.

"I can't go," he said, stumbling back into his bedroom. "To Tilly's."

"What?" Greer's voice lifted slightly. "Why?"

Hayes flopped onto his bed, catching his breath. "The stupid Songbird Strangler, that's why."

"Can you sneak out?"

Hayes rolled onto his back, the faint green glow of his old ceiling stars staring down at him. "My parents will find out. You know Dad."

"You're right. The downfall of having a journalist as a parent. I don't want to go if you can't," Greer said.

Hayes propped up on his elbow. "Come here instead. My parents said we could stay in the brig. Tilly doesn't want to come, but it would be cool if you did."

"I'd love that," Greer said, "but . . ."

"But what?"

"Troy and Tilly will be pissed if we don't show."

"Please, Greer." Hayes swung his legs over the side of the bed and stood. "Come over. Otherwise, the night's ruined. Maybe we can go to the Prices' and get Troy and Tilly. I think she left her phone off the hook."

"I'll get them," Greer replied. "It's easier for me to pick them up since I'm only five minutes from her house."

Hayes tried to think of a reason they should go together, but he couldn't. If Tilly was mad at him, maybe it was best that Greer did the convincing. "Okay. But you've gotta talk Tilly into coming. Please don't bring her through the house, though. She's already had too much to drink. Park and come around to the—"

Hayes froze when he turned and saw a figure standing in his doorway. He put his hand to his heart. "Dad! You scared me. How long have you been standing there?"

"Not long." Red held up his keys. "Heading out. Last call for requests."

Hayes's fingers tapped the edge of the phone, his stomach knotting at the thought that Tilly might not come over. "Um, pretzels, Doritos, and some Dr Peppers would be great."

"Hot Pockets!" Greer screamed into the phone.

"And Hot Pockets," he told his dad, pulling the phone away from his ringing ear.

"Got it," Red said. "Want something sweet too? Those Keebler cookies?"

"Sounds good, Dad. Thanks." Hayes wasn't sure if Red hadn't heard his comment about Tilly's drinking or if he just wasn't making a big deal of it. Either way, Hayes was grateful his dad had devised a decent Plan B for the night.

Hayes brought the phone back to his ear. "I'm gonna grab some sleeping bags and blankets and set up things for us. You go get Troy and Tilly and bring them back here."

"I'll do my best," Greer said. "If we aren't enough to convince her, maybe the Hot Pockets will be."

Hayes smiled. "Thanks, Greer. See you soon."

# CHAPTER 13



**2024**

"No luck on the class rings," Melrose said, sinking into the chair across from Joaquin. "The company only keeps records for five years, so there's no way to track how many size twelve sapphire rings went to Bluesummer seniors in 1986."

Joaquin set his glasses on a pile of case files that teetered like a seesaw. "That's what I was afraid of. Did you call the high school?"

"They also don't keep any class ring records. Wouldn't even give me a list of 1986 seniors. But the paper must have posted the graduates' names. Or I can find a yearbook at the library."

"Good idea. Then you can start with anyone born in September."

"Yeah, but then what?" Melrose asked. "Call 'em and ask for their ring size? Tell them we're checking to see if they're the Songbird Strangler?"

Joaquin considered his answer. "It's all about how you frame it. We aren't necessarily trying to find the Strangler—just prove the ring alone wasn't enough probable cause for a search since others had the same design."

"I get that." Melrose tapped the desk. Her nails were cut short and painted a Barbie pink shade. "But," she continued, "it's possible that one of those men with that size and color ring is the actual Strangler. Why would they want to help us?"

"Maybe the one who *doesn't* want to help is the one we need to look more closely at," Joaquin said.

"I've also been calling jurors from Troy's trials," she said. "Most don't want to talk or still stick to their verdict, but a couple have doubts."

"That's great." Joaquin nodded. "Every bit helps."

Melrose pulled a piece of paper from her pocket. "This is Greer Sheridan's cell. I planned to call her today. Wanna eavesdrop?"

Joaquin checked the clock.

Melrose locked eyes with him. "What? Got a date?"

Joaquin felt heat in his cheeks. "Yeah, with Luca, but not for another half hour."

"Plenty of time." Melrose pulled a pen from her pocket. "Put her on speaker."

"I'm going to let you do the talking," Joaquin said as he dialed.

The phone sat on speaker between them, its red light blinking. Melrose clicked her pen twice before the call connected.

"Hello?" a woman's voice crackled through the speaker.

Melrose cleared her throat. "Mrs. Sheridan?"

"Speaking."

"Hi. My name is Melrose Reed, and I work for Joaquin Ramos." She waited a second as if Joaquin's name would ring a bell for anyone.

*Someday*, Joaquin thought. If he got Terrell out, the world would recognize his name.

"Mr. Ramos is Troy Terrell's new post-conviction lawyer."

Greer's sigh carried through the speaker. "Are you the woman who called my father-in-law?"

"Yes," Melrose said. "But—"

"Red's ill," Greer interrupted. "Cancer. Terminal. He's not up for any interviews."

"I'm so sorry," Melrose spoke softly. "I hadn't heard."

Joaquin hadn't either. Maybe that explained why Red Sheridan had remained silent as yet another execution date for Troy Terrell approached.

"He didn't want to make a fuss about his diagnosis," Greer went on. "Contrary to what you may think, Red Sheridan doesn't like media attention. He's a crime writer, and he solved a crime a long time ago. He doesn't want the spotlight on him."

Joaquin smirked. *Could've fooled me.*

"I apologize for bothering him," Melrose said. "But today, I was calling to speak to you."

The radiator hissed under the window, filling the office with dry heat and a faint smell of burnt dust. Joaquin rubbed his thumb along a coffee ring on the desk, waiting, half convinced Greer had hung up.

"No thanks," Greer finally said, her tone clipped, defensive. "I already told the police everything I could about that night."

"Would you mind telling us?" Melrose asked, reaching across Joaquin's desk to grab a legal pad.

Another long pause, punctuated only by a faint exhale over the speaker.

"I've moved on," Greer said. "It was so long ago, I barely remember the details now."

Even if Greer's voice hadn't cracked, Joaquin would have known she was lying. Trauma, like she had experienced, seeped under your skin, burrowed into your brain, and became a part of you.

"Mr. Ramos and I are finding a lot that's dodgy," Melrose said. "You're a journalist. Don't you want to uncover the truth?"

"I *know* the truth," Greer said, sharper now. "Troy killed Tilly."

Melrose jotted something down, the pen's scratch loud in the small office. "We understand why your father-in-law and the police reached that conclusion, but we've found evidence that suggests otherwise."

"Okay," Greer said slowly. "I'm listening."

"What if I told you the semen sample taken from Tilly's body didn't belong to Troy?" Melrose said without missing a beat.

Joaquin blinked, unsure if he'd misheard. "What?" he mouthed.

"I'd say you're lying," Greer said. "The evidence was lost before DNA testing was possible."

Melrose raised her eyebrows. "So, you *are* following the case?"

"I'm a journalist," Greer said. "Technically retired—but you never really retire from this job."

"This is going to turn into quite a story, Mrs. Sheridan. You could have an exclusive."

Greer laughed once, humorless. "I've *had* an exclusive since the night it happened. I understand you are just doing your job, but Hayes wants to put this all behind us."

Joaquin and Melrose exchanged a glance. "Hayes does," he mouthed.

Melrose softened her tone. "Greer . . . Troy cares about you. He speaks highly of you. I believe Red Sheridan made a terrible mistake—one that could cost Troy his life. Would you be willing to meet and talk in person? No pressure. Just a conversation."

"I don't know . . ." Greer's voice faltered.

"You know Troy better than we do. Your instincts are the reason your career was so successful. Picture Troy from 1986. Not the one in Red's book, not the media version. The one you shot Roman candles with that night. Do you believe he was capable of killing Tilly—and four other women before her? A murder spree that began while he sat next to you in senior English? With instincts like yours, how did you never suspect Troy was a monster?"

There was another long pause. Joaquin could hear Greer's breath, uneven but deliberate, as if she were weighing every word.

"Are you still there, Mrs. Sheridan?" Melrose asked.

"I'm free Friday morning," Greer said, the tremor in her voice settling into something more certain. "Where should we meet?"

Joaquin and Melrose were listing questions for Greer when they heard Luca Moretti's booming voice greet Bernie in the hallway.

"He's early," Joaquin said, rising from his chair. The stacks of papers shifted as he moved, sending a small avalanche of notes to the floor. "Hopefully with good news."

Luca filled the doorway before he spoke—a wall of confidence in a pressed shirt. He didn't wait for an invitation into Joaquin's office. He strode in, tall and broad-shouldered, and extended a hand toward Joaquin—but his eyes immediately found Melrose.

Joaquin started to introduce them, but Luca dropped his hand and reached for hers. Joaquin raised an eyebrow, caught off guard by the casual familiarity. Even more so when Melrose gave Luca a quick once-over.

"I was wondering when I was finally going to meet you," Luca said, settling into the chair beside her.

"Same," Melrose replied, brushing a stray lock of hair behind her ear. "Your reputation precedes you."

"Don't trust anything this guy says about me." He pointed his finger at Joaquin, and Melrose glanced at his hand. Was she checking for a ring?

She scooted to the edge of her chair. "Should I leave you guys alone or—"

As much as Joaquin wanted to say yes, there was no reason to send her away. "No, you're good," he said, masking his irritation. He looked at Luca. "Any good news?"

Luca crossed one leg over the other, angling toward Melrose. "Afraid not. Titus recanted."

Joaquin crumpled in his chair. "He recanted his recant? Carter's dead. Who got ahold of Titus?"

"Someone with the DA, I'm sure," Luca said. "But hey, chin up. You and I both know these jailhouse informants carry little weight when it comes to overturning convictions. We've always needed more."

"We need the DNA," Joaquin said.

"I've been at the courthouse all week digging through old evidence boxes, but no luck. Supposedly, there's more in a few storage facilities and at the police station."

"It's insane that states can store crime evidence wherever they damn well please. For all we know, our box is in the basement of some abandoned K-Mart," Joaquin said.

"You'd be surprised how common lost evidence is." Luca reached into his pocket. "I brought you this, though." He pushed a tiny slip of paper toward Joaquin.

Joaquin picked it up. "1100 Red Rose Lane?"

"Bruce Ford's address. Ollie's dad, remember you asked me to investigate him?"

"Okay, yeah. Find anything interesting?"

Luca flashed a grin. "Always. Turns out Ollie's dad has quite a record. Assault and battery, and he's a registered sex offender."

"You're kidding? Was he habitual or—"

"Only one incident on record," Luca explained. "Sorry, I haven't found many details yet. The registry wasn't established until ninety-one, and while Texas allowed retroactive additions, the information is sparse."

"I can look into him," Melrose offered. "I'm already looking into Ollie."

Luca's gaze lingered on her just a moment too long, and Joaquin felt a twinge of irritation.

"This makes so much sense," Joaquin said, pointing to the note Luca had brought. "He might have been involved."

Luca showed his palms. "Easy there. It might be a coincidence. But in any case, I called him, and he agreed to meet with us on Friday morning. Said he and his son have nothing to hide."

Joaquin pocketed the paper. "I'll be the judge of that. Friday, you said?"

"Yep. Figured we'd meet up here and go together." He looked at Melrose. "Interested?"

Joaquin's mind raced. He needed a reason to keep Melrose busy on Friday. But before he could come up with one, she shook her head. "Already got another meeting."

"That's right," Joaquin said too eagerly. "She's meeting with Greer Sheridan."

Luca raised his eyebrows. "Nice." He looked back at Joaquin. "Sorry, I don't have more for you. I got your message on the class rings, but haven't looked into it. DPAP's got me working on a few other cases, too."

"Not surprised," Joaquin said. "Seems they're stretched pretty thin. They didn't assign me a paralegal either."

"Well, that's a blessing in disguise," Luca said, winking at Melrose.

Joaquin fought the urge to kick him under the desk. Luca had always been a good investigator—but sometimes he was insufferably smarmy.

"I'm handling the class rings, Luca," Melrose said. Joaquin didn't like the way she said his name. What kind of name was Luca, anyway? Like some soap opera character.

"Josten's doesn't keep records," Melrose continued. "But I'm working through a list of the class of eighty-six."

Luca pointed at Joaquin. "Ever thought about ditching that guy and working for me?"

"We're both working for the same organization," Joaquin said, keeping his annoyance in check.

"I'm just saying we'd make one hell of a team," Luca said, smiling at her again. Those teeth gleamed under the fluorescent office light.

"Anything else you needed, Luca?" Joaquin asked.

Luca finally tore his eyes away from Melrose. "I should ask you that, I suppose."

"Still, the DNA." Joaquin tapped his pen against his desk.

"You know I'm doing all I can. I'll search every abandoned K-Mart in Texas, but if it's gone, it's gone."

Joaquin held up a hand. "It's *not* gone. It can't be."

"I assure you, it can be," Luca said. "Knowing how crooked Kevin Carter was, it wouldn't surprise me if he destroyed it."

"Or hid it," Joaquin said.

Luca shrugged. "Stranger things have happened."

Joaquin stood, giving Luca the signal to follow suit, but instead, Luca turned his body toward Melrose. "So, Melrose Reed, tell me a little about yourself."

# CHAPTER 14

**July 4, 1986**

"Where do you think you're going?" Keaton looked up from his Zelda game. He lay sprawled across the couch, strawberry-blond hair falling over his forehead, green eyes sharp and assessing.

Greer's stomach tightened as she hoisted her duffel bag over her shoulder. "What's it to you?"

"All those years of us being responsible for you," Zach said, lounging on the beanbag, orange fingers digging into Cheetos puffs. His hair stuck up at odd angles, and the tilt of his jaw gave him a slightly more playful, relaxed expression than his twin.

"Right. Well, you two have fun finding the Triforce or whatever." Greer grabbed her keys from the hook by the door.

Keaton handed the controller to his brother and stood. "You said you weren't driving." He stepped closer. "When I bought you the booze, you said—"

Greer cut him off. "Chill. I didn't drink any yet."

Zach sank deeper into the beanbag, resting his foot on the scuffed coffee table cluttered with soda cans and Keaton's gaming guides. "Sure you haven't."

Greer leaned over the couch toward him. "Wanna smell my breath?"

"No thanks," Zach said. "I'll leave that to Hayes."

Greer threw her keys at him. "Shut up."

"Are you sure you're good to drive?" Keaton's stare was intense, scanning her for signs of anything off. She hated it when he tried to play the caring older brother. He'd lost that right a long time ago.

"Gah, enough with the third degree. I haven't been drinking, and I'm staying with Tilly."

"That why the lipstick?" Zach asked, tossing the keys back.

Greer caught them. "It's lip *gloss*."

"So Hayes is still dating her?" Keaton asked.

Greer sighed. "Yeah. Who cares?"

"She sucks, Greer." Zach paused the game and rolled off the beanbag. "I know she's cheated on Hayes. For a fact."

"Shut up, Zach. You aren't helping." Keaton's eyes flashed with anger.

Greer instinctively stepped back. "Don't believe everything you hear," she said, desperately wanting to know what Zach knew. "Look, I gotta go."

"Mom knows you're staying at Tilly's?" Zach asked.

"Stop acting like a dad. Yeah, Mom knows."

"Mom knows what?" Jessie Collins asked, stepping out of the hallway, her strawberry-blonde hair a softer, wavier echo of Greer's.

Greer sighed. Between her brothers and mom, she might not spend time with Hayes after all. "That I'm staying at Tilly's."

Jessie smoothed a hand over Greer's hair. "How were the fireworks?"

"Awesome."

"And what is your plan for the rest of the night?" Jessie asked Keaton.

Greer eyed the door as her brothers told their mom about the friends they'd invited over. What was up with this? Her mom never questioned their plans. Greer sensed she was about to get busted.

"And what about you and Tilly?" her mom asked, fixing her attention on Greer.

"We're just hanging out. Watching movies, doing makeup, the usual. I need to get going," she said, touching the doorknob.

"So you won't be going *anywhere* else? I don't want you kids on the road tonight. Lots of crazies are out, and most of them end up at my ER."

"Don't worry. We'll stay put." Greer forced a smile, keeping her voice light, but her stomach twisted as she hugged her mom goodbye. Every word felt like a tightrope—one slip and her lie would be obvious.

Sliding into the driver's seat, she adjusted the mirror, heart still racing. As she started the engine, she wondered what she could say to convince Tilly to come with her. She wasn't sure she wanted to.

A firework burst as she drove toward Tilly's, filling the night with a brilliant blue flash. It was followed by another, gold shimmering down like a gentle rain.

The car seemed stifling. Greer pulled over and stepped out onto the roadside, surrounded by exploding fireworks. Tonight felt different, the air charged with more than explosive chemicals.

Tonight, Greer had the chance to be alone with Hayes—right after he'd fought with Tilly, who, according to her brother, had cheated on him. She imagined him leaning against the doorway, tense and frustrated, the kind of quiet anger only she could soothe. Maybe she'd make him laugh, and he'd pull her close, brushing a strand of hair from her face.

Her stomach tightened at the thought, a mix of longing and nerves twisting together. She should just hop back in the car and head straight to Hayes's house.

But then her mind flipped to Troy. He wouldn't wait forever. Eventually, he'd leave Tilly's and swing by her place—or even Hayes's— wondering why they hadn't shown, ruining the perfect night she had pictured.

The solution dawned amid the scream of a bottle rocket: tell Tilly she was sick, catch Troy alone, beg him to let her have the night with Hayes. Troy had to understand—he just had to. A red firework, almost heart-shaped, burst overhead. It had to be a sign. She jumped back in the car and sped toward Tilly's house.

Troy kept checking the clock, growing impatient. What was taking Greer and Hayes so long?

Sounds drifted from the kitchen: cabinets opening and closing, items clinking into cups.

He looked around the Prices' living room. It reeked of wealth—floral couches, velvet drapes, ferns by the window. Troy had never been comfortable around rich people except for Hayes and his dad. Red never talked down to Troy; he'd get his hands dirty with the hogs and pay for things Troy's folks couldn't.

"Here you go." Tilly emerged from the kitchen, handed him a glass of blue liquid, and set another on the coffee table. "One for me, one for you."

"Looks like you're missing two," Troy said, sniffing the drink. "For G and Hayes."

"Hayes isn't coming, and Greer's not big on fruity drinks."

"Wait, Hayes isn't coming?"

Tilly swirled her drink with the tiny straw, the ice clinking in the crystal glass. "Not unless he finds some backbone and stands up to his mommy."

Troy sipped cautiously. The drink scorched his throat like chlorine. "What's in this?"

"It's called Sex in the Driveway. I used Daddy's Balkan Vodka."

He took another taste and set the glass on the lacquered coffee table, its mirrored surface reflecting the soft glow of the chandelier. "Anything besides vodka?"

"Peach schnapps and blue curaçao."

*Booze on booze.* Troy checked the time again. Ten more minutes. If G and Hayes were no-shows, he was gone.

"So what's next?" Tilly asked, reclining on the cream velvet loveseat, her manicured fingers tapping the armrest. "Want to play a game? Truth or dare?"

Troy took another drink. "Let's wait for G."

"Greer, Greer, Greer. How long have you been in love with her?" Tilly asked, finishing her drink.

Troy froze mid-sip, the glass trembling slightly in his hand. "What?" His voice was sharp and defensive. Had Greer told her about their kiss— a single, vulnerable moment that changed nothing? "I'm not in love with her," he said.

"You are! You're always asking about her. *When's G coming? Where's G?* It's like you don't care about anyone else."

"I'm here now," Troy said, even though he knew it was a terrible example. Because Greer had five minutes to get there, or he was gone.

"Yes, you are." Tilly leaned further back on the couch, spreading her legs slightly. "Truth or dare."

"I don't wanna play," Troy said.

"Two truths and a lie, then." Tilly jumped up. "After a refill."

"I'm good," Troy insisted, but Tilly was suddenly beside him, nudging his hand with the drink toward his mouth.

"Finish it," she urged.

Troy complied, unsure why Tilly had so much power over him. Her perfume filled the space, and her leg brushed against his—daring him.

He watched her walk into the kitchen, her miniskirt hugging her in all the right places. "I'm gonna call G," he said.

Tilly appeared again, lifting her shirt over her head.

He looked for half a second, then turned away. "What the hell, Tilly?"

At his words, she laughed and lowered the shirt back down. "Relax. I'm just gonna change into my swimsuit. If you want to leave, just leave." She turned, lifting her hair and exposing her smooth neck. "Can you help me first, though? I don't want my necklace to get wet."

Troy stepped closer, his fingers brushing her skin as he unclipped the necklace. Goosebumps rose under his touch.

Tilly disappeared into the hallway, and Troy felt a wave of dizziness wash over him. Was he too drunk to drive? He needed to call Greer and tell her to hurry.

In the hallway, he spotted the phone knocked off its base. "Your phone was off the hook," he called out.

Tilly emerged from her bedroom in a tiny blue bikini. "Must have bumped it," she said.

He tried to look anywhere else, furious at himself, at Hayes's parents, at Greer for putting him in this position—drunk and alone with Chantilly Price.

"Don't call Greer's house!" Tilly snatched the phone away. "She told me her mom is sleeping before her shift."

"But G should already be here," he said through gritted teeth.

Tilly used her free hand to cover her eyes. "I'm so dumb. I totally forgot she offered to buy snacks."

Troy tilted his head. "Are you sure? How did you *just* remember?"

"I'm foggy. No doubt thanks to that Sex in the Driveway." Tilly winked. She put the phone back in the cradle. Taking his hand, she pulled, urging him to come. "Swim with me."

Troy shook his hand free. "It's dark, Tilly."

"The pool has lights."

"I didn't bring a swimsuit."

Tilly stopped and placed her hands on his waist. "What size are you? I can check if my dad has any."

A fluttering sensation stirred in his chest at her touch. "It's fine, Tilly. I don't want to swim."

She moved her hands to the bottom of his shirt, raising it. "Take off your shirt and get in. Those basketball shorts will dry."

He swallowed hard. "Tilly, stop." He pushed his shirt back down.

"Have it your way." She turned to unlatch the sliding glass door.

Troy stepped outside and watched as she dove into the pool. He lowered himself onto the concrete. He was conflicted—angry that Tilly was coming on to him yet strangely excited about it. Maybe he was dreaming again—one of those Tilly fantasies he'd never admit to.

Above them, fireworks hissed, flashed, and popped from all directions. He loved fireworks, but that wasn't why this was his favorite holiday. He loved it because of the memories he'd made with his friends. Now he was drunk, Greer and Hayes were MIA, and he was fantasizing about having sex with his best friend's girlfriend.

"Ready to play two truths and a lie?" Tilly asked.

Troy hesitated only a moment before dipping his feet in the water. "Sure. Why not?"

Greer knocked harder on Tilly's front door. Troy's truck was parked out front, but Tilly's Jeep could be anywhere since the garage was closed. Fireworks painted the sky red and gold while parents shouted warnings from porches. Not even a serial killer could stop Texans from lighting up the sky.

A burst of rockets shot across the street, hissing and popping as sparks fountained into the air. No wonder Troy and Tilly hadn't heard her knocking. Maybe it was better this way—no chance of sharing Hayes with either of them tonight.

Greer grabbed a pen and notebook from her car and scribbled a quick note to Troy:

*Hayes can't come here, so he asked me to stay at his place tonight. We tried calling and coming here to tell you. You guys can come over, or if you want to do me a big life-changing favor, maybe you won't. I'll owe you BIG. Love, G.*

She slipped the note under Troy's windshield wiper. As she turned to walk back to her car, another crackle of fireworks filled the air, followed by deeper booms. Then Tilly's scream sliced through the noise.

Greer froze. The Strangler could move unnoticed beneath all this noise. Shaking and dizzy, she bolted back to the door and tried the knob—locked.

"Call 911!" Greer tried to shout, but her voice came out hoarse and weak. She cleared her throat and tried again, but then she heard a splash, followed by Tilly's boisterous laugh. Was she swimming?

Confused, Greer circled around the side of the Price home and peered through the slats of the wooden fence. After a few minutes, she stepped back, rubbed her eyes, and muttered, "Are you freaking kidding me?" before pressing her face back against the fence.

# CHAPTER 15



"These trees are the best part of Bluesummer," Joaquin said, rolling down his window. Pines stood tall and green among oaks losing their luster, the woods easing quietly toward winter. The scent of pine needles and damp soil drifted in as the Jeep bumped over uneven dirt, dust swirling around the tires. The steady crunch of gravel grounded Joaquin, a steady rhythm against the swirl of thoughts in his head.

"Didn't you grow up near the Redwood Forest?" Luca asked.

"Only went once." Joaquin thought about the expression of pure awe on Glory's face as they drove through the trunk of the Chandelier tree. "I grew up in Bakersfield."

"So, it's the country life for you?"

"Never imagined I'd say this, but yeah. I've gotten too used to falling asleep to the sound of crickets."

"They have apps for that—nature sounds," Luca said, then nodded toward the back seat. "Melrose not joining us?"

"We told you she's meeting with Greer Sheridan."

"No, she's not." Luca pointed up the road. "Turn right on Oakmere, then left."

"What do you mean she's not?"

Luca adjusted his seatbelt. "Greer backed out."

Joaquin frowned. "How do you know that?"

"Well, I was with Melrose last night when Greer texted," Luca admitted with a sheepish grin. "Sorry, I figured she would text you."

Joaquin scrolled through his messages, searching for something that wasn't there.

"There's your turn," Luca said.

Joaquin swerved onto the street. Whom Melrose dated was none of his business. He told himself that twice, but it didn't stop the flicker of something sharp and unwanted in his chest.

"She's young, Luca."

"Who's young?"

"Melrose." Joaquin parked in the Fords' driveway.

Luca unbuckled. "She's thirty-two. Not that it matters. It was strictly professional."

Joaquin opened his door. "Professional. Sure."

Luca paused, watching Joaquin over the hood. "Hold up. Do you two have something going on?"

"No," Joaquin answered too quickly. "She's my employee."

Luca grinned. "Ah, so you've got a little crush. Fair enough."

Joaquin tugged at the collar of his jacket. "A crush? I'm not a teenager."

"Adults get crushes, too," Luca said.

"I don't have a crush on anyone. I'm just saying, be careful with Melrose. She's a good person."

"And I'm not?" Luca flashed that megawatt smile. "Wait, don't answer that."

Joaquin exhaled, then stepped around the Jeep. His boots scuffed the gravel as he made his way up the narrow dirt path toward the trailer. The late-morning sun glinted off the peeling aluminum siding, casting sharp angles across the warped wooden steps.

A low growl stopped him cold. A pit bull stood near a copse of stunted oaks at the edge of the yard, teeth bared, straining against a chain. Sweat prickled along Joaquin's neck.

"Ziggy won't hurt ya," a deep voice said. "He's as friendly as a porch cat."

Joaquin turned to see an older man with thin, graying hair and a stocky build standing behind the screen door.

"Doesn't sound friendly." Joaquin laughed weakly. "You must be Mr. Ford?"

"Name's Bruce. Come on in."

Joaquin drew in a slow breath, trying to calm his racing heart as the dog's low growl faded behind him.

"So you love crickets but fear dogs?" Luca whispered, sidling past with a smirk.

Joaquin and Luca stepped inside, the door groaning behind them. The trailer smelled of cigarettes and musty wood. Dust motes drifted through shafts of sunlight slipping past the crooked blinds. The floorboards sagged in places, and the linoleum was scuffed and worn.

Bruce nodded toward the couch. "Sit." His voice was calm, measured, but his sharp eyes studied them as they lowered themselves onto the cushions. He leaned back in his recliner. "So you're here about them murders?"

Luca nodded. "Yes, sir. We read the police questioned your son."

Bruce gave them a long, appraising look. "Yeah, but Ollie got cleared."

"Why did they suspect him?" Joaquin asked.

Bruce glanced at his chipped coffee mug, tracing the rim with a thumb. "Because of an incident around the same time. Guess he snuck into the locker room. Got caught before any girl even undid her ponytail. He liked to scare people—kids' stuff, games."

"But he wasn't a kid," Luca said. "He was what? Twenty-three?"

"Twenty-two," Bruce corrected, rubbing a hand over his stubbled chin. "He's got a disability. That kind of thing—it's a game to him."

"What about the other accusations? Peeping through windows? Just more games?" Joaquin asked.

"Rumors," Bruce said. "Ollie liked to roam around, look for 'treasures' as he called 'em. People saw him and jumped to conclusions."

"Is he home?" Luca asked, eyes scanning the narrow hallway.

"At work." Bruce pursed his lips. "I didn't want this dredged up. Ollie had nothing to do with them killings."

"Any alibis?" Luca pressed.

Bruce's fingers drummed on the arm of his chair. "Home," he said firmly.

Joaquin narrowed his eyes. "During all the murders?"

"Yep. Police already checked. I vouched for every night."

*Convenient*, Joaquin thought.

"Even on the Fourth?" Luca leaned forward. "You stayed home *all* night?"

Bruce pulled the lever on his recliner, sitting up with a creak. "Sure did. Ollie worked at the supermarket until five. We picked up Taco Bell and rented a Frankie Avalon movie, like always. My boy likes routine. Fireworks spooked him, so we made popcorn and watched the movie. He crashed before it ended."

"Can't say I blame him. Wasn't a fan of sixties movies either," Joaquin said.

"Oliver's a beach fan. I wish I'd taken him to see the ocean, but you know how it goes. Never enough time, never enough money."

"Mind if I take a look at his room?" Luca asked, glancing around the cramped trailer.

Bruce crossed his arms. "Not without a warrant. I don't go in there. He's a grown man."

Joaquin's eyes drifted to the streaked windowpane. The overgrown yard beyond blurred in the pale November sun. "You said Ollie liked to explore. Was he in the woods often?"

"He never wandered too far out. Not to the bower if that's what you mean."

Luca slapped his legs. "Well, we should be leaving, but my two cups of morning coffee caught up with me. Mind if I use your bathroom first?"

"First door on the right," Bruce said.

*Leaving?* Joaquin shot a glance at Luca. They hadn't questioned Bruce about his sex offender status or the assault and battery charges. No way they were going anywhere.

Joaquin scooted to the edge of the couch. "Would you mind answering some questions about your own criminal record?"

Bruce raised his eyebrows. "Hmm. So it's not *just* Ollie you've been looking into."

"We've found some things during our standard investigation. I mean no offense."

Bruce waved a hand dismissively, lips pursed. "It's nothing I ain't heard before. Yeah, I got into a few scuffles."

"And the other charge?" Joaquin asked.

Bruce's nostrils flared, jaw tightening. Joaquin had struck a nerve. "You mean the mess with Ollie's mother?"

Joaquin cocked his head. "His mother?"

Bruce gave a bitter laugh. "Wow, and I thought you lawyer types did your homework. Beverly Bray. She was a freshman; I was a senior. We were in love, but her parents hated me. When she got pregnant, they made sure I paid the price." His voice tightened. "I was in jail when Ollie was born. Bev's parents made her turn him over to the state. Took a mess of years to get custody back. We ain't seen hide nor hair of Bev since."

Joaquin dropped back against the couch cushion, bewildered. How had Luca missed this? How had Melrose? Too busy having drinks together to do their jobs?

"Texas has addressed cases like that now," Joaquin said softly. "It's called the Romeo and Juliet law. You could file to be removed from the registry."

"You ready, boss?" Luca stood by the door.

"Yeah," Joaquin said, springing to his feet, glad to escape the dust and stale odors. "Thanks for your time, Mr. Ford. We'll be in touch if we have more questions."

Joaquin stepped past Bruce and beat Luca to the door, ignoring the pit bull still lounging near the trees. He slid into the Jeep and slammed the door, the echo sharp in the quiet driveway.

Luca climbed into the passenger seat, giving Joaquin a sidelong look. "What's got you so worked up?"

"Why didn't you tell me the details about why Bruce is on the sex offender registry?" Joaquin snapped.

Luca blinked. "What are you talking about?"

"I assume that's why you were ready to leave without talking about it. I'm supposed to be a big-shot lawyer, and you made me look like an idiot."

Luca laughed. "First, you're not a big-shot lawyer. Second, I didn't check Bruce's rap sheet because Melrose said she'd handle it."

He was right. Melrose was supposed to look into that. He fired off a text: *Are you at the office? We need to talk.*

He turned back to Luca. "I thought you'd do some basic research. Or were you relying on Melrose to brief you during your date?"

Luca rolled his eyes. "It wasn't a date. And Bruce's crimes don't matter. He didn't kill anyone."

Joaquin tapped the steering wheel. "I agree."

"Now, the only question is, did he know his son was a murderer or not?" Luca asked.

Joaquin turned. "Huh?"

"Think about it, Joaquin. What was found at the bower?"

Joaquin blew out a breath. "Bones. A memento from each victim."

"What else?"

Joaquin's phone buzzed. A text from Melrose: *Hey, so sorry. Not feeling well. Took a sickie. I called Bernie, but I should've texted you, too.*

He tossed the phone into the console, her Australian slang suddenly grating. *A sickie, huh? Must have had too many drinks with Luca.* The car suddenly felt suffocating.

"What else was found at the bower?" Luca repeated.

Joaquin flicked off the heater. "The class ring, teeth, hair, blood, two birds from the wind chimes . . ."

"Bingo." Luca snapped his fingers. "The birds, but *not* the dolphin. Seaglass wind chimes with a chipped dolphin were taken from Erin Llewellyn's home. So the Strangler had those wind chimes but didn't leave a piece at the bower like with the other pairs. Why?"

"I assumed it didn't go with the bird theme he was going for. Once the papers dubbed him the Songbird Strangler, he ran with it."

"Or maybe the killer kept it because of an obsession with the ocean?"

Joaquin suddenly understood. "You went to Ollie's room, didn't you? And found the dolphin?"

"It was locked. Who locks their bedroom door when they aren't in it?"

"Bruce mentioned giving Ollie his privacy," Joaquin said. "And considering everything the killer did, was Ollie capable?"

"Have you seen Oliver Ford? He's built like a linebacker."

"I meant mentally."

"Stranger things have happened," Luca said. "The Baton Rouge Serial Killer had an IQ that labeled him disabled."

"Well, no judge will give us a warrant to search someone's bedroom based on a vague statement from his dad and a hunch about some dolphin behind a locked door."

"Then we'll find another way," Luca replied.

Joaquin chuckled. "Like breaking and entering?"

"No, I'd like to keep my license. Let's pay Ollie a visit at the grocery store next week. Maybe he'll talk to us."

"Alright. I need to pick up some groceries, anyway. I'll ask Bernie about my schedule."

"Bring Melrose along," Luca added. "She may come in handy. She has a way of making people feel comfortable."

Joaquin's phone buzzed again—*Are you free now?*

He dropped his phone and rolled down the window, letting the crisp breeze wash over his face. Above him, the pines and oaks held their quiet vigil, unconcerned with the messy world at their roots.

So many questions pressed on him. Was Ollie Ford really the Songbird Strangler? Had Bruce helped him cover it up? Were Luca and Melrose going to date? Had he embarrassed himself in front of Luca with his jealousy, like he'd embarrassed himself in front of Bruce? Could he save Troy Terrell? How could he play the hero when every mistake felt like proof he wasn't one?

The road stretching ahead of him reminded him just how far he still had to go.

Bluesummer was just waking when Joaquin pulled into the lot the next morning, gray light flattening everything it touched. Melrose's car sat in its usual spot. He was surprised to see her there so early—no doubt trying to make up for yesterday.

Inside, the office was cold and still. He turned up the heater and hesitated at Melrose's door.

She looked up from her desk, her movement tentative. "Good morning," she murmured, her voice barely carrying over the low hum of the computer and the soft hiss of the heater.

"Morning. Feeling better?"

"Much. Figured I'd come in early to catch up. I tried calling, texting . . ."

"Yeah, I saw." Joaquin shoved his hands in his pockets. "I was busy."

"Sorry. I should've called your mobile about being sick. Figured Bernie would pass it on."

"I didn't go to the office before my meeting. I wish you'd have at least warned me that Greer had backed out."

She scrolled on her phone. "Didn't I?"

"Nope," he said, feeling the tight knot of irritation in his chest tighten.

"I could've sworn I texted," she muttered.

"Look, I get you were busy with Luca, but—"

"It's in my drafts." She held the phone up. "And what exactly did Luca say?"

"Look, it doesn't matter if you date him or drink with him or whatever. I just felt foolish that he knew something about my case that I didn't."

Melrose crossed her arms. "*Your* case? So it's not *his* case, too? Or *mine?*"

Joaquin considered reminding her he was the lead attorney, but she was right—the case belonged to all of them. "Yes, it's *our* case. Forget I said anything. The text didn't send, and we've all been hungover."

"Excuse me? That's not what happened. Not that what I do outside office hours is your business."

Joaquin rocked on his heels. "You're right. It's just . . ." He stopped. "Forget it."

Her eyes narrowed, darkening. "It's just *what?*"

"Watch out for Luca. I heard he cheated on his ex. He's a great detective, but is not exactly faithful in relationships."

Melrose smirked. "Trust me, he's not the first womanizing bloke I've ever worked with. I can handle myself."

Joaquin sat on the loveseat across from her desk. "Right, of course you can."

She let her gaze sweep over him. "And I'm not *at all* interested in him."

Joaquin met her eyes. "Sorry I brought that up."

"No worries, but can we stick to business?" She grabbed a file folder and sat next to Joaquin. Her hand brushed his, a tingle rising up his arm. So much for proving he could *stick to business.* "I got a 1986 yearbook and listed all the male graduates. Then I checked which ones are still living."

"How many are we looking at?" Joaquin asked.

"Over one hundred. I'm working on gathering phone numbers. Should I be honest about why I'm calling?"

Joaquin rubbed the stubble on his chin. "What if you said you were from Jostens and doing a survey?"

"Do companies still do that? Call? And why would any company care about class rings from nearly forty years ago?"

"They don't need to know we're only calling the class of eighty-six," Joaquin said.

Melrose tapped her pen against the file. "I bet if we could incentivize the survey, most of these guys won't think twice. The only issue is privacy laws."

"You're right. We'd have to disclose what we plan to use their data for."

Melrose sighed. "So we'd just throw in some fine print? This data may be used to determine if you're a serial killer?"

"I'll get Luca's thoughts, but the class ring search might be a dead end," Joaquin said.

Melrose closed the folder. "How was the meeting with the Fords?"

"Ollie wasn't home, but Bruce mentioned his son has this fixation on the beach. He collects anything ocean-related. It got Luca thinking . . ."

"About the dolphin wind chime?" Melrose asked. "The one *not* at the bower."

"Exactly. Seems like a long shot, especially with Ollie's disability. And Bruce's past charges aren't the smoking gun I hoped." He glanced at the carpet. "I guess you didn't have time to check into him?"

"Damn!" Melrose smacked her forehead. "I'm so sorry. I knew I was forgetting something."

"Not a big deal," Joaquin lied, leaving out the details of the humiliation he'd experienced at Bruce's smug words. *I thought you lawyer types did your homework.* "And just because his criminal history isn't as seedy as I expected, doesn't mean he's not involved," Joaquin continued. "People will do a lot to protect their kids."

Joaquin thought of his own parents after Glory's death. The lies they'd told the police, the lies they'd told themselves, the lies they were *still* telling themselves.

"Are you going to plan another visit?" Melrose asked.

"Yeah. It might be best to visit Ollie in person, away from his dad."

"Doesn't he work at Murphy's Market? He's loaded my groceries a few times. He seems like a real gem, honestly."

"So did Ted Bundy."

Melrose playfully hit his leg. "Is that your only comeback?"

Joaquin smiled. "Maybe Ollie's innocent, but I figure if we can get him talking about his collection, maybe we can bring up the dolphin. Luca and I are going tomorrow, but it might be best if you came. You'd be less intimidating."

Melrose hit his leg again, harder this time. "Excuse me?"

Joaquin raised his hands. "Okay, you're intimidating. But you also make people comfortable," he said, even though he felt anything but comfortable sitting this close to her.

"Alright," Melrose said. "I'll have a chat with him."

Joaquin looked more closely at her. He noticed dark circles under her eyes and a pink rash at her temple, partly hidden by makeup. For the first time, he wondered if she'd actually been sick. "Are you *really* feeling okay?"

"I'm fine."

"You look tired."

Melrose huffed. "Wow. Thanks. So I look like shit."

He stared into her eyes and swallowed a million words he wanted to say but knew he shouldn't. "You don't look anything close to shit, ever."

She sighed. "I wasn't hungover from that drink with Luca, but I am ill."

"Then go home. I'll bring you chicken soup."

She wrinkled her nose. "Ugh. I hate chicken soup."

"The stuff from the can is gross, but my mom's is amazing. She gave me the recipe—I could try to make it for you."

Melrose shook her head. "It's not that kind of sick. I have fibromyalgia, an autoimmune disease. I manage a lot of the symptoms with medication. Botox works wonders for the migraines, but the worst part is the brain fog—it makes me forgetful."

Joaquin thought about the background check she was supposed to do on Bruce Ford and the unsent message in her phone's drafts folder. "I see."

"This isn't an excuse. My job is my responsibility. So I deserve an ear-bashing."

He inched closer to her. "A text still in drafts is not a big deal, Melrose."

"But the next one might be." Her bottom lip trembled, and her eyes glistened. "I've got to be more careful and keep better notes. That's why Oswald gave me the boot. I forgot something important."

He nudged his knee until it brushed hers, then said, "I'm sorry."

She kept her head down. "It was an important brief."

"Did Oswald know? About the fibromyalgia?"

"No." She swatted away a tear, and Joaquin reached for a box of Kleenex.

She took a tissue and blotted under her eyes. "I didn't want him to pity me. I don't want you to either."

Joaquin took in her steady focus and quiet strength, the way she pushed herself, carrying her burdens without complaint. It made him respect her—and worry for her at the same time. "I don't pity you," he said. "I admire you. But stay home when you need to. We have no set hours. Just get the job done."

"Thanks, Joaquin," she said. It was the first time she'd used his first name, and he liked how it sounded, colored by her accent.

"I'd better get back to work," he said. As he was about to move, Melrose smiled—full and genuine, not a half-smile or smirk. Another first.

"You said you weren't gonna smile till Troy was free," Joaquin teased.

"Consider this preemptive."

Joaquin wiped his damp palms on his pants, feeling her gaze linger. "I was kinda hoping it wasn't about Troy Terrell at all," he admitted, surprising himself.

The bang at the door was a less welcome surprise. "Knock, knock," Bernie said, opening it a crack.

Joaquin jumped up, his face flushing. "Come in."

Bernie's head peeked through the door. "Hunka Burning Love is on the phone."

"Huh?" Joaquin smoothed his jacket.

"Eye Candy Extraordinaire? Hottie McHotface? The Italian Stallion?"

*Luca*, Joaquin realized. "Can you take a message?"

Bernie shook her head. "Tried. Says it's urgent."

The word *urgent* sent a jolt of tension through Joaquin. He weaved around a stack of boxes to Melrose's desk. "Transfer the call in here," he said.

He hit the speaker button. "Hey Luca, I've got you on speaker. What's up?"

"I found the DNA!"

Joaquin froze, caught between disbelief and the dangerous pull of hope. "Not funny, Moretti."

"I'm not joking." Luca's voice was breathless. "We have the evidence."

"Where was it? Did Carter hide it?"

"I don't think so. Gwinn Barns had it."

Joaquin glanced at Melrose, trying to gauge if he should recognize the name, but Melrose just shrugged. "Who the hell is Gwinn Barns?" he asked.

"State lab analyst who had promoted the serology," Luca explained. "She broke protocol and didn't return the slides with the semen to the sexual assault evidence kit. She has them both, along with the hair and blood samples."

"Are they still good?" Melrose moved closer to the phone. "I mean, can they be tested?"

"Not the hair. Gwinn said there's no root tissue attached. But the semen and blood, yeah, I think it's possible," Luca said.

Joaquin grabbed his head. "How the hell did you do this, Moretti? I could freaking kiss you, man. Come by the office and fill us in."

"I'm in Houston, so that kiss will have to wait. I'll drop by first thing tomorrow."

Joaquin's heart was still racing after he hung up. He glanced at Melrose. "Thank God for broken protocol."

Melrose's fingers drummed lightly against the desk. "But will there be issues with the chain of custody or the sample's integrity?"

"We'll deal with that as it comes," Joaquin said, catching his breath.

"We've *got* to tell Troy in person," Melrose said. "This news deserves more than a phone call, yeah?"

"You're right." He met her gaze again and gave a shy smile. "Road trip it is."

Less than two hours later, they were back on the cramped bench at Polunsky Unit. Joaquin winced at his offhand comment in Melrose's office: *I was kinda hoping it wasn't about Troy Terrell at all.* What had he been thinking?

Melrose, however, was still beaming. Her smile was probably more about the DNA breakthrough than about him. Joaquin, despite the good news, couldn't summon a smile. Doubts gnawed at him. What if DA

Claire Hench refused the testing? She seemed reasonable, unlike her predecessor, but no district attorney wanted to admit the state had imprisoned an innocent man. If she refused, a judge would decide—and Texas courts had a reputation for placing unusually high barriers on post-conviction DNA testing. Even with a ruling in their favor, would DPAP have the budget?

Troy's eyebrows knit together in confusion as they brought him into the legal booth. Joaquin picked up the phone before Melrose had the chance, holding it so both of them could hear.

"What's going on?" Troy asked. "Everything okay?"

"Everything's great," Joaquin responded, his tone upbeat. "We got some important news about the DNA evidence."

"What about it?" Troy asked.

Troy stiffened, muscles taut, expression unreadable.

Curiosity and unease pricked at Joaquin, but he forced himself to stay calm. "It wasn't destroyed," he said. "Luca found the DNA."

Troy swallowed. "All of it?"

Joaquin's stomach sank. Why didn't Troy sound relieved? "Yeah, all of it. Blood, semen, hair—everything."

Troy hung his head. Melrose's smile vanished. She must have realized what Joaquin had—he was right to doubt, right to focus on violations of procedure and not actual proof of innocence.

"Talk to us, Troy," Melrose said softly, though her tone carried an edge.

Troy looked up, his eyes hollow. "Does anyone else know?"

Joaquin met his gaze with a steely, unwavering stare. "The DA will know soon enough. The serologist is required to return the evidence to the state."

"And they'll test it right away?"

"Not necessarily," Joaquin said. "But it's gonna look real damn bad if we don't push for it to be. Look, man, you've gotta shoot straight with me. Tell me why you're acting like this isn't good news."

Troy faced Melrose, his eyes welling up with tears. "It was an accident, a mistake."

Shock and a bitter sense of betrayal surged through Joaquin, tightening his chest. "You're saying . . ."

"Don't test the DNA," Troy whispered.

"Damn it!" Joaquin slammed his fist on the table. "Why not, Troy? Why shouldn't we test it?"

Troy slumped, face buried in his hands. "Because . . . it's mine. The DNA is mine."

# CHAPTER 16

**July 4, 1986**

"What the hell, Tilly? I said I didn't want to swim!" Troy wiped water from his eyes and saw Tilly inches from his face.

"Oh, come on. Little old me couldn't pull you in against your will." She wrapped her legs around him. Troy glanced at her lips, droplets of water clinging to them.

Troy pushed her back gently, heart racing. "Stop . . . let's get out." His fingers lingered on her arms, and he felt a stubborn tug to stay, even as his brain screamed this was wrong.

Tilly raised an eyebrow, smirking. "Oh, you want to take this inside?"

Troy forced himself to step back. *Focus, Troy. Don't do something stupid.* "N . . . no," he muttered, barely audible.

"Fine. Back to the game. My turn." She lowered herself so the water hit right under the lips Troy was still staring at. "Number one: I won a dozen baby pageants before I was two. Number two: on vacation, I met Brooke Shields at a snow cone stand. Number three: I've never slept with anyone besides Hayes."

"Brooke Shields is the lie," Troy said.

"Nope, she ordered coconut with cream, just like me." Tilly went underwater and came back up, shaking water from her hair.

"No pageants," Troy said.

"Wrong again. Tons of the trophies are boxed up in my closet if you want proof." She locked eyes with Troy as if daring him to ask about the lie she'd told—about never sleeping with anyone besides Hayes. As far as Troy knew, Hayes and Tilly hadn't broken up, so either someone came before him or she'd cheated. Not his business.

"Okay, here's mine," Troy said. "One: I can sing the ABCs backward. Two: strawberries make me break out in a rash. Three: I take a bubble bath every Sunday night."

Tilly laughed. "I've seen you eat strawberries, so I'm gonna say the first one was a lie."

"Wrong," Troy said. "Third one."

Tilly swam closer. "Well, darn. I was enjoying the visual of Troy Terrell in a bubble bath."

Troy backed against the wall of the pool. "The only baths I've ever taken were ice ones for football."

"We can fix that." Tilly put her mouth underwater and then rose, spitting water like a fountain. "Mom and Dad have one of those jacuzzi tubs."

Tilly drifted closer. Troy knew he needed to leave the pool, but stayed pressed against the edge as Tilly lifted his shirt. "Take this off so it can dry."

Troy tugged off the shirt and tossed it onto the concrete. Tilly stayed close, pressing her chest against his. He liked how she looked with water dripping from her hair, liked the closeness of their bodies; he liked it all too much.

Troy gently pushed her back. "Your turn," he managed.

"Hmm, okay. Number one: I still sleep with a stuffed animal. Number two: I can hold my breath underwater for two minutes. Number three: I think I'm pregnant."

"What?" Troy clutched the pool's edge. "That's not funny, Tilly."

"What's not? Which one's the lie?"

"The last one's a lie."

"Nope, the second one. I can't hold my breath for shit." She held her nose. "Time me," she said, going underwater.

Troy grabbed her hand and pulled her back up. "Are you pregnant, Tilly?"

She averted her gaze, shoulders hunching. "I haven't taken a test yet."

"Why not?"

She turned her head and tugged at her ear, allowing the water to drain. "Well, first, I didn't want to be seen buying one—everyone in this town knows me. And second, I guess I'm afraid to find out." Her voice had lost its flirtatious edge.

"Have you told Hayes?"

"No!" Tilly shoved Troy. "And you better not either."

"Why not? Hayes would want to help figure this out."

Tilly turned away from Troy. "There's nothing to figure out, Troy. *If* I'm pregnant, I can't keep the baby. I'll be lucky to pass my college classes without having to find a babysitter."

"I understand," Troy said. "But you still need to talk to Hayes. He'd want to be there for you—"

"I'm breaking up with Hayes, okay?" Tilly's voice trembled.

Troy grasped both of Tilly's shoulders, gently turning her toward him. Her eyes were brimming with tears. "Tilly, no. Hayes loves you. I understand you're scared, but that's not a reason to ruin a good thing."

"It's not about the pregnancy scare. I've known for a while that our relationship won't last. We've both changed. There's a reason most people don't marry their first love, right?"

"Hayes is looking for rings, Tilly."

Tilly squeezed her eyes shut and shook her head. "There's someone else, Troy. I love someone else, and I think the baby is his."

Troy froze, his mind scrambling. "Wait . . . what? Who . . . who is it?"

"I'm done talking about this. It's too cold to talk about this." She swam to the edge of the pool and climbed out.

Troy followed and scanned the pool chairs for a towel to wrap Tilly in. "You're shaking," he said, pulling her close to his body for warmth.

She continued to convulse in his arms. Troy wasn't sure whether crying or the cold was to blame. It had been a long time since he'd seen Tilly this honest, this vulnerable. Water from her hair dripped as she pressed her mouth against his ear. "How long have you wanted me?"

Troy briefly clenched his hands. "Tilly, don't—"

"How long?" she asked again. "I'm just curious."

"A while. Since around sophomore year."

Tilly pulled back, looking into his eyes. "I've got you beat," she sniffled, then wiped the back of her hand across her nose. "It was eighth grade for me."

*Eighth grade.* Before Hayes. Troy couldn't deny how good that made him feel. Chantilly Price, who could have had anyone, wanted him.

"And what is it about me that made you feel that way?" Tilly asked.

Troy chuckled. "Come on, Till. You know you're gorgeous."

Tilly took a small step away from him. "Ugh. Of course."

"What?" Troy put his hand on Tilly's chin and raised her head. "What's wrong with that?"

"It's all people see." Tilly flopped into a patio chair. "All they've *ever* seen. Guess how often I've been told I should be a model?"

Troy squatted in front of the chair. "Tilly . . . I . . ."

"Hundreds!" she interrupted. "What if I don't want to model? Maybe I want to be a nurse or a hairdresser." She threw up her hands. "Or a goddamn glassblower."

"You'd be an awesome nurse or hairstylist, but I'm not sure you've got the heat tolerance for glass blowing. You pass out pretty much any time the temperature hits a hundred degrees."

Tilly laughed and swatted away a tear. "That only happened twice." She rubbed her eyes. "I know what you're thinking. Poor little rich girl, right? Sometimes, it feels like I can only be what others want. Like I can't live for myself. What if I want to skip the hour of skincare? What if I want to eat something besides a salad? That's why I fell for this other guy. He's the first person who's ever told me I was smart and talented. He sees me for who I really am."

Troy hesitated, his chest tight. "Then . . . you should break up with Hayes. You deserve someone who sees you—really sees you."

Tilly shook her head, eyes downcast. "It's too late. He's done with me. I promised months ago I'd leave Hayes, but I never did."

Troy swallowed, searching for the right words. "I bet you'll meet someone at college who notices those things about you. Who appreciates your confidence, the way you carry yourself, the way you throw yourself into things. I've always noticed. I just . . . never said it."

Tilly looked down, a shy smile tugging at her lips. Her fingers fidgeted with her swimsuit strap. "Thank you for telling me that."

"And you're really generous," Troy added. "Always picking up the tab, helping others with your family's connections . . . even sending those handwritten birthday cards. It's always meant a lot."

Tilly giggled, the playful glint back in her eye. "Don't go giving me a big head now."

Troy stood from his squat, wincing as his knee twinged. He extended his hand. "Come on, girlie. You're still shaking. Let's go inside."

As he helped Tilly to her feet, she stumbled into him, and their lips brushed. Heat flared in his chest. He knew it was wrong, but nothing felt more right. He meant to pull away, but his fingers found her wet hair, and his mouth moved with hers. They broke apart when a massive firework exploded overhead. Troy noticed a flicker of movement behind the fence. "We shouldn't be out here. People might—"

"Then come inside," Tilly replied. "Please, just hold me."

Without waiting for a response, she turned back to the house. Before Troy could second-guess himself, he followed.

# CHAPTER 17

2024

"Do we still need to do this?" Melrose asked as she drove Joaquin and Luca to Murphy's Market.

"Can't hurt," Luca replied, lounging in the middle of the backseat.

Melrose glanced back. "Buckled?"

"Nah, I like to live dangerously," Luca said with a smirk.

"So you're saying I'm a bad driver?" Melrose shot back, catching his eye in the mirror.

"No, not at all, but remind me, are speed limits optional in Australia?"

Joaquin folded his arms. They were flirting right in front of him.

"Getting something out of Ollie feels more important than ever after Troy's little confession yesterday," Luca said.

"Don't remind me." Joaquin massaged his temples. "I swear if I catch him in one more lie."

"You won't," Melrose cut in. "He thought the DNA was gone. And you heard him—he's not afraid to test the Wendy Knott evidence. I'll admit, for a minute, I thought things were about to go pear-shaped. When he called it an accident, I was afraid he meant . . ."

"That her murder was an accident," Joaquin finished. "Me too. Sex doesn't happen by accident."

"Bad choice of words. He meant the sex was a mistake," Melrose said. "But hey, not all bad news. Tilly thinking she was pregnant by some other guy is a new twist."

"She wasn't, right?" Luca asked. "The autopsy would've shown."

"I'd think so," Melrose said. "But Tilly's belief that she was pregnant adds motive for both Hayes and the mystery man."

"We need to find this guy and talk to him," Luca said. "In a town like Bluesummer, someone had to know who Chantilly Price was seeing on the side. I can't believe Troy never told anyone about this."

"He says he did, but the police dismissed it. The files show no follow-up—they'd decided Troy was guilty."

Luca tapped Joaquin's seat. "What's the status of the DNA testing?"

"Heard from Hench this morning," Joaquin said. "She won't object as long as the state agrees to the lab and we cover the cost."

Luca hit his seat harder. "Nice work. Guess she's not as crooked as Carter."

Joaquin adjusted his sunglasses as sunlight flickered across the hood. "Don't celebrate yet. The lab you recommended quoted eight grand."

Melrose's head snapped toward him, her ponytail brushing her shoulder. "Eight thousand? Why not use the state lab? Gotta be cheaper."

"It'll take longer," Luca said. "This lab's one of the best in Texas. I know the guy running it—he'll prioritize us."

"Okay, that's a win, but can DPAP afford eight grand?" Melrose asked.

"Doubt it," Joaquin said. "But hopefully, they can swing the two-grand advance."

"And the rest?"

Joaquin rested against the window. "Hell if I know. Fundraisers? I could take on a few divorces." The thought alone intensified his headache.

"I'll talk to Phil," Luca said. "Might get him to drop the price."

Melrose tapped the steering wheel. "We'll figure it out. We need DPAP's media liaison to draft a statement—something that makes it clear Tilly and Troy were involved. If we wait until after the DNA results, it'll look like we're scrambling if there's a match."

Joaquin slapped the dashboard. "How could he hide something this big?"

"I know he lied," Melrose said, "but he wouldn't push so hard to test the Wendy Knott evidence if he were guilty."

"I hate to be negative, but even if it's not Troy's DNA in the Wendy Knott sample, one conviction is enough for the needle," Luca said. "Best-case scenario? We get someone else's DNA in *both* samples."

"We should get Troy to do an interview," Melrose suggested. "Explain what happened with Tilly."

"The Texas Department of Criminal Justice might not approve it," Joaquin said. "And even if they do, I'm not sure it'd help. Troy comes off cold."

"He's private," Melrose said. "We can coach him."

Joaquin let out a short laugh. No amount of coaching could make America believe a convicted serial killer.

"And why do we need this dolphin?" Melrose asked, pulling into the parking lot. "If we've got potential Strangler DNA, why not test Bruce and Ollie for comparison?"

"We will," Luca said. "But we still don't know for sure if we'll get a profile. Maybe the Strangler didn't assault his victims. Tilly had consensual sex that day—maybe Wendy did too."

"And we don't have much of a sample," Joaquin explained. "It might not be enough to test. But if we find that dolphin from the Llywelyn wind chimes in a former suspect's room? I'd feel a hell of a lot better."

"Fair point," Melrose said, shifting into park.

"Leave it running for me, will you?" Luca asked.

"You're not coming?" Joaquin turned in his seat.

"The three of us might make Ollie suspicious," Luca said. "You two will blend in—just a couple grocery shopping."

Joaquin unbuckled his seatbelt, pleasantly surprised that Luca hadn't suggested Joaquin be the one to stay in the car.

"Shouldn't you come with me, Luca?" Melrose asked. "Aren't you better at getting info?"

Joaquin pursed his lips. So Luca hadn't sidelined him, but Melrose had. Even better.

"Ollie's shy," Luca said. "I might spook him." He waved them off. "Go on, see what happens."

Joaquin strode toward the store, staying a few steps ahead of Melrose. At the cart bay, he yanked at one, but it stuck. He pulled harder, lifting it slightly, but it wouldn't budge. Heat crept up his neck.

"Hey, relax," Melrose said, effortlessly freeing a cart from the adjacent row. "Do we really need a buggy?"

He'd planned to buy groceries with Luca, not Melrose. It felt too intimate having her watch him load TV dinners, compare body wash, and stock up on antacids. "We need to buy enough to justify carryout," he said as they pushed through the sliding glass door.

"Why not grab some lollies for the office?" Melrose suggested.

He tilted his head slightly, trying not to laugh. "Lollies?"

"Sweets, candy," she clarified with a grin. "We'll need a sugar hit to keep us going." She nodded toward the registers. "That's Ollie, right? Lane five?"

Joaquin glanced at the man bagging groceries. He was tall and hulking, the sort who looked like he could handle himself in a fight. Yet, despite his imposing presence, his demeanor suggested no rage or even annoyance as he cheerfully packed the groceries, his mop of white hair obscuring his eyes.

Still, what could you really know about someone just by looking at them? The FBI profile painted the Strangler as a man with a deep-seated hatred for women—maybe thanks to a controlling mother or the absence of one. They likely faced romantic rejection, too. Ollie had been given up for adoption, and Joaquin doubted the high school girls had been kind. The profile fit.

"Alright," Melrose said, steering the wobbly cart toward the coffee aisle. "Let's get a move on, yeah?"

They moved through the supermarket tossing chips, candy, granola bars, coffee pods, and sparkling water into the cart. Fluorescent lights hummed overhead, casting a stark glow on the neatly stacked shelves. "Iris" played softly over the speakers, its lyrics echoing a longing for Melrose that felt both silly and dramatic as Joaquin stocked a rickety grocery cart with gummy bears.

Melrose steered toward the checkout lanes. "So, what's the plan? Ollie might end up doing a takeaway for someone else once he carries out the woman in line's bags. There are three baggers, and they rotate."

Joaquin eyed the customer in front of them. "That's maybe four bags' worth. She'll carry them herself."

"And if she doesn't?"

"Trust me," Joaquin said, beginning to unload the cart.

But when Ollie placed the few bags back into the woman's cart and started pushing it, she didn't stop him.

"Unbelievable." Joaquin sighed and tossed a bag of chips onto the conveyor belt. "Seriously, is everyone that lazy?"

"Don't judge," Melrose said. "Maybe she's got a disability." She glanced over her shoulder. "Oi, stop loading."

Before Joaquin could ask why, Melrose spun toward the aisles, standing on her tiptoes. "Where's that kid?" she asked with exaggerated annoyance. Turning back to the belt, she swept their items back toward them. "Here, you go ahead," she told the man behind them, placing a divider in front of their groceries. "We sent our son off for cereal, and he's taking his sweet time."

The man chuckled. "Cereal's an important decision. I don't mind waiting."

Melrose slid their cart aside. "You've only got a few things." She nodded at the red basket he was carrying. "We've practically bought out the whole shop."

"Well, thanks." The man smiled at Melrose, barely acknowledging Joaquin.

"Son, huh?" Joaquin asked.

"Just give me a hand," Melrose said, loading more items onto the belt.

The man ahead carried his single bag out of the store, passing Ollie, who was heading back to aisle five. *He likes routine*, Joaquin recalled Bruce saying. Thank goodness for that.

Joaquin stepped to the credit card machine and pulled out his wallet. "Say, you guys don't have any beach-themed birthday supplies, do you?"

The young cashier didn't look up as she robotically scanned the groceries. "Party supplies are on aisle nineteen."

"Yeah, we saw them, but nothing beachy."

She snapped her gum. "Well, it *is* November."

"I know, but my friend here is from Australia. It's almost summer there."

The cashier raised an eyebrow. "Uh-huh."

"Anyway, she loves all things beach-related—has quite the collection. I wanted her birthday to be extra special this year, but I guess I should've shopped in July."

"Guess so." The woman punched a few buttons on the register. "One hundred twenty-seven dollars and six cents."

Joaquin slid a card into the chip reader and glanced at Ollie. His expression revealed no interest in Joaquin's beach comment as he packed bags into the cart.

Joaquin figured he'd have to be more direct as they led Ollie across the parking lot. But as they reached Melrose's vehicle, Ollie took the bait. "I like the beach too," he said.

*Bingo.*

"Are the beaches awesome in Australia?" Ollie drew out the words.

"So awesome," Melrose answered. "Which beach is your favorite?"

Ollie looked down. "The ones in movies, I guess."

"She has this huge beach collection," Joaquin interjected as Melrose raised the liftgate.

Ollie's eyes lit up. "Me too!"

Joaquin picked up a case of water from the bottom of the cart. "What beach things do you have in your collection?"

Joaquin noticed Luca subtly angling himself to listen in.

"Umm, shells and stuff," Ollie said, quickly loading the bags. He was being too efficient.

"What other things?" Joaquin asked, intercepting a bag from Ollie and deliberately stalling as he set it in the cargo area.

"Beach chairs, beach movies, beach balls, driftwood," Ollie listed.

"What about—"

"Oh!" Ollie's sudden exclamation startled everyone. "And my favorite—a starfish."

"That sounds cool," Joaquin said as Ollie picked up the last bag from the cart. They were out of time. "What about dolphins? Like glass or metal ones?" He nodded toward Melrose. "She has tons of dolphins."

Ollie set the last bag into the car. "I wish. I love dolphins." He mimicked a dolphin's click. Joaquin hated to admit it, but Ollie's childlike enthusiasm was making it difficult to picture this man so much as hurting a sand flea, much less being a serial killer.

Melrose pulled a twenty from her wallet. "Thanks for the carryout. This should buy you a proper dolphin figurine."

"Oh, wow!" Ollie's eyes widened as he took the bill. "I don't think I'll spend it. If I save enough, I could go to the beach. Maybe I'll even see a *real* dolphin!"

Joaquin noticed tears in Melrose's eyes. She reached into her purse again. He needed to stop her before she handed over her debit card and PIN. "Time to go." He nodded toward the back seat. "We need to get little Luca home for a nap."

"What?" Luca turned sharply as Joaquin slammed the liftgate.

"I'm not doing that again," Melrose said once inside the SUV. She wiped mascara from under her eye. "He's a sweet man."

"Come on, Melrose," Luca said. "We have to follow all leads."

Melrose gripped the wheel. "He said he doesn't have the dolphin, and he doesn't. If you two don't want to leave that poor man alone, that's on you, but I'm done."

Joaquin wasn't sure why Melrose was so upset, but when a tear slipped down her cheek, he touched her shoulder. "Hey, I'm sorry if—"

Before he could finish, she pushed his hand away and cranked up the radio.

Joaquin lowered his sunglasses and reclined his seat as Beyoncé's "Texas Hold 'Em" blared through the speakers. The upbeat rhythm clashed with the mood—both inside the car and in his head. Nothing had gone as planned, but if his parents had taught him anything, it was that you play the hand you're dealt.

Refusing to fold, he opened his notes app and started working on tomorrow's to-do list.

# CHAPTER 18

**July 4, 1986**

Greer's tire scraped the curb as she pulled up to the Sheridan home. The last half hour was a blur, too surreal to be real, but it was. The darkness and slats of the Prices' fence obscured much of what had happened, and the fireworks drowned out most of the conversation between Troy and Tilly, but Greer had seen enough: a game, a kiss, an invitation inside.

She could have stopped them. *Should* have stopped them, but she hadn't. Instead, she'd come here to tell Hayes. Why? To hurt him? To make him end things with Tilly and turn to her? She wasn't sure she could face those kind blue eyes and shatter what was supposed to be a perfect night—and a perfect future.

A knock on her window jolted her.

"Didn't mean to scare you," Red said, moving to the back door to grab her bag. Greer eased her door open, steadying her racing heart. "Sorry. Just spacing out."

Red pointed to the house. "Dr Pepper's on ice. Hot Pockets are in the freezer. Hayes is in the brig. In order of importance."

"Thanks." Greer noticed the notebook tucked under his arm. "Did we kick you out of your writing cave?"

"Nah. I was gonna watch a movie, but thought I'd brainstorm on the porch first. Thought the fresh air might help."

"Only if you consider sulfur and smoke fresh air."

Red took a deep breath. "I do. I actually love it."

"Me too," Greer said. "But most nights, I'm at a rink that smells like smelly feet and nacho cheese. My standards are low."

Red laughed. "Well, you've always liked fireworks. Another thing we have in common."

"Yep. Sparklers and serial killers." She nodded at his notebook. "Any new leads?"

"Afraid not. And based on the timeline between his kills, I figure we've only about three weeks to solve this case before there's a fifth victim."

"You'll solve it," Greer said as they walked up the stone driveway, past perfectly trimmed hedges and the softly glowing lanterns along the path. "You'll do what our incompetent police force can't."

"And what the FBI can't?" Red asked, a half-smile tugging at his lips.

"Yeah, them too."

Red set her bag on the porch swing and pulled out a pack of cigarettes. "I should stick to writing about solved cases. In this situation, you need to be first to print. Once there's an arrest, my book has to be the first on my agent's desk."

"You need to be the one to write this," Greer said.

"Well, thanks for the vote of confidence." Red lit a cigarette. "How's everything going? All set for school?"

"Yep, all set."

"And you're living on campus, right?"

The fireworks stopped, leaving only the sharp click of Red's lighter, followed by the soft hiss of the flame.

"I decided it makes more sense to live at home," Greer explained. "It's close enough to drive, and I can save more money."

"Hmm." Red took a puff.

Greer pressed her lips together, tugging at the hem of her sleeve. Her mom had worked hard to make college possible—Red didn't need to feel sorry for her.

"Well, you're going to be a hell of a journalist," he said. "Those articles you wrote for the school paper were damn good."

"Really? Thanks for reading them. Got any advice?"

Red blew out a puff of smoke. "Get the story. You're talented, but you were stuck with boring topics: objections to reading material, debates about standardized testing."

Greer crossed her arms, a mix of pride and discomfort washing over her. She thought those articles were hard-hitting, but she was impressed he had read them at all.

"I mean no offense," he added, taking another drag. "You've got talent, but you need a better story. The story is everything."

"I'll keep that in mind," she said, reaching for the screen door. She hesitated. "Does Joanne know you're smoking again?"

Red exhaled, offering a small smile. "I mostly quit. Let's not make a thing of it, alright? Everyone deserves a vice, right?"

Greer sighed. "Your secret's safe with me, but it's bad for you, Red."

He gave a small, tired laugh. "I know, I know. I'll finish this one, then the only smoke I inhale tonight will be from the fireworks. Deal?"

"Deal." She smiled. "Thanks for letting us all hang out tonight."

"Anytime, Greer." Red handed her the duffel bag. "You've always been like a daughter to me. If you need anything—advice, references, money for a dorm room, whatever—just ask."

"I'll be fine, really," Greer said. Despite the irritation at Red's pity, she couldn't help but smile at the thought of being his daughter.

Hayes jumped from the couch when Greer walked in, his eyes searching behind her. The disappointment that flashed across his face when he saw she was alone didn't escape Greer's notice.

"Where's Troy and Tilly?"

Greer shut the door too hard, making the dartboard mounted on its back rattle. "Tilly didn't want to come. She's wasted."

Hayes shoved his hands into his pockets. "And Troy?"

"Sick," Greer said, dropping her bag by the door.

"But his truck isn't at his place," Hayes said, a sharp edge in his tone. "Is he still at Tilly's?"

Greer bit her lip. "He's waiting for her to pass out so she doesn't drive."

"Oh." Hayes furrowed his brow. "What were they doing?"

"Watching TV," Greer said, forcing a casual tone.

"Were they sitting next to each other?"

"Come on, Hayes. Let it go."

"Did you tell her that her phone was off the hook?"

Greer sank onto the leather couch. "Sorry, I forgot."

"Greer! I need to be able to check on Tilly. I don't like the idea of her being alone overnight."

Greer felt a twist of sadness tighten in her chest. "If you're going to sulk, I'm going home." She stood. "Because it feels like I don't matter."

"I want you here." Hayes rubbed his forehead. "I wanted us *all* here."

She put a hand on his shoulder. "I get you have a vision for how things should be, but sometimes things don't go as planned. People get drunk. Parents say no. We can still make the best of tonight."

Hayes put his hand on hers. "I'm glad you're here," he said, his voice gentle.

Goosebumps spread over Greer's arms as he looked into her eyes.

"So, what should we do?" Hayes asked, pulling his hand away. "Dad got Hot Pockets."

Greer sat on a pillow in front of the TV. "Let's talk first. Did you decide about Cornell?"

Hayes dropped down next to her. "Yeah, I'm not going."

"What? Why not?" Greer edged closer.

"It doesn't make sense. Why go to school to be a farmer? Why make less money?"

"Because you'd be doing something you love."

"I love architecture too," he said defensively.

*And Tilly*, Greer thought. *You're doing this for her.* She clapped her hands together once. "Okay, it's settled. When do you leave for UT?"

"Six weeks," Hayes said, shaking his head. "Crazy, right?"

Greer picked at the shaggy carpet. "I'll miss you."

"I'll miss you too." Hayes touched her knee.

Hayes didn't move his hand away. Greer wondered whether she should tell him she loved him or lean in and kiss him. What had held her back all these years? Was it just Tilly or the fear of ruining their friendship?

Either way, she didn't care anymore. Their friendship would change when he left for college, and she couldn't care less about Tilly's feelings after what she'd seen tonight.

Before she could act, Hayes stood. "Want to play *Punch-Out*?"

"*Punch-Out*?" Greer wiped her lips with the back of her hand.

"Fine. *Mario Brothers* it is. Want a snack first?"

"No thanks," Greer said. She sure didn't need Hot-Pocket breath when kissing Hayes.

"You sure? I'm going in anyway."

"A Coke would be great."

He winked. "You got it."

Once Hayes left, Greer checked her reflection in the tiny bathroom. She wished she had brought a hairbrush. She hurried back when she heard Hayes stomping outside.

When he entered, his face was flushed, and his hands were empty.

"What's wrong?" Greer asked.

"Troy's truck *still* isn't in his driveway."

Greer picked up the controller. "He'll be home soon."

The door slammed with a thunderous noise.

"Sorry," Hayes said. "But Tilly mentioned Troy's been staring at her."

She rolled her eyes. "Come on, Hayes. Tilly thinks every guy is looking at her."

Hayes leaned back, arms crossing over his chest. "What's that supposed to mean?"

"Exactly what I said. Tilly thinks every guy wants her." The words came out sharper than she had intended.

"Well, they probably do."

Tears welled in Greer's eyes. "But nobody wants me, right?"

Hayes flinched. "That's not what I said. Of course guys want you."

"Who?" Greer swatted away a tear. "Name one."

"Ronald West." Hayes stepped closer. "Not that he deserves you. Where's this coming from?"

"That's the thing." Greer's voice hardened. "Every time a guy showed interest, you said he wasn't good enough."

"Well, they weren't good enough," Hayes said. "You're my best friend. I don't want you to settle."

"But at the same time, *I'm* not good enough for you, right?" Her voice wavered, and she blinked hard, refusing to look away from him.

Hayes opened his mouth, then closed it. "It's not like that," he said. "It's just . . . I've always been with Tilly."

"But you had to know," Greer's voice hardened. "You had to know how I felt. At least once in the past decade, you had to know!"

Hayes looked at the ceiling, unable to meet her eyes.

"So, is that a yes?"

"I've wondered," Hayes said quietly. "But I was never sure. You never said anything."

"And if I had?" Greer pressed.

"Greer . . ." Hayes took a step toward her. "I think you're great. The best. And so pretty."

Greer held up a hand. "Just stop."

"No!" Hayes grabbed her hand. "It's all true."

For a moment, Greer dared to hope. They were holding hands, lips inches apart. But his eyes were filled with tears. "There's no reason I shouldn't feel that way about you," he said. "But I don't."

Greer dropped his hand and stepped back.

Hayes touched her cheek. Greer wanted to scream at him to stop, but she let him wipe away her stupid tears.

"I'm sorry," he said, his voice breaking. "I'm just being honest."

Memories swarmed Greer—staying on the phone with Hayes after a fight with Tilly, comforting him on his sixteenth birthday when Tilly hadn't shown up. Greer always hoped he'd realize her loyalty and love her for it. But now she knew it was all a fantasy. His cold words looped in her mind.

*Just being honest.*

"Greer, please say something."

Outside, fireworks boomed, and Greer knew she'd never hear them again without reliving this night. She grabbed her bag and pushed past Hayes into the backyard.

Not wanting Red or Joanne to see her crying, she ran to the fence. She fumbled with the latch as Hayes approached—slow and calm like a horror movie villain.

"Stop, Greer. Let's talk. We've always been able to talk about everything."

The latch wouldn't open. She tossed her bag over the gate, then climbed.

"Greer!" Hayes yelled. "You're going to hurt yourself!"

She stumbled toward her car, keys slipping from her fingers like the stupid girl in every horror movie. She found them and opened her door just as Hayes unlocked the gate.

She should have left, but she couldn't resist rolling down her window as Hayes approached. "Just so you know," she said calmly, "you were right to be worried about Troy and Tilly."

Before he could respond, Greer twisted the key in the ignition and slammed her foot on the gas. The tires screeched as she sped away, leaving Hayes and the night behind.

# CHAPTER 19

**2024**

"Troy claims he pulled onto his street at 11:15 p.m." Joaquin stood before a dry-erase board. Its surface crisscrossed with names and times as he pieced together a Fourth of July from nearly forty years ago.

"And Red confirmed that's when he talked to Troy," Melrose said, swiveling her chair. "No wonder Troy was acting weird. He'd slept with Chantilly."

Joaquin capped the marker and pointed at the board. "Greer called 911 at 11:55. If Troy is telling the truth about leaving Tilly's at 10:35, that leaves a one-hour, twenty-minute window for Tilly's murder."

"Right, but wouldn't it have had to be when Greer arrived?" Melrose asked. "Why else would the Strangler leave Tilly's body behind?"

"Well . . ." Joaquin hesitated, shoving a handful of overcooked popcorn into his mouth. "Nah, forget it."

"Spit it out. What are you thinking?"

Joaquin walked toward the thermostat. "I'm thinking it's too hot in here. Too late. Let's call it a night."

"I'm not tired," she said, rubbing her shoulder.

"But you're hurting," Joaquin observed.

Melrose rolled her neck. "Just a bit stiff. Now, spill it. What's on your mind?"

Joaquin lowered the thermostat and loosened his tie. "I still can't shake this suspicion Tilly wasn't killed by the Strangler."

Melrose folded her legs beneath her. "Back to this? Fine, let's explore your wild theory—the one where Troy isn't a serial killer and only murdered Chantilly."

Joaquin perched on the desk. "That doesn't make Troy the killer."

"Hayes then? The mystery guy she was seeing?" Melrose asked, handing him a bag of pretzels.

Joaquin popped one into his mouth and chewed thoughtfully. "What about Greer?"

"Crossed my mind," Melrose admitted. "She was upset with Hayes. According to his interview with the cops, they had a massive blowup. He rejected her, but I can't see her strangling her best mate over it."

"Me neither." Joaquin glanced back at the board. "So what about Hayes?"

"Alibi."

"Yeah, but it's from his folks," Joaquin pointed out. "Hayes was in the detached apartment. How would they know if he left?"

"Joanne Sheridan claims she had his keys to keep him in," Melrose said.

Joaquin returned to the board, the dry-erase marker clicking softly as he tapped it against his palm. "What if Greer knew about Troy and Tilly? Maybe she saw them together."

"Troy did mention seeing movement by the fence," Melrose said.

Joaquin planted his hands on his hips, studying the timeline on the board. "If she had seen something, she'd have told Hayes. Then he'd have a motive."

"She would've," Melrose agreed. "Hayes rejects her and says he loves Tilly. Greer's angry and embarrassed, and the only way to ease her hurt is to see Hayes's reaction when she tells him Tilly's cheating."

Joaquin wrote Hayes's name under the suspects column with a question mark.

"But if Greer knew about Troy and Tilly, she never said," Melrose said.

Joaquin capped the marker. "They were probably all lying. The cops should've dug deeper, been tougher on Hayes and Greer."

"They had their guy," Melrose said. "Remember, Troy was wearing new shoes."

"Huh? New shoes?"

"Troy had new shoes when they questioned him," Melrose explained. "The cops latched onto that like it meant something, saying he'd tossed the old pair after getting Wendy's blood on them. Red even told them he was the one who bought those shoes before the murder, but of course, they didn't care. Bet not one of those pricks would've noticed if blood was dripping from Hayes Sheridan's beige Sperrys."

Joaquin thought about Hayes. The FBI profile suggested the Strangler knew the woods—another clue used to point at Troy. But Ollie liked the woods. Maybe Hayes did, too. They were literally in his backyard.

"But I still think it'll be tough to pin it on Hayes," Melrose's voice broke through his thoughts. "He admitted he and Tilly had had sex that day, so if DNA matches, it's not a smoking gun—*unless* his DNA also shows up in the sample from Wendy's underwear."

Joaquin noticed Melrose rubbing her arm. "You alright?"

"Sometimes the sun and bright lights irritate my skin. Spent some time in the yard yesterday." She rolled her sleeve back, revealing a rash.

Joaquin pointed at the fluorescent bulbs above them. "Do these lights bother you?"

"Not much. I usually keep a jacket on; I just got a little warm."

Joaquin switched the thermostat to AC.

"You don't have to do that," she insisted. "I'm fine."

"We'll get the lights changed." Joaquin flipped both switches off, plunging the office into darkness. Only the desk lamp remained, casting a soft glow.

Melrose laughed. "Come on, Joaquin. We can't read the board now."

Joaquin switched one light back on. "How's this? Better?"

"Don't make a fuss about me. I'm not going to catch on fire."

"I want you comfortable. Say something if you're not."

Melrose crossed her arms. "I made my discomfort clear when I told you I'm not harassing Ollie Ford again."

"Understood," Joaquin replied, though he thought a few questions and a twenty-dollar tip hardly constituted harassment.

"I get you had to consider him a suspect," Melrose said, "but there's no way that poor man could have done what the Strangler did."

"I'm inclined to agree, but Luca's convinced otherwise."

"Well, I want no part of it," Melrose said firmly.

"I'm sorry I put you in that position. I should have talked to him myself. Luca and I just thought—"

"Thought that since I'm a woman, I could bat my eyelashes, and he'd confess to murder?"

"No. I thought you'd make him feel more comfortable; you're naturally nicer than we are." He raised his hands. "Again, sorry."

Melrose leaned forward, resting her elbows on her knees. "It's not *entirely* your fault it got under my skin. Remember when you asked why we moved to the States?"

"So your folks could care for your grandparents, right?"

She drew in a slow breath, eyes fixed ahead. "Well, that's not the *entire* story."

Joaquin sat in the chair next to her. "I'm listening."

Melrose steepled her fingers. "After Year Eleven, I worked with my friend Mady at a takeaway joint called Pizza Palace. We had a coworker, Ted Jennings. He was a bit older and intellectually disabled. We were awful to him."

Joaquin sensed where this was going. He was all too familiar with childhood regret. "We all do stupid shit when we're kids."

"But I knew better," Melrose said. "I wanted to be popular like Mady. Plus, I had a massive crush on another coworker, Ellis. He and Mady would pull pranks on Ted and rope me in. They'd have me invite Ted to eat with me while they hid under the table and tied his shoes together— cheeky stuff like that."

"So, indirect involvement on your part?" Joaquin asked.

"That's how I justified it," she said, pulling her knees closer. "But Ted trusted me. He'd confide in me about what they were doing, never suspecting I was part of it. Near the end of the summer, we went too far," Melrose said, blotting her eyes with a tissue. "Ellis sent Ted into the freezer and locked the door behind him. It wasn't long, but it felt endless hearing him bang and scream. When I finally went to open the door, Ellis kissed me, saying he'd dreamed of doing that all summer. Lies I wanted so badly to believe."

Joaquin handed her another tissue. "What a creep."

"Ted told," Melrose continued. "Mady and Ellis said it was an accident. The door sometimes closed on its own. The manager asked how we hadn't heard Ted screaming. Ellis said we were outside on break. I played along. I'll never forget the look Ted gave me. He was so hurt . . . betrayed. They later reviewed security footage. The three of us got fired."

Joaquin scratched the back of his neck, gaze dropping for a moment before returning to hers, unsure how to respond. "Man, I'm sorry," he finally said. "Did you talk to Ted after?"

Melrose sighed. "I wish that were the worst of it. Ellis and I started seeing each other, but it was so he could get me to help them get back at Ted. Mady was going to the police, claiming Ted had touched her inappropriately. They wanted me to back it up."

Joaquin's eyes widened. "That's a pretty serious revenge plan."

"I refused to lie, so Ellis dumped me. After Ted got arrested, I told my parents everything. Mom took me straight to the cops. Year Twelve started, and Mady spread awful rumors about me. I spiraled. My parents decided to move us to the States."

Joaquin scooted closer. "I'm sorry you went through that, but you should be proud of doing the right thing."

Melrose huffed. "Finally."

"Better late than never."

Melrose fidgeted with a delicate gold ring on her pointer finger. "So I guess when I was talking to Ollie, it brought all those feelings back. I felt like bait again."

Joaquin stared at his shoes. "I'm so sorry, Melrose."

"I get it's not the same. You're not trying to set up an innocent man."

"You're right. I just want the truth."

Melrose wiped her nose. "Me too. I hope Ollie and his dad aren't involved. I hope Ollie gets to visit the beach someday. I hope Ted Jennings got his job back and still loves making pizzas."

Joaquin placed his hand on her knee, surprised when she rested hers on his.

"Thanks for listening to my sob story," she said, withdrawing her hand. Joaquin followed suit reluctantly. "People like Ted and Ollie need allies like you," she said.

"Guess you've heard of Joe Arridy?" Joaquin asked.

Melrose shook her head.

"Arridy was executed back in the 1930s. He had an IQ of forty-six. Loved trains. Chose ice cream for his last meal. He played with his toy train and ate ice cream until they led him to the chamber."

Melrose recoiled. "So they executed someone with the mental capacity of a child?"

"Yeah. What's worse, they coerced Joe into a false confession. He was pardoned eventually, seven decades too late."

Melrose shook her head. "That's the problem with the death penalty. It's irreversible. This shows how crucial the work you're doing for DPAP is."

"*We're* doing," he corrected. "Important work we're doing. Couldn't do it without you."

Melrose smirked. "Sure you could."

"I wouldn't want to." He locked eyes with her. Something magnetic in her gaze pulled him in. He edged closer, and she did, too. But as their lips almost met, hesitation gripped Joaquin. He was her boss. This could ruin cases, ruin careers.

He stopped, standing abruptly. "I'm sorry."

Melrose pulled back. "No, I'm sorry. I'm exhausted, and you were so kind and . . ."

"It's fine." Joaquin adjusted his tie. "Not a big deal."

Melrose stood. "I should head home."

"Yeah, it's late. We're both out of it. Let's resume this—I mean, resume work—tomorrow."

"Same time, same booth?" Melrose asked, her voice casual. They'd fallen into the routine of having breakfast together before work, a habit Joaquin now questioned.

"Nah, let's just meet here. I'll have Bernie grab donuts."

"Oh." Melrose's tone dropped as she grabbed her things and headed for the door. "See you in the morning then."

He froze for a beat, chest tight, eyes tracking her as she moved toward the door. Fingers fidgeting at his sides, Joaquin swallowed hard, not wanting the night to end like this. "Melrose, wait."

She looked up, her eyes steely, mouth set in a firm line. "Yes, Mr. Ramos?"

*Mr. Ramos?* So they were back to this? Joaquin hated the sound of his own name. He hated his weakness for leaning in for that kiss—and his strength for stopping it.

He stepped aside. "Have a good night," he whispered, watching the carpet until he heard the office door slam shut.

# CHAPTER 20

**July 4, 1986**

Troy rolled down his window and took another random turn onto a country road. He didn't want to go home; he wasn't in the mood for questions about why his night ended early. But heading back to Tilly's wasn't an option, and he definitely couldn't face Hayes. So, he kept driving, letting the roads take him wherever.

He turned the radio down, letting the crunch of gravel and the faint pop of fireworks in the distance fill the quiet. The truck bounced over the uneven road, but he didn't ease up on the gas. He loved the rush of speeding down a dirt road, experiencing every bump and dip as he swerved around potholes and rocks. He imagined a map spread out on the passenger seat, picturing himself somewhere far away—driving along a breezy beach in Bora Bora or navigating a majestic mountain pass in the Alps—anywhere but Bluesummer.

Troy replayed the night. There was no excuse for what he'd done. He'd known exactly where things were headed before he followed Tilly into her bedroom.

Hayes could never find out. If he did, their friendship would be over, and Troy would lose Red, too. And Greer would back Hayes, no question. Judging by the note on his windshield, no one else mattered to her.

Troy glanced at the gas gauge, a knot forming in his stomach. The needle hovered close to empty—too low to run away to Bora Bora or the Alps. Too low to go anywhere but home.

He turned onto his street, surprised not to see Greer's car outside the Sheridan house—and even more surprised by the figure on their porch.

He squinted, leaning forward when his hand slipped and hit the horn. The sudden blare startled him, causing him to jerk the wheel and send his truck skidding. He eased off the gas, took a few steadying breaths, and slowly pulled into his driveway.

He was rushing into his house when he noticed Red walking toward him. *Shit. Shit. Shit.*

Troy lifted his hand in a half-hearted wave. "Sorry about the horn. Have a good night."

But Red didn't turn away. "Why would anyone be worried about noise tonight? Are you alright, though? You were driving all over the place."

"Got dizzy," he said, hoping Red wouldn't smell alcohol on his breath. "Must be coming down with something."

"So, I guess that means you won't be joining Hayes in the brig tonight?"

Troy's gut twisted at the mention of Hayes. He stepped back, covering his mouth, grateful when only a small burp escaped.

Red smiled, the streetlight catching the lines around his eyes. "Too much to drink?

"I'm sorry. I didn't—"

Red waved him off. "You're an adult. If you can fight in a war, you can drink a beer or three. But hey, call me next time you need a ride. Better safe than sorry."

"Yes, sir." Troy glanced at the Sheridan home. "Wasn't Greer staying the night?"

Red exhaled. "That's a mystery I'm trying to solve. She was here earlier. I took a shower, came back out, and her car was gone. I checked—Hayes was still in the brig, but his keys weren't where he usually leaves them." Red turned toward the house. "Now I'm wondering where Greer went and if Hayes is sneaking off to join her. Got any intel?"

Troy shook his head.

"Is Tilly coming over?" Red asked. "That's where you're coming from, right?"

Troy shoved his hand into his pocket, jangling his keys. "I was there for a bit. Hayes and G didn't show, so I left."

Red tilted his head. "But didn't Hayes tell you the plan had changed? He must have, since you knew Greer was supposed to be here."

*Damn.* No wonder Hayes never got away with anything. "Right. Hayes called while I was at Tilly's and said the plans had changed. But Tilly was tired, and I was . . ."

Red leaned in just a fraction, eyes narrowing. "Sick?"

"Yeah. So I decided to head home and sleep it off."

"That's wise. But I sure don't like the idea of Tilly being alone with all this Songbird Strangler business."

Troy could sense Red's judgment. He tightened his grip on the keys.

"I bet that's where Greer went," Red speculated. "And I'm sure Hayes is sneaking off there, too." He sighed. "I should let him. Better that the girls aren't alone."

Troy didn't know where Greer was, but he was pretty sure she wasn't at Tilly's. And if Hayes showed up there, he wouldn't like what he'd find: Tilly's wet swimsuit on the tile floor, Tilly passed out in bed, smelling of sex, and Troy's Old Spice aftershave.

"Welp, I'm not going to worry about it," Red said. "I'll go inside and watch my movie. Pretend I don't hear Hayes's truck pull out. The less I know, the better. That boy had better hope he gets home before his mom wakes up." Red clapped Troy on the shoulder. "Get some rest and remember next time . . ." He mimicked holding a phone to his ear.

"Will do." Troy pulled the keys from his damp shorts and tried to be quiet while unlocking the door. But when he stepped inside, he noticed the kitchen light on.

"Still awake, Pops?" Troy tried to sound casual.

"Home so soon?" Troy's mother stood in the kitchen doorway, tightening her robe belt. "I thought you were spending the night with all those especially white friends of yours on this especially white holiday. When you think about it, in 1776, independence was just for white men. It's no surprise that—"

Troy didn't let her finish. "Ma," he choked out, folding himself into her frail frame. His hands trembled against her back, and the tension he'd carried all night slipped with a quiet shudder. Dottie froze for a heartbeat, lips parting, before she wrapped her arms around him. Troy's knees weakened, and a soft, helpless sob escaped him.

She pulled back. "What's wrong, baby? Are you okay?"

Her concern made him cry harder. He held on tighter, so tightly it seemed her delicate bones might snap. But somehow, Dottie Terrell found strength when Troy needed it most.

She pressed a kiss to his hair, murmuring, "It's going to be okay. I've got you."

Troy let himself sink fully into her embrace, the last of the night's armor falling away. For the first time in a long time, he felt safe.

Greer sat in her driveway listening to her Tears for Fears tape and trying to stop her own tears long enough to make it past her brothers and their friends. She didn't want to be home but had nowhere else to go. She couldn't face Tilly and say, "Sorry, I confessed my love to your boyfriend, and he rejected me." Not that Tilly had reason to care after what she'd done. As for Hayes's house, Greer knew she could *never* go back.

She gave herself until the end of "Mad World" to get it together. When the song finished, she turned off the car, wiped her eyes, and hurried inside. The living room smelled of pizza and beer, and the loud commentary from her brothers' friends nearly drowned out the chaotic video game sounds.

She turned down the hallway, thinking she was in the clear—until Zach called her name.

She stopped but kept her back to him.

"What are you doing home?" Zach grabbed her shoulder and turned her around. "Have you been crying?"

"No," Greer said, forcing a laugh.

"Your eyes are red." He sniffed her shirt. "Were you smoking pot?"

"Leave me alone!" Greer snapped, stepping toward her room. Zach followed.

"You can't just come home and not tell me what's going on," he said, leaning in the doorway. "Did you and Tilly get into a fight?"

"What's your deal?" Greer tossed her bag on the bed. "Since when do you care?"

"That's a shitty thing to say. I've always cared about you."

Greer squeezed her eyes shut. She should have known that coming home was a mistake. "I'm sorry. It's just—"

"Wait, are you the one who called Keaton?" Zach interrupted. "Did you ask him to pick you up?"

"I haven't called anyone."

Zach glanced toward the living room. "He answered the phone, then took off. It's been like forty five minutes."

"Well, if you haven't noticed, Keaton's pretty much a lunatic," Greer said.

"Hey, don't say that. He's just been a little messed up since Tara gave back the ring."

Greer rolled her eyes. Keaton had been messed up long before that, and she and Zach knew it better than anyone. But she wasn't up for a fight. Coming home had been a mistake. Even sleeping in her car seemed better than the third degree. "Well, it was probably Tara calling," Greer said. "She does that now and then to screw with his head."

"He's been drinking, Greer." Zach ran a hand through his hair, jaw tight. "He shouldn't be out driving, especially if he's upset. And you shouldn't be either. You both promised Mom."

"Chill. I haven't had anything to drink." Greer's fingers fumbled as she pulled open a drawer. "I forgot my swimsuit and came home to get it."

Before Zach could speak, the front door opened. He poked his head into the hallway, squinting. "Keaton? Where the hell did you go, man?"

Greer stiffened, watching Keaton push past Zach with a huff. He kicked at a stray sneaker in the hallway. "Needed some fresh air."

"Yep," Greer said, stuffing the swimsuit into her bag. "Tara strikes again."

"Some holiday this turned out to be!" Keaton shouted, his voice fading as his door slammed with a bang.

Zach pressed his forehead against the doorframe, letting out a long breath. "Great. Guess one of us should talk to him."

"Not it." Greer swung her bag over her shoulder. "Like I said, I just needed my swimsuit. See you tomorrow."

Greer hesitated at the end of her driveway, unsure which direction to go. There weren't any good options, but anything was better than going back to Hayes—or sitting at home with her brother's drunk friends and dealing with Keaton's girl drama.

She drove aimlessly for a while, trying not to think about Hayes. Eventually, without fully meaning to, she found herself near Tilly's street and noticed that Troy's truck was gone. Maybe he'd gone home. If she showed up and apologized, there was still a chance of salvaging their plans. She needed to do something—*anything*—to get her mind off Hayes Sheridan.

As Greer attempted a U-turn, she noticed Tilly's back gate, the one she had pressed her face against an hour ago, was wide open. Tilly wouldn't leave it like that, especially if she were home alone.

Greer parked, circled to the side of the house, and was about to close the gate when she spotted the back sliding glass door ajar.

She hesitated. The teens across the street had gone inside. She could knock on their door and ask them to call the police, but was it necessary? She'd seen Tilly and Troy go inside and knew what they were doing. In moments like that, locking the door might not be a priority. But why hadn't Tilly come back to secure it? And why did Troy leave without making sure Tilly was safe?

Greer took a few slow steps into Tilly's backyard, hyperaware of her surroundings and flinching at every firework. She took a deep breath, inhaling the hot and sticky summer air.

As she reached the back porch, she peeked through the open door.

"Tilly?" she called. No response. She tried again, but the silence was unsettling. She couldn't leave the door open, and she couldn't lock it from the outside. She had to go in.

Cursing Tilly under her breath, Greer stepped into the Price home and locked the sliding glass door behind her. She maneuvered around Tilly's wet blue bikini, taking in the living room—two empty glasses on the coffee table, condensation dripping from them—leaving rings of water on the wood, just like the blue bikini had on the floor.

"Tilly?" she called again as she moved toward the bedroom. The only response was the boom of fireworks.

Tilly's bedroom door was cracked. Greer knocked, then peeked inside. She saw a foot—hot pink toes sticking out from under the comforter. "Tilly?" Greer pushed the door open. Tilly lay on the bed, the comforter pulled to her chin. The air conditioner kicked on, sending a chill through the room and slamming the door behind Greer. She jumped.

"Too much to drink?" Greer asked. She'd seen Tilly this way before, so far gone you'd swear she was dead. Greer didn't blame Troy for bailing, but she was going to give him a piece of her mind about leaving the damn back door wide open.

As Greer turned to leave, something made her pause. She moved closer to the bed. Tilly lay too still, her skin drained of color. A cold weight settled in Greer's chest as she leaned in. Tilly wasn't breathing.

Greer yanked back the comforter and stumbled away. A phone cord was wrapped around Tilly's throat. She stumbled into a shelf, and a music box clattered to the floor, croaking out half a note before falling silent.

The room spun. Greer ran to the door, hands trembling, fumbling with the knob. It wouldn't turn. "HELP!" she screamed, her voice raw.

The room closed in, the air thick and heavy. She was seven again, trapped on the Zipper at the county fair—hands raw from pounding the cold metal cage, begging it to stop.

Greer forced herself to take slow, deliberate breaths to steady her racing heart. She had escaped that spinning cage; she'd escape this one, too. Tilly's words from years ago echoed in her mind: *It sticks sometimes.*

With a burst of strength, Greer threw her shoulder into the door. It flew open, sending her tumbling into the hallway. She sprinted through the house and back into the night, her cries for help cutting through the summer air.

# CHAPTER 21



Joaquin shot up in bed, caught between the remnants of his nightmare and reality. Had the dream woken him, or something else? His skin was clammy. He stripped off his damp undershirt and turned the pillow over.

"Different night, same twenty-something-year nightmare. The screams, the blood, the tiny coffin.

A text alert beeped, dragging him from the darkness. It must've been what pulled him from the dream, and he was grateful. For years, he'd set alarms throughout the night just in case he needed an escape from *that* dream. He'd stopped years ago as the nightmare became less frequent. What had triggered it tonight? Perhaps Melrose sharing her own trauma had stirred something deep within him.

*Melrose.*

Joaquin buried his face in his hands, recalling their almost-kiss. Why had he been such an idiot? He turned up the brightness and saw the text was from her. Sitting up, he reached for his reading glasses.

*Sorry to text so early. I've been up all night with a fibro flare—the migraine is brutal.*

Joaquin quickly typed back. *Hate to hear that. Don't worry about work today. Is there anything I can get you?*

*No, thanks.*

He collapsed back onto the bed, wondering if Melrose was actually sick or just uncomfortable with him. He texted again.

*Are you sure there's nothing I can do?*

The reply came fast. *Find a smoking gun that proves Troy's innocence.*

Joaquin smiled. That didn't sound like someone feeling harassed by her boss, now did it? *Oh, is that all? LOL. I'll check on you later.*

He second-guessed the LOL. Maybe an emoji would've been better. His niece had told him no one used LOL anymore.

He waited a few more minutes, hoping she might respond, then finally swung his legs over the side of the bed. Might as well get moving.

Bernie was already at her desk reading the newspaper when Joaquin arrived at the office. He dropped a box of donuts on her desk and several bags from Home Depot on the floor in front of it.

"Yum, what's the occasion?" Bernie asked, opening the box.

"Got up early." Joaquin grabbed a donut. "Spent an extra half hour in the gym. Figured I should cancel that out."

"Did Melrose text you? About her migraine?"

"Yeah. I bet it was these damn lights. I read they can trigger migraines." Joaquin picked up a bag. "I stopped by Home Depot for these filters." He pulled out several rolls of blue paper with cloud patterns. "I'll put them above her desk first. If they work, I'll get them for the whole office. If not, could you ask Dan what bulbs would be best for her?"

Bernie raised an eyebrow. "Dan's a retired electrician, not a doctor. And this isn't my place to say, but you're doing a lot for a woman who's temporary help."

Joaquin shrugged. "I just want her to be comfortable."

"Comfortable . . . in your bed," Bernie muttered under her breath.

"Hey!" Joaquin dropped the filter. "I heard that."

"I know you did. Look, you're obviously smitten, but you're her boss."

Joaquin bent down and grabbed the filter, setting it on Bernie's desk with more force than intended. "I'm aware, Bernadette."

"Uh-oh. You used my trouble name." Bernie bit into her donut. "You should understand by now, I call 'em like I see 'em. Nothing to be mad about. Melrose feels the same."

Joaquin straightened. "What makes you say that? Did she say something?"

"She doesn't have to, Romeo. I've been around the block. Look, it's fine. All I ask is that you wait to screw her until the case is over. Can you manage?"

Joaquin huffed. "I can wait much longer than that."

Bernie brushed the sprinkles off her desk. "That's probably nothing to brag about."

Heat burned up Joaquin's neck and ears. "I mean, it's not going to happen. Now *or* when the case is over." He grabbed the filters again. "Now, where the hell is the ladder?"

Bernie stood. "Let me. You do some work. Preferably billable."

"We're fine," he assured her. "DUIs slow down in the fall. It's almost Christmas-theft season."

"And New Year's divorces," Bernie added. "Just sayin'."

"No way. I hate family law. And you're still getting your paycheck."

"And the day I don't is the day you'll find my chair empty." She gestured to a pile of unopened bills on her desk. "Hey, at least if the lights get turned off, you won't have to worry about these damn filters."

Joaquin picked up the bills. "I'll take care of these. And I'll make sure you get a Christmas bonus, too. Meanwhile, set those down. You don't need to be on the ladder."

Bernie swung a light filter roll at him, connecting with his chest. "I should slap you for that."

"You did," he said, rubbing his breastbone. "Now, where do we keep the—"

The phone ringing interrupted him. He looked at it before shifting his gaze back to Bernie. "You gonna get that?"

"I'm busy," Bernie said, waving the light filter roll. "And since when do we open before 8:00, anyway?"

Joaquin sighed deeply before reaching across Bernie's desk to answer the phone. "Joaquin Ramos, attorney-at-law."

"Hello," a crisp voice answered. "Is Ms. Reed available?"

"Sorry, she's out today." Joaquin grabbed a pen from Bernie's desk and searched for a sticky note. "Can I take a message?"

"Is this Mr. Ramos?"

"Yes." Joaquin tried to place the voice.

"Oh, hello. This is Greer Sheridan."

Joaquin dropped the pen. "Mrs. Sheridan. Hi."

"I'd spoken to Melrose Reed. We'd arranged a meeting, but I had to cancel." Greer's tone was clinical.

Joaquin pushed the donut box aside and sat on Bernie's desk. "Yes, she told me."

"I'd like to reschedule."

Joaquin jumped up. "That's great. Ms. Reed won't be in today, but if you don't mind talking to me—"

"I'm free all day," Greer interrupted.

Joaquin glanced at the appointment book on Bernie's desk. "Looks like my schedule is clear until 9:45."

"I'll be right there." The line went dead before Joaquin could give her the address.

"Glad someone answered," he called to Bernie. "That was Greer Sheridan."

"No kidding?" Bernie said from behind the ladder she was trying to maneuver out of the closet.

Joaquin took the ladder from her. "She's on her way." He sniffed the air; traces of last night's burnt popcorn lingered. "Spray some Lysol." He set the ladder in Melrose's office, then rushed to his own desk, frantically straightening until Bernie appeared in his doorway less than ten minutes later. "Looks like the guest of honor has arrived."

"Already?" Joaquin closed a few files and reached for the potpourri on the bookshelf. He agitated it with his fingers, trying to awaken a smell that hadn't existed in twenty years. He dumped it in the trash, adjusted his jacket, and entered the lobby.

Greer Sheridan shook Joaquin's hand. Tall and thin, with strawberry-blonde hair falling past her shoulders and soft bangs slanting across her face, she met his gaze head-on. Blue eyes shone bright and direct, freckles visible beneath light foundation, fine lines tracing the corners of her eyes and mouth. He led her from the lobby to his office, motioning to the chair in front of his desk.

"I'm ready to start when you are," she said as he sat.

"Before I forget, please take one of my business cards." He gestured to the holder on his desk. "It's got my cell phone number."

As Greer placed the card in her wallet, Joaquin opened the drawer where he kept his recorder.

"I'd like this to be off the record," Greer said, as if she could sense that was what he was reaching for.

He closed the drawer. "No problem. Can we start with why you're sure Troy is the Strangler?"

"I'm actually not so sure anymore." Her gaze flicked toward the diplomas on the wall, then back at him. "It's possible I've never been sure."

Joaquin blinked rapidly, trying to process her words. "I'm glad to hear that, but if you had doubts, why did you testify against him?"

"I testified about what happened that night." Greer's words had a hard edge.

"Not *just* about that night. You said Troy had a temper—volatile, you called him."

Greer shook her head. "That's what the police called him. They kept pressing me. When I finally admitted Troy had a temper, they asked if he could be volatile, and I said yes."

Joaquin leaned back slightly in his chair, folding his arms. "What do you mean by 'Troy had a temper?' Don't we all?"

"Please don't talk to me like a lawyer. Sure, but Troy was notorious. He got benched plenty for yelling at his coach or a ref."

Joaquin exhaled. "On the football field? Come on, Ms. Sheridan, that's—"

"Not just on the field," Greer cut in. "After the first game Troy missed because of his injury, I found him alone in the locker room—knee locked in that bulky brace, an ice pack melting onto the floor. He was slamming his fists against the lockers, screaming that it wasn't fair, that his life was over."

Her voice dropped. "I tried to calm him down, but he grabbed a helmet and hurled it at the lockers. It scared me. I turned to leave, and he grabbed me—hard." Her fingers brushed her arm, a faint tremor running through her hand.

Joaquin sat up straight, resting his hands on the desk. His eyes narrowed slightly. "Surprised Carter wouldn't ask you to recount that."

Greer stared at the carpet. "I didn't tell the police."

"Why not?"

"Because after he grabbed me, he hugged me and cried." Her voice softened. "I cried too. I knew football wasn't just a hobby—it was his ticket out of Bluesummer." She pushed her bangs back. "Then . . . I don't really know how it happened, but we kissed."

"Ah." Now, it made sense. "You knew it wouldn't hold up under questioning."

She shifted. "I could hear them now: 'So, Ms. Collins, you were so scared you kissed him.' I didn't want to share those details in court with Hayes. It was a onetime thing when Troy was in a vulnerable spot."

Joaquin nodded. "I appreciate your honesty, Mrs. Sheridan. Is there anything else you didn't share with the police? About Troy? About that Fourth of July?"

Greer rested her elbow on the arm of the chair and pinched the bridge of her nose. "When I showed up at Tilly's the first time, I didn't just knock on the door and leave. I snuck around to the side of the house and watched Troy and Tilly through the slats. I watched them flirt, make out, and go inside."

"Wait." Joaquin raised a hand. "You saw them and didn't tell the police?"

"Well, at first, I didn't believe Troy could hurt Tilly, and I didn't want to make it worse for him. But mostly, it was always about Hayes. It would have hurt him too much to know that Tilly had cheated on him."

"So you *never* told Hayes?"

"I yelled something when I left his house so angry that night," Greer said. "That he was right to worry about them. But if Hayes heard, he never asked me about it."

Joaquin bounced his toes under the desk, a thought forming. *Hayes. Motive. Bingo.* "This is good news."

Greer recoiled. "Good?"

"I'm sure you've heard we found the DNA. It's being tested now. Troy admitted the DNA from Tilly's sample could be his, but he claims they were consensual sex partners. No one will believe him, but they might believe you."

Greer waved her hands. "No. Sure, it looked like Tilly invited him in, but I have no idea what happened after. I don't know what Troy did to her."

Joaquin leaned forward, his voice calm but insistent. "Yes, you do. Drunk or not, you knew Troy Terrell. He was your friend. He wouldn't hurt Tilly."

Visible color rose in Greer's cheeks. "Troy had been acting differently. Distracted."

Joaquin took a steadying breath. He needed Greer on their side. "Okay. Is there anything else you can tell me that might help? Any strange cars around Tilly's house?"

Greer shook her head. "No, nothing like that."

"When Tilly and Troy stepped inside, did you notice if they closed the back door?"

"I didn't," Greer said. "I bolted. But it was open later that night. Either they left it that way, or it was unlocked. Unless the Songbird Strangler had the alarm code."

It wasn't lost on Joaquin that she'd just suggested someone besides Troy was the Strangler. "Okay," he said. "You left Tilly's, went to Hayes's house, then back to Tilly's?"

"I stopped at home before going back to Tilly's."

Joaquin looked down at the file, reviewing her testimony. "At Tilly's, you came in through the open back gate and went inside through the open back door."

Greer looked away, eyes filling with tears. "Have you ever been in a room with a dead body, Mr. Ramos?"

A lump formed in Joaquin's throat. "Yeah. I have."

"Someone you loved . . ." Greer's voice cracked.

"Yes."

She met his gaze. "I'm sorry. It's horrible—the shock." She wiped away tears.

Joaquin pushed a box of tissues toward Greer. She pulled out several and blotted her face. "You don't have to talk about finding her," he said. "Let's fast-forward to the 911 call. You made it from the neighbor's house?"

"Yeah." Greer tore off a corner of the tissue in her hand. "Couldn't exactly use the Prices' phone with the cord missing."

"About that." Joaquin raised a finger. "It never made sense. Troy and Tilly presumably sleep together in her bedroom, but he goes to the living room to find a strangulation device. Sure, the phone in Tilly's room was cordless, but he could have used anything in there."

Greer crossed her legs. "The prosecution didn't know they'd slept together. They thought Tilly had gone to bed, thinking Troy had left. But he grabbed the cord, waited until she was nearly asleep, then snuck in and caught her by surprise, as he did with his other victims."

Joaquin's mind raced. How had Greer convinced herself that Troy killed Tilly? Was she delusional or covering for someone else?

"Red had another theory, though," Greer added. "I'm sure you read his book."

Joaquin shook his head. "I checked it out from the library, but haven't had time for fiction."

Greer smirked. "Red didn't get everything right, but the book's hardly fiction."

Outside, the clouds shifted, and sunlight streamed through the window, illuminating specks of dust and pretzel crumbs on Joaquin's desk.

"Well, give me the cliff notes version of the chapter on Tilly's murder," he said, turning his chair to lower the blinds.

"For starters, Red didn't believe it was premeditated. He assumed Troy got angry for some reason when they were having drinks in the living room and snapped."

"So he killed her in the living room and staged her body in bed?"

Greer tore another piece of tissue. "That's what Red believed. It was based on the phone call. He assumed it had to be made from the living room because the Prices' bedroom door was locked, and the phone in Tilly's room wasn't working the night of the murder."

Joaquin frowned. "Phone call?"

"The living room telephone had been off the hook most of the night. Hayes tried to call, but around 10:45, either Tilly or Troy must have noticed because someone tried to call me from her house."

Joaquin pursed his lips. He didn't remember reading anything about phone records in Troy's trial transcript, nor were they mentioned in any appeal paperwork.

"It could have been Troy, I guess," Greer continued. "Asking where I was. But if so, why did he hang up so quickly? Before it rang on our end? My brothers were home. They would have heard it."

Joaquin tried to piece it together. "So you think it was Tilly trying to call you, and she got interrupted?"

Greer's hands shook. "Maybe she was scared because Troy was angry, working himself up like he did that day in the locker room. She tried to call me for help, and that set him off. He ended the call and . . . and . . ."

"And strangled her with the phone cord?" Joaquin asked.

Greer used the wadded tissue to wipe her nose. "That's what I told myself. Now I'm not sure. I've been thinking about how the phone wasn't pulled out of the wall like I'd expect in a struggle. The police version—that it was purposely removed and taken to Tilly's bedroom to kill her—

makes more sense. But if they're correct about her time of death, someone called me five minutes before she was killed."

"How did Red see the phone records?"

"The district attorney, I guess," she said, pulling a fresh tissue from the box. "You must have them somewhere."

Joaquin nodded, though he was fairly certain he didn't. If Carter had evidence he withheld from Troy's counsel, it would be a clear Brady violation—good news for Team Troy. "Okay, did you call anyone else while at the neighbors' house? Besides 911?"

"Just Hayes."

"And did he answer?"

"His mom did. He didn't have his own line."

"And did she get Hayes on the phone?"

Greer shook her head. "I didn't get a single word out. I heard sirens, so I hung up."

"But you're certain he was home? You're sure he didn't follow you after you left his house?" Joaquin asked.

"He wanted to," Greer said. "Or so he told me later, but he couldn't find his keys. Turns out Joanne had taken them so he wouldn't sneak off."

"How did he act after Tilly's death?" Joaquin asked.

"Hayes? He was beside himself. He was going to propose. Had been shopping for rings."

Joaquin motioned to Greer's hand. "But he bought you one instead?"

Greer moved her hand to her lap. "What does that have to do with anything?"

"Nothing. I'm just wondering if he shares your doubts about Troy's guilt. Wondering if he's okay you're here."

Greer picked up her purse. "I don't have to ask my husband's permission to be anywhere."

"Right. Sorry. Bad choice of words."

She unzipped a compartment in her purse, presumably to get her keys. Joaquin regretted having made that comment about the ring.

"Hayes doesn't know I'm here, nor that I'm having doubts," she said, pulling out a tiny ziplock bag. "And he doesn't know about this."

Joaquin narrowed his eyes, but Greer's fingers covered the bag's contents.

"So I have a three-year-old grandson," she continued. "Silas. We call him Si. He's obsessed with pirates and treasure. Hayes bought him a real metal detector for his birthday." She laughed. "A three-hundred-dollar metal detector for a three-year-old. Anyway, we take it out to the woods sometimes."

"The woods as in—"

"As in *the* woods, yeah. Despite the horrible things discovered at the bower, I have good memories from there with my friends. Si recently found one of those tacky gold bracelets we always wore."

"That's . . . neat," Joaquin said, unsure where this was heading.

"I kept Si yesterday." Greer gripped the ziplock bag tighter, her knuckles turning white. "With the recent rain, I figured we could dig up some treasures."

Joaquin tapped his desk. "Okay. And?"

"And we did." She opened her hand and dropped the bag on Joaquin's desk.

He picked it up and saw a class ring with a blue sapphire in the center, "Class of 1986" inscribed on the side. His eyes widened. "Is this what I think it is?"

"It doesn't mean it's Troy's." Greer's voice quavered. "It's as generic as can be. But I remember Troy's lawyer claiming he'd lost his in the woods." She clutched her purse against her abdomen. "And if this is his . . ."

"Then it's someone else's at the bower," Joaquin finished, unable to tear his eyes away from the ring. "We have to take this to the cops, and you need to tell them everything you told me about seeing Troy and Tilly in the pool."

Greer stood and snatched the bag from Joaquin's hand. "Give me a day or two."

Joaquin leaped from his seat. "Absolutely not. This is evidence. You're a journalist; you have an obligation."

Greer stuffed the bag back into her purse. "I'm going to turn it in. I just need to talk to Hayes first."

Joaquin pressed his fingers against his temples. "Greer, you can't—"

But she was already jogging toward the front door. Joaquin followed. "Greer!" He caught the door just as she pushed through. "Wait! Let's talk about this."

"After the holiday," she said, climbing into her car. "I promise."

"Well, that didn't look like it went so hot." Bernie waited for Joaquin as he stepped back into the lobby.

"It actually did," he replied. "We might have hit the jackpot— possible Brady violation and fresh evidence." He flopped onto the floral-patterned green couch.

"Fill me in *after* your meetings," Bernie said, walking to her desk and holding his appointment ledger. "You're booked solid for the rest of the morning."

Joaquin glanced at the schedule, each line feeling heavier than the last. "Nope. You'll have to cancel them."

She put her hands on her hips. "Like hell I will."

He stood and approached her desk. "Greer mentioned Red saw phone records from the night of Tilly's murder. I'm pretty sure they aren't in Troy's files. I need to comb through everything before I contact the district attorney."

Bernie snorted. "You've got some nerve. I've already rescheduled these clients twice. We need this money, Joaquin. Trust me."

Joaquin stepped back. "Fine, I'll look through everything tonight."

Bernie groaned. "Just bring a few files, and I'll see what I can find while you're meeting with clients. I got the damn filters up in Melrose's office while you were in there yakking. I'll go put the ladder away and get to work."

Joaquin smirked. "You said you weren't going to help with the Terrell case."

"I could be persuaded," she replied, "for some of your mom's coconut pudding."

"She's making some for Thanksgiving. You and Dan should come."

"Dan's out of town. Hunting with his brother."

"Well, all the more reason for you to come with me." He shoved his hands into his pockets. "I was thinking of inviting Melrose, too."

Bernie crossed her arms. "Of course you were."

"Come on, Bernie. Her folks live in Australia."

"Whatever. It's your call. Just be careful, boss. *Very* careful."

"I appreciate your concern, but I am being careful. This isn't some meet-the-parents thing." He wrapped an arm around her shoulder. "Think of it as a company Thanksgiving party."

"Mm-hmm." She pulled away and walked into Melrose's office. "At this rate, the Christmas party will be at your wedding reception," he heard her say over the clunk of the ladder closing.

"Still heard that," he called after her.

"Still know you did."

# CHAPTER 22

**2024**

Greer Sheridan scrubbed at the remnants of dinner stuck to the pan, but the stubborn noodles refused to budge.

"Let's soak it," Joanne suggested as she dried the last of the silverware.

Greer ignored her mother-in-law and scrubbed harder. She'd get these noodles off the pan; she'd get these ghosts out of her head.

Since meeting Joaquin Ramos that morning, scrubbing one image from her mind proved impossible—Tilly's lifeless body. Completely still beneath a pink fuzzy blanket, then just as still in a turtleneck matching her rose-pink coffin.

Greer remembered Troy standing over that coffin, leaning down as if whispering a secret in Tilly's cold, dead ear. Had he even cried? Greer couldn't remember.

"Greer? Are you okay, honey?"

"Yep, all good." Greer turned off the faucet.

"Red wants to fry turkey on Thanksgiving." Joanne hung the dish towel on the oven door. "Not that he has the strength, but you can't tell that man anything."

"Hayes will do it," Greer offered.

"We girls should make it in the oven like we used to. Whaddaya say?"

Greer dropped the soggy sponge into the sink. "Either way is fine, Joanne." *I couldn't care less, Joanne.*

"We'd have to get up early to have it ready by lunchtime. At least four."

Greer kneeled at the cabinet under the sink, searching for a stronger sponge.

"Yes, I know it's early for you, but there's so much to do for Thanksgiving," Joanne continued. "I've always been envious of how late you can sleep."

Greer wanted to say not everyone went to bed at 7 p.m., but why bother? Joanne didn't mean anything by it. Or maybe she did. Either way, there was no point in biting back. A passive-aggressive mother-in-law was the least of her worries.

"My roasting pan is here somewhere." Joanne spun around the kitchen. "Unless you didn't unpack it. I still can't find any of my things."

Greer slammed the cabinet door. Joanne still had a chip on her shoulder about moving in. She'd understood living alone wasn't possible anymore, not after Red's cancer diagnosis and hip replacement, but she'd assumed Greer and Hayes would move in with them. In many ways, it made sense—their house was bigger and had acres of woods for their grandson to explore. But Greer had realized living at Red and Joanne's would never feel like home. She'd always be a guest. Joanne seemed to feel the same about being here. Greer had tried to be welcoming. Red and Joanne had their own bedrooms, connected by a Jack-and-Jill bathroom. Being on the other side of the house from Greer and Hayes offered privacy, but her in-laws still seemed uneasy about the new arrangement.

Greer turned on the hot water, resigned to letting the pan soak.

"Is your mom joining us for Thanksgiving?" Joanne asked.

"No, she'll be with my brothers and their families in Dallas. Last I heard, the girls are going there too," she added, referring to her twin daughters.

"Oh." Joanne put a hand to her chest. "You and Hayes should go. Red and I can manage."

They couldn't. Greer knew it, and Joanne did, too. "It's fine. My family will all be here for Christmas."

"Won't having the girls back home be nice?" Joanne smiled.

It would be nice. Not long ago, children filled those rooms and shared that Jack-and-Jill bathroom. Now, those giggling girls were gone—Quinn was married with a child, and Farren was working on her master's in Corpus Christi. And Caleb, well, he'd been gone the longest, not in a house across town or a beachfront condo, but resting at Bluesummer Cemetery. It was hard to imagine that her curly-headed preschooler would be thirty now.

Caleb was always on Greer's mind, especially at this time of year. Would he be coming home for Thanksgiving? She liked to think so. It was easy to idealize a version of someone who never existed. Caleb never broke the neighbor's window with a runaway baseball or became a brooding teenager. She'd never caught him sneaking out or yelled at him about a failing grade. He died young and perfect.

"Add some brown sugar to your Thanksgiving list," Joanne said. "I'd like to make a pecan pie for Hayes; those were always his favorite."

"Will do," Greer replied, though Hayes always claimed her mom's coconut pies were his true favorites. But that was Hayes—always wanting everyone to feel special.

Greer checked the clock. He should be home by now, and she needed to talk to him. Hopefully, Joanne would head to her room; this conversation couldn't wait. Before Greer could offer to help Jo to bed, the front door swung open.

"Sorry I'm late," Hayes said, shedding his jacket and briefcase. "Did I miss dinner?" He wrapped his arms around Greer.

"Saved you a plate," Greer said, sinking into his embrace. While the old electricity might be gone, nothing felt more comforting than being in his arms. She pulled back to meet his gaze. Hayes Sheridan still looked young and handsome, thanks in part to the hair dye that Greer touched up for him every month. His bright blue eyes still sparkled, and the deep creases from years of smiling added to his charm.

Yet weariness clouded his face, hidden beneath that smile. He'd spent over thirty years in a high-stress job—one Greer hoped he'd retire from soon. They'd faced their share of sadness, too: Tilly, Caleb, Red's diagnosis . . . and Ally Swanson, a long-ago betrayal that still pricked at Greer's chest.

Hayes kissed her quickly before grabbing Joanne's walker and pushing it toward her. "You shouldn't be on your feet, Mom."

Joanne waved it away. "I can make it to the couch."

The couch. Greer stifled a sigh. She shouldn't be upset; it was Joanne's living room, too. Still, she missed the comfortable routine she'd settled into with her husband.

"How was your day?" Hayes asked.

"Eventful. Want to go for a walk?" Greer asked.

Hayes glanced toward the window. "Now? It's dark."

"Just around the cul-de-sac." Greer tossed him his jacket and grabbed her own.

Hayes took hold of Greer's hand as they walked. "It's been a while since we did this. It's nice."

"Yeah, it's been a whirlwind month getting your parents settled."

Hayes squeezed her hand. "Thanks for taking such good care of them."

They walked in silence, the chilly air smelling of chimney smoke. "So, you mentioned an eventful day?" Hayes finally said. "What's up?"

Greer bit her lip. "Well, a few days ago, I got a phone call from Troy's new attorney's office."

Hayes kicked a stray leaf. "And you told them you had no comment, right?"

"Right." She'd get to the part where she changed her mind soon enough.

"Tell them to call our attorney with any more questions. You have Rick's number, right?"

"They found the missing DNA evidence, Hayes."

He stopped mid-step. "Tilly's?"

"And Wendy's. They're testing it now."

Hayes resumed walking, frowning. "How'd you know?"

"Some contacts at the paper got wind of it," she lied.

"Okay. So if it's not Troy's, then what?"

"I don't know. It might help his case, but they're not sure that the Strangler sexually assaulted his victims. The semen on Wendy's underwear could belong to her ex-boyfriend, or even a new one, and Tilly's might—"

"Be mine," Hayes interjected. "But that doesn't mean Troy didn't kill them."

"I know. But doesn't any of this bother you?"

Hayes dropped her hand. "Doesn't any of *what* bother me?"

Greer clenched her teeth. Hayes's condescending tone definitely *bothered* her. "Oh, I don't know. How about the fact that Troy had an alibi for Andrea's murder?"

"Says the school janitor. Come on. He was friends with Troy's dad. He covered for them."

"And Troy was our friend. Do you really think—"

"Yes," Hayes said. "Greer, we've talked about this."

*Not nearly enough*, she thought, frustration bubbling beneath the surface.

"This attorney should've never called you," Hayes said, walking faster. "It's got you all mixed up."

Greer struggled to keep up. It frustrated her that after all these years, she was still chasing him.

Hayes stopped and turned. "Why are you doing this?"

"Doing what? Having a conversation?"

Hayes made a sweeping arm gesture. "Drudging all this shit back up."

"He's going to die in January, Hayes," Greer raised her voice. "And there's real doubt, but that doesn't bother you?"

"He's not dying anytime soon. It's been delayed how many times? And if he is, no, it doesn't bother me. Did it bother you when Tilly died?"

Greer clenched her fists. "That's a shitty thing to ask. You know what that did to me."

Hayes shrugged. "I thought I did, but you seem to have a newfound sympathy for her murderer."

She pounded a fist against her thigh. "Troy is our friend!"

"*Was* our friend!" His anger rang out, a sharp contrast to his usual calm. He rarely raised his voice—not when the girls broke curfew or swiped his credit card, not when he was passed over for a promotion, not during those heated arguments in the early years of their marriage. He saved his anger, his passion, for Tilly and Tilly only.

"We should check on Mom." Hayes strode back toward their home. Greer followed, pulling her coat tighter as the wind picked up.

At the door, he faced her. "Look, I'm sorry," he said, calmer now. "But Dad worked hard on that case. It killed him when the evidence pointed to Troy. He tried to convince himself that he was wrong. Do you think he'd go to the police if he weren't sure?"

"I understand he was sure," Greer said, "but people make mistakes."

"Redman Sheridan makes fewer than anyone I know. And Troy's not the only one who might be dead in January. Maybe you should think about that."

Greer's ears pounded. "If you didn't notice, I quit my job to focus on your parents."

Hayes raised his hands. "Okay, sorry, that wasn't fair. But honestly, I don't understand you sometimes."

"I don't understand you either," she shot back. "Don't you think this is worth investigating?"

"It's being investigated. That's what his lawyer is for. You don't need to get involved."

*You don't need to get involved.* How many times had Greer's mother said that to her growing up? "That curiosity is going to get you in trouble, young lady." Well, it had a time or two, but it also earned her a thirty-year career and a pension.

"My testimony helped implicate Troy—how different he'd been, his temper."

"You were being honest," Hayes said. "All of it was truthful."

Not wanting to look Hayes in the eye, Greer focused on the porch light and its firework-green glow. Her testimony hadn't been entirely truthful. She'd kept to herself what she saw through the fence slats—kept it to herself for nearly four decades.

"Why did you lie and say you talked to Troy and Tilly?" Hayes had asked in that cold, sterile hallway at the police station the day after Tilly's murder. "If I'd known they didn't answer the door, I would have gone back and . . ." He'd stopped there, but Greer heard the unspoken words: *I would have gone back and saved her.*

Greer later learned that Troy claimed he and Tilly had only swum for about ten minutes, and then she'd gotten tired, so he left.

Greer had initially convinced herself that Troy might be telling the truth. She'd seen enough to know they hadn't gone inside because Tilly was tired, but maybe, once inside, Troy had come to his senses and immediately left. Maybe Tilly, upset or drunk, had forgotten to close the door.

But as much as she tried to believe Troy, the timeline didn't add up. Even if he hadn't stayed until 11:00, as the police claimed, Troy testified that he left at 10:35—ten minutes after Greer saw them leave the pool.

She knew what had happened during those ten minutes. She'd always known. And now, with the DNA evidence, the world would know too. No one would entertain the idea of consensual sex unless Greer told the whole truth about what she'd witnessed.

"I see the wheels turning, Greer. What are you thinking?" Hayes said, bringing her back to the present, back to their front yard.

"I'm thinking that you don't get to tell me not to get involved. I've been involved since the night I found my best friend dead."

Hayes turned away. "I don't want to talk about this," he said, reaching for the door. He stepped inside but turned back, whispering, "Do not get involved."

Frustration surged through Greer. She wanted to push through the door and tell him the class ring in her purse might belong to Troy. But she couldn't with Hayes on the couch, pretending to watch *Wheel of Fortune* with his mom. Instead, she marched past them and pulled Joaquin Ramos's card from her purse.

*I'm taking the ring to the police on Friday*, she texted. *I'm ready to help Troy in any way I can.*

# CHAPTER 23

**2024**

A light dusting of snow covered Joaquin's windshield as he drove toward Tyler for Thanksgiving. He told himself to enjoy today, forget the stacks of work at the office.

Melrose yawned from the passenger seat, prompting Joaquin to do the same.

"Late night?" Bernie asked pointedly from the back seat.

"We had a lot of work to do," Joaquin answered. "Finished shortly after midnight."

Bernie tsked. "My momma always said nothing good happens after midnight."

Joaquin adjusted the speed of the windshield wipers. "Something good *might* have happened. We searched every file, and there's no mention of the phone records Red Sheridan discussed in his book."

"Ah, so that spells trouble for the DA's office?" Bernie asked.

"Possibly," Melrose said, massaging her temples. "Prosecutors have to disclose evidence that could help the defendant, but maybe they didn't think the phone records mattered."

Joaquin understood Melrose's practicality, but he wished she would summon a little more optimism. "Yet somehow Red Sheridan saw them."

"Yes, and he used them to build his theory that Troy was the killer. If there were proof of Troy's innocence in those records, Red would have noticed."

"Sheridan might have missed something, or maybe he was covering for—"

"So what happens next?" Bernie interrupted.

"I'll request a file review with the DA first thing Monday," Joaquin replied.

"Weren't the records destroyed?"

"Only the evidence, not the case file. I'm interested in what's in those phone records. I'm beginning to think I'm alone in that interest."

"I am interested," Melrose said. "I'm just saying, don't get your hopes up. These phone records have been our sole focus for the last two days, and we still need to pursue all other leads." She shook her head, tapping her fingers against the dashboard. "Can you not handle anyone challenging you, or is it only when it's a woman?"

Joaquin huffed. "What I can't handle is—"

"Can you two cool it? It's Thanksgiving."

Melrose reached into her purse for a bottle of Motrin. "Right, sorry. I'm just cranky."

"And you have a headache," Joaquin pointed out.

"I missed my Botox appointment a few days ago. No big deal. Rescheduled it for Tuesday."

"Is it my fault you missed it?" Joaquin asked. "Melrose, you need to tell me when you have appointments. Your health comes—"

"Relax, you were in court. I had planned to go, but got busy." She yawned again.

"Well, your erratic sleep schedule is my fault." Joaquin stretched his neck. "We should have wrapped up earlier so you could be well-rested and enjoy today."

"I will enjoy it. I'll enjoy anything that doesn't involve digging through eight boxes of musty files. Thanks again for inviting me."

"Of course. Mom's excited. I haven't visited since I took the case."

"And she's okay with you dragging along your coworkers?" Melrose asked.

"Are you kidding? My parents love to feed people. At this point, Mom wouldn't care if I brought my laptop and worked at the table during lunch."

"You did bring your laptop," Bernie said. "I saw it in the back."

"Well, that's just in case we happen to get the DNA results back. That's an emergency. Mom will understand."

"Results already?" Melrose asked. "It's only been a few weeks."

Joaquin turned onto his parents' street. "Luca said it might come back quickly. I'm being optimistic." He wasn't sure if he believed it, but saying the words out loud helped.

The familiar gray-brick house came into view, its windows aglow with warm, golden light spilling onto the freshly shoveled walkway. Joaquin eased the Jeep to a stop, tires crunching against the gravel, and cut the engine. The quiet hum of the vehicle gave way to the soft whistle of wind through the bare trees. Before they could reach the door, it swung open, and a figure appeared in the warm frame of light.

"You're home!" Isabel Ramos exclaimed, kissing both of his cheeks.

She peered behind him. "And this must be Bernadette and Melrose! Come in, come in!" she said, ushering them through the door with enthusiasm.

As always, the house was immaculate, filled with the aroma of Caribbean thyme and the warm scent of a Pink Sands Yankee Candle flickering on the coffee table.

Luis Ramos emerged from the kitchen, wiping his hands on his apron, but before Joaquin could greet his father, his youngest niece, Camila, barreled into his arms.

Joaquin scooped her up with a grin. "*¡Mira quién llegó!* My little princess, Cami! Where are your brother and sister?"

"Glued to their phones," Luis said, hugging his son. "You know how teenagers are these days."

Luis greeted Bernie and Melrose. "We're so glad to have you here. We've never met any of Joaquin's Texas friends."

"That's because I don't have any friends outside work," Joaquin said, setting Camilia down.

"You work too hard," Isabel said, cupping his face. "Take off your coat. Sit."

Helping Melrose with her peacoat, Joaquin's fingers brushed her arm. Something about the small gesture felt intimate, like he was bringing a girlfriend home. Across the room, Bernie raised a knowing brow. "Don't worry about me; I've got it," she said, shrugging off her own jacket.

Joaquin hung the coats while his dad led Bernie and Melrose to the living room. "Today, you'll meet Ashley, our oldest, and her husband, Favian. They had to make a Kroger run—I forgot mangoes for the cranberry mango sauce. I know what you're thinking, but it's delicious."

"After that coconut pudding Joaquin brought to the office, I'll eat anything you two cook," Bernie said.

"Made some yesterday. It's in the fridge." Isabel took Camila's hand. "Come, Bernadette. We'll show you the recipe."

Joaquin eased onto the couch, leaving an empty cushion between himself and Melrose.

Once Isabel was out of sight, Luis snuffed out the candle. "Smells like a goddamn Jolly Rancher," he said, waving away the smoke. "Anyway, Ashley and Favian live in Dallas. He's the assistant district attorney."

Luis said "assistant district attorney" like he was proclaiming his son-in-law was the Messiah. Joaquin fought the urge to roll his eyes. His parents didn't quite grasp why he'd want to represent criminals when he could be locking them up like their son-in-law.

"They have three children," Luis continued. "Camila, whom you just met. Her big sister Avril is fifteen, and Bryan is fourteen. Easy to remember: ABC. Now, Mia, my other daughter, is in California with her five kids." He held up a hand, fingers spread wide, ready to list them all.

"Pop," Joaquin cut in, "I don't think she needs a full roster."

Luis lowered his hand. "Right, right, sorry. My wife says I'm a chatterbox. So, how about you tell me a little about yourself, Miss Melrose?"

As Melrose started to answer, Isabel reappeared, patting her leg. "Continue, *mija*. I'm borrowing my son."

Joaquin followed his mom to the hallway. "What's up?"

"She's pretty, *niño*."

"Thanks, Mom, but Bernie's taken."

Isabel scoffed. "I'm talking about Melrose. Pretty, and she's a lawyer like you, so she's smart."

Joaquin sighed. "Paralegal, but yeah, she's incredibly smart . . . and yes, very pretty. But I told you, she works for me."

"Is she Catholic?"

Joaquin pinched the bridge of his nose. "I don't know, Mom. That's not the kind of thing you ask an employee."

"Are you even Catholic anymore?" Isabel crossed her arms. "When's the last time you went to Mass?"

Before Joaquin could scramble for an answer, the front door opened.

"Must be Ashley and Fabian," Isabel said.

"Saved by the mango," Joaquin muttered, nudging her. "Go help Dad with the sauce. We'll talk later."

The table overflowed with food, leaving little room for plates. Traditional Thanksgiving dishes like green bean casserole and mashed potatoes sat alongside Puerto Rican favorites—pigeon peas and rice, fried plantains, and *pavochón*.

Luis stood at the head of the table, carving knife in hand.

"The turkey looks amazing," Melrose said.

"*Gracias*," Luis said, slicing a piece. "It's *pavochón*—turkey cooked like roast pork. The stuffing's got plantains and pork rinds."

As the food was passed around the table, the low hum of the TV in the living room drifted into the dining area—news speculation on Cabinet picks for the president-elect's next administration.

Ashley's face tightened. She gulped her wine in one go, lowering the glass with a sigh. "Four more years of—"

With a dramatic flourish, Luis dropped the carving knife onto the board.

Joaquin's fingers tightened around his glass. *Here we go.*

"Don't say that *el payaso*'s name in my house," Luis said. "*¡Por el amor de Dios!* Floating pile of garbage. His name contaminates the air more than your mother's stinky Jolly Rancher candle."

Isabel stood. "*Siéntate*. Luis. I'll turn off the television before you throw the turkey at it."

Luis sank into his chair and took a sip of wine, his shoulders relaxing. "Forgive me," he said, passing the tray of meat to Melrose. "No more politics from this old chatterbox."

Melrose leaned in with a wry smile. "You're in good company. Can't stand the bloke myself."

Luis chuckled, his eyes twinkling. "Ah, I like you, Melrose. After dinner, come join me for a cold one on the patio. We'll have a proper shit-talking session."

"You'll have *what* on the patio?" Isabel's voice cut through the conversation as she paused in the doorway, crossing herself.

"Your famous coconut pudding, of course."

Isabel sighed, taking her seat. "Pray for this meal, and try not to let the news give you heartburn."

As his father stumbled through grace, Joaquin kept his eyes open, gaze drifting around the table. His thoughts wandered to Glory. Would she resemble Ashley—tall, with delicate features and sleek hair—or take after their mom and Mia, short and stout with tight curls? Would she have followed their parents to Texas like he and Ashley or stayed in California like Mia? Knowing Glory, she'd be somewhere else entirely, carving out her own path.

"How's the case coming?" Favian's words pulled Joaquin out of the sea of what-ifs he was so often drowning in.

"Good." Joaquin shoveled rice into his mouth. "The clock's ticking, but the appeal's almost ready."

"Think you have a shot?"

"I hope so. As you know, after a conviction, the presumption of innocence flips. It's an uphill battle. Innocent people on death row are among the unluckiest in the world."

Favian cut Camila's turkey. "So, you actually believe he's innocent?"

"Tío Joaquin is helping a bad guy?" Camila asked.

Ashley set her fork down. "Who told you that?"

Camila shrugged, but her sideways glance at her father didn't go unnoticed.

Heat crept up Joaquin's face. "No, sweetie. Mr. Terrell's not a bad guy."

"Anyone want more wine?" Luis chimed in, topping off his own glass.

Joaquin locked eyes with his brother-in-law. "I get the public has this warped idea that prosecutors are the good guys and defense attorneys are the bad ones. It's politically popular to fund your salary, but not the salaries of public defenders. But I don't appreciate you feeding those ideas to my nieces and nephew."

Favian opened his mouth, but Ashley grabbed his forearm, shooting him a pointed look—a clear warning to stay quiet. One Joaquin knew his brother-in-law would not heed.

All the adults at the table looked uncomfortable. The teens, for once, weren't looking at their phones. Joaquin was about to change the subject when Favian turned toward Melrose.

"I guess you share my brother-in-law's belief that Troy Terrell isn't the Songbird Strangler?"

Joaquin tensed. Luis groaned from across the table.

"Don't bring her into this," Joaquin said firmly.

Favian wiped his mouth with his napkin. "I meant no disrespect, Ms. Reed. It's just that I trust our judicial system. If two juries and countless judges found him guilty despite numerous appeals, well—what's that saying? Where there's smoke, there's fire?"

"I understand why you'd assume that," Melrose said. "And I get why you trust the system. You seem like a decent bloke who wants to get the right guy, yeah?"

Favian nodded. "Absolutely."

"Well, not everyone is like you. Some cops, some judges, some DAs—they just want to get *a* guy."

Favian crossed his arms. "So you're suggesting what? That they target someone they don't like? Plant evidence?"

"It's not usually that malicious," Melrose said. "Most of the time, it's a rush to judgment. You know better than anyone that there's immense pressure to find a suspect, especially in heinous cases. Pressure from up top, from the community, and even from the victims' families. And here in Texas, judges don't get elected unless they run on tough-on-crime platforms. If they don't enforce the death penalty or, heaven forbid, actually overturn a death penalty case, they won't have a hope of winning reelection."

Favian nodded. "I won't pretend that rushing to judgment doesn't happen. Look at Marcellus Williams—the prosecutor actually tried to stop his execution. Cases like that are why my office has a Conviction Integrity Unit. My job is to seek justice, not rack up convictions."

"Yet prosecutorial success is still measured by conviction rates," Joaquin muttered.

"These plantains are just wonderful," Bernie interjected. "What are they seasoned with?"

Before Isabel could answer, a small voice piped up. "But what if you represent a guilty man, and he goes free?" Avril asked.

Joaquin smiled at his oldest niece. "Then the state didn't prove its case. Our founding fathers believed it was better for a guilty man to go free than for an innocent one to be imprisoned."

Avril glanced at her father, waiting for an argument.

"Your *tío* is right this time." Favian buttered his roll. "The burden is on the state to prove guilt beyond a reasonable doubt."

"Wait, did you just admit my brother is right?" Ashley put her hands to her cheeks in mock surprise. Laughter rippled through the table, easing the tension.

"More importantly," Isabel chimed in, "our founding fathers believed in Thanksgiving!"

"Kinda," Joaquin said. "It wasn't a holiday until Lincoln, but Washington and Adams declared days of gratitude." He sipped his wine.

"Jefferson, on the other hand, opposed making it a holiday, believing it violated the separation of church and state."

Isabel rolled her eyes. "My son, the lawyer-slash-historian. All I'm saying is if the Pilgrims and Native Americans could find peace, so can a defense attorney and a district attorney."

Joaquin's nephew, Bryan, raised his hand. "That's actually a bad example. The Wampanoags welcoming the English settlers turned out to be a huge mistake that led to genocide."

"It's true," Avril added. "Most tribes consider today a day of mourning."

Isabel threw up her hands. "Happy now, Luis? All your 'vote blue no matter who' nonsense? Our grandchildren are woke!"

The table broke into laughter, with even Isabel eventually joining in. Luis stood, placing his hand on his wife's shoulder. "You know what we can all agree on? Dessert! I'll be back."

"Your family is a riot," Melrose said as they drove back toward Bluesummer. "Thanks again for inviting me."

His chest warmed as he stole a quick glance at her. "They liked you—especially Mom."

Bernie cleared her throat from the backseat, a wordless reminder that Joaquin's comment sounded more like something said to a girlfriend than a coworker. Or maybe she was just telling him to focus on the road.

Melrose smiled. "Even though I'm Episcopalian?"

"It's okay. Bernie back there made up for it."

Bernie leaned forward. "Twelve years of Catholic school taught me a thing or two. I'm not as active as I used to be, though. Probably can't take communion since I'm shacked up with Dan."

Joaquin glanced at her in the rearview. "Yeah, for like forty years. Doesn't the church recognize common-law marriage?"

Bernie shrugged. "Hell if I know."

Joaquin slowed as he turned onto the highway, the roads slicker than he'd expected.

Melrose straightened. "Looks pretty slushy; might be black ice under there. Maybe we should've taken your parents up on their offer to stay the night."

"I considered it," he said. "But with Ashley's family visiting, I figured there wouldn't be much room. I guess we could have gotten a hotel room." He caught himself. "Two hotel rooms, I mean." He glanced back at Bernie. "Three rooms."

Bernie snickered.

"Two would've been fine," Melrose said. "I meant Bernie and I could share one."

"Right, of course." Joaquin gripped the wheel tighter. "If it gets too slick, I can always—" His phone chimed, cutting him off.

"Is that an email?" Melrose asked.

"It's probably nothing," Joaquin said, more to himself than to her. "Just a Black Friday coupon or CVS reminding me to refill my blood pressure meds."

"Or it could be the DNA results," Bernie said.

"Yeah, or that." Joaquin pressed against the seat, struggling to pry his phone from his too-tight jeans.

"I take back what I said about the DNA results," Bernie added. "Please don't kill us over a Groupon."

"Let me help," Melrose said, tugging the phone from his pocket.

Joaquin shivered at her touch. "Check it for me? The Outlook app."

"I need your thumb," Melrose replied.

Joaquin removed his hand from the steering wheel, and Melrose took it, pulling it toward her. Was it his imagination, or did she hold on longer than necessary to unlock the phone?

He turned the heater off, the car now silent except for the squeak of the wipers.

"Well?" Joaquin asked, breaking the silence.

Melrose held up a hand. "Shhh, I'm reading."

"Reading what?" He leaned in closer. "A Black Friday doorbuster or the DNA results?"

"Neither."

"What then?" He eased off the gas, realizing he was speeding.

"*The Tribune* is publishing an article about the lost DNA. They want a comment from you."

"Dammit!" Joaquin hit the wheel. "Who leaked it?" He already knew the answer. "*The Tyler Tribune?* That's where Greer Sheridan used to work."

"Doubt it was Greer," Melrose said. "She said she'd turn in the ring. She's on our side. The media were bound to find out. Told ya we needed to prep a statement."

"I know, but—"

"This is our chance to control the narrative," she said, setting his phone on the console. "Get the truth out before it spirals."

His fingers drummed nervously against the steering wheel as he recalled Greer's text from days ago: *I'm ready to help Troy in any way I can.* He forced himself to breathe, trying to push down the tension coiling in his gut.

*Well, Greer,* he thought, *here's your chance to prove it.*

# CHAPTER 24

**2024**

Greer's stomachache wasn't from Thanksgiving—she'd hardly touched her plate, too restless with anticipation for tomorrow.

Tomorrow morning, she'd cook breakfast, send Hayes off to work, give Red his medication, and then take the ring to the police station. And if Troy's attorney pulled the right strings, she'd have one more stop.

But Joaquin Ramos's text made clear that wasn't enough.

*We need you to speak to the media. You won't be alone.*

Greer knew Joaquin meant to be reassuring, but a near-stranger by her side didn't make her feel less alone—especially knowing this would alienate her from her husband and her family. Red's reaction worried her most. He'd initially been Troy's fiercest defender.

She could still see Red—usually so calm in a crisis—storming into the interrogation room, furious that the police were questioning Troy again.

"Now calm down, Redman," Detective Adams had said. "Troy's not a suspect. We just have a few questions—"

"Shove those questions up your ass," Red had shot back at a man he once shared morning coffee with, who sat in the pew ahead of him every Sunday.

Red dismissed how Troy had acted that Fourth of July in his driveway. He convinced himself the scent on Troy's skin wasn't Tilly's perfume. A few days later, while helping swap the ignition switch, he overlooked the blood in Troy's truck—after all, even a scrape could leave traces. The ring found at the bower was easy to downplay; it looked like Troy's but was too generic to be certain. When the cops discovered Tilly's charm bracelet there, too, Red told himself that wasn't what Troy had been jangling in his pocket minutes after Tilly's death.

Instead, he pushed police to investigate Ollie Ford or Wendy's ex, Derek Reynolds, who grew up next door to Nicole Garcia, the first victim. The FBI didn't suspect Troy. Why should he?

Then, on one humid August night, Red woke up gasping for air, his chest tight with panic. The hospital called it an anxiety attack. He brushed it off with a laugh, blaming a boo hag—the skin-shedding campfire creature he liked telling stories about, who fed on the breath of sleeping victims.

But it happened again. And again. As if all those ignored doubts had grown into something monstrous, feeding off him.

Joanne convinced him to go to the police. Detectives asked Troy's parents for his class ring paperwork and deduced the ring at the bower was his. A search of his truck revealed that it was not his blood type on the floorboard, but Wendy's. His dental impression matched the bite mark on her shoulder. That was when Red knew: he couldn't make any more excuses for Troy Terrell.

The panic attacks stopped. He'd slain the boo hag. But he'd lost a son in the process.

Red never spoke to Greer about the case. She only knew how he came to his conclusion by reading his 1988 bestseller, *Son and Songbird: The Shocking True Story of Serial Killer Troy Terrell.*

Not everyone believed Red had suffered. "If it hurt so much, why write a book?" her brother Zach had asked.

But Greer understood the power of the right story. After years of telling others' truths, Red finally had his own.

What would it do to him to learn he'd been wrong? This wouldn't just discredit his career—it would break his heart.

Still, she couldn't let them kill Troy to spare her father-in-law's feelings. Greer hoped she might shield Red from the news. He used the TV only for old movies. He loved true crime podcasts but had no idea how to download them—Greer curated every playlist.

"Can you please be still?" Hayes rolled over, his voice groggy. She hadn't noticed he'd stopped snoring. He flipped his pillow with a sigh. "Hard to sleep with you flopping around."

Greer bit her tongue. He'd toss and turn, too, if he looked at this objectively.

She grabbed her pillow, slipped out of bed, and stopped at the hallway closet for a blanket and melatonin. Not the first time one of them had slept on the couch. Wouldn't be the last.

The office was dim, lit only by the bluish glow of the router light. The ceiling fan hummed faintly. Coffee mugs cluttered the desk, papers stacked in uneven piles beside a dying peace lily. The couch was comfortable enough, but as she sank into it, a heaviness settled over her. She couldn't tell if it was the weighted blanket or if her own boo hag had come to visit.

Greer had been in prisons before—plenty of them. She'd stared down hardened criminals, honest-to-God monsters, through security glass and across scuffed-up tables. She'd asked sharp, probing questions designed to break their defenses. Some had threatened her, some had lashed out, but she'd never been scared. Not until now, waiting for Troy.

That morning, Joaquin Ramos had caught her off guard. "Troy listed you on his visitor list when he first got here," he had said. "Ten friends or family—guess he never thought to take you off."

Had Troy been waiting for her? Expecting her to visit? Regret tightened her chest as the officer led Troy into the booth. He looked so familiar yet so startlingly different.

She wasn't sure what reaction she'd expected, but his easy, genuine smile wasn't it.

She smiled back, her hand unsteady as she lifted the cold, heavy phone.

"Good to see you, Greer." The warmth in his voice surprised her.

"Greer?" She laughed. "I don't think you've called me that since we were nine."

His smile deepened, crinkling the corners of his eyes. Those lines hadn't been there the last time she saw him—nor the gray in his hair or the bifocals on his nose. "I wasn't sure if we were still on a one-letter basis," he said. "But you'll always be G to me."

Greer's eyes burned. She pressed a palm to her lips, holding back a sob. "I'm so sorry, Troy."

He softened his expression. "Hey. Didn't mean to upset you. I'm glad you're here," he said, his gaze lingering for a moment. "You look good. Different."

"Yeah, I had a lot fewer wrinkles the last time you saw me."

"That makes two of us." He chuckled. "And your hair—it's different, too."

Instinctively, she tucked a strand behind her ear. "Yeah, I grew it out in college."

"And it's blonde."

"Highlights." Her mother's voice echoed from years ago—*Greer, honey, why are you trying to look like Chantilly Price?*

Troy smirked. "I got highlights, too." He dipped his chin, pointing to the gray threading through his hair.

Greer laughed, full and long—the way she always had with him.

"How's your mom?" he asked.

"Not bad. Just a little harder for her to get around these days." Her voice dropped. "I was sorry to hear about your parents."

"Yeah. It was for the best that Pops passed before the trial. Not sure he could've handled it. Didn't think Ma would either, but she did." His voice flattened. "Funny, isn't it? All this pushed her to get clean. Silver lining, I guess."

"I'm glad. Did she get to visit often?"

"Ma worked two jobs to cover my legal fees, but yeah, as often as she could. And Vic too—he still comes almost every week."

*Vic.* She and Troy had planned to crash at his place that Fourth of July. Had they stuck to that plan, Greer would have been Troy's alibi—not his accuser.

She adjusted the phone against her ear, the coiled cord brushing against her wrist. The booth was cold, all hard edges and white cinderblock, and the sharp scent of bleach mixed with the memory of that night turned her stomach.

His tone turned casual. "Vic's on my witness list. Five are allowed . . . for the execution."

Cold swept through Greer's veins.

"Mr. Ramos, my lawyer, will be another," Troy continued. "His assistant, too, if she's willing. And . . . I'd like you to be there. That's why I never took you off my list. You've always been after the truth, G. I figured someday you'd find it."

Her chin trembled. "I don't think I can watch that, Troy. Why would you want me there?"

"The victim's families will be there. I don't blame them for the hate they'll bring. The guards, too—they don't care about me. Texas doesn't let the chaplain in the chamber anymore. That room will be full of pure hate. I thought it'd be nice to have a little counterbalance."

"Your lawyer says you've got a good chance at a stay of execution."

Troy's voice sharpened. "I don't want another stay."

Greer flinched.

He sighed. "Sorry. But do you know what that means? Another year in here. Twenty-three hours a day in a piss-and-metal-smelling pod. My only company? Cockroaches, a radio, library books, and my maps."

Maps. Troy had always obsessed over them—always planning an escape, a way out.

"I sleep on a mattress with a stain I don't want to know the origin of. Some mornings, my back hurts so badly I have to roll off it. I've forgotten what outside even feels like. Birds, grass . . . they're as foreign as the places on my maps. This ain't a life, G."

"We have to get you out," she said, voice firm despite the lump in her throat. "Think about what's waiting for you."

Troy removed his glasses, trying to rub a smudge away with the sleeve of his jumpsuit. "I'd love to get on a plane and see those faraway places on my map. Hell, I'd be happy with a run through the woods of Bluesummer. But Texas wants me dead. I don't want a stay just to get another execution date. I'd rather they killed me now. Put me down like an old, sorry dog."

The words hit her like a blow. He sounded so calm, so certain, and it made her sick. "Stop. We'll get you out."

"How?" His eyes held hers steadily, sharp and wary. "Did Mr. Ramos tell you about the DNA? That the semen is probably mine?"

"Yes. And I know what I saw, Troy."

His brows knit. "What?"

"That night. I saw you and Tilly in the pool. Heard you flirting. I'm going to do an interview. I'll tell the world what I should've told the police—that it was consensual."

Troy shook his head. "Why didn't you say anything back then?"

"For one, I didn't want to hurt Hayes, and I also thought it might make you a suspect."

"Yet you said I had a volatile temper, didn't you?" Troy's voice rose, confusion in his tone.

"The cops put those words in my mouth. You know how they were. But if I'm being honest, you do have a temper. I mean, you're yelling at me right now."

Troy slumped back. "Sorry, G. I just—"

"I'm trying to make up for it," Greer interrupted. "Make up for my testimony. Make up for having a career as a journalist, yet failing to look at your case objectively. I turned over the ring and am doing the interview. I . . ." She faltered, the words catching in her throat. *I'm betraying my husband*, she thought.

Troy pressed his palm to the glass. "Mr. Ramos told me about the ring. Thank you."

Greer hesitated, then lifted her hand to meet his. "I'm sorry, but I have to get going—it's a two-hour drive, and I still need to make dinner. I'll come back when I can stay longer."

"Bring your husband." A grin tugged at the corners of his lips. "A little birdie told me you married Hayes."

"I did." She smiled, her cheeks flushing.

"I'd love to catch up with him." Troy's expression turned curious, cautious. "I assume he's on the same page as you with all this?"

Greer swallowed hard. "I'll . . . um, see what I can do." She pushed back her chair, standing quickly before Troy could ask for one more impossible thing.

# CHAPTER 25

Joaquin pushed away from his desk and lowered his mask for the last watery sip of Diet Dr Pepper.

"I told you to take that off," Melrose said. "I'm not worried about some little cold."

"It doesn't bother me," he said, raising the mask. "I've been coughing a little. Better safe than sorry." He blinked several times, then rubbed his eyes. "The words on the screen are blurring together. Time for a break."

Melrose straightened. "I can type if you dictate."

Joaquin's stomach rumbled. How could he be hungry? Crumpled wrappers from both lunch and dinner littered the trash, and his extra-large waxy cup left a ring on the desk.

The explanation came as Melrose glanced at her watch. "Wow, already eleven."

"Eleven? Go home." Joaquin stood, stretching his back.

"I'm not tired. We're pressed for time—we need to give this our best shot."

"Alright, but I need more caffeine. Want anything?"

She waved him off. "No, go. You're the one who needs a pick-me-up."

Joaquin grabbed an energy drink from the fridge and sat at the kitchen table, sliding his mask beneath his chin as he cracked open the can. The air hit his lungs, sharp and clean. He wasn't used to wearing a mask anymore. The snug fit and the slight warmth with each breath were noticeable after so long without one.

Joaquin unwrapped a muffin, his eyes drifting to the pot of coffee Melrose had made earlier. He wouldn't make her a cup, not with the cold lingering, but he remembered how she liked hers—one sugar, a splash of cream. He'd picked up on the little things. How she hated ketchup on burgers, but dunked her fries in it. How her brown eyes had tiny flecks of gold. How her accent sharpened when she got fired up, vowels stretching just a little longer. Details a boss shouldn't notice about an employee.

He couldn't shake the memory of that night on the loveseat, the way they'd sat so close, their faces inches apart. Who could say what might have happened if he hadn't stopped it? He'd considered bringing up what had happened . . . what had *almost* happened, but why make things awkward when Melrose didn't seem upset? She'd gone to Thanksgiving with him. She obviously wasn't uncomfortable.

Joaquin slid his mask back on and washed his hands before heading back down the quiet hallway to the office. He sank into his chair across from Melrose.

"So we still need to include Titus's recant, right?" she asked. "Even if he's back to his original bulldust story?"

"Right. Even if he claims the recant was a lie, we still have his signed affidavit."

Melrose unscrewed her water bottle. "So, DNA, the ring, Titus—what else?"

"Failure to investigate alternate suspects," Joaquin said, brushing muffin crumbs off his shirt.

"Meaning Ollie Ford?"

"Not just him. Wendy Knott's ex boyfriend, who lived next door to the first victim, and possibly . . ."

"Hayes Sheridan?" Melrose finished.

"I don't think he's a serial killer, but since Troy and Tilly slept together and Greer hinted it to Hayes, maybe he confronted her, and things went wrong. Hopefully, the DNA results will be in by the time we file and give us those answers. DPAP will be paying for a while, but it's worth it if it gives us another suspect. If results come in too late, we'll file a supplemental petition."

"Are you going to mention the phone records?" Melrose asked.

"The goddamn phone records," Joaquin muttered. He'd spent an entire day combing through the district attorney's case file, only to find no trace of the records—no subpoenas, no logs, nothing. "Yeah, I'm including it. Red Sheridan obviously saw them. Carter had to be the one who showed him." Joaquin spun his chair in frustration. "Those records contained something Carter didn't want to be exposed."

"Could Greer get Red to explain how he saw them?"

"We've got a better chance of Carter clawing his way up from hell to hand us those records than Red Sheridan admitting he got it wrong." Joaquin's throat tightened. He coughed, turning away to pull his mask down and take a sip of water. After a few long gulps, he cleared his throat. "And apparently Greer's never even brought up the case with Red," he said, his voice hoarse. "It'll raise eyebrows if she asks, 'Hey, Red, how'd you sleep? Also, how'd you get the phone records from the Price house the night of Tilly's murder?'"

A sharp car horn blared from outside, slicing through the quiet stillness of the night. Melrose rose from her seat, moving to the window to investigate.

"Hopefully, Luca finds something," she said, stretching. "Though he's still hung up on Ollie Ford."

*He's hung up on you*, Joaquin thought.

Melrose sat back down. "Luca says we should talk to Ollie again."

"Does he now?" Joaquin pressed his lips together. "Did you set him straight?"

"Not as strongly as I did with you, but I made it clear I won't be tagging along for any more visits."

"No need. Luca's keeping a close watch on them. With the DNA news, we need to make sure they don't flee."

"Ollie was at work this weekend," Melrose said. "Doesn't seem like they're going anywhere."

"Doesn't seem like they're taking their trash out, either," Joaquin said.

"Huh?"

"Luca checked their trash bin a couple of times since the DNA story broke. It's been empty."

Melrose held the papers like a shield. "The city might have just emptied it."

Joaquin shook his head. "Nope."

Melrose set the papers down. "You think they're keeping all their rubbish inside? Why would they do that?"

"You know why. They don't want their DNA for comparison."

"Or maybe they don't make much rubbish. Ollie and his father live pretty simply."

Joaquin smirked. "Melrose, even a simple life produces trash." He lifted the overflowing trash can from under his desk.

She crumpled a paper and lobbed it at him. "Alright, it's a little dodgy."

Joaquin caught the paper, stuffed it into the bin, and slid it back under the desk. "The police disagree. Just like they don't think the ring Greer found is worth investigating."

"Luca knows dumpster diving on private property is illegal in Texas, right?" Melrose said, chewing on a pen. "Even if he found DNA to test, the court would throw it out—and he could lose his license."

"Come on, we're talking about Loophole Luca. He'll figure it out. Who's to say he didn't find it in the alley or accidentally take the wrong water bottle when we visited the Fords' trailer?"

Melrose unwrapped a Pop-Tart. "You know, it's been hard to go back to this junk food after your parents' Thanksgiving spread."

Joaquin smiled. "You're welcome back anytime. My family loved you."

"I had a great time," Melrose said. "Not sure if you noticed, but your mum pulled out an old scrapbook while you were doing the dishes."

"Ugh, sorry. How embarrassing."

"No, they were great. Loved the one of you and your little sister with that terrifying Easter Bunny."

Joaquin felt a shift in his expression. He tried to hide it, but somehow Melrose caught it immediately.

"Sorry," she said, taking a bite of the frosted pastry. "I shouldn't have brought her up."

"It's okay. Honestly, I hate that we never talk about Glory."

Melrose finished chewing. "We can talk about her now."

Joaquin let out a shaky breath, his lips vibrating as he drummed his fingers on the desk. Did he want to relive the worst moment of his life at half-past eleven, with the motion still unfinished? Not really. But it felt like he'd opened a door he couldn't close.

"Glory was four years younger than me, and we were close," Joaquin said, his gaze drifting past Melrose as though seeing something far away. "Sibling relationships can be complicated. They were with my older sisters—still are. But not with Gloria." He gave a hollow laugh. "It's easy to say that when someone's forever five years old. Glory might've grown into a pain-in-the-ass teenager like Mia, or married a pain-in-the-ass district attorney like Ashley."

"Only five?" Melrose's tone was soft. "Was she ill?"

Joaquin's throat tightened, tears filling his eyes. "It was an accident," he whispered. "A pit bull attacked her."

Melrose covered her mouth. "Oh, Joaquin. That's . . . horrific."

"It was my fault," he whispered, the words slipping out before he could stop them, a tear dampening the edge of his mask.

"Your fault?" Melrose shook her head. "No one could expect any child to fight off an angry pit."

"But he wasn't angry, not at first," Joaquin said. "The owner kept him tied up. We usually avoided the street—Glory was scared of animals. But one day, we stayed too long at the park and cut through. The dog wasn't tied up."

Melrose stood and walked over to the bookshelf, grabbing a box of Kleenex. "Still not your fault," she said, placing the box in front of him. "That's an irresponsible owner."

Joaquin pulled out a tissue, using it to dab at his eyes. "He was staring at us, barking so damn loud. Pop had always told me never to run from a dog, but I thought he was going to charge at us. I looked for a stick, but all I found were rocks."

"So you threw one?" Melrose asked.

"Yeah. It missed, but the pit backed up, so I thought it worked. Threw another one. The next thing I knew, he was charging. Happened so fast." Joaquin's stomach twisted. "That's not the worst of it." He took a sip of water, then crushed the bottle in his hand. "I took a step back."

"That's instinct," Melrose said quickly.

"No. It's cowardice. I put Glory closer to danger than I was." Joaquin lowered his head, the weight of the memory crushing him. "All these years,

I still hear her screams." He paused, chest tight. "I called for help, but it was too late."

"I'm so sorry, Joaquin," Melrose said softly.

"My uncle killed the dog."

Melrose nodded, her expression serious. "Standard procedure when an animal kills a child."

Joaquin lowered his mask to wipe his nose, and then quickly pulled it back. "Yeah, I get it. But I still wonder whether he deserved it. I mean, you talk about instinct when I took that step back," Joaquin said. "Wasn't the dog acting on instinct? When I threw rocks at him?"

Melrose opened and closed her mouth, as if unsure of how to respond.

"I've thought about that dog a lot. Too much. I hate him, but as time's gone on, I've had to admit it wasn't all his fault. It's like these men on death row. The public wants them dead, and I get it, Melrose, I do. But we have to ask, 'Why did they end up where they did? Who raised them to be violent? How many people threw rocks at them?'"

"You're right," Melrose said, her tone thoughtful. "The link between child abuse and violent crime is indisputable. I've done research on it and—" She stifled a yawn.

"Hey, I'm sorry for keeping you so late." Joaquin ran a hand through his hair, trying to shake off the heaviness pressing in on him. Telling her about that night had left something raw and hollow inside, like he'd dragged out the horrible truth and set it on the table between them. "Let's call it a night—or a morning. I'm gonna crash on the couch."

Melrose stood. "Here?"

Joaquin clicked save on his document. "Yeah. I live out in the boondocks, and it's a drive."

Melrose began to straighten the files, but he waved her off. "Don't bother. We'll pick back up tomorrow, anyway." Joaquin pushed his chair back, adjusting his mask. "I'll walk you out—at a safe distance, of course."

Melrose's voice softened, her expression serious. "I want you to know it means a lot that you're wearing the mask. It's probably unnecessary, but it's such a kind gesture. During the pandemic, people were so bloody ugly about masks—calling others sheep and all, it's rare to see such thoughtfulness."

Joaquin shrugged, a slight flush creeping up his neck. "It's no big deal."

"It is to me," Melrose said, giving him a soft smile. "I'd hug you, but I guess that would defeat the purpose."

Joaquin chuckled, rubbing the back of his neck, his eyes briefly meeting hers. "Yeah, probably not a good idea." He shifted his weight, working up the courage to say, *Maybe next time*, when she spoke again.

"Seriously, though, are you going to be okay staying alone tonight? Recalling trauma is tough, and sometimes you don't want to be alone."

Joaquin skated a finger along his jaw, unsure what to say. He didn't want to be alone, but he couldn't guilt Melrose into sleeping on the other couch in the waiting room in her business attire while he coughed all night. "I'm good."

He swore he saw a flicker of disappointment in her expression. "Unless you want to stay. There's another couch, and I've got extra toothbrushes and stuff."

He winced. *Extra toothbrushes and stuff? Smooth.* "I mean, I get you may not want to drive in this, umm . . . condition . . ." Joaquin wondered why he couldn't stop vomiting words.

Melrose grinned, one eyebrow arched. "Condition? I'm tired, not drunk. Let me grab my purse."

As she disappeared into her office, Joaquin rested his forehead against the doorframe, resisting the urge to bang his head against it.

He waited until her taillights disappeared, then locked the door behind him.

Too tired to bother changing clothes, he collapsed onto the couch, pulling a throw blanket over him. He closed his eyes, knowing the nightmare that was waiting for him, but to his surprise, it never came.

# CHAPTER 26

Greer decided to wait until their Sunday lunch to tell Hayes about her interview with Troy's attorney. Church had a way of brightening her husband's mood.

"Come on, Silas, it's time for kids' church." Quinn held out her arms, but Silas clung tighter to Greer.

Quinn crouched to meet her son at eye level. "Remember how much fun you had last week?"

Silas shook his head. "Fun's all gone."

Greer stifled a laugh. The right thing was to pry his fingers from her shirt and tell him to obey, but what was the harm in staying? Caleb had been the same, never wanting to leave her side. On the last morning of his life, he'd cried and begged not to go to preschool.

If only she'd let him stay home.

"Can't he stay? He'll be good for Nana, won't you, Si?"

"Pinky promise," Silas said, holding up a tiny finger.

Quinn's shoulders tensed, but before she could respond, her husband, Rafael, turned from the pew ahead. "Let him stay with your mom."

"Thank you," Greer mouthed to her son-in-law as Quinn stomped back to her seat.

To her right, Hayes's gaze burned into her. The blaring organ cut off whatever disapproval he was ready to voice—not that he needed to. She knew what he was thinking.

*You never let our girls stay with us during church.*

He wasn't wrong. After Caleb's death, it took countless therapy sessions—and a carefully balanced mix of antidepressants—to find the will to get out of bed. Let alone dote on two little girls who'd always seemed to prefer their daddy, anyway.

"Nana!" Silas exclaimed, his voice echoing a bit too loudly for church.

Quinn spun around in her seat, her eyes narrowing.

"Shhh." Greer pressed a finger to her lips. "Quiet voices, like little church mice."

Greer considered slipping Silas her phone. He adored *Sweet Smash Mania*, a silent distraction. But Quinn was militant about screen time—ironic, given how much TV she'd watched as a kid. That was how it went, though, wasn't it? Children grew up and made a show of being better parents than you ever were.

Digging a pen from her purse, Greer slid a hymnal under the bulletin. "Draw a picture for Nana," she whispered. "Stay quiet, and I'll give you gum when Pastor Foster starts speaking."

Gum—another Quinn restriction, which made it the perfect bargaining chip.

Greer stood and stared blankly at the hymnal Hayes held between them. This church, these hymns, this congregation—it had all become her husband's sanctuary after Caleb's death. He'd found solace in the stained-glass windows, metrical choruses, and stern sermons. Greer wished she could, too. But no matter how hard she tried, she felt . . . nothing.

Sometimes, it seemed like Hayes had forgotten Caleb. After his death, it was as if he wanted every trace of him gone. Greer fought to keep the bedroom untouched, but practicality won with twins on the way.

Everything had been packed up except Caleb's favorite stuffed animal, Kiki, a well-loved koala.

Kiki still sat on Greer's nightstand—its chewed-up, faded fur a reminder that Caleb had once existed. And the preschool paintings Caleb had made still clung to their refrigerator. To this day, Hayes couldn't look at them, his gaze dropping to the floor whenever he reached for the milk.

Hayes Sheridan, the great avoider.

Their grandson didn't at all resemble Caleb. Silas had his father's dark curly hair and tan skin. But Silas was just as sweet and loved her every bit as much. It was his love, Greer suspected, that had brought her back to life.

The end of worship ushered in Greer's least favorite part of the service: greeting your neighbors. Did these neighbors have any idea how they'd wounded her with their ridiculous platitudes?

"Now he'll be able to watch out for you."

"God needed another angel."

The worst came when they learned she was pregnant with the girls. "God has given you back double for the loss." They said it so casually as if Caleb could be replaced. As if he were a ruined sweater replaced by a buy-one-get-one-free sale.

She had wanted to scream that, given the choice between Caleb and the two strangers inside her, she'd choose Caleb.

"They mean well, honey," Red had said. "They're goddamn fools, but they mean well."

He was right. That was why she had shown up every Sunday, waking at the crack of dawn to wrestle Quinn and Farren into matching dresses with frilly socks. Why she had watched Hayes take up the offering and agreed to let him tithe ten percent of their income. Greer wasn't thrilled about a God who wanted her son and her money, but at least the church did good for the community—feeding hungry children, revitalizing struggling neighborhoods, and helping single mothers. Their denomination was inclusive, allowing women to pastor and steering clear of tying salvation to who you voted for. The youth group had given their girls a sense of belonging during those awkward teenage years. But mostly, she came because it mattered to Hayes.

So much of her life had been spent trying to please Hayes Sheridan. Greer had always considered herself a feminist, preaching independence to her daughters, never realizing how much of her life she'd spent acquiescing to her husband's desires. The big wedding she never wanted. Staying in Bluesummer. This church. Giving up her job.

She sat beside Silas, who looked at her expectantly. Pulling a piece of Trident from her purse, she checked that Quinn still faced forward before slipping it to him. Knowing the gum alone wouldn't occupy him for the entire sermon, Greer pulled out her grocery list and drew a quick tic-tac-toe board on the back. "Do you want to be Xs or Os?" she whispered.

"Bananas," Silas said with a serious nod as he tried to sketch one in the right corner square, his little brow furrowed in concentration.

Greer kissed the top of his head, and an image of Troy Terrell surfaced—of the grandchildren he'd never hold. This joy, this love, this life had been stolen from him.

And she bore part of the blame.

She glanced around the congregation, wondering how their pro-life stance applied to a black man on death row.

She was about to find out.

Because sitting quietly while the government killed an innocent man was not something that even Hayes Sheridan could convince her was for the best.

"Already putting up the tree?" Hayes reclined in his chair and pointed the remote at the TV.

Greer paused her holiday playlist and pulled out an earbud. "Why wouldn't I?"

"You usually wait till the last minute."

He was right. Greer had always struggled with Christmas. The tree and presents had been set up the day Caleb died. So now those same decorations were a constant reminder of the worst time in her life.

"Buy a new tree," Hayes had suggested two years after Caleb's death when he walked in to find Greer on the floor sobbing, artificial tree limbs scattered around her. "New ornaments, too. Or screw it. The girls are still babies. They don't get what Christmas is." Hayes didn't understand that she wasn't putting up the tree for the girls but to honor Caleb. He had loved holidays.

"Did you enjoy the sermon today?" Hayes asked, taking a sip of his beer.

Greer sighed. "It was . . . fine."

Hayes lowered the volume. "Maybe it's not a good idea for Si to stay with us during service. I'm sure it's distracting."

Finishing the final strand of lights, Greer shrugged. "Church is your thing, not mine. I welcome a little distraction."

The TV volume lowered again. "Well, what is *your* thing?" he asked.

Greer hooked a silver bauble onto a bare branch. "Right now, Christmas trees. Then, dispensing medication, followed by cooking dinner."

Hayes pulled the recliner lever and stood. "Don't cook. Let's order pizza." He walked closer. "If caring for my parents becomes too much, we can hire someone full-time. I know the hospice nurse only comes a few times a week."

Greer shot him a pointed look. "Jo hates pizza. And I'm fine—I want to help your parents. I just . . . sometimes I miss my job, my coworkers. It's strange not having a life outside this house."

Hayes scratched his forehead. "So you want to go back to work?"

Greer kneeled, rifling through a box of ornaments. "I don't know. Maybe. I need something of my own again. I've been considering doing freelance work or maybe starting a podcast."

"Where's this coming from?" Hayes asked, a mix of curiosity and concern. "What made you interested in podcasting?"

Greer sighed. "I listen to podcasts all day. Maybe I'd make a good host. It sounds like something I'd enjoy."

"Okay, let's buy you the equipment. You've got plenty of true crime stories. And . . ." He winked. "You've always had that sexy voice."

Greer blushed. Even after all these years, Hayes could still make her feel like a lovesick teenager.

Hayes picked up a snowman ornament and fiddled with the hook. "Does this just go anywhere, or do you have a system?"

"Anywhere," she replied, but redirected his hand when he tried to hang it on the end of a branch. "That one's heavy. Put it further back."

He chuckled. "Tell you what, I'll hook 'em, you hang 'em."

"Deal," Greer said. They worked together for a few more minutes before she gathered enough courage to continue the conversation. "For the podcast, I might like to feature stories of death row inmates."

Hayes shook his head. "If you're talking about Troy—"

"I saw him," Greer blurted.

The sound of an ornament crashing to the ground startled her. She looked at Hayes, confused to see him still holding a nutcracker ornament. "Ugh," she muttered, realizing the broken ornament had fallen from her own hand.

"I thought we decided we were done with all this Troy Terrell business." Heat had entered Hayes's tone.

"No, *you* decided." She stepped around the shards. "Let me sweep."

Hayes reached to hang the nutcracker ornament on a high branch. "His lawyers got to you, didn't they?"

Greer pulled out her phone and opened her photo album. "No, they didn't get to me. This got to me." She held the screen out for him to see.

Hayes leaned in. "A class ring?"

"I found it. When Si and I were metal detecting. Troy always said he had lost his ring in the woods. We found this one in the woods."

"Okay. So what?"

"So if this is Troy's ring, it's not his that was found at the bower."

Hayes studied the picture, then handed the phone back. "And how can you be sure this one is his?"

"I can't," she admitted, slipping her phone back into her pocket. "But I took it to the police."

"So let them do their job."

"But they're not doing anything!" Greer snapped.

"Then there's nothing to be done. Trust law enforcement."

"Come on, Hayes. I've learned a thing or two about crooked cops in my career."

Hayes crossed his arms. "So, what's your plan? I know you already have one."

"For starters, I'm going on *Breakfast with Texas* alongside Troy's attorney."

Hayes's nostrils flared. He ran a hand over the back of the recliner, leaving a faint smear on the leather. "Everyone we know watches that, Greer."

"A big audience is the point. There's a story coming out, and we have to get ahead of it."

"We, huh?" Hayes's neck tensed, the cords standing out as his Adam's apple bobbed. "What story do *we* need to get ahead of?"

"The DNA results."

Hayes exhaled, frustrated. "I still don't understand why that involves you speaking. Why can't you let the DNA speak for itself?"

Greer's legs weakened, and she sank into the couch. "It's not that simple."

Hayes trailed behind her. "Why? Because the DNA might be mine? That won't make me a suspect, Greer. I was her boyfriend."

Greer shook her head. "Not because it's yours. But because it's Troy's."

Hayes blinked, the words hanging in the air. "I don't get it. You've been saying he's innocent."

"I haven't been honest about that night," Greer said.

Hayes sat beside her. "I know you weren't honest with *me* then, but you told the truth when questioned. That you went to Tilly's house, knocked, and left when no one answered."

"That's not the whole story. I didn't leave. I snuck around to the side of the house and saw them in the pool."

"Okay . . . so you watched them swim?"

Greer bit her cheek. "Not *just* swim. They were flirting."

Hayes laughed bitterly. "You must have misunderstood."

"No," she said firmly. "Tilly kissed him."

Hayes shot to his feet. "That's bullshit."

"I'm telling the truth," she insisted. "I didn't hear every word, but what was happening was obvious. Tilly kissed him, and when they got out of the pool, she invited him inside."

Hayes's face turned pale. "You're sure about this?"

Greer nodded.

He sank back into the seat next to her. "Why didn't you tell me?"

Greer leaned forward, fingers steepled. "I wasn't sure how. At first, I didn't want to hurt you. They'd both been drinking, Hayes—it probably didn't mean anything to either of them. But later . . . I got angry." She swallowed. "After you rejected me. That's why I yelled that you should be worried about them as I was leaving."

"I didn't hear what you said. The fireworks were too loud." Hayes stared at his empty palms. "You've had all these years to tell me. Why haven't you?"

Greer's chest tightened. She hadn't told him because she loved him too much to make his life hurt more than it already had. "I was *trying* to protect you," she whispered.

"Well, you should've told the police. Because this doesn't clear Troy—it makes him look guiltier."

"I don't think he did it, Hayes."

He hung his head. "Don't go on TV and say this in front of millions. It's embarrassing for me and tarnishes Tilly's memory."

Greer reached for his hand. "I lied, Hayes. I have to make it right. If I don't, no one will ever believe Troy didn't assault her if the DNA turns out to be his. Please try to understand why I have to do this."

Hayes sat frozen, and Greer felt a tear fall on their joined hands. She moved closer to comfort him, but he pulled away, standing abruptly. "I'm going."

"Going where?"

He put on his jacket, jerking it angrily into place. "I don't know."

"Hayes—" Greer stepped toward him, but he raised a hand to stop her.

"I need some space." He stepped back, shoulders tense. "Just give me some goddamn space."

The door slammed, rattling the walls. Greer stood there, her heart in her throat, as the sound of his boots faded into the night.

She grabbed a broom and swept up the broken glass. December was always like this—fragile, like the ornaments themselves. She and Hayes hadn't had a good one in years. Not since Caleb died. Every year, they danced around each other's sharp edges, snapping over the smallest things, both too broken to bridge the gap.

She pushed the earbud back in, letting the Christmas playlist that had lifted her spirits earlier play on. But now, every note felt heavy, and each cheerful lyric seemed to pull her deeper into sadness.

Dropping the broom, Greer pressed her back to the wall. Her breath hitched, and she slid down until she was sitting on the floor. Her fingers fumbled through the box of decorations until they closed around Caleb's stocking. Pulling it close, she buried her face in the soft fabric as sobs overtook her. Johnny Mathis crooned on, his warm voice painfully at odds with the cold ache in her chest.

It was beginning to look a lot like Christmas indeed.

# CHAPTER 27

"Five already?" Melrose grabbed her purse and a few files.

"You outta here?" Joaquin asked, masking his disappointment. He'd grown used to her late-night company at the office.

"I figured I'd work from home," she said, words tumbling out faster than normal.

Something felt off. He noticed the bags under her eyes—she hadn't been herself all day. "You sure you're okay? Hope I didn't get you sick."

"I'm fine. Just have stuff to do at home."

"Need help? I'm pretty handy with small repairs."

"Oh, nothing like that, just some laundry. Bit of a boring night, yeah?"

*Laundry.* Might as well have said she was rearranging her sock drawer. At least if Melrose had a date, it wasn't with Luca, who was due here soon for a meeting. Joaquin had planned on ordering pizzas, but maybe, like Melrose, he needed a break from the office. He texted Luca: *Wanna meet at Texas Roadhouse instead?*

Joaquin followed Melrose into the lobby. She said goodbye to Bernie and disappeared through the front door.

Joaquin turned to Bernie. "Do you think I've been working her too hard?"

Bernie put one arm through her sweater. "Why are you asking me? Ask her."

"I did, but she insists she's fine."

Bernie wrestled the other arm in. "Then I'm sure she is. Listen, I typed out the motions and left them in your box to sign. Then I sent out the billing. Your calendar's clear on Monday. Tuesday, you're in Dallas for the interview. Wednesday, a new client meeting at 8:30."

Joaquin watched Melrose's car pull out of the lot. "She seemed in a hurry to leave."

Bernie dropped her arms. "Do you hear yourself? You're worried you're working her too hard, but also mad she's not working late on a Friday."

"I'm not mad. I'm just telling you, something's not right."

Bernie brushed past him, powering down the paper shredder. "Could it be because you ordered her to fetch you coffee today?"

"Huh?"

Bernie sighed. "When I got back from lunch, she was making coffee in the kitchen. Said you asked for a cup."

Joaquin replayed the afternoon in his head. *Right. She said she was grabbing a snack. I asked if she'd bring me a cup of coffee. Totally normal.* "I didn't order her to do anything. She was headed to the kitchen. I asked if she'd bring me a cup."

"Well, you'd already drunk the whole damn pot I made," Bernie said. "So she made more."

Joaquin adjusted the collar of his shirt. "Did she say something or—"

"Didn't have to." Bernie sat on top of her desk. "I saw it all over her face. Listen, I come from a different time. Fetching coffee for your predecessor was half of my job. But it's 2024. Melrose is a college-educated paralegal. If I'm not here to make your coffee, I bet you can manage."

"I didn't think about—"

"Of course you didn't!" Bernie peered over the rim of her glasses. "You wouldn't ask Luca to fetch your coffee, would you?"

Joaquin hesitated. "No, but—"

"Did you know women are twice as likely to be asked to make coffee at work? It's not a gender-specific role, Joaquin."

"I get that. I've made coffee." Joaquin planted his hands on his hips. "The only reason I wouldn't ask Luca is that he doesn't work here."

Bernie stood. "Do you like Big Macs, Joaquin?"

*Big Macs? What the hell now?* The absurdity sharpened his tone. "Huh?"

"Do you like Big Macs?" she repeated slowly.

"They're alright."

"Do you think that's a good name? Big Mac?"

Joaquin frowned. "What's this about?"

"The McDonald's bigwigs wanted to call their new sandwich the Blue Ribbon Burger." Bernie scoffed. "Lame, right? Luckily, a twenty-one-year-old secretary suggested calling it the Big Mac. What do you suppose those executives did?"

"Promoted her?"

Bernie jabbed a finger into Joaquin's chest. "Laughed in her face. But eventually, the name stuck."

"So she got the last laugh?"

"Nope. She *got* to go back to the coffeepot. No raise, no new title, nada. Didn't get credit until 1985. Guess what they gave her then?"

He had a feeling of where this was going, but hoped he was wrong. "A big check?" he asked.

"Nope. A plaque!" Bernie spat the words out. "An ugly-ass plaque."

A plaque. Of course. His gut twisted. The story wasn't about a burger. It was about patriarchy. It was about him. "That sucks."

"Damn right, it does. And it probably *sucks* to have a bachelor's degree and be making your boss coffee on *your* lunch break. Hell, what's next? You want her to fetch your slippers and the newspaper? If you haven't noticed, it's still a man's world, Joaquin. I've given up hope that we'll ever have a female president in my lifetime."

"Hey, I voted for a woman . . . twice," Joaquin said.

"Well, I'll engrave your name on a plaque," Bernie said, her voice dripping with sarcasm. She stepped closer, eyes locking with his. "Ever considered that Melrose is exhausted from doing all the work, knowing your name will be in the papers if Terrell is freed? Maybe she's tired of playing the game—tired of making coffee."

Joaquin put a hand on Bernie's shoulder. "Alright, I get it. I'll be more mindful. But she seemed off before the coffee."

Bernie shot him a pointed glance, her eyes hardening. "Leave her alone, Joaquin." She paused long enough for the words to land. "And I mean that in every possible sense."

He opened his mouth to protest, but Bernie cut him off, flipping off the overhead lights. "Have a nice weekend," she said, her voice final. "I'll lock the door behind me."

"Think you could've picked a louder place?" Luca called out over the twangy music and a nearby screaming toddler.

"It's Friday night," Joaquin said, scanning the chaos. "Name a place that won't be loud."

He arched an eyebrow, tilting his head slightly. "Uh, your office."

"Does my office have these?" Joaquin tipped his beer bottle toward the plate of boneless buffalo wings between them.

"Sure," Luca said. "It's called takeout."

Joaquin tore open a complimentary bag of peanuts. "Well, I needed to *take* myself out of there. I practically live in the office now."

"At least you've got a good-looking roommate," Luca said, raising his eyebrows. "Any time I've passed the office after hours, there have been two vehicles in the lot, and one of them isn't Bernadette's."

"Well, we're up against a lot of deadlines." Joaquin cracked a peanut and set the shell on the edge of the appetizer plate. He could never bring himself to drop it, despite the steakhouse's signature peanut-dusted floors. His mom's obsession with cleanliness had left its mark.

"Mm-hmm." Luca picked up his menu. "Where is she tonight?"

*Organizing her sock drawer.* "She's busy—chores and stuff." He resisted the urge to steer the conversation toward coffee, sexism, and Bernie's earlier tirade.

Luca clapped his hands together. "Alright, I'm gonna cut to it—are you interested in her?"

Before Joaquin could respond, the server returned. Joaquin listened as Luca rattled off what had to be the most carb-loaded meal on the menu.

"Just a burger and fries for me," Joaquin said, forgetting what he had planned to order.

As soon as the server walked away, Luca's eyes sharpened. "So? Are you?"

"Of course not. She's my employee."

"Okay, good." Luca spread butter onto a roll with deliberate care.

Joaquin popped another peanut into his mouth, his fist tightening around the shell. *Good?* The word lingered. "Why do you ask? Are *you* interested?"

Luca took a slow bite of his roll, chewed, and swallowed before answering. "Yeah, actually, I am."

Joaquin opened his fist, letting the shell drop to the ground.

"I promise I won't ask her out until we're done with this case. Just wanted to make sure you're cool with it."

Across the restaurant, a server announced a customer's birthday, prompting cheers and applause.

Joaquin rubbed his forehead. Luca was right; it was too loud here. And too hot. He tugged his shirt away from his chest in short, irritated bursts, trying to air out the sticky fabric. The mix of yeasty bread, beer, and vinegar from the wings churned in his stomach—or maybe it was the thought of Luca and Melrose.

He looked over at Luca, tearing through another roll. How the hell did he eat like that and still have a six-pack?

Luca wiped his mouth with a napkin. "Enough about that. Let's get down to business. I know I was sold on Ollie and Bruce Ford, but I finally think it's time we shift our focus."

Joaquin set his beer aside and reached for his water, squeezing a wedge of lemon into the glass. "To who?"

"Hayes Sheridan. Remember you told me Troy said Hayes and Wendy were close?"

"He didn't say *close*," Joaquin replied. "He said they worked on a big science project senior year."

"Okay, but it's still a connection between victims four and five. So, I did some digging."

Joaquin leaned forward, elbows on the table. "And?"

"So far, I can't find any connection to Andrea. But Hayes and Erin had been in school together since elementary. They had trig together senior year." Luca's brow lifted. "But Hayes told the cops he didn't really know her."

"Well, yeah," Joaquin said. "He might not have been close to Erin. Did you talk to everyone in all your classes?"

"Okay, I'll give you that. But let's talk about Nicole Garcia."

The name of the Strangler's first victim snapped Joaquin to attention. "Hayes knew Garcia?"

Luca reached into his jacket pocket and tossed a folded paper onto the table.

Joaquin unfolded the paper, which appeared to be a printout of a photo from someone's Facebook page. It showed a grainy image of a large group of high schoolers in front of a Pineview Baptist Church bus. "Church camp?"

"Yep. Nicole Garcia's parents posted it on her tribute page."

Joaquin scanned the photo, eyes settling on Nicole—her long black hair cascading around her face, a soft smile on her lips. But the Sheridans were Methodist, and none of the lanky boys in the group looked like Hayes. "I'm not following."

Luca twirled his straw. "Look behind the kids—in the bus."

Joaquin squinted, then froze. Sure enough, through the bus's front door window, he spotted someone standing on the steps—jet-black hair catching the light, unmistakably Hayes Sheridan. "Strange," Joaquin said. "Why wasn't he in the group pic?"

"I had the same question, so I started digging," Luca said. "First stop was the former youth pastor, Dex Henley. Turns out Red Sheridan was the one driving the bus for that trip. He got his CDL so he could take the Methodist kids to church camp every year. When the Baptist church driver had a family emergency, Red stepped in."

Joaquin set the photo down, leaning back. "So Hayes tagged along? What year are we talking?"

"Summer of eighty-five."

Joaquin glanced at the group photo again. "Looks like half the town went to that camp. Who's to say Nicole and Hayes crossed paths?"

Luca smirked and slid a Polaroid across the table. "I paid a visit to Nicole's parents. Unlike the other victims' families, they're open to the idea that Troy might be innocent. They let me borrow Nicole's scrapbook. I didn't find much, but look at this."

Joaquin snatched the Polaroid, brow furrowed as he studied it. A pale blond teen with braces flashed a peace sign by the ocean. "This isn't Hayes."

Luca sighed. "Look again. In the water."

Joaquin scanned the photo again. There, in the ocean, were a boy and a girl. Nicole was on Hayes's shoulders, laughing down at him while he returned her smile.

"Holy shit," Joaquin murmured. "Did the youth pastor remember seeing them together?"

Luca shook his head. "Henley didn't remember them spending time together and never saw Hayes at their church again after the trip. But it doesn't mean something didn't happen at camp—something that burned out in a bad way."

Joaquin studied the photo again, the weight of its implications sinking in as the server delivered their food. "Weren't Hayes and Tilly dating that summer?"

"So what?" Luca quipped, cutting into his chicken fried steak. "You're telling me you never cheated on a girlfriend in high school?"

"I've *never* cheated," Joaquin replied. "Unless you count in court."

"This is something." Luca took a bite. "Even if he didn't talk to some girl from trig class, he knew the one sitting on his shoulders."

Joaquin crunched a fry. "Why lie to the cops?"

"That's what I'm going to find out. Pastor Dex might not know what happened after lights out, but you can bet your ass those kids did."

Joaquin squirted mustard onto his burger. "Nice work, man." He wasn't hungry, but brought the burger to his mouth, anyway. His phone buzzed.

*Melrose.* Setting the burger down, he slid out of the booth. "Excuse me," he told Luca.

"Hello?" Joaquin moved through the noisy restaurant, searching for a quiet corner. "Melrose?"

"I'm here." Her voice wavered. "Are you busy? You sound busy."

"Just grabbing a bite with Luca. What's up?"

"I need to have a chat with you," she said, her voice trembling.

Joaquin stopped mid-step. "Are you alright?"

A muffled sob came through the line.

"Melrose, talk to me," he urged, weaving through waitstaff and patrons to reach the door.

"I haven't been honest with you," she confessed.

"What do you mean?" Joaquin pushed through the crowd and stepped outside. The night air did little to cool the heat creeping up his neck, his pulse hammering in his temples.

"Meet me at the office when you're finished," she said. "Alone. Got something to show you."

Joaquin's heart sank as the call disconnected. He stood beneath the flickering neon of the restaurant's sign, staring at his phone in a daze.

Whatever Melrose had to show him, he had a feeling it was about to change everything.

# CHAPTER 28

"You alright, kid?" Greer was barely off the floor when Red shuffled in behind her, steadying himself with his walker.

She swiped under her eyes, hoping to erase any telltale streaks of mascara. "Yep, just decorating the tree. Did you need something? Why didn't you ring your bell?"

"Nah." Red eased himself onto the couch with a grunt. "I wanted to check on you."

Greer's ears burned. Red had probably heard everything. "Sorry if I woke you."

"This is your house. Smash ornaments, yell at my son—make as much noise as you want."

Greer grabbed a throw pillow from the loveseat. "Here, let's get you propped up."

"Don't fuss," Red muttered as Greer tucked the pillow behind his back. It pained her to see him looking so frail. What started as a doctor's visit for heartburn, nausea, and vague stomach discomfort turned into a devastating stage four stomach cancer diagnosis.

She sat beside him. "Did you hear what we were arguing about?"

When Red shook his head, Greer exhaled in relief. She needed to remember to keep her voice down now. Explaining everything to Red felt even more daunting than confronting Hayes.

"But if you want to fill me in, I'm all ears."

Greer shook her head. "Better save it for therapy. Get my money's worth, you know?"

He frowned. "You're still seeing that shrink?"

"Dr. Nick, yep—twice a month." Greer started therapy three weeks after Caleb died and had never stopped. At first, Hayes wasn't thrilled about it.

"Couldn't you have picked a female therapist?" he once grumbled.

She'd shut him down with a single sentence: "Couldn't you have picked a male receptionist?"

Hayes never mentioned Dr. Nick again.

"Well, I guess that's the norm now. Glad it's helped you." His eyes drifted to the mantle, landing on Caleb's stocking. "I know you wanted Hayes to go with you, and it's my fault he won't. Things were different in my day, honey. We were taught to keep our feelings to ourselves, and I raised Hayes to do the same."

"You did great with him. We all have our issues."

"I sure tried to do better than my dad."

Red's father had passed before Greer met Hayes. Hayes never knew him, and Red rarely spoke of him. But maybe as Red's life neared its end, that had changed.

Greer took a chance. "What was your father like?"

"Horrible," Red said without hesitation. "Abusive."

Greer sank a little deeper into the loveseat, eyes flicking to the string of garish Christmas lights draped across the mantle. "I'm sorry," she said.

Red scratched at his face with a jagged nail, and Greer made a mental note to clip them later. "As heartbroken as I was when my mom took off, I didn't blame her. Well, not for leaving anyway—just for not taking me with her."

Greer remembered the time she had left Hayes to live with her mom. She didn't take her girls either. It never crossed her mind then, something she was ashamed of now. But at least she didn't leave them with someone like Red's father.

"Well, you understand what it's like to be abandoned by a parent," Red said.

Greer nodded. "Yeah, but I was so young I don't remember my dad. My life was probably better without him." She nudged Red. "After all, I had you."

A soft smile tugged at the corners of his mouth, his eyes crinkling with something like pride. "If I remember right, you took care of yourself."

"No way, Red. You were always there. Remember that father-daughter dance in middle school? Tilly talked about it for months. As much as I tried to act like I didn't care, I did."

"Of course you did," Red said.

"So, Joanne took me to get a dress. She curled my hair, and you took me to the dance—total princess treatment."

"Well," Red said with a chuckle, "now you're feeding me and emptying this bag of piss I have to carry around. I'd say taking care of you was a lot easier by comparison."

Greer laughed. "Least I can do. You were so good to me, Red, so good to all of us."

Red averted his gaze, his expression clouding. "Not *all* of you."

"What do you mean?"

Red sighed. "Troy. As much as I tried to help, it wasn't enough."

Greer froze, unsure how to respond. Why was he thinking about Troy? Did he catch something on the news, or was he lying about not overhearing her argument with Hayes?

"They're about to kill him, right?" Red asked, his voice heavy.

Not if she could help it. "Well, a date is set for January. But Troy's got a new lawyer now. He's supposedly good."

Red gripped the blanket on his lap. "To say my emotions are mixed is an understatement. Troy was like a son to me. Imagine if you found out your boy had done such horrible things."

Greer's eyes drifted to the red stocking hanging from the mantle, Caleb's name embroidered on it in green cursive. She couldn't imagine her sweet boy ever doing anything monstrous. Not Caleb. Not ever.

"I didn't want to go to the police," Red said after a pause. "You know that, right? Joanne pushed me. She saw what keeping it all bottled up was doing to me."

"That must have been hard."

"I didn't want to write the damn book either. My agent kept pushing me, and offers kept rolling in." He threw up his hands. "Listen to me—guess I'm more of a pushover than I'd like to admit."

"You had to write the book," Greer assured. "You were a crime writer. This was your big break. Someone was going to write about it—why not the one who lived it?"

Red gave a wry smile. "It takes a lot of courage to be in our profession. I know I told you a thousand times, but it's true. Journalism is not a job for someone who wants to be liked. A good journalist ruffles a lot of feathers on their way to the truth. The truth has to matter more than anything or anyone."

*Even your husband*, she thought. *Your daughters. Your church. Your father-in-law.*

The silence that followed was heavy. Greer's thoughts drifted to the text from Troy's lawyer about the missing phone records. *Ask Red how he knew Tilly called you that night.*

"Well, all this talking wore me out." Red slapped his thighs, cutting into her thoughts. "Naptime for me."

As Greer helped Red to his feet, he gripped her forearm firmly. "Don't worry about Hayes. He'll get over whatever's got his dander up. He'll remember you're the best thing that ever happened to him and be home in time for dinner."

Greer wondered if she really was the best thing that had ever happened to Hayes. Or a consolation prize?

Red must have sensed doubt because he spoke again. "What? You don't believe me?"

Fidgeting with her wedding ring, Greer hesitated before replying. "Sometimes I wonder what would've happened if Tilly . . ." She trailed off, unable to say it aloud. But Red understood.

"Wouldn't have lasted," he said. "They weren't right for each other."

Greer studied the floor. "That Fourth of July, I told him how I felt. He said he didn't feel the same about me." Her voice cracked. "That's why I left your house so fast that night." She swallowed hard. It seemed childish to still be insecure decades of marriage later.

"Hayes told me about that eventually," Red said. "But he also told me how he chased after you."

Greer let out a strained laugh. "Oh, yeah—chased me all the way to the driveway."

Red shook his head. "He wanted to go after you. Got his keys and everything. He would've driven around looking for you if I hadn't stayed up to watch a movie."

Greer pinched the bridge of her nose. *Why am I dredging this back up? It doesn't matter anymore.* "You need to rest." She moved to his side, placing a steady hand on his back to support him as he maneuvered the walker toward the bedroom.

By the time they reached the bed, Red was weak and winded. Greer eased him down, fluffing his pillow before helping him settle in. "Here," she said, holding a glass of water with a straw to his lips.

Red drank without protest, then let his head sink into the pillow. His eyes closed almost immediately, and his breathing evened out. Greer turned to leave but stopped short when she heard a low grunt, something that almost sounded like her name.

She turned back. "Did you say something?"

Red's eyes fluttered open. "I'm sorry Hayes didn't follow you that night," he murmured. "But I'm sure glad he caught up with you eventually."

Greer let herself smile, the tension in her chest easing a bit as she straightened and closed the door behind her.

Greer pulled out her cell phone. No missed calls, no texts. She considered texting Hayes, but he was the one who left, who needed *some goddamn space*, so she tossed the phone on the coffee table.

She stared at the tree she'd spent the afternoon decorating. It looked beautiful, warm, and inviting—like a picture from a holiday card. But her life was no Christmas card. The perfect facade couldn't mask the cracks running beneath the surface.

From behind her, a door opened. Greer turned to see her mother-in-law clutching her robe. "Did you need something, Joanne?"

"Just wondering if you might bring a few of those boxes from storage tomorrow?"

Greer tilted her head back slightly. Joanne had refused to get rid of at least half of her possessions, even though they both knew she'd no longer need them. "Is there something specific you need?"

"Well, yes." Joanne glanced down at the floor before looking back. "I want to start scrapbooking again. I thought I could use the leftover materials from the girls' books to make something for Silas."

Greer felt guilty about being annoyed. "That would be nice, Jo. I'll find it tomorrow. Any idea which box it's in?"

Joanne tapped a finger on her lip. "It's been so long since I used them, I'm not sure, but I might have stored them in Red's office. Oh, and while you're at it, can you find my recipe box?"

"I'll look. First thing tomorrow."

Joanne thanked her and said goodnight, but instead of returning to her room, she glanced around uneasily. "Is Hayes still not home? He doesn't normally work on Sundays."

Greer breathed a sigh of relief that at least Joanne hadn't overheard all Red had that afternoon. "Hayes will be home soon," she said, willing it to happen.

Joanne nodded, seemingly satisfied, and turned back into her room.

Greer leaned over the coffee table to check her phone again. Nothing. She stood. Now was as good a time as any to look for that box.

Grabbing the keys to the storage unit, Greer stepped outside. The moment she set foot on the back patio, a wave of calm washed over her. The air smelled faintly of pine and wood smoke from the nearby fire pit, grounding her in the present while stirring memories of lazy afternoons spent here with the kids. This was her favorite part of the house. Hayes had brought her vision to life with a pergola that balanced sun and shade during the day and a fire pit to keep things warm long after sunset. Little touches like fairy lights, comfy furniture, and a soft rug created the cozy atmosphere she had longed for during those chaotic early days of motherhood.

But she hardly spent any time out here anymore. Pine needles littered the floor, and the cushions, musty from neglect, were in desperate need of a wash.

One detail of the patio had been a surprise for Greer—the porch swing. Not just any swing, but the one from Red and Joanne's patio.

Hayes had refinished it, moved it here, and engraved their names on the armrest.

How long had it been since anyone had sat on it? Greer hesitated for a moment before carefully lowering herself onto the swing, the wood creaking as she leaned back. She closed her eyes, listening for the familiar sounds of East Texas, but the night was as quiet as her phone.

Her fingers traced the engraving: *Hayes and Greer, 1-1-89.* The date of their first kiss, on this very swing. It was their junior year of college, and Hayes and Greer had all but lost touch after her decision to attend Texas Tech instead of following him to the University of Texas.

Hayes hadn't come home the summer before, so it had been a year since they'd seen each other. On a whim, Greer accepted Red's invite to their New Year's Eve party. When her eyes met Hayes's across the room, she knew something had changed. She could now recognize the look of a man interested in a woman—something she'd given up hoping to see from Hayes.

What had changed? Was it her longer hair? The blonde highlights? The fitted jeans and off-the-shoulder black sweater she'd worn? Or was it the rose-pink lipstick Hayes Sheridan would soon smear? It might have been something deeper, too—a realization of how much he'd missed her, their shared trauma, a longing for the comfort he'd only experienced with her. All these years later, she'd never bothered asking. They'd sat on the back porch swing for hours, knees touching, as they caught up. Greer glimpsed two chicken pox scars on Hayes's forehead she'd never noticed before. It was maybe the first time she'd realized that Hayes Sheridan wasn't perfect.

Despite all the signs of interest she'd recognized—the intense eye contact, flushed skin, and playful touches—she was still taken aback when, just before midnight, Hayes asked, "So, are you seeing anyone?"

"Yes," Greer had answered. She'd been seeing Tate Adams, a fellow journalism student, for the past six months.

Hayes looked at the pavement. "Is it serious?"

"No," Greer said, because how serious could it be if she still felt this way about Hayes?

Then, as if they were in some cheesy rom-com, a firework exploded above them. Hayes looked at his watch—a silver Fossil that hung loosely on his wrist, making him look more grown-up somehow. "Someone's a little early," he said.

Another premature firework, set off much closer, startled Greer. Hayes touched her leg. "You okay? Don't you love these things?"

"Not anymore," she'd said. "Now they take me back to . . . well, you know."

"Yeah, I get that," he said, just as Red and Joanne's party guests began the ten-second countdown to 1989.

"But I also think there's a way we could redeem them," he said, angling his body toward hers. The blare of noisemakers and cheers of "Happy New Year!" erupted from inside the house. More fireworks boomed, and Hayes Sheridan's lips met hers for the first time.

The memory of that night still made Greer smile, even tonight. A night after angry words, slammed doors, and silent phones.

Greer forced herself off the swing. She was being overly sentimental. As she picked up the keys to the storage, her father-in-law's words from earlier came to mind: *He wanted to follow you. He got his keys.*

Greer froze. But hadn't Joanne taken Hayes's keys that night? That was what he'd told the police, what Red and Joanne had corroborated. That there was no way Hayes could have left the house that night because Joanne had his keys.

A knot formed in Greer's stomach. Either Red was misremembering, or the Sheridans had all lied to the police.

# CHAPTER 29

After Melrose's urgent call, Joaquin asked the server for a takeout box and left in a rush, offering Luca the flimsy excuse of needing to meet with a client who'd been picked up for drugs again.

Racing to the office, Joaquin parked beside Melrose's SUV and hurried inside, his pulse hammering. "Melrose?" he called, the word coming out sharp and unsteady. "Is everything okay?"

Melrose emerged wearing a pink and black checkered pajama set and white tennis shoes. The makeup had been scrubbed from her face, and her hair was pulled back in a loose knot.

"I'm sorry," she said, glancing at the to-go bag. "You could've eaten first."

"No, I really couldn't, Melrose." Joaquin set the bag on Bernie's desk. "You called me crying." He took a step closer, his eyes searching her face. "I'm worried. What's going on?"

Melrose gestured toward the couch. "Can you sit?"

Joaquin's hands grew cold, a tingling sensation creeping up his fingers. He rubbed them together, trying to shake it off. "Whatever this is, it'll be okay. We'll figure it out."

Melrose took a slow breath, then lifted her purse from the floor. She hesitated before pulling something wrapped in paper towels from a side pocket.

She took a few unsteady steps toward him, unwrapping the object with trembling hands. When she placed it in front of him, it only took a second for Joaquin to recognize it—the chipped-tail dolphin that had been missing from the Llywelyn's wind chimes.

Joaquin shot to his feet. "Where did you get this?"

"I'm sorry."

"*Where* did you get this?" Joaquin demanded, louder now.

"Ollie Ford," she said, barely above a whisper.

Joaquin's heart pounded. "When?"

"A few days ago."

He exhaled, trying to process it. This explained her recent distance. He studied the dolphin. "Where were you when he gave you this?"

"At the grocery store, he remembered me."

"Okay, good. I bet the cameras caught that. Pray they haven't deleted it already." His gaze sharpened. "Did Ollie say anything else?"

"He said that he'd forgotten he had it, but that he wanted to give it to me since I'm such a fan of dolphins. It was very sweet."

"He's a killer, Melrose. That's what this means."

"You don't know that."

"I do," Joaquin said. "And so do you. Otherwise, you wouldn't be so reluctant to show this to me. You shouldn't still be touching it." He turned toward the kitchen. "There are gloves in there. Let's bag it up."

"Joaquin, the police can't recover fingerprints after all this time," she said, wrapping the dolphin back in the paper towels.

"What are you doing?" Joaquin asked.

Melrose slid it into a zippered compartment in her purse. "I don't think we need to turn it in."

Joaquin poked his tongue into his cheek. "Have you lost your mind?"

Melrose eased her purse over her shoulder, brushing against the stack of magazines on an end table. "It might not even be the right one."

"It's got the chipped tail, Melrose. Come on."

"Well, it doesn't matter. Ollie didn't kill anyone," Melrose said.

"Okay, Bruce, then. Either way, this is huge."

"No, not Bruce either. If you'd stop jumping to conclusions and listen, I'll tell you the rest of the story."

Joaquin leaned against the edge of Bernie's desk. "Alright, I'm listening."

"I asked Ollie where he got it. He said he'd found it ages ago. He's got a huge box of treasures he's found in the woods."

Joaquin stared without blinking. "Come on, Melrose. I know you've got a soft spot for the guy, but you're too smart to believe he happened to stumble across this piece of evidence. The cops have searched those woods a hundred times."

"Well, they missed Troy's ring, didn't they?" she shot back.

Joaquin stormed into the kitchen, yanked a ziplock bag from the drawer, and slammed it on the counter. "Bag it. We have a legal obligation."

"Even if it puts another innocent man in prison? Did Luca tell you about the picture he found with Hayes?"

Joaquin dropped the bag to the floor. "Why are you talking with Luca?"

"Why are *you* so insecure? We're all on the same team."

"Well, that's what I thought, but that death grip on your purse suggests you might be playing for Oliver Ford's team."

Melrose pulled out her keys. "You know, you run your mouth about Red Sheridan wanting to be famous for solving the case. And how, in his zeal, he ruined someone's life. Now you're doing the bloody same thing! You don't want the truth; you want to be the one who cracked the case."

Joaquin's jaw tightened. "You don't know what you're talking about. Unlike you, I'm willing to put my emotions aside and look at every angle.

Lawyers have to lead with their heads, not their hearts." He turned away, hands on his hips. "Leave the dolphin, or you're fired."

From behind him, he heard the sound of a zipper opening and keys rustling.

"No need," Melrose said. "I can't work with you."

Joaquin whipped around to see the dolphin and Melrose's office key on the countertop. "Come on, you're being childish," he said.

Melrose picked up the dolphin, still wrapped in paper towels. "Childish? That would be smashing it to bits."

For a second, Joaquin thought she might. He'd never seen such darkness in her eyes. But instead, she grabbed the ziplock bag from the floor, placed the dolphin inside, and held it out to him. "You don't need me. You've got your evidence. Case closed."

"Melrose—"

"Take it!" She shoved the bag closer to his face.

As soon as he grabbed it, Melrose pushed past him and out the front door.

Unable to calm his shaking hands, Joaquin set the bagged dolphin back on the counter. What in the hell had just happened? Before he could make sense of it, his phone buzzed in his pocket.

He wondered if it might be her, but instead, Luca's name flashed on the screen.

"What's up, Luca?"

"You still at the jail?" Luca's voice crackled through the line.

Joaquin braced himself against the counter. "Just left. Why?"

"Have you checked your email?"

"No. Why?"

"Check it," Luca said. "Then meet me at your office."

Joaquin ended the call and opened the Outlook app on his phone. His eyes scanned his messages until he spotted the email in question. His fingers slick with sweat, he struggled to tap the message open. Finally, it loaded. Joaquin's eyes widened.

To: joaquin.ramos@ramoslawfirm.com
CC: morettil@dpap.org
From: alcoplabs@results.com
Subject: DNA Results

Dear Mr. Ramos,

Thank you for trusting Alcop Labs to perform your recent DNA testing. The results are waiting for you on our secure server. Please create a username and password to review the results . . .

# CHAPTER 30

Greer kept touching the back of her neck, still startled by how bare it felt. She adjusted the rearview mirror for another look, hardly recognizing herself. She hadn't worn her hair this short since middle school, but the chocolate brown bob suited her.

"You look hot," Jade, her best friend and hairdresser, had said, spinning her to face the mirror. "Like Uma Thurman in *Pulp Fiction*."

What was it her mom always said? "Don't cut your hair when you're sad." But Jade disagreed. "It's just hair," she'd said. "If you hate it, we'll fix it."

Hayes hadn't come home last night. On her way to the hair appointment, Greer drove past his office. His Toyota Tacoma sat in its usual spot. He must have slept on his office couch. At least, she hoped he had.

So when she turned onto their cul-de-sac after running errands and spotted his truck in the driveway, her breath hitched. Hayes never came home for lunch.

She fluffed her hair, then reached into the backseat for the Best Buy bags.

As soon as Greer stepped through the door, the scent of meat cooking hit her. The cumin and chili powder gave it away—Hayes was making his famous fajitas. Hopefully, this was his way of apologizing.

Joanne rose from the couch when Greer walked in. "Goodness gracious, I barely recognized you."

Greer dropped the bags and touched the back of her hair. "Do you hate it?"

Joanne's lips pressed into a thin line, eyes flicking away. "No, honey. It's darling. Just . . . different."

Hayes stepped into the living room, metal tongs in hand. His chest stiffened, and he blinked at Greer. "Wow, I was going to ask where you've been all morning, but I guess mystery solved."

Greer said nothing. So much for an apology.

"I'll go check on Redman," Joanne said, clearly eager to escape the tension.

Greer waited until she heard Red's door close before continuing. "I didn't realize you'd be home for lunch."

Hayes walked back into the kitchen. "Obviously."

Greer followed him. "Well, seeing as you didn't bother coming home last night, can you blame me?"

He froze mid-step, the tongs clattering slightly in his grip. "Look, I don't care what you do all day, but what if my parents had needed something?"

"They both have my number and the number of the home health agency."

Hayes slammed a cutting board onto the counter and yanked the cabinet closed, his jaw tight. His eyes flicked to hers, vulnerable for a brief instant before the tension returned. "Might've been hard to rush home with dye in your hair."

"If I'm such a bad caretaker, fire me and hire a full-time nurse."

She bit her tongue, stopping herself from adding—make sure she's not young and blonde. She'd promised Hayes she wouldn't bring up Ally Swanson again.

Hayes exhaled slowly, shoulders slumping a fraction as he sliced a bell pepper. "You're not a bad caretaker. It's just . . . I came home to apologize, and I guess it didn't feel great you weren't here."

"Imagine my night. I didn't want to do that again—sit at home wondering if you'd be coming home. So, Jade got me in for a hair appointment, then I went to Best Buy for podcasting equipment."

Hayes tossed the pepper core into the trash. "So you *are* doing a podcast? I didn't realize that was already decided."

Greer rested her arms on the counter. "You said get the equipment. Told me I had the voice for it? Remember?"

Hayes nodded, peeling an onion. "Where are you setting it all up?"

"In the office."

"I thought we were putting a guest bed in there," Hayes said, reaching for a dish towel. "For when Si spends the night or Farren comes home."

"There's a sofa in the office, and a few air mattresses in the closet," Greer replied.

"We should've moved into my parents' house. We'd have more rooms."

"We don't need more rooms," Greer said, leaving unsaid what Hayes already knew—that Red wouldn't need his room much longer. "I'm not even close to starting the podcast yet," she added.

"If you're not ready to start, why'd you buy all the equipment?" Hayes asked, the knife moving faster than necessary through an onion.

It was a fair question, and Greer wasn't sure how to answer. There was a chance she'd done it for the same reason she'd cut and dyed her hair—as her own little act of defiance against Hayes Sheridan.

"Jade's salon is across from Best Buy, so I thought, two birds, one stone."

Hayes placed the knife on the counter and rubbed the back of his neck, eyes meeting hers. "I came home to apologize, and I'm being an ass."

Greer couldn't tell if the tears in his eyes were from the onion or from a heartbreak that mirrored her own.

He wrapped his arms around her. "I'm sorry, Greer," he murmured into her freshly dyed hair. "It's just . . . all this stuff with Troy, on top of my dad's health, and Christmas is always hard." He pulled back, looking at her. "I saw Caleb's stocking hanging up when I came in, and it hurt. Doesn't it make you sad to see it?"

"I'm sad no matter what," Greer said. "I want us to acknowledge him."

Hayes held her tighter. "Fair enough." When he pulled back, he tucked a strand of hair behind her ear and smiled. "This looks nice."

"I know you like it better long." She left out the part about how he seemed to prefer blondes.

Hayes turned back to the pan. "A woman's hair is her prerogative."

Greer pulled out a barstool and sat. "Are you off for the rest of the day?"

"Sure am," Hayes said, wiping his hands on a towel before flinging it over his shoulder. "Can I take you on a date—a movie after lunch?"

Greer fought the urge to be catty, to comment about how that would involve leaving his parents alone. Hayes was trying. She could try, too. "Sure." She forced a smile. "Sounds fun."

Greer couldn't sleep. Maybe it was the adrenaline from the dumb action film Hayes had chosen, the basket of breadsticks she'd devoured at Olive Garden for dinner, or the overwhelming ammonia smell of her hair.

Once Hayes started snoring, she slipped into the living room. Her equipment still sat in bags by the couch. Would anyone listen to a podcast about exonerated death row inmates? Maybe—if her first guest was Troy Terrell.

Was it wrong to think about that already?

Probably, but an exclusive with Troy could launch her post-retirement career. One good story could be the difference between clawing up the charts and skyrocketing straight to the top.

But Troy had to be exonerated first. Hayes hadn't mentioned Troy, the podcast, or her upcoming *Breakfast with Texas* interview at dinner, and she hadn't brought up Red's claim about the keys. She figured they'd altered their story to avoid suspicion that Hayes had left the house that night. While she believed he hadn't, the lie still bothered her.

She needed a distraction. She might as well look for Joanne's scrapbooking supplies after abandoning the search the night before.

Out back, she unlocked the tool shed—now Red and Joanne's storage unit—and pushed the door open. Dust swirled as she yanked the cord; the air reeked of fertilizer, gasoline, and rusted tools.

She found three large boxes labeled "Red's office." She shifted a stack of paint cans aside and swept away some sawdust with a broom to create a space to sit.

She dug through the first box but found only books and office supplies. She sighed. Hayes should've been more ruthless when packing and forced Joanne to part with more of their junk.

She noticed a brown accordion file at the bottom of the box and pulled it out. *Intruder in the Valley* was scrawled across it in Red's messy handwriting. Greer realized this file must have contained the notes he'd used to write his debut book. Not scrapbook supplies, but something far more interesting. She set it aside, wondering if he had a similar file for each book he'd written—wondering if there was one about Troy.

Greer ripped open the second box, oddly let down to find Joanne's scrapbooking supplies instead of more of Red's brown accordions. With a sigh, she closed it and shoved it behind her, planning to take it back inside later. But she couldn't stop now—she still had to check the third box.

Sure enough, the third box held five more accordions—one for each of Red's books. Greer spotted the one labeled *Son and Songbird* and picked it up. She paused before opening it. These were private notes. She should ask Red first.

Most days, she didn't feel fifty-six, but getting off the floor was a different story. She stumbled as she tried to rise, barely catching herself as the accordion tumbled from her arms.

"Good one, Greer," she mumbled, bending to collect the file and scattered papers. When she picked up the Southwestern Bell bill, she assumed it was one of the Sheridans' old phone bills misplaced. But when she looked closer, she saw the name Larry Price on the yellowed paper— Tilly's father. The dates listed for the phone calls made her realize what this was and why Red had it in his book file. This was how he knew Tilly had called Greer's home. It wasn't subpoenaed by the state or Troy's lawyer; it had been provided to Red by his friend, Larry. Greer found the phone call in question on the second page of the bill. Her hands shook when she saw it in black and white: the 10:45 p.m. phone call made to Greer's childhood phone number.

At 10:45, Greer had been with Hayes, ready to pour out her heart. Troy said he'd been driving down back roads, trying to come to terms with what had happened with Tilly. And what was Tilly doing? Calling Greer. Why? Was she wondering where her friend was, or was she scared about something? Did she see a strange car outside? Hear a noise from another room? Greer would never know, and the uncertainty still knotted her stomach. She nearly shoved the bill back into the file when something beside the phone call caught her eye. Under the "minute" column: the number four. That meant the call to Greer's house had lasted four minutes. But how could it, when she hadn't been home?

She blinked to clear the spots from her vision as the answer hit her, bringing more questions. Which brother spoke to Tilly that night? And why had they kept it a secret?

# CHAPTER 31

Joaquin slammed his hands against the steering wheel in the prison parking lot. The leather absorbed most of the impact, but his palms still stung. His eyes burned worse—like they were packed with salt. He hadn't slept since seeing the DNA results the night before.

"There's good news here," Luca said from the passenger seat. "The semen sample taken from Wendy Knott's clothing excludes Troy as the donor. We'll test her ex; if that fails, CODIS first, then forensic genealogists. Ancestry sites are cracking cases left and right."

"For what, another eight grand?" He reversed and hit the gas.

"Troy's DNA in Tilly's sample isn't a surprise," Luca added, clicking his seatbelt. "Sure, we hoped otherwise, but it's not the end of the world. We'll share the results in our interview and control the narrative."

Joaquin realized Luca was right on both counts. They'd braced for the confirmation about Troy and Tilly. But the third test—that was the gut punch. "Well, good luck spinning a narrative about how Wendy Knott's blood ended up in Troy Terrell's truck," Joaquin said.

Luca sighed. "It *might* be Wendy's blood. Certainty comes only if they exhume her body and get a sample."

"It's hers, Luca. A sample from her isn't necessary—they have her parents' DNA. The relationship test is enough to prove it."

Luca pointed to a speed limit sign. "Wanna slow down a little, hotshot?"

"Not really," Joaquin said, though he eased up on the gas pedal, anyway.

"If he's lying about Wendy never being in his truck, he's damn convincing," Luca said, leaning an elbow on the center console. "The shock on his face seemed real. This could be a setup. Wendy's body had already been found, so Bluesummer PD had her blood. And you're telling me Troy moved a bludgeoned body and left only a speck of blood in his truck? Looks like we've got a dirty cop or two involved."

Joaquin gripped the steering wheel a little tighter, eyes on the road. "Yeah, well, good luck convincing most of the public that a shiny piece of metal pinned to someone's chest doesn't automatically make them the good guy."

"Well, I don't see another option. Melrose can come up with something."

Joaquin winced. Clearly, Luca hadn't heard she'd quit. But "quit" didn't tell the whole story—he'd let things spiral and threatened to fire her before she walked out.

"What? What's that face about?" Luca asked.

Joaquin filled Luca in on Ollie, the dolphin, and Melrose.

"I'll talk to her," Luca said. "She was just angry. She won't give up on Troy."

Joaquin checked his phone again. No response to the three texts he'd sent this morning. Melrose had certainly given up on him.

"I can take the dolphin to the cops today," Luca offered. "I'll ask Melrose to come. She's got to realize they'll have questions for her."

Joaquin slumped in his seat. "The cops won't do anything with the dolphin. Just like they didn't with Troy's ring."

"You just focus on the interview," Luca said. "Speaking of which, we need to see if Greer can meet with us. Practice the interview questions."

"I'm too busy," Joaquin said. "I need to file the motion before the interview, so I'll be in Tyler on Monday. That leaves today and tomorrow to add the dolphin and DNA stuff." He swallowed hard, his throat aching from holding back tears. "I'm so behind. Bernie's helping, but everything's piling up. And now with Melrose gone, it's gonna get worse."

"How can I help?" Luca asked.

Though Joaquin was almost drowning in his own self-pity, he hated Luca's. "You've got your own job to do. Speaking of, anything in the Fords' trash can yet?"

"Nope. Thinking I'll shift focus to Murphy's Market instead. I've seen Ollie show up with a lunch bag, so he must eat in the breakroom." He sighed. "So yep, that means I'm digging through a bigger trash can now."

Joaquin pictured the industrial-sized dumpsters behind the supermarket and couldn't help but laugh at the thought of Luca—tight polo, pressed slacks, and glossy dress shoes—rooting around in them. The mental image made him laugh, and soon Luca joined in. For a moment, the weight on Joaquin's chest lifted. Despite the jealousy he'd harbored over the past month, he realized how glad he was to have Luca in his corner. These days, Luca and Bernie were the closest things Joaquin had to friends.

Joaquin was surprised to see Bernie's car in the parking lot. "She must've left something at the office," he told Luca. But before they got out of his Jeep, Bernie walked out the door holding a ziplock bag containing the glass dolphin. "Is this what you needed, sugar?" she asked Luca.

"Yes, ma'am. Thank you."

Joaquin glanced between them, looking for answers, but Luca slapped him on the back and opened the door of his silver Mustang. "I'll take care of this. Call me if you need anything."

"What are you doing, Bernie?" Joaquin rubbed his head. "It is Saturday, right?"

"It is." Bernie pushed back through the office doors.

Joaquin followed her inside. "Then why are you here? And how did you know Luca needed the dolphin?"

"Must've been ESP."

Joaquin thought back to the drive from the prison—Luca texting furiously in the passenger seat. "Did Luca ask you to come?"

Bernie sat and adjusted her computer monitor. "He did."

"He shouldn't have done that. It's the weekend."

"I'm aware. Luca also mentioned you've got to be in Tyler on Monday to file the habeas. That was news to me."

"Last-minute decision. Filing before the interview makes us look more prepared—ahead of the game."

"What happens after you file?"

"The state has fifteen days to respond. Then the Court reviews any unresolved issues, makes findings, and sends it to the Court of Criminal Appeals."

"And you've got a good shot?"

"Not sure. A second habeas is a tough sell, and this is technically a third. But finding the missing evidence should be enough for the court to reconsider the case."

Bernie put in an earbud and started typing again. "Go to your office and dictate what I need to add to the habeas. I'll finish the orders for our other cases while you do."

"Bernie, you don't need to—"

"And after you're done dictating, take a nap. You look like hell."

Joaquin stretched out on the couch and covered his face with a pillow.

"I said *after* you get your work done," Bernie said.

Joaquin groaned into the pillow.

"For goodness' sake," Bernie said. Joaquin heard her chair roll away from her desk. "Listen, I won't even put this on my timesheet. What's the matter?"

Joaquin pulled himself into a seated position. "Oh, I don't know. Not only do we have to convince the public that Chantilly Price had consensual sex with Troy Terrell, but I also have to suggest the police planted Wendy's blood in his truck. Meanwhile, I'm ninety-eight percent sure Troy is lying to me, and that this case is going to end my career. I should withdraw as counsel."

Bernie glared at him, unblinking. "Well, boo-fucking-hoo. I knew you were a drama queen, but not a quitter."

Joaquin slouched. "Well, Melrose quit, so why can't I?"

Bernie froze. "She what?"

"She quit," he said, waving a hand. "I don't want to talk about it. There's too much work to do."

"Yeah, I know," Bernie said. "Why do you think I'm here? To give you a motivational speech?"

Joaquin sank lower into the couch. "Maybe I could use a little motivation."

"Okay, Joaquin. You want motivation? Here you go. I don't understand why you took this case. But whatever the reason, you did it against *all* my warnings. You did it at the expense of your other clients' cases, and I've picked up the slack."

"You're right, you're right. I'll give you a raise after—"

"I don't want a raise," Bernie interjected. "I want you to get off that couch and finish what you started. Don't let those fat-cat government bastards kill our client."

Joaquin raised an eyebrow. "*Our* client?"

"Well, hell, Joaquin. I pay attention. You've got me believing in this case, in this cause. If you give up now, Troy Terrell's not the only person you're disappointing."

Joaquin watched, dumbfounded, as Bernie rolled back to her computer and resumed typing. She was right. This was just a setback. All cases had them, and he needed to stop feeling sorry for himself. He stood, ready to thank Bernie, but noticed she'd put both earbuds in.

So, he thanked her wordlessly, picking up the dictation recorder off her desk and getting to work.

Joaquin usually passed commute time with audiobooks, but today, he couldn't focus. Scanning radio stations, he stopped on Taylor Swift's "Fortnight" and scream-sang the bridge, feeling every bit of Post Malone's angst—because Taylor wasn't the only one who wouldn't pick up her phone.

Joaquin checked his phone. Still nothing from Melrose. With a sigh, he tossed it onto the passenger seat, grabbed his Styrofoam cup, and chugged the last of the bland coffee. He was running solely on caffeine, but the motion was finished and packed into a plastic document envelope. He wouldn't mail it. Joaquin trusted the postal service about as much as he trusted the justice system. Too many lost letters, too many lost lives.

This was the longest petition Joaquin had ever written. Troy's original writ had been 192 pages—Joaquin made sure this one was longer at 201 pages. Some motions needed brevity, but not this one. This was the "kitchen sink" motion, a last-ditch effort to save a life. He could only hope it was enough.

Of course, he hadn't done it alone. There was no way it would've happened without Bernie, Luca, and Melrose. At the thought of Melrose, he reached for his phone again. Nothing.

He started to put his phone down, but hesitated. Should he text her one more time? Let her know he was filing the motion?

Before he could overthink it, he opened their text thread and dictated:

*Hey Melrose, sorry to bother you, but I'm heading to Tyler to file the motion. It got me thinking . . .*

He stopped, then erased it. Now wasn't the time for a "kitchen sink" text. Instead, he tried again.

*Look who's riding in my passenger seat.*

Joaquin leaned over to take a picture of the motion, but a horn blared, snapping his focus back to the road and the car inches from his door. His entire body tensed as Taylor and Post Malone's harmonies were drowned out by a jarring cacophony of screeching tires, crunching metal, and shattering glass. The airbag collided with his face just before everything went quiet.

# CHAPTER 32

Greer wandered the winding paths of Klyde Warren Park, scanning for Zach. When she told Hayes she was heading to DFW a day early to visit her brothers, he hadn't argued—not even about the interview. Still, she knew he disapproved. The girls must have heard because both texted, insisting Greer was making a mistake.

Was she?

When Troy's attorney called about the DNA results, old doubts crept back in. The findings pointed to him, but there were still too many loose ends to accept that. Like that four-minute phone call.

"Wanna slow down there? Some of us have short legs."

Greer looked up to see her brother's familiar sparkling smile.

She pulled him into a hug.

He stepped back, giving her the once-over. "Did you do something with your hair?"

"Yeah, covered the gray." Reaching up, she tousled his wavy locks. "You should try it sometime."

"Hey, at least I have some—unlike our brother." Zach smirked as he resumed walking, and Greer fell into step beside him. "Speaking of Keaton, why didn't you invite him?"

A winter breeze whispered through the barren trees lining the walkway, their branches swaying and creaking in the cold. Greer tugged her sweater tighter against the chill. "Because I have something big to talk about, and I didn't know how he was doing."

Zach stopped. "Big? Are you okay?"

Greer kept moving. "Yeah, it's nothing health-wise or anything."

Zach quickened his pace to match hers. "Well, Keaton's in a pretty good place right now. Samantha said he was doing some outpatient treatment program."

"Well, Sam's a saint," Greer said. She'd always admired her sister-in-law's patience and steady calm.

"You hungry?" Zach asked, nodding toward the line of food trucks along the park, the smoky tang of grilled meats and sweet wafts of fried dough drifting over to them.

Greer shrugged. "I could eat."

Zach headed to a ketchup-red and mustard-yellow truck. "You've gotta try these corn dogs." She reached into her bag, but Zach waved it off. "I got it."

Greer glanced around as they waited for their food. The park was an unusual yet peaceful oasis above the eight-lane freeway, its lawns, flowers, and busy walkways creating a space that blended nature and urban life in a way that just worked.

"Should we sit?" Greer asked once the vendor handed them each a corn dog.

"Wait." He gestured toward the condiments. "You've gotta add mustard for the full effect."

Greer set her drink down and held her corn dog under the ketchup dispenser, pushing the pump.

"Still gotta do everything opposite of me, huh?" Zach teased, squirting mustard in a zigzag across his corn dog.

"I've always hated mustard. You know that."

"You could squirt motor oil on this thing, and it'd still taste good."

Greer grabbed her drink and napkins, nodding toward a table. "Come on, let's sit and talk."

The orange table wobbled as she set down her drink and tray. "So, you ready for your close-up?" Zach asked.

Greer looked away. "Don't talk with your mouth full."

"Okay, Mom. Sorry, Mom." Zach wiped his lips with a napkin. "So, back to this big thing you wanna talk about. What's up?"

Greer straightened her legs under the table, then bent them again. "I found the Prices' July phone bill while going through Red's things. I'm guessing they gave it to him when he tried to piece the night together. Anyway, I noticed a call at our house."

"Yeah, that's not news. Red assumed she was trying to call you when Troy . . ." He stopped. "Well, you know."

"Why didn't he notice the call lasted four minutes?"

Zach's forehead furrowed. "Did the machine pick up?"

"We didn't have a machine then. Plus, you were home. Wouldn't you have heard the phone ring?"

"Yeah, I guess so. But Tara was the only one who called."

Greer leaned forward. "But did Keaton say it was Tara?"

Zach thought for a second. "No. He didn't want to talk, so . . ." He shook his head. "Shit."

"What?" Greer asked.

"It could have been Tilly."

"Why would Tilly and Keaton have a four-minute conversation? One that made him run out of the house?"

Zach sighed. "Look, don't kill the messenger, but Tilly and Keaton dated for a while."

Greer froze. "What do you mean? She was with Hayes."

"Tilly always liked Keaton. You knew that." He gestured at her untouched corn dog. "You gonna eat?"

Greer took a reluctant bite. It tasted good, but the revelation about Tilly and Keaton had killed her appetite.

"Tilly did have a crush on him," she said, sipping her lemonade. "But when we were little girls."

"That year he came home for spring break and never went back," Zach said. "I guess Tilly called when you weren't around. They talked for a while—she told him he deserved better than Tara and admitted she'd always had a crush on him. That kind of thing boosts a guy's ego when he's vulnerable."

"But she was with Hayes!" Greer repeated.

"I get it, Greer. I told Keaton he was playing with fire, but he was crazy about her. He bought her a custom diamond necklace shaped like a key." He paused, waiting for Greer to catch on. "Key, as in Keaton."

The key necklace. Greer remembered Tilly wearing it that summer and how she'd sent Hayes into the woods to find it.

"Tilly promised she was breaking up with Hayes," Zach went on. "When Keaton realized that wasn't happening, he ended things. She supposedly took it hard."

"When?" Greer shivered, curling slightly in her seat. "When did he break up with her?"

"Want my jacket?"

"No, I'm fine."

"Are you gonna eat the rest of your corn dog?"

Greer pushed it toward him. "When did they break up?"

Zach wiped some ketchup off her corn dog with a napkin. "Early June, maybe?"

Greer sat back, stunned. "Months of secretly dating, and I never noticed. How is that possible?"

"No clue. I didn't ask for details. But by the Fourth of July, they were done. I assumed it was Tara calling. I mean, she had just a few weeks before."

"Maybe Tilly and Keaton weren't done," Greer muttered, pulling her sweater tighter. "Tilly was wearing that key necklace the day she died."

Her mind raced. If Tilly had called Keaton, what would she have said to upset him? Where had he gone? And if it was all innocent, why hadn't he told anyone?

"This changes everything," Greer said. "We know Keaton has a propensity for violence."

Zach stopped mid-bite. "Come on. Maybe he took roughhousing a little too far, but it was normal brother stuff. Well, except for . . ."

"Except when he was choking me?" Greer's voice faltered as she recalled that terrible winter day. She'd been sitting at the kitchen table making Valentines—cutting hearts out of construction paper—when, suddenly, she was on the tile floor with Keaton's hands around her throat. She remembered nothing in between, nothing that could've explained the outburst. Thankfully, Zach had heard the crash and likely saved her life.

"That was his meds, Greer." Zach crossed his arms. "He didn't remember doing it. Mom took him to the doctor, and they got his dose regulated."

"It wasn't *just* his meds. He's always had something dark inside him. Maybe he's been violent with Samantha, or ex-girlfriends, or even strangers . . ."

Zach leaned back slightly in his chair, arms tightening across his chest. "What are you suggesting? I mean, I understand you don't believe Troy killed Tilly, but you don't have to sell out your own brother to prove it."

"I'm not selling him out!" Greer snapped. "I'm trying to make sense of this huge revelation that he was possibly the last person to talk to my best friend before she was killed. I'm not sure why I'm even talking to you about it. You've always defended Keaton. I'm calling Samantha."

"Don't call Sam with this garbage theory," Zach muttered, pressing his fingers to his temple. "She's been through enough."

"Meaning what?" Greer pressed. "Have you seen Keaton hurt her?"

"No, but after he was hospitalized, Bonnie and I helped Samantha with some repairs. There was a hole in the wall. I assume from Keaton."

"And did y'all ask her about it? If he ever hit her?"

"Of course. You know Bonnie," Zach said, a smirk tugging at his lips. "She's a fixer—why do you think she married me?"

"And what did Sam say?" Greer asked.

"She swore he never touched her, but she admitted he'd broken more than drywall around the house."

"What an asshole."

"Well, we all have our demons," Zach said.

"You remember that Christmas at my place when the twins were little? Hayes asked Samantha if they planned to have kids. She said it wouldn't be fair to bring children into their mess of a life. I always thought it was because of Keaton's depression, but now I'm wondering . . . what if it was about his abuse?"

"Greer, stop," he said, his mouth full, crumbs flying. "I mean, listen to yourself. You're suggesting our brother's a serial killer." He glanced around. "Keaton Collins. He's an accountant!"

"So was John List. He was a family annihilator who—"

"I don't wanna hear about John List." Zach shook his head. "Look, it doesn't matter if it was Tara calling or Tilly calling. Keaton went for a drive to cool off."

Greer leaned forward on the table, causing it to wobble again. "We should at least ask him about it."

"*We*? No way. Bringing it up might set him off. Set him back."

Zach had a point. Anything seemed to set Keaton off. She couldn't let herself truly believe he'd killed Tilly, but he might have been the last person to talk to her. Greer needed to hear what had been said during that conversation.

"So, are you going to drop it?" Zach asked.

Under the table, Greer crossed her fingers—like they always did when lying to each other as kids. "Sure," she said. "Consider it dropped."

Greer texted Keaton, setting up lunch at his office the next day—he never liked crowded, noisy places. Then she called Hayes, hoping for a quick, surface-level conversation before bed.

"Hi, babe!" Hayes's cheerful tone eased some of her tension.

Greer stretched out on the lumpy hotel bed. "Just letting you know I'm back at the hotel."

"Good deal. Did you have a nice visit with your brothers?"

"Yeah, just Zach today. Meeting Keaton tomorrow."

Hayes yawned. "Glad you called—I was about to text. Brad's out with the flu. He needs me to cover some client meetings in Austin. Big project. I'll be gone all week."

"Wow, Austin. Long drive. When do you leave?"

"Crack of dawn tomorrow."

Greer rolled to her side. "I won't be home till late tomorrow night. What about your parents?"

"Quinn and Si are going to hang out here till you're back."

"How nice of her," Greer said, trying to mask her jealousy. Quinn would have balked if Greer had asked.

As Hayes rambled about his trip, relief washed over her—he'd be gone, giving her space to think and sort things out without his probing questions. But relief gave way to guilt. What kind of wife was this, glad her husband was leaving? At seventeen, she'd never have believed Hayes Sheridan could wear out his welcome.

His voice pulled her back. "You still sure about the interview?"

Tension stiffened her muscles. "I'm here, aren't I?"

"I just want to make sure you've thought about how it'll affect Dad. The girls."

*Affect you*, Greer thought. She sat up. "Hayes, I'm not saying your dad was wrong or that Troy's innocent. I'm telling the truth about what I saw in the pool. That's all."

Hayes sighed. "I don't want to argue."

"Then don't." She glanced at the clock. "If you're leaving early, you should get some sleep."

"You're right. I'm exhausted. I'll call tomorrow."

"Okay. Goodnight." She was about to hang up when his voice softened.

"Greer."

"Yes?"

"I love you."

"Love you, too." A strange weight hung in the air. She wanted to say more, something to bridge the growing gap between them, but all she managed was a quiet: "I'll talk to you soon."

Still wide awake, she powered on her laptop. She had checked it daily since the DNA results, waiting for the story to leak. It hadn't. Seems the world would learn about Troy and Tilly tomorrow morning—when Joaquin Ramos and Greer revealed it to the viewing public.

She opened Facebook. She hadn't checked her page in months, growing weary of the election posts.

Farren's latest photo showed her with a new boyfriend. Greer hadn't met him, but he looked nice. Scrolling further, she found a collage Farren had posted last month. "Happiest of birthdays to my amazing Mama," the caption read. Warmth spread through Greer's chest. She hadn't been the best mother, but Farren never held it against her. Amiable, quick to forgive—so different from Quinn, who tallied every failure.

Greer commented on the post and then checked Quinn's page. There were a few new pictures of Silas she hadn't seen. She saved them to print for Joanne's scrapbooking.

She was about to log out, but hesitated, drawn to search for one more name.

Ally Swanson's profile picture hadn't changed. She was still sitting on that swing, blonde hair flowing, feet kicked out—a pose more suited for a four-year-old than a forty-two-year-old woman. Forty-two. The same age Hayes had been when he slept with her, back when Ally had been only twenty-eight.

Hayes had mentioned they'd hired a new receptionist, but said he doubted she'd last. She wasn't catching on. A few months later, he let her go. Greer never thought twice. She'd never worried about Hayes cheating. He was the most loyal person she knew.

Until he wasn't.

One night, after the girls were asleep, he confessed his secret to Greer.

It had only been once. He'd been drunk. It meant nothing. He made sure Ally was transferred right after. He'd never spoken to her again. Could they move on? Forget it happened?

But Greer pressed for details, journalist instincts overriding self-preservation. He answered every painful question. It happened after the company Christmas party—the one Greer missed because Farren had come down with the flu. So, while Greer was scrubbing vomit from the bedroom carpet, Hayes was having sex with a twenty-eight-year-old.

When Greer asked if Ally could be pregnant, Hayes assured her he'd used protection. That was when Greer realized he wasn't telling her the whole truth. A condom meant premeditation. It suggested what Greer had suspected all along: that while they'd only slept together once, and maybe that was the end of their affair, it hadn't been the beginning of it. There had been stolen glances, flirtations, late-night chats—something that prompted one of them to carry a condom to a company Christmas party.

Her final question caught him off guard. "Why did you tell me?" she cried. "If it meant nothing, why say anything?" She had always believed knowing the truth was better, but in that moment, she wished Hayes had kept his damn mouth shut.

"I've been convicted." He sniffled. Convicted—one of those trendy new church words that made her itch.

Greer packed her bags that night and showed up at her mom's door. She slept fitfully in her old bed, her mind racing. In the middle of the night, she logged onto her mom's computer to search for Ally Swanson.

What struck her most was how much Ally resembled Tilly—blue doe eyes, pale skin, petite frame, long satiny hair. A painful reminder that Greer had always been Hayes's second choice.

Yet, she eventually forgave her husband. They had children. She loved him.

He was so grateful, telling her she could ask anything, even check his phone. But she never did.

Still, she searched for Ally. Every few months, first on Myspace, then Facebook.

Through her searches, Greer learned that Ally married a surgeon but divorced before having kids. She probably lived on alimony. How else could she afford elaborate nails, platinum hair, and perky breasts while working reception at an H&R Block in Oklahoma?

Greer adjusted the fluffy hotel pillows behind her back, settling in to check what Ally had been up to since her last search. The newest post on her profile appeared only three hours ago. Greer read it, then slammed the laptop shut. It couldn't be. She must have read it wrong. Hands tingling, she opened it again. The words remained unchanged.

*Surprise, surprise, Texas friends, I'm in Austin for the rest of the week! Hit me up if you wanna hang.*

# CHAPTER 33

Joaquin struggled to open his eyes. The harsh overhead lights stabbed at his skull, amplifying the throb in his head. Pain radiated through his body, making every movement feel like static electricity. He shut his eyes again.

"Joaquin?" a familiar voice beckoned.

He opened his eyes and squinted, making out a man's figure beside the bed.

The chair beside him squeaked as it rolled back. "Nurse, he's awake," the man said into the hallway.

*Luca*, Joaquin realized.

Though Joaquin wanted to respond, to stay awake, he shut his eyes again. But the darkness didn't last long. A flashlight pierced it, cold fingers lifting his eyelids.

"Sir, can you hear me?"

"Yeah. What happened?"

"There was an accident," a nurse replied. "Do you know where you are?"

"A hospital?" Joaquin croaked, tasting the metallic tang of blood on his tongue.

"What's the date?"

"Uh . . . December . . . something. Monday, right?"

The nurse nodded. "My name is Conner. I'll be taking care of you. Any pain?"

Joaquin tried to shift in the bed. Flashes of agony shot through him. "Yeah," he admitted.

"Where?" Conner asked, pressing his icy fingers against Joaquin's wrist.

"Everywhere. Mostly my head."

Conner adjusted the stethoscope around his neck. "We'll get you something for that."

Joaquin swallowed, his throat feeling full of glass. As soon as Conner left to get water, Luca stood and pulled out his phone. "Your parents went back to the house to get your dad's blood pressure meds. I'll text them you're awake."

Joaquin forced himself to sit up. "How long have I been here?"

"About four hours."

"I ran a red light, didn't I?" Joaquin remembered the text, the picture, the blaring car horn. "And I'm in Tyler?"

Luca nodded.

"Was anyone else hurt?"

Luca stood, stretching his lower back. "Just cuts and scrapes."

Joaquin's hand fluttered to the side rail, gripping the cold steel. "Shit. The motion!"

"It took a trip through the windshield, but it survived. It's filed."

Joaquin exhaled shakily. "I guess I should've buckled it in."

Luca chuckled. "Kinda surprised the damn thing didn't kill you. Talk about a deadly projectile."

Luca stepped aside as the nurse returned with a cup of water. Joaquin took a few sips through a straw and winced; lifting his arm sent a sharp jolt of pain through his shoulder. He wiped his mouth and glanced at Conner. "So, when can I leave?"

"That's up to the doctor. I'm guessing she'll keep you overnight for observation."

"No." Joaquin pressed his fingers to his temple. "I have something important for work tomorrow."

Conner gave a sympathetic nod. "You can discuss that with the doctor. I'll make my rounds, but call if you need anything."

As soon as Conner was out of earshot, Joaquin looked at Luca. "I'm *not* missing the interview. I don't care if I have to yank this IV out myself."

"Relax. The interview's handled."

"Tell me you didn't cancel, Luca. The results will leak and—"

"Melrose and I are doing the interview with Greer," Luca interrupted, his voice cutting through Joaquin's panic.

The soft, rhythmic beep of the heart monitor filled the silence. Joaquin's gaze drifted toward the door. "Melrose?" he asked, his tone softening. "Melrose changed her mind?"

"I'll let her fill you in on that."

"Wait, she's here?"

"She stepped out," Luca said, glancing toward the doorway, "but she's been here all day—except when she left to file the motion."

More memories rushed back—Friday night at Texas Roadhouse, Luca saying he was going to ask out Melrose. Joaquin's ribs tightened. "So, she's here with you? Like with *you*?"

Luca's brows furrowed, his sneakers squeaking as he shifted. "No. She came because she was worried. Yes, I planned on asking her out, but I think she has feelings for someone else."

He opened his mouth to ask for more details, but paused when he spotted Melrose in the doorway. He lifted a hand. "Hey."

Melrose stepped closer, fingers twisting the strap of her purse. "I'm so glad you're awake."

Luca cleared his throat. "I need to make a phone call. You two can have a few minutes before Mom and Pop Ramos get back."

"Is Mom freaking out?" Joaquin asked. "They've never handled hospitals well—not since Glory."

"Yeah, you scared the hell out of them, but the doc assured 'em you're in the clear. I was glad Luca talked them into leaving to get your dad's meds. They needed a break."

Joaquin motioned to the chair. "You wanna sit or . . ."

"I'm good." Melrose's gaze flicked to the heart monitor, watching the steady rhythm for a beat before smirking faintly. "You know you didn't have to crash a car to get my attention."

"Apparently, I did. I mean, you're here." Joaquin glanced at the ceiling. "Should you be, though? With these lights?"

"I'll be fine. Do you remember how the accident happened?"

"I remember I was texting you."

"Joaquin!"

"I know, I know. But it's been eating at me, how things ended."

Melrose hesitated, taking a small step closer. Her voice dropped. "I wanted to talk to you, too, but I was embarrassed about how I carried on. I'm sorry."

"You? No way. I'm the one who's sorry."

Melrose reached out, her hand brushing his shoulder. The warmth of her skin seeped through the hospital gown. "I think we're both allowed to be sorry." She pulled back, straightening her spine as if she needed to recompose herself. "But hey, I'm available for rehire, if that's something you're interested in."

Joaquin struggled to focus, his thoughts swirling. Whether it was the injury or the weight of the moment, the words escaped unexpectedly: "I am interested—interested in you."

Melrose's lips parted in surprise, then curved into a teasing grin. "The doctor might want to review that CT scan again."

"I'm not joking, Melrose. There's something between us—I've felt it for a while. And maybe I'm way off, but I think you have, too."

Melrose gave a long, low sigh. Joaquin tried to read her expression and her body language, but neither gave him any clues. Finally, she spoke, her voice quiet. "Of course I have."

Joaquin tipped his head back, relief settling in. "Alright," he murmured, heart racing. "Then maybe I should be your boyfriend instead of your boss."

"That's not a good idea," Melrose said, absentmindedly tugging at her necklace.

The words hung in the air, thick and suffocating. Joaquin poked his tongue against his cheek, exhaling slowly. "I see."

Melrose moved the chair closer to his bed and sank into it. "I mean . . . I want this job. My focus needs to be on helping Troy."

"Okay," Joaquin said, forcing a laugh to mask the tightness in his chest. "Sorry, I wasn't thinking. Is it too late to blame the concussion?"

Melrose's expression softened. She placed her hand over his. "I'm flattered. I think we could be good together. But—"

Joaquin pulled his hand back. "No need to explain."

"If it weren't for this case . . ." She stopped, squeezing her eyes shut. "It's not the right time for us to be sidetracked. Do you understand?"

Joaquin nodded, the sting of rejection easing a little with her words. "So you're saying if . . ."

She rose, turning toward the window as if she needed distance. "I'm saying if things were different . . ."

"Then things could be different," Joaquin finished.

Melrose turned back, her eyes glistening. "Yes," she whispered. "Then things could be different."

"Ma'am?" Conner's voice came from the doorway again. "Sorry to interrupt, but Mr. Ramos's parents are in the lobby. Only two visitors allowed at a time."

"Right, of course." Melrose grabbed her purse and walked back to Joaquin's bed. She reached for him, fingers hovering above his hand before she pulled back. "Take care of yourself, Joaquin. Troy needs you."

Before Joaquin could ask if she'd be back, Melrose was already at the door. He opened his mouth, wanting to call out, to get her to turn around, to say something more—but when he blinked, she was gone.

Joaquin squinted, the studio lights as blinding as the hospital's fluorescent ones the day before.

"You sure you're up for this?" Melrose asked, her warm, minty breath brushing his ear as she tucked a few unruly curls into place.

"Getting here was the hard part," he replied, referring to the early-morning drive to Dallas after his release from the hospital. "Now I just sit, drink coffee, and answer questions."

"And try not to sound cocky." Melrose held up a finger. "Confident, not cocky."

"Yeah, yeah." Joaquin glanced at the empty seat next to him at the mock kitchen table, where he and Greer would be interviewed over a fake breakfast. "Where is she?"

"Still in makeup." Melrose pulled out a chair and sat across from him. "She's pretty nervous."

Joaquin understood. He glanced around the broadcast room, taking in the monitors, cameras, and green screens. This setup was more intimidating than he'd expected.

"So, when are you going to be honest with her?"

"Huh?"

Melrose lowered her voice. "That Hayes Sheridan is a suspect?"

"Not while we still need her," Joaquin replied, his tone steady.

"Doesn't that bother you?" Melrose asked, her eyebrows knitting together. "Greer would never help if she realized you were looking into her husband."

"It doesn't bother me. Look, I understand your sympathy toward Ollie Ford, but I didn't realize it would extend to every single suspect."

"I don't have sympathy for Hayes Sheridan, but I do like Greer. I don't want her thinking we've betrayed her," Melrose explained.

"The only way she'll find out is if we discover Hayes is guilty."

Melrose straightened, tugging down her suit jacket. "Okay, don't be mad, but I met with Bruce Ford on Sunday."

Joaquin drummed his fingers on the tabletop, the plastic cutlery and fake toast between them rattling slightly. "Melrose, why?"

"Because I wanted to convince him and Ollie to do DNA testing, to exclude them as suspects in Wendy's case."

Joaquin tilted his head back, chin jutting forward, the studio lights warm on his face. "And let me guess . . . they won't?"

"Wrong," Melrose said firmly, leaning slightly forward, a spark of triumph in her eyes.

"Are you kidding?" Joaquin huffed, incredulous. "This makes no sense. They wouldn't take out their trash so we could get a DNA sample, and now they're going to hand one over?"

"Bruce doesn't trust the police. He thinks the cops are out to get him. After seeing Luca snooping around his trash can, he started burning most of their rubbish in the fireplace. He was afraid someone might take his or Ollie's DNA and plant it as evidence. He didn't understand DNA testing or the safeguards in place to ensure its accuracy. When the cops showed up—"

Joaquin raised a hand. "Wait. The cops came?"

"Saturday. Bruce didn't answer, but I explained they were there to question him about the dolphin Ollie gave me."

"Are you insane, Melrose? Not only could he have killed you, but you also gave him time to come up with a story about the dolphin."

"Bruce didn't know anything about the dolphin. But he had Ollie show me his room. There were trinkets everywhere, Joaquin. The room is full of the treasures he's found in the woods. So I managed to talk Bruce into havin' a word with the cops and going in for voluntary DNA testing. We should have the results in a week."

Joaquin sighed. "I admire how kind you are, but has anyone ever told you that kindness doesn't always make for a good lawyer?"

She stood. "Guess it's a good thing I'm a paralegal."

Melrose moved aside as a production assistant miked Joaquin, while another guided Greer to the seat beside him. Joaquin couldn't tell if the makeup and lights made her look so pale or if nerves were to blame. He patted her arm. "You're going to do great."

"What if they ask me about finding Tilly's body?" Greer's voice trembled. "I can't talk about that—"

"They won't. We've got an agreement," Joaquin reassured her. "And if they ask anything you're not comfortable with, you don't have to answer. I'll take the lead."

Greer rolled her shoulders and let out a long breath. "Okay. Ready or not . . ."

From off-camera, a producer called, "We're live in five . . . four . . . three . . ." The red light above the camera blinked on.

Joaquin squinted against the glare, the studio lights harsh on his temples, each pulse syncing with the ache in his head. He flexed his fingers against the laminate tabletop to mask the tremor running down his arm and forced that jury-winning smile across his face. *Focus. Breathe.*

"Welcome back to *Good Morning Texas*," Clara Rayburn said, her warm Texas drawl filling the studio. Her honey-colored hair caught the light as she leaned forward. "I'm Clara Rayburn, and today we're joined by attorney Joaquin Ramos and journalist Greer Collins to discuss recent developments in the case of the Songbird Strangler—a case that has reopened old wounds in this small Texas town."

"Thank you for having us," Joaquin said smoothly, letting his fingers rest lightly on the tabletop, pretending it grounded him. "We believe this case highlights why the system needs checks and balances—especially when a man's life is on the line."

Clara gestured toward the monitors displaying faded news footage of Bluesummer. "For viewers who may not be familiar, back in the 1980s, the quiet town of Bluesummer was rocked by a series of murders that left the community shaken . . ."

Joaquin glanced at Greer. Her hands gripped her coffee mug like a security blanket, knuckles whitening. *Look up. Breathe.* He wanted to remind her—and himself.

"Mr. Ramos, recently missing DNA was found and tested. What can you tell us about that?" Clara asked.

"Yes. The DNA results confirm that my client Troy Terrell's DNA was present in the Sexual Assault Evidence Kit performed on Chantilly Price," Joaquin said, lifting a finger for emphasis. "But context is everything. DNA alone does not prove guilt or tell the full story of what happened that night."

Clara shifted her gaze to Greer. "You were Tilly's best friend, correct, Mrs. Sheridan? And the one who found her body that fateful Fourth of July?"

Joaquin's chest tightened. They'd agreed not to talk about that. But Greer answered firmly, hands still wrapped around her mug. "Yes, I did. And I stayed out of the public eye for decades," she continued. "But what

I personally witnessed that night was Troy and Tilly swimming, flirting, kissing, and then going inside for a consensual encounter."

Clara crossed her legs under the table, leaning slightly forward. "Why haven't we heard this before?"

"I was scared," Greer said quietly but firmly, the studio microphones picking up every word. "I didn't want to harm anyone—especially Hayes Sheridan, Tilly's boyfriend at the time and my husband. Speaking up then could have caused pain and confusion. But I can't live with the secret any longer . . . the truth matters. Troy matters."

"And it was your father-in-law who helped build the case against Terrell?" Clara asked.

"People make mistakes," Greer said, voice steady.

Joaquin exhaled, momentarily forgetting the ache behind his temples. She was nailing it.

Clara's gaze sharpened. "But blood from another victim, Wendy Knott, was found in Troy's truck. How do you respond to that?"

"Yes, it was found there," Joaquin said evenly, the studio lights glinting off the table. "But it wasn't in the semen sample from her clothing. We need to determine whose semen it was. And while I can't discuss specifics regarding the speck of blood in the truck, investigations are ongoing, and circumstances strongly suggest alternative, possibly sinister, explanations for that evidence."

"Are you suggesting police mishandling?" Clara asked.

"There are gaps in the chain of custody that haven't been fully explained," Joaquin said, clasping his hands together. "Look, Mrs. Rayburn . . . nothing here is simple. We've filed a habeas corpus motion— over two hundred pages outlining why this case deserves another day in court. DNA is significant, but it does not tell the full story. Evidence, testimony, and alternative leads all matter. We are currently awaiting

DNA results from another former suspect, one who was recently discovered to have missing evidence in his home."

He forced himself to keep his gaze on the host, careful not to glance at Melrose off to the side, who surely didn't want any mention of Ollie. Joaquin didn't care—he was here to create doubt in the public's mind, planting every seed he could.

Clara's brow furrowed. "What evidence?"

Joaquin leaned in, fingers interlaced on the table. "I can't provide any more details at this time. All I'm asking for is enough time for a thorough review before any irreversible action is taken."

Clara straightened, taking a breath. "Wow, well, thank you both for sharing this information. We did reach out to the state for comment, but as of this recording, they have not responded."

Greer set her mug down, the subtle thump drawing all eyes to her. "I need to say something more."

Joaquin's stomach tightened. *She's going off-script.* Every instinct screamed panic, but he forced a calm expression.

"Yes, go on," Clara said, surprise flickering across her face.

"If Troy is executed without a full understanding of the circumstances, it cannot be undone," she said, her eyes bright and unflinching as they scanned the studio, as if daring anyone to look away. "The boy I knew, the man I see today—he deserves fairness. What's pro-life about the death of an innocent man?" She leaned forward slightly, her voice gaining intensity. "Whether or not you want to accept it, justice in this country is not equal. Black men are disproportionately represented on death row, and far too many have been wrongfully convicted. Mistakes happen. Corruption happens—I've seen it firsthand in my career as a journalist. Once the state acts, there's no taking it back."

Her shoulders squared, she let her gaze settle on Joaquin for a heartbeat before returning to the cameras. "I'm late to this conversation, but I'm all in for Troy Terrell. I won't stay silent just because the truth is inconvenient—even if it means challenging the very narrative people I love the most helped create."

Joaquin's chest lifted slightly, a flicker of heat behind his ribs—pride, sure, but a pinch of envy too. She was owning the room in a way he hadn't expected.

Clara adjusted her notes, glanced at the camera, and said, "Thank you, Mrs. Sheridan, and thank you, Mr. Ramos. Clearly, there's more to come as this case develops, and we expect to hear much more as the days tick closer to Mr. Terrell's scheduled execution."

The red light above the camera clicked off. Greer exhaled, shoulders relaxing, relief and determination softening her features. Joaquin wanted to reach over, slap her hand in a victorious high-five, but kept it contained. This interview might not be enough to completely sway the public or erase the weight of the evidence—but it was a damn good start.

# CHAPTER 34

Greer wiped her greasy fingers with a napkin from the bag. She glanced around Keaton's office. "Got a trash can somewhere?"

"Already finished?" Keaton eyed his own Styrofoam box, still full of chicken fingers and fries.

Greer laughed. "Despite the show being called *Breakfast with Texas,* there's no actual eating. Those pastries on the table are props." She crumpled the napkin and tucked it into her box. "Not that I had much appetite. I was a total wreck."

"You did great," Keaton said.

"Oh, you watched it?"

Keaton tore the corner off a ketchup packet. "Of course."

A heater in the corner rattled to life, adding to the already stifling warmth of the office. At least the noise muffled the sound of printers and laughing coworkers outside Keaton's door.

"I'm glad Troy's lawyer made it to the interview," Greer said, pushing the conversation forward. Things never flowed naturally between her and Keaton. "Joaquin had a car accident yesterday and was barely released in time."

Keaton popped a fry into his mouth. "Ramos came across . . . I don't know, arrogant?"

"Yeah, he kinda is," Greer admitted, "but he seems to be a good attorney."

"Are you staying in Dallas tonight?" Keaton asked. "Sam would love to see you. We could have dinner—and invite Zach and Bonnie, too."

"Hayes is in Austin." Greer's stomach churned at the thought of Ally Swanson. "Quinn's staying with Red and Joanne, so I have to get back."

"How's Red doing?"

Greer shook her head. "Not good."

"Sorry to hear that," he murmured, eyes briefly meeting hers. "Red always treated me well."

"You worked for him, right?"

Keaton set down an unfinished chicken strip. "Yeah. He noticed I was struggling and wanted to help. Later, he got me a more stable job there in Bluesummer."

"And now here you are." Greer gestured around the office. "Transferred to the Dallas branch. Big time."

Keaton gave a muted laugh. "I wouldn't say that. The company's been good to me, though, despite my struggles."

"You seem to be doing well," Greer said, hoping her reason for being here wouldn't unravel him.

Keaton wiped crumbs from his lap, his movements stiff. "The medication and therapy have helped."

"Told you therapy wasn't so bad," Greer said.

"My therapist said retiring would've been a mistake. She advised cutting back hours—something about saving my sense of purpose."

"Smart therapist," Greer said. "So far, I don't recommend retirement."

"Sounds like you've got plenty to keep you busy," Keaton said, tapping a pen against a stack of forms. "Helping with the Death Penalty Abolition Project and all."

Greer twisted her hands in her lap. Keaton's lunch break wouldn't last forever. Time to get to the point. "Yeah, that's why I'm here."

Keaton cocked his head. "Yeah. I saw the interview, remember?"

"No, I mean *here*, talking to you." Greer focused on the jacket draped over Keaton's chair. "I found the Prices' phone bill from July 1986 while sorting through Red's things." She shifted her gaze to her brother. Was it her imagination, or did a line of sweat suddenly appear on his forehead?

"Okay," he said, taking a handkerchief from his pocket and wiping down his mostly bald head. "It's hot in here, isn't it?"

"That call from Tilly's house to ours . . ." Greer continued. "Tilly didn't hang up like Red assumed. She talked to someone for almost five minutes."

Keaton swallowed. "Probably a mistake. The eighties weren't exactly peak technology." He forced a laugh.

"Zach told me about you and Tilly."

Keaton slammed both hands on the desk, making the papers jump. "Are you serious? He had no right!"

"I'm not mad, Keaton. I just want to understand why you lied."

He opened a drawer and tore the wrapper off a roll of Tums, popping two into his mouth. "By then, it was over between us, Greer. I had nothing to do with—"

"Of course not. But something she told you might help solve the case."

"You never leave well enough alone." Keaton hesitated, rubbing the back of his neck. "Look, she called me because she thought she might be pregnant. I figured you'd find out sooner or later. But it doesn't change anything."

The elevator dinged outside Keaton's office, the sound reverberating in Greer's ears. "Wait, what?"

Keaton ran a hand down his face. "She swore it was mine and was terrified—sobbing. She hadn't done the test yet, so I bought one and took it over. It came back negative. Then Tilly tried to kiss me. I told her it wasn't a good idea—that I loved her, but she was with Hayes. She'd made her choice."

Greer thought back. "So that's why you were so upset when you came back home?"

Keaton tapped his desk with two fingers. "You understand why I couldn't tell the police, right? They'd think I killed her. The murders started right after I came back to Bluesummer."

Greer's body stiffened. She hadn't made that connection before, but Keaton was right. The murders *had* started around the time he had returned to Bluesummer. But that didn't mean anything. Sure, he'd been in a dark place, but he wouldn't have . . . he couldn't have.

"You believe me, don't you?" he asked.

Greer glanced at her brother, face slick with sweat, and his hands shaking. "Of course. Breathe, Keaton. Everything's okay."

"You can't tell anyone, Greer. Not Mom, not Zach, not Troy's lawyer . . . not the police."

"But you saw Tilly alive after Troy left her. Do you remember how long you stayed?"

"Just long enough to get the test results. Ten minutes tops. You saw me come home. What time was that?"

Greer didn't remember all the details, but she knew what she'd do tonight—construct a timeline. One thing was for sure: Tilly hadn't died as early as the police had theorized.

The office air hung thick and stagnant. Greer grabbed a notepad from Keaton's desk and used it to fan herself. "If you'd told the police, it would've cleared Troy."

He banged his fist on the desk. "And implicated me!"

Greer leaned back, her body tensing.

"Sorry." Keaton raised both hands. "But the police conducted a thorough investigation. As did your father-in-law."

*Not that thorough*, Greer thought. Everyone had somehow missed that tiny four-minute annotation on the Prices' phone bill.

"There was evidence against Troy," Keaton continued. "Especially with this new revelation that they apparently slept together before she called. That was news to me. If I had believed he was innocent, I would've spoken out. But I've always believed he returned that night and killed her."

Greer reached for the scarf draped loosely around her neck, twisting and twirling the fabric. "Troy didn't go back."

Keaton shook his head. "You can't be sure of that."

"We have to go to the police, Keaton."

The suggestion made her brother jump to his feet. "Absolutely not. They'll arrest me."

"No, they won't. The police have the Songbird Strangler's DNA from semen found in Wendy Knott's underwear. Provide your DNA, and they can clear you."

"I'm not going to the police." Spit flew from Keaton's mouth. "And if you do, I'll deny it. I'll say you have an axe to grind with me, that you're making it up to get Troy off." His words rushed out, his eyes frantic.

Greer needed to get out of here. She reached for her purse.

"Do not leave," he growled. "Not until we figure this out. Sit back down."

"I'll call you later," Greer said, backing toward the door. "When you calm down."

She burst into the hallway, a sharp blast of cooler air hitting her as she jabbed the elevator button nonstop until the doors finally slid open.

As the elevator lowered, Greer's stomach dropped with it. As much as she didn't want to admit it, she was afraid of her brother.

Greer's bedside clock read the exact time she'd found Tilly dead.

Years ago, she told her therapist she kept seeing that number—on her office clock, on the microwave, glowing from her phone when she woke at night. Dr. Nick had called it a trick of the mind. Greer glanced at the time dozens of times a day, but only noticed 11:55 because it meant something to her. He mentioned that many people who lived through the September 11 terror attacks often noticed the time 9:11.

Greer rubbed her eyes, feeling the weight of exhaustion settle in. She'd been up since 4 a.m., and the day had been emotionally draining.

Since slipping away to her bedroom early, pretending to have a migraine, Greer had been trying to construct a timeline. She'd left Quinn to clean after dinner and administer Joanne and Red's evening medications before returning to her own home. Greer had even said no when Si asked if he could stay the night—something she never did.

This was too important to ignore. This could prove Troy's innocence. But there were still too many gaps, too many unknown times. What time had she left Hayes's house? How long had she sat in her driveway, crying to Tears for Fears before going inside? The entire night until 11:55 was a blur.

She needed help. Red was the obvious choice, but would it upset him to learn he'd been wrong? Or—worse—had he known all along? If so, who was he protecting?

Figuring it out would have to wait. Her eyes were heavy, and her focus was slipping. She set her clipboard and pencil on the nightstand and switched off the lamp.

Reaching for her phone charger, she hesitated. Hayes hadn't texted her all day.

She told herself he was busy, but he always sent a goodnight message when he was away, no matter how hectic his schedule was.

Quinn was mad at her for the interview—maybe Hayes was, too.

Greer checked her message thread with Hayes just to be sure. Nothing since last night. She should put the phone down—get some sleep.

Instead, she opened Facebook.

She scrolled to Ally's profile, not expecting anything new. But two hours ago, she had posted a picture of two drinks on a small table—red wine and a pink cocktail with an orange floating on top. Beyond them, Austin's skyline glittered, neon reflecting off glass towers.

One of those rooftop bars Hayes liked.

Greer's pulse ticked up, a hollow feeling settling in her chest. She blinked hard, refocusing on the caption:

*#austinskies #blueeyes #butterflies.*

# CHAPTER 35

Joaquin rubbed the side of his head, wincing as the ache throbbed behind his eyes. He skimmed the email from District Attorney Hench. "According to law enforcement, there are no matches in CODIS," he read aloud, yanking off his reading glasses and tossing them onto the desk.

"CODIS isn't the end-all," Luca said. "I've spoken to a Houston genealogist, Maya Whitmore. She can use GEDmatch to find partial DNA matches, build a reverse family tree, and identify suspects based on age, location, and other factors."

"So you're talking some Golden State Killer-type shit?" Joaquin asked.

Luca slipped his phone into his jacket. "In theory, yeah. Hopefully, Maya can find something. And since your interview, momentum's building, 'Free Troy' is trending, donations to DPAP are coming in— enough to cover DNA testing."

Joaquin offered a faint smile. "Now we just need the public—and Wendy Knott's parents—to demand the police officially reopen the case." He clasped his hands behind his head. "But her parents won't return my calls. They've got to be wondering whose DNA that is, whose ring was at the bower, and who these alternate suspects we alluded to in the interview are."

"Admitting they were wrong has gotta be tough," Luca said. "It is easier to pretend the semen came from a secret boyfriend, that it was

Troy's ring at the bower, and that Greer Sheridan found someone else's. Or that Ollie Ford really stumbled onto that dolphin during one of his little expeditions."

"Well, I'd rather still believe in Santa Claus, too," Joaquin said. "But by ten, I found too many holes in the story."

"I'd offer to visit the Knott family, but Melrose is the better choice. She got Ollie and Bruce swabbed, which saves me from dumpster diving at Murphy's Market."

Joaquin chewed the end of a pen. "So, where to next? Hayes Sheridan's trash can?"

"Would be easier if Greer brought us something. Have you told her about the picture of Hayes and Nicole yet?"

"No. We can't afford to lose her support."

"It would be easier to lose her support than lose the case, but—" Luca trailed off, his attention shifting. "I think I just heard the bell on your front door."

"That you, Melrose?" Joaquin called, wincing as he shifted, the movement pulling at the back of his skull.

"Unfortunately for you, it's not," Bernie yelled back.

Luca smirked. "So, you and Melrose are . . ."

"Working together," Joaquin said, keeping his tone flat. Anything else would be a distraction. He felt a low, persistent ache in his chest but shoved it down.

"Well, the case won't last forever."

Joaquin's face warmed. He'd thought the same, had felt the pull, the spark—but for all he knew, Melrose's insistence on keeping things strictly professional was only an excuse. Maybe the careful boundary she maintained around him was proof that he'd misread every glance, every small smile. He wanted to believe she felt something—but doubt whispered it was all in his head.

"I agree it's better to wait," Luca said. "Gives you time to get your strength back. You're in no shape to sweep anyone off their feet, let alone roll them around in bed."

Joaquin smirked. "If I weren't a gentleman, I'd have a comment about that."

Luca chuckled. "Come on, look at you. You're practically in traction."

"Traction? My arm's in a sling, and I have a headache, is all."

A series of quiet beeps came from inside Luca's jacket. "Hold on," he said, pulling out his phone. "It's Greer."

Joaquin listened as Luca's responses bounced between okays, wows, and a surprised "You're kidding," his curiosity growing.

"Put it on speaker," he mouthed, but Luca waved him off.

"I'm glad you called, Mrs. Sheridan," Luca said. "I'm at Joaquin's office now. Can you come by? That works. See you then."

As Luca hung up, Joaquin's pulse quickened. "Well? What's going on?"

Luca tilted his head. "Forget Hayes Sheridan's trash can. I think we've overlooked a third suspect."

An hour later, Greer sat in Joaquin's office. His whiteboard was covered with a timeline of the events of July 4, 1986.

Their timeline exposed gaps in Keaton Collins's story. He claimed he had left Tilly's at 11:15, leaving forty minutes for someone else to kill her before Greer arrived. But a quick Google search revealed that pregnancy tests in the eighties took thirty minutes, and Keaton had claimed he stayed long enough to get the negative results. When they worked backward from

Greer's timeline—factoring in when her path crossed Keaton's—it became clear her brother had stayed at Tilly's longer than he'd admitted.

Joaquin took a step closer to the board. "If we're right and Keaton left Tilly's at 11:35 or 11:40, that leaves just ten or fifteen minutes for someone else to kill her and leave before you arrived." He looked at Greer.

"It's possible, isn't it?" she asked, pushing down the memory of Keaton coming home furious.

"Is it possible?" Joaquin repeated her question. "Sure. Likely? No, I don't think so."

"That's not for us to decide," Melrose said, snapping the lid of an Expo marker back on. "But it proves it couldn't be Troy. Red and his mom both testified that Troy was home at 11:15. Keaton was at Tilly's then."

"And Troy obviously had left by the time Tilly called Keaton to come over at 10:45," Luca interjected. "So what Troy said about leaving by 10:35 and driving around until 11:15 actually adds up."

"He told the truth." Melrose turned to Joaquin. "Told ya."

Excitement buzzed in the room, thinly masked for Greer's sake. Proving Troy's innocence should have felt like a win. Instead, it cast a shadow over her brother. It was like finding a key to unlock a treasure chest, only to discover it was actually Pandora's box waiting to unleash even more chaos.

Melrose sat beside Greer. "Thank you for telling us this. You've done the right thing."

Greer's hand shook as she swiped at a tear, her thoughts clawing for escape routes, for possibilities that didn't end with her brother's guilt. "It doesn't have to be Keaton. It can't be." Her voice wavered, barely steady enough to form words. "What about Ollie Ford? He could've been near her house, seen Keaton leave, and—"

"We are still looking at all suspects," Joaquin interjected.

"All?" Greer's chest tightened, her mind careening toward the one name she hadn't let herself think about: *Hayes*. Hayes in Austin with his mistress. "Who else is a suspect?"

The subtle exchange of glances between Luca, Melrose, and Joaquin set her nerves on edge. *Do they suspect my husband? Should I?*

Joaquin's voice broke through the rising panic. "Mrs. Sheridan, we need to have an honest conversation about that."

When Joaquin reached for a manila envelope, Melrose slammed her hand against the whiteboard, her voice sharp. "Joaquin! Look at the bloody timeline. There's no one else it could be."

"We're still missing something," Joaquin said, his voice tight with frustration. "Why would Red Sheridan have the phone record showing the four-minute call and not turn it over to the police?"

"He probably didn't notice it," Melrose said.

"Or it didn't fit the story he created—that Troy strangled Tilly while she tried to make that call." Joaquin's eyes darkened. "He's covering for someone. And we have to ask—why would he cover for Keaton Collins?"

Luca stood, tugging at his collar. "Let's not do this now."

"I want to see it," Greer said. A knot of anxiety tightened in her chest. "Whatever it is."

Joaquin perched on the edge of his desk. "Mrs. Sheridan, did Hayes know any of the victims?"

Greer's stomach churned, and she pressed a hand to her mouth, fighting the rising nausea. *They did suspect Hayes.* "Erin was our valedictorian, so yeah, everyone knew her, and Wendy Knott was his lab partner senior year. They did this experiment together . . . blood typing. He didn't know Andrea or—"

"Nicole Garcia?" Joaquin interjected.

"No. She was older."

Joaquin pulled a Polaroid from the folder and handed it over.

The photo showed a teen she didn't recognize standing on a beach. But behind him, there was Hayes, waist-deep in the water, with Nicole Garcia perched on his shoulders, smiling down at him. They looked at ease, as if they had shared countless moments like this, carefree and intimate. A jolt of dread raced through her veins.

Worse than the suggestion Hayes had been involved with Nicole Garcia was the fact that he was now a suspect in a series of brutal murders. A serial killer's first victim was often someone close, someone personal. Hayes had denied knowing Nicole. Yet in that photo, they clearly seemed to know each other—maybe a little too well.

"Greer." Luca's voice pulled her from her thoughts. "We aren't saying your husband is a suspect per se," he said. "But it looks like he may be a liar."

# CHAPTER 36

"Hayes *isn't* cheating on you," Jade said from the treadmill beside Greer's. "He adores you."

Greer increased her speed. "Both can be true. He's cheated before."

Jade tugged at her bright blue ponytail. "So they're both in Austin. So are like a million other people."

"Don't forget the red wine, blue eyes."

"Lots of people drink red wine and have blue eyes. Hayes slept with her once. It wasn't some epic love affair that left them pining for years."

Greer's legs burned. "I'm not saying it was. They might've just met for sex."

Jade wiped her face with a towel. "If it were, would he take her to a bar? Let her post on Facebook. Come on, Greer, I get he screwed up, but all these years of loyalty have to count for something."

"Seems disloyalty isn't new," Greer muttered. "I saw an old picture of Hayes. Maybe he cheated on Tilly, too."

"Are you seriously bringing up high school?"

Greer increased her pace.

Jade hit the stop button on Greer's treadmill.

"Hey!" Greer jumped onto the side rails.

"It's too loud in here," Jade said, pointing to a speaker blaring a song by Imagine Dragons. "Let's grab a milkshake."

"We haven't burned off enough for a milkshake."

Jade swiped her bangs aside. "Well, a Diet Coke, at least."

Greer grabbed her water bottle. "Fine. Let me shower."

"Thank God. I only come to the gym to talk to you, but it's hard to talk when you're running like a crazy person."

Greer smiled. Sometimes, Jade was the only one who could make her smile. Hayes had never understood their friendship. Jade, who smelled like cigarettes, swapped boyfriends like hairstyles; Jade, who flew to DC for protests and had a giant "Smash the Patriarchy" decal on the back window of her 2004 Ford F-150.

"It's not that I don't want you to be friends with her," he'd once said. "I just wonder why you can't also be friends with some ladies from church. Why won't you at least try the women's ministry events?"

"Because they're not like me, Hayes. I don't want to decorate tables, have tea parties, or go on a Christmas tour of homes. That's not me."

"Hayes didn't call me the night of Ally's post," Greer said as they waited for their drinks. "Last night, our call was like two minutes."

"Come on, Greer. If you're not convinced Hayes is working, it won't be hard to find out, right? You're a reporter. Dig."

"Used to be a reporter. Now I'm a caretaker and wannabe podcaster," Greer replied, staring out at the asphalt, letting the hum of the old engine fill the pause.

"Oh, shut up," Jade said. "Once a reporter, always a reporter, and you're going to find the real Songbird Strangler. Imagine the satisfaction."

Greer turned to the window, hiding her tears before Jade could see. Yes, she might have found the Songbird Strangler, but it wasn't satisfying—not at all.

She discreetly wiped away her tears, unsure of what had triggered them. Her marriage? Her brother? Her father-in-law dying in his bed?

Troy, set to die next month? Her daughters, who believed she'd failed them? Her son, whom she knew she had failed? A little of everything?

"Hun? Are you crying?" Jade asked.

The carhop arrived, giving Greer time to pull herself together.

"Shoot. I should've tipped him, huh?" Jade said.

Greer sipped her Diet Coke. "I never know anymore. I even saw a tip jar at the drive-through window at Taco Express yesterday."

Jade poked her straw into her drink. "Next thing you know, I'll have to tip the friendly teacher's assistant who opens the car door when I drop my granddaughter off at preschool. Maybe if we paid people a livable wage . . ." She trailed off, taking a long drink of her cherry limeade and setting it in the console. "Anyway, what's the plan? Are you going to confront him or—"

"Or what?" Greer asked.

Jade blew out a breath. "Look, I don't buy that he's cheating on you, but as part of my best friend duties, I don't mind spying. Can't till Sunday, though."

Greer gave a short laugh. "How can you spy? Hayes knows your truck." She reached over to fluff her best friend's turquoise ponytail. "And no offense, but you don't exactly blend into a crowd."

"So I'll go undercover. Switch trucks with my dad. Wear a wig."

"And if you see them together, then what?"

"That's your call, hun. I can throw wine in his blue eyes, lock a feral cat in his truck, or just tell you and let you handle it."

Greer recalled the question she'd asked Hayes when he confessed his secret to her: *Why did you tell me?*

Her grip tightened around her cup, the Styrofoam squeaking.

Did she want to know if her husband was back in Ally Swanson's bed? She wasn't so sure.

"This is silly." Greer released her grip on the cup. "I'm sure there's nothing to worry about."

"Exactly what I've been saying," Jade said, putting her truck in reverse. "Some things are just coincidences."

"You're right." Greer swirled her drink absentmindedly. "I'm going to let it go," she said, knowing full well she was lying to herself.

Greer checked Ally Swanson's Facebook again as she pulled into the prison parking lot. There had been no updates since the blue eyes and wine post.

Jade's words from yesterday echoed in her mind—not the reassurances about Hayes, but the advice: *You're a reporter. Dig.*

An idea hit her. Contact Maggie Dawson—Hayes's supposedly too-sick-to-travel coworker's wife. They weren't close, but Maggie was on Greer's Facebook friends list. She found her profile and typed:

*Hi Maggie. Wanted to check on Brian. Do you need anything?*

Grabbing Troy's vending machine quarters, she reached for her purse—but her phone chimed with a Messenger notification. She opened it immediately.

*You're so sweet to check on him. Brian's feeling a tad better but is still weak. Sorry Hayes had to cover for him.*

Greer leaned back, relief flooding her. Why hadn't she done this sooner? She quickly texted Hayes.

*Love you.*

The reply came almost immediately: *Back at you—got anything fun planned today?*

Greer hesitated. She couldn't tell him she was here to visit Troy—their friend who'd spent decades in prison, while the potential real

Songbird Strangler had been an usher at their wedding, slept in their guest room at Christmas, and was called "uncle" by their kids. Instead, she typed:

*About to have lunch with Jade.*

*Sounds like fun. If everything goes well, I might come home tomorrow. I'll call you tonight.*

Greer shifted in her seat. Knowing Hayes wasn't in Austin to see Ally Swanson didn't completely ease her mind. She started typing again.

*Saw an old picture of you today. I didn't realize you were friends with Nicole Garcia.*

She deleted it. This wasn't a conversation for text. Instead, she sent a single heart emoji.

With six minutes left before visiting hours, Greer opened Facebook again. She meant to scroll, but instead, she typed Ally's name.

A new post appeared at the top. Ally was tagged.

*This is Danica, Ally's sister. Has anyone heard from Ally? She said she was meeting a guy in Austin she's been talking to. She promised to call afterward, but she hasn't responded in over forty-eight hours!! It's not like her. If you know anything, please reach out. We love you, Al. Call us!*

Greer checked her watch. "Half an hour already? Time flies when I'm here."

Troy shook his head. "Can't say the same. Time moves like a glacier for me here."

Greer glanced around the booth. "Well, you won't be here much longer, right?"

Troy rattled his Dr. Pepper can and took a last sip. "The only thing slower than a glacier is bureaucracy. But no, I won't be here much longer.

Pretty soon, I'll walk out of these doors—most likely on my way to Huntsville for a three-drug cocktail that stops my heart."

"You're not going to Huntsville. You're walking out those doors and going wherever the hell you want."

A grin spread across his face. "Guess where I wanna go?"

"Whataburger?"

He laughed. "Okay, yeah, that too. But I was thinking about the stadium."

"Bluesummer High's stadium?"

Troy scratched his cheek. "Yeah. Weird, I know."

"That's not weird. You were an amazing football player."

Troy shook his head. "It's not that. It was being together beneath those lights every Friday night. Hayes and I on the field, Tilly cheering on the sideline, you in the stands with your clarinet. All doing our own thing but still together. That felt special."

"It *was* special." Greer's voice cracked.

Troy closed his eyes and spoke softly. "I keep having this dream. I'm a kid again, running through the woods behind the farm—dodging logs and tangled roots, with the smell of wet dirt and pine all around me. I hear birds calling and animals rustling through the underbrush." He exhaled, blinking back tears. "I never know how to feel when I wake up. Happy I had the dream, or sad that it's just a dream." A single tear traced his cheek. "Will you spread my ashes there?"

Greer swallowed hard. "Sure—in another thirty years. No problem."

Troy wiped the tear. "Damn. Sorry for being a bummer."

Greer shook the bag of quarters. "Nothing a candy bar won't fix. Want another drink?"

Troy patted his stomach. "Trying to fatten me up?"

"Please, you're still in high school shape."

He chuckled. "Plenty of time for push-ups."

Her smile faltered, and the fluorescent lights above flickered faintly. She dropped her gaze to the table. "Troy . . . I'm sorry."

"Hey." He tapped the glass. "You didn't put me here."

"I didn't stop it either."

Troy pressed his palm to the glass. "It's okay, G."

Greer raised her hand to meet his. "Remember that last Fourth of July? Holding hands, watching fireworks over the lake?"

"Of course. It was epic."

"I didn't appreciate it enough," Greer said. "I stood between you and Tilly, wishing I were next to Hayes and holding his hand."

Troy smirked. "Color me surprised."

Greer stared at the floor. "I didn't realize I had my whole life to hold Hayes's hand. That was my last chance to hold Tilly's. My last chance to hold yours."

"Well, if they release me, you can hold my hand and walk me out," Troy said.

Greer met his eyes. "I will. That's a promise."

Troy nodded. "Then help me find a job? I tried taking college courses, but they shot that down. Said I wasn't here to be rehabilitated."

Greer tapped her foot. "When you get out, Texas will owe you millions. Forget a job—get a passport."

Troy rolled his eyes. "Come on, G."

"I looked it up. You're entitled to eighty thousand dollars per year of wrongful incarceration. Plus health insurance."

"It's not automatic," Troy explained. "You have to apply, and they can deny you. They only pay if you're declared 'actually innocent.'"

Greer frowned. "I don't get it."

"They can overturn my conviction—say there wasn't enough evidence. But that's not the same as proving I didn't do it. Without that declaration, I get nothing. The system's not broken; it was designed this way."

Greer huffed. "That's such crap."

"I'll be alright," Troy said. "I'll work. Work at Allsup's, drive a trash truck—doesn't matter."

Caleb had always loved watching the trash truck. Every Monday and Thursday, Greer would take him outside to watch them dump the bin. It was one of their little routines—just like going out every night to look at the moon. Caleb had adored the moon. He once told her he was going there. Greer sometimes imagined Caleb had grown up to be an astronomer, astrophysicist, or astronaut. But the comfort of that fantasy was always short-lived. Her boy wasn't on the moon; he wasn't even working at the Allsup's down the street. He was gone. He'd never be anything but gone.

"You okay, G?" Troy leaned closer.

"Sorry. Something you said reminded me of my son. He passed away a long time ago."

Troy's voice softened. "I'm so sorry. Was he sick?"

"No. Freak accident. He fell off the playground equipment at preschool."

"Preschool?" Troy exhaled. "That's terrible."

"He didn't want to go that day. I almost let him stay home, but I was behind at work. Plus, Hayes thought he should get used to being away from me." She wiped her tears. "Caleb clung to my blouse at drop-off. I didn't make it to the hospital in time, so that was the last time I ever saw him alive."

"It wasn't your fault," Troy said softly.

*No*, Greer thought. *It was Hayes's fault.* An unfair blame she still couldn't shake. "For a long time, I got stuck on all the what-ifs. What if I'd just kept him home? You hear stories like that—people who miss disasters by pure chance. A flat tire. A forgotten wallet. One small twist in the day, and everything's different."

Troy shook his head. "That's trying to make sense of the senseless. Like thinking God spared one person but not the next. How does that even make sense?"

Greer dabbed her eyes. "You sound like my therapist."

"It's good you talk to someone. Does Hayes?"

Greer rolled her eyes. "Just that guy upstairs."

Troy smiled. "Nothing wrong with that either. I was lost when I first got here, but faith gave me hope. Prayer brought me peace."

"I'm glad," Greer said. "It never worked for me."

Troy nodded thoughtfully. "Well, if you're ever willing to give it another try, I could sure use a miracle."

Greer smiled faintly, then glanced toward the clock on the wall. Visiting hours were slipping away, but neither of them seemed ready to end the conversation. The talk drifted, circling from old memories to the case.

"You don't really think Keaton did it, do you?" Troy asked, brow furrowed.

"I'm not sure," Greer admitted. "He had been secretly dating Tilly, and he was the last to see her alive. When he came back from her house, he was distraught."

Troy let out a slow exhale into the phone. "Tilly did tell me there was someone else, and that she might be pregnant. Do you think Keaton would take a DNA test?"

"He won't respond to me. Zach either."

Troy sighed. "As much as I hope you're wrong, I appreciate you risking this for me."

"If Keaton had told the truth about going to Tilly's, you wouldn't be here," Greer said. "The truth needs to come out, whatever it is." As she said it, she wondered if a part of her wanted it to be Keaton, just so it wouldn't be Hayes. Her mind flashed to the picture of Hayes with Nicole Garcia and the Facebook post about missing Ally Swanson. She couldn't shake the memory of Hayes volunteering at the Terrell farm all those years—volunteering to slice open pigs' throats.

Troy tapped on the glass again. "You good?"

Greer shook her head. "Sorry, yeah. Your lawyer said I could do a DNA test. If mine's a close match to what they found on Wendy's clothes, they can test Keaton discreetly. Ollie and Bruce Ford were tested, but I doubt it's them. Do you know if they're looking at anyone else?" She twisted her wedding ring.

Troy broke eye contact. "Not anyone they should be."

"Hayes?" Greer asked.

"They didn't want you to know. They were worried you'd stop helping."

"They're probably using me for information about Hayes," Greer said. She didn't add the rest—that it was the price of being married to a man with secrets.

"Ramos has always suspected him," Troy said. "No proof, just a picture with Nicole and some BS theory."

"They showed me," Greer said. "I remember now—Hayes went to South Padre with his dad that year. Never mentioned knowing Nicole, though."

"Can you blame him?" Troy asked. "The cops were trying to pin Tilly's death on him."

"What?" Greer frowned.

"He overheard Red telling Joanne the police were trying to gather enough evidence to arrest Hayes—that he was suspect number one."

Greer rubbed her temple. "He never told me this."

"Why would he? That theory faded, and I became the prime suspect."

"Right," Greer replied, but her mind couldn't help but linger on the timing—how perfectly convenient it had been for Hayes. Red had never mentioned in his book that Hayes had been a suspect. It made her wonder if Red's real motivation for claiming he'd solved the case wasn't so much about the book deal but about protecting his son.

"It's just a picture," Troy said. "Captures a single moment—might be the only time they ever interacted. Hayes would never cheat."

Greer fought the urge to correct him, to reveal the story of Hayes's missing mistress. Instead, she said, "He could have. We all have secrets."

Troy waved his hand. "Well, even if he hooked up with Nicole, so what?"

"Then he had a relationship with three of the victims."

"Three?" Troy shook his head. "He and Wendy were lab partners. That'd be like me saying you had a relationship with everyone you worked with on the school paper."

Greer shrugged. "You can't work with someone that much and not get close. She was at his house a lot and—"

The guard's voice cut in. "Time's up, Terrell."

The words hit like a cold splash of water. Greer didn't like the sound of that.

# CHAPTER 37

"Hate to say I told you so." Melrose slid a piece of paper across the desk.

Joaquin scanned the Fords' DNA results, then looked up, catching the glint in her eyes. "No, you don't."

"You're right. But I was sure it wasn't Ollie."

Joaquin shrugged. "We had to check. That dolphin was big."

"A big coincidence. Ollie found it in the woods, just like he said." Melrose eased into the chair opposite Joaquin.

"You okay?" he asked. "You sat down like I do after leg day."

"Well, my superpower is getting pain and stiffness without doing a single leg press. Fibromyalgia stuff."

"Do you need the day off? Or maybe—"

"I'm fine," Melrose cut in. "Don't make a fuss."

Something tightened in his chest watching her straighten, pretending she was fine. "Sometimes it feels like I don't make enough fuss. Honestly, it's easy to forget you're sick because you . . . well, you . . ."

"Hide it so well?" Melrose finished. "I've had a lifetime of practice masking my symptoms. If I had a dollar for every 'You don't look sick,' I'd be retired on a beach somewhere—still in pain, but with a cocktail."

"That's not what I mean. I understand you're sick, I just—" He stopped, struggling for the right words.

Melrose tapped her pen against her notebook, the soft rhythm filling the quiet hum of the office. "No worries," she said finally. "Can we get back to work?"

Joaquin nodded. "Okay, so you were right about Ollie. What else is that sharp intuition of yours saying? Keaton Collins? Hayes Sheridan?"

"I have no clue, but poor Greer either way. Hopefully, the genetic genealogist is piecing together a family tree. In the meantime, we can file a successive petition about the police timeline errors."

"Too bad Keaton lawyered up. No way he's signing an affidavit about going to Tilly's now." Joaquin moved his mouse to wake his screen. "In better news, the AP ran our story, mentioning the four jurors from Troy's second trial who are now second-guessing their verdict. Thanks to you."

"Did you see Kim Kardashian reposted DPAP's tweet about the upcoming protest?" Melrose asked.

Joaquin's fingers froze over the keyboard, eyes wide. "Seriously? Any chance she'll come? She visited Rodney Reed on death row."

"Already trying. DPAP's media guy is trying to reach her publicist. Bit of a long shot, but hey, stranger things have happened."

Joaquin tried to focus on scrolling through Kim's tweets, but his gaze kept drifting back to Melrose. Her rose gold necklace caught the light, the teardrop pendant resting elegantly at her collarbone. She toyed with the chain absentmindedly as she read something on her phone. *Speaking of long shots*, he thought.

"Got any plans for Christmas?" Melrose asked, slipping her phone into her jacket pocket.

"Just going to my parents'. You?"

"Not going to my parents'. Promised them I'd visit next year—unless I'm busy saving someone else from death row."

"What's Christmas like back home?" Joaquin asked.

"Bloody hot—of course, December's summer in Australia, so Santa's more likely to wear boardies than a suit. It's too warm for a roast, so we stick to cold seafood and beers at the beach."

Joaquin's recent Christmas fantasies had involved cozying up with Melrose by a fire, but swapping that for lying on a beach with her, sipping a cold beer, didn't sound too shabby either.

Joaquin tugged at his shirt collar. "You're welcome to spend Christmas with us this year. My parents would love to have you again. My other sister and her family will also be there this time." He paused, studying Melrose's expression. "No pressure, but if you don't want to be alone . . ."

"Who said I'd be alone?"

"Please tell me you're not spending it with Luca," Joaquin teased, his tone flirty, but Melrose's smile suggested she didn't mind.

"Close," she said. "Visiting Troy in the morning, then dinner with Bernie and Dan."

"Lucky them." Joaquin held her gaze longer than he meant to.

"Yes, lucky us," a raspy voice interrupted.

Joaquin tore his gaze away from Melrose to find Bernie standing in the doorway. "Mrs. Sheridan's here. Should I send her in, or are you two . . . busy?"

"Send her in." Joaquin stood, and Melrose slid her chair a few inches closer to the wall.

Greer walked in and gave them a quick nod. Without waiting for an invitation, she pulled out a chair and sat.

"So, what's this about?" she asked, looking from one to the other.

Joaquin eased back into his own seat. "We got the results in, and the DNA taken from Wendy Knott's clothing doesn't belong to Bruce or Ollie Ford."

"Oh." Greer bounced her foot against the carpet. "So you need me to provide a DNA sample?"

"That would be helpful," Joaquin said. "But it'd be more helpful if your brother would."

"Neither of my brothers is speaking to me. Mom will find out what's going on soon enough since I'm clearly not welcome at Christmas in Dallas." She twisted the hem of her skirt. "If I'm wrong about Keaton, I've destroyed my family. If I'm right, I've still destroyed my family."

"It might rule him out," Melrose said. "But it'll help Troy if we have a witness who saw Tilly alive after Troy went home."

"Are the police doing anything?" Greer asked. "I gave my statement, but no one's returning my calls. Can't they make Keaton give his DNA?"

"Only with an arrest or a warrant," Joaquin said. "They still think Troy's the guy. But we've got a mystery DNA profile and a forensic genealogist working it. We'll see what shakes out."

Greer's shoulders hunched as if she were trying to shrink into herself. "What if I got it wrong? What if it's not Keaton?"

*Then we might need your husband's DNA*, Joaquin thought. He pointed to the whiteboard behind Greer. "Then back to the drawing board."

"They'll stop the execution, right?" Greer asked. "Until all the DNA testing is done?"

"Not always," Melrose said. "Less than a decade ago, Arkansas executed Ledell Lee for the murder of Debra Reese—even though the Innocence Project and the ACLU filed motions for DNA testing. The court denied them."

"It was later tested four years after his death," Joaquin added. "Another man's DNA was found on the murder weapon."

"So, two murderers with no consequences," Greer said. "Whoever killed Debra Reese and the State of Arkansas."

"And the latter had scheduled eight executions over eleven days," Melrose said. "All because the state's lethal injection drugs were about to expire."

"Yep," Joaquin said. "It's like when I was a kid, and Mom saw bananas turning brown and started mashing them. Expiration dates are a good reason to make banana bread, not to kill human beings." He shook his head, then glanced up. "Anyway, are you going to the protest?"

Greer gave a curt nod.

"Can you talk Hayes into joining you? PR-wise, it'd be great to see Red Sheridan's son supporting Troy."

Greer fidgeted with her watch. "I . . . um . . . don't think so."

"Any specific reason he doesn't want to help Troy?" Joaquin asked.

Melrose shot him a disapproving glance, but he continued. "I get it's hard facing that his dad got it all wrong. I just assumed that with the recent developments involving Keaton, he might reconsider."

Greer's voice tightened. "I haven't told him yet. He got in late last night. I'll have to soon enough, or he'll start questioning why we're not spending Christmas with my family. Not to mention Keaton could be arrested."

Something was off. Greer seemed jittery. Whenever her husband was mentioned, she stumbled over words or babbled.

"The police won't arrest your brother without conclusive DNA proof. Would you help get a sample from Hayes?" Joaquin raised his hands. "Just to rule him out. If Troy is declared innocent, the case reopens. They'll look at Hayes first—he was the boyfriend."

"Like an empty water bottle?" Greer asked.

"Or hair, nail clippings, toothbrush—whatever's easiest," Joaquin said.

Greer rubbed her forehead. "None of this makes sense. Troy says Wendy was never in his truck . . . so the cops planted her blood. And supposedly Hayes was suspect number one—so why target Troy?"

"It wasn't only the cops who could've had Wendy's blood—her killer could have had it too," Melrose said.

"But blood dries fast," Greer said. "Fresh blood in a tube needs an anticoagulant. That's not the kind of thing a killer walking the streets would have. Someone with access to medical supplies had to plant it."

"You're picturing some crooked cop with a vial, dripping Wendy's blood in Troy's truck like a *Law & Order* episode," Joaquin said. "By the time they found Wendy, her body had already started decomposing. They didn't collect any fresh blood—just dried flakes that had to be scraped off."

"And there was hardly any in Troy's truck," Melrose said. "The police report even calls it 'blood flakes,' and the photos match. If it had been fresh, it would've soaked the carpet. So yes, the cops had her flakes—but so did her killer. And with a pair of tweezers, it would've been easy to plant."

Greer leaned forward, head in her hands. "Maybe . . . my brother found out Tilly slept with Troy and set him up." Tears welled, and she wiped them away. "These last few days have been hell, realizing my brother could be a killer—that he let Troy go to prison, to death row. But if he set him up . . . he's a psychopath."

Joaquin and Melrose exchanged a look. Melrose rested a hand on Greer's knee. "All we know is Troy's innocent. And that's enough. It's not our job to solve the case."

Greer looked up. "But it makes sense. You're right; I was picturing the cops with a vial . . ." She stopped. Her eyes widened, and her breath became heavy.

"Greer." Melrose lowered her voice. "Are you alright?"

Sweat beaded on Greer's forehead. She flapped her hands as if to fan herself. "I . . . I . . ." She stood too fast, stumbling.

Melrose slowly stood. "Greer, please wait. You don't look—"

But Greer was already running out of the office.

# CHAPTER 38

Greer uncapped the red marker, hovering it over the blank poster board. An article on her phone listed anti-death penalty slogans— *EXECUTE JUSTICE, NOT PEOPLE. COMPASSION, NOT CRUELTY. KILL THE DEATH PENALTY.* She knew no slogan could untangle something this complicated, but Joaquin had said she didn't need to change minds—just make them look. With a sigh, she wrote something simpler: *FREE TROY.*

Capping the marker, she grabbed her phone. The Google alert for Ally Swanson had yielded little—just one brief article on her disappearance. She checked again, then scrolled through Ally's Facebook page, her breath catching every time the page refreshed. No new posts. No answers. Just more worried comments piling up.

Greer glanced at the red marker smudges on her hands and reminded herself that even if Ally were safe, it wouldn't necessarily clear Hayes. She couldn't shake the image burned into her mind since last week in Mr. Ramos's office—two vials of bright red blood sitting in a small dorm fridge.

Near the start of the summer after senior year, Greer remembered reaching into Hayes's mini fridge for a Coke. Her hand froze midair when she accidentally bumped the door to the small freezer compartment on top. Inside, vials filled with blood and neatly wrapped in white labels stared back at her. "What the hell?" she asked.

"Mine and Wendy's." Hayes crunched a chip, unfazed. "For the Science Olympiad experiment."

"Okaaaay, but school just ended. Why is it still in your freezer?"

Hayes shrugged. "It's infectious waste. Gotta ask Dad if I can toss it."

Had he tossed it? Or had he done something else with it? He had Wendy's blood. He had access to Troy's car. But the experiment was in May. Wendy died in July? Could frozen blood even last that long? Long enough to plant?

"What are you doing?"

Greer jumped. "Hayes!" A hand flew to her chest. "You scared me." Inhaling, she forced a casual tone. "Just looking at tacky protest slogans," she said, subtly closing Ally Swanson's Facebook page.

Hayes's eyes locked onto the poster. "So, you're doing this?"

"Yep. Headed to the courthouse in an hour." Greer looked up, hopeful. "Wanna join me?"

Hayes twisted off a water bottle cap, taking a long drink. "This'll make the news."

"Yeah, hopefully. But Red doesn't watch the news. Neither of your parents mentioned my *Breakfast with Texas* interview."

Hayes glanced at the sign. "You're making protest posters in their home, Greer."

"In *our* home. In *my* office," she corrected. "Red and Jo never come in here unannounced. It's not like I do this at the kitchen table during dinner."

Hayes slammed the bottle back like he'd run a marathon. His chest rose and fell rapidly, eyes narrowing. "You've been different since I got back. Distant. Then Quinn tells me we're not spending Christmas in Dallas? That was news to me. What's going on?"

Greer's shoulders tensed. "I found a phone bill."

Hayes tossed the empty bottle into the trash. "Our cell bill? Not like I hide them." He cocked his head. "Are you going through my calls or something?"

"Of course not," Greer said, trying to decipher whether that was guilt—or maybe fear—in his voice. "It was in Red's research files. We knew Tilly called my house that night, but everyone missed that someone *answered.* Someone picked up—and talked to her for four minutes."

Hayes sank onto the couch. "But you said you didn't speak to her on the phone that night."

"I didn't." Greer rocked slightly. "Keaton did."

"Keaton?" Hayes ran a hand along the back of his neck.

Greer hesitated, then finally said quietly, "They were seeing each other."

Pain flickered across Hayes's face. He opened his mouth, but Greer cut him off.

"Long story short, Tilly thought she was pregnant. She called my house, asking Keaton to bring a test. He did. Meaning he saw her after Troy left."

Hayes shot upright, shaking his head, fists curling at his sides. "Wow, I'm not surprised your crazy brother made up this fantasy, just surprised *you* believe it."

Greer stood, brushing off her jeans. "Why would he lie? Something that implicates him? Zach confirmed it. And Troy said Tilly also told him about the pregnancy scare that night."

Hayes raised his hands, voice tight, shoulders hunched. "Wait— you're still talking to Troy?" His face darkened. "Nope. Forget it. I won't listen to any more of this. If Tilly had thought she was pregnant, she would've told me." He jabbed a finger into his chest, then ran the other hand through his hair in frustration.

"It just makes me wonder if my brother had something to do with—"

Hayes cut her off. "So now you think your brother is a serial killer?"

"I . . . I'm not sure what to think," Greer admitted, mind racing—the vials of blood, the beachside photo of Nicole and Hayes, the Facebook post from Ally Swanson's sister: *Has anyone heard from Ally?*

"When I said you'd been different since I got back, I was being nice. You've been different for a while. Ever since that goddamn attorney called."

"Oh, excuse me for trying to save our friend when it's obvious he didn't kill anyone." Greer threw up her arms. "Deny it all you want—there are doubts. But you're more worried about your dad being wrong than about your best friend getting executed."

"You're my best friend!" Hayes snapped, pacing a half-circle across the room, hands gesturing wildly. "Or you were. Now, you're a stranger. And it's not just Troy—it's everything. The hair, Caleb's stocking. You've changed. Even Quinn's noticed."

Greer narrowed her eyes. "Has she now? Funny, Quinn didn't seem bothered when she called thirty minutes ago, asking me to watch Silas Friday night. But glad to hear you two talk about me so much."

Hayes shook his head. "This is ridiculous. There's no talking to you when you're . . . when you're—"

"When I'm talking back?" Greer stepped closer. "When I'm not hanging on every word you say?" Her voice rose, spittle hitting Hayes's cheek. "Sorry, I'm not seventeen anymore. I'm not Tilly!"

Hayes closed his eyes and wiped his face.

When he opened his eyes again, Greer saw a rage she had never witnessed before—not even on the football field. His skin was flushed, and his lips pulled back to reveal his teeth. Her gaze dropped to his hands, clenched into trembling fists.

Was this the last version of Hayes Sheridan that Tilly had ever seen?

He stepped closer, then another step, eyes darkening, breath growing heavier. Instinct urged Greer to retreat, but she planted her feet and met his gaze head-on. She wouldn't let him see her fear.

At the last second, Hayes veered right, pushing past her. The door slammed, and Greer flinched. She forced herself to relax, her breathing slowing. Then, she picked up the protest sign and grabbed Hayes's empty water bottle from the trash can.

"How are you feeling?" Greer asked, noticing the sling still cradling Joaquin's arm.

"Not too bad." He lifted a hot pink poster attached to a wooden stick. "Still got one good sign-holding arm."

A stiff wind swept through the courthouse parking lot, making the cardboard signs clatter like restless birds. Greer tugged her sweatshirt down over her hands.

"Are you cold?" Melrose asked. "There's coffee."

"I'm fine. Just ran out without my coat."

"Here," Luca offered, taking off his leather jacket.

Greer held up a hand. "I'm not taking your coat."

"Fine." Luca slipped his arm back through the sleeve. "There's a heavier jacket in my car. Come on, let's walk."

They hadn't gone far when Luca stopped. "I wasn't going to mention this until later, but the lab analyzed your DNA sample against the Wendy Knott evidence."

Greer's pulse quickened. "And?"

"The DNA doesn't match."

She expected relief to hit her like a wave—her brother wasn't a serial killer. But instead, the silence hung heavy, and she couldn't bring herself to smile.

"Greer? Are you okay?"

"Yeah, sorry, this is great news. Looks like I have a lot of apologizing to do."

They started walking again toward Luca's Mustang, where he grabbed a North Face jacket. It swallowed her. Her thoughts swallowed her, too. If it wasn't Keaton's DNA, did that mean it was Hayes's? She thought about the water bottle in her car, just a few rows down. She opened her mouth to tell Luca about it, but couldn't force out the words. Hayes wasn't a monster. He wasn't. He had never been violent, not even as a testosterone-charged teenager. But Greer had read enough about serial killers to understand duality was possible. She was familiar with Bundy, BTK, and the Green River Killer—family men who led seemingly normal lives while hiding dark, violent secrets.

"Are you sure you're okay?" Luca asked, glancing at her as they walked back toward the gathering crowd. "Joaquin told me about you running out of the office last week."

Greer huffed. "Come on, he called me, and I told him I was fine. I just got a little overwhelmed."

Luca looked at her incredulously. "If you don't want to talk about it, that's okay, but you clearly are *not* fine."

An unexpected tear slipped down Greer's cheek. "If I ask you to look into something for me, can you? Confidentially?"

Luca rubbed his stubbled chin. "I can try."

Greer wiped away another tear. "Ally Swanson."

"Okay. Who's she?"

"A woman missing out of Austin."

Luca's expression was blank. "Okay. Did you know her or—"

"Hayes did," she choked out. "They had an affair. Ages ago."

He blinked, jaw tightening for a moment, then gave a small, steady nod. "Okay. Let me see what I can find out. Try not to think the worst. I'm sure she's fine."

Greer turned on her phone's front-facing camera to check her mascara. "Thank you," she said softly, wiping beneath her eyes before heading back to Joaquin and Melrose.

"Are you still good to talk to the media?" Joaquin asked.

Greer zipped up Luca's jacket, grateful for the warmth as the wind picked up. "Yeah, I'm good."

"And Hayes?" Melrose asked. "Think he'll speak to the press, or is he just here for support?"

Greer shook her head. "He wouldn't come. I asked, but—"

"Wait, that's not Hayes?" Joaquin asked, pointing toward the parking lot. "Leaning against that red truck?"

When Greer's eyes met Hayes's, he didn't smile but lifted his hand in a slight wave before taking a few tentative steps toward her.

Greer wove through the crowd. What if Hayes had seen her take the water bottle? What if he knew what she was doing with it?

Her fears melted away when she noticed what was draped over Hayes's arm—her black puffer jacket.

"Thought you might need this," he mumbled. "But I see someone already beat me to it," he added, pointing to the jacket she was wearing.

Greer unzipped the oversized coat and slid her arms out of the sleeves. "This belongs to Luca. He's part of Troy's legal team. But I'll be glad to trade it for a coat that doesn't smell like it's been soaked in cologne."

Hayes helped her into her jacket, then opened the door of his truck. "The radio said rain was possible, so I brought your umbrella. Don't want the ink on your poster to smear."

Greer raised her eyebrows. "You sure about that?"

"I am," he said, closing his door. "Look, I'm sorry for how I've acted. How selfish I've been. Whether Keaton was involved, there's a good chance Troy's innocent. All I've been worried about is my dad looking bad."

"Greer!" From across the parking lot, she heard Joaquin calling her name. "We're about to start."

"I've gotta run," Greer said. "But thank you for the coat and umbrella. Let's talk more when I get home."

Hayes's eyes darted around the parking lot. "I was thinking of staying. I don't want to talk to the media, but if it's okay, I'd like to stay."

With his words, the weight of months of tension lifted from Greer's body. "Yes, please. It would mean a lot to me, to Troy."

Hayes wrapped his arms around her, kissing the side of her head. "I'm sorry."

"Me too," Greer whispered.

He pulled away from her. "Guess we'd better get over there." He held up his empty hands. "I don't have a sign."

"We've got extras." Greer took his hand. "Come on, let me introduce you to the team."

"Thanks again for coming," Greer told Hayes as he helped her into her car.

"It was enlightening." Hayes squeezed her hand. "I'm sorry about everything, Greer. Sorry I said all that about your changing. It's okay to change your mind, your hair, your Christmas decorations. I should be supportive and . . ."

"Hayes, you don't have—"

"No, let me finish, please. I just checked on Mom and Dad—they're fine. How about we grab lunch and take a drive? I found a place for sale outside town and wanted your opinion. It could make a great retirement home—plenty of rooms for future grandbabies, ten acres if I decide to raise a few animals," Hayes said. "There's even a detached apartment perfect for Mom or a studio for you. Oh, and I've been looking into better equipment than what you bought. Do you still have your receipt?"

"Hayes, you don't have to do this. It was just a fight," Greer said. He had always overcompensated after any disagreement they'd had.

Hayes shifted his weight from one foot to the other, voice low and careful. "Considering how I've acted the past few months, it's the least I can do. Meet you at Quiznos?"

"Sure." Greer watched Hayes walk back to his truck. She needed to wait till he was gone to give the water bottle to Luca.

She opened Facebook and froze at a new post atop Ally's page. Greer's breath caught as she read.

*Hey guys, it's Ally! So sorry I've been MIA. I met an amazing guy, and we did a thing . . . a Vegas thing. My daddy always said when it's right, you just know, and well . . . we did! Can't wait to share more soon. Sorry for disappearing—dropped my phone in the pool and had to get a new one, so I was off the grid for a bit. I didn't mean to scare anyone. XOXO #whathappensinvegas #goingtothechapel #eloped*

Greer pressed her palm against her heart and let her head fall back against the headrest. Hayes hadn't killed Ally Swanson. He hadn't even had dinner with her.

Greer's brother wasn't a murderer, nor was her husband. She needed to get a grip. Everything was going to be okay.

She crushed the water bottle in her hand and tossed it in the trash before heading to lunch with Hayes.

# CHAPTER 39

Joaquin handed Bernie a glass of apple cider. "Thanks for coming yesterday. It meant a lot."

Bernie smirked. "Don't get all mushy. I only showed up hoping Kim Kardashian might make an appearance."

"We tried. Not exactly a Kardashian, but Hayes Sheridan was a surprise."

"No kidding. Guess he's finally come around?"

Across the room, "Rockin' Around the Christmas Tree" blared louder. "Time to get this party started!" Luca shouted. He wore a sleeveless red vest with no shirt underneath and a pair of fuzzy red-and-white Santa pants, somehow managing to look both ridiculous and entirely confident. Between that and Bernie's flashing Christmas light necklace, Joaquin felt seriously underdressed. Even Melrose had on reindeer ears. When Luca suggested a small after-work Christmas party, Joaquin pictured drinks and a couple of meat and cheese trays—not costumes, tinsel covering every inch of the lobby, or a mistletoe branch he'd been dodging all night.

"I wouldn't say he's come around." Joaquin raised his voice over the music. "Pretty standoffish, but at least he showed."

"At least who showed?" Luca popped open another beer, refilling Joaquin's cup.

"Hayes Sheridan."

Luca crushed the can, aimed for the trash, and missed. "Wouldn't put him in a *Team Troy* shirt just yet. He's our last suspect standing."

"You should be at *his* Christmas party, digging his solo cup out of the trash," Melrose said, appearing behind them. "Can we turn the music down?"

"Please," Bernie added, covering her ears.

"You two are no fun. Fine—but you're not skipping the games," Luca said, his voice carrying over the holiday music.

"Games?" Melrose eyed him. "What games?"

"Reindeer games," he said, pointing at her headband.

Melrose groaned. "Reckon I'll need a drink for this."

"Atta girl. But come help me set up first."

Joaquin watched them head to the kitchen, relieved to see Melrose also steering clear of the mistletoe.

He motioned to Bernie. "Hey, come to my office for a sec."

Bernie pressed a button on her necklace, speeding up the lights. "Forget it. I'm officially on Christmas break."

"It's not work. I want to give you something."

In his office, he grabbed a card from his desk.

Bernie shook her head as she opened the envelope. "This better only be a card—we agreed, no gifts." She skimmed the holiday message, then found a check inside. "Joaquin, no."

"Don't tell Luca or Melrose," he said as she unfolded it. "I can't do this to everyone yet, but once the trial's over—"

"Are you serious?" Her eyes flicked between him and the check. "No way you can afford this."

"Sure I can."

She adjusted her glasses and read the memo. "In lieu of a plaque? What's that supposed to mean?"

"In honor of Esther Glickstein Rose," he said. "She named the Big Mac but never got the credit she deserved, and I don't want the same thing to happen to you. You've kept this office running and handled the heavy lifting on every other case while I focused on Troy. You've always had my back, and I wanted to acknowledge that."

Before he could react, Bernie hugged him, then pulled away, wiping a tear. "Thank you. Looks like Dan and I finally have enough for that Alaskan cruise."

"But not yet," Joaquin said, raising a finger.

"Not yet," she agreed. "Not until Troy walks out of prison."

She reached for a tissue on the windowsill but grabbed a small box instead. "What's this?" she asked, studying the flip-flop ornament.

Joaquin stuffed his hands into his pockets. "I wanted to give Melrose something to remind her of home since she can't go back for Christmas."

Bernie set the box down. "So when you said you didn't get anything for Melrose or Luca, you meant you didn't get anything for Luca."

"Come on, Bernie, it's just a generic ornament."

From the lobby, Darlene Love's voice swelled, pleading for her baby to come home for Christmas.

"Come on," Joaquin said. "Let's go see what kind of torture Luca's cooked up for us."

As much as Joaquin hated to admit it, Luca's games had been fun. Holding open a trash bag, Joaquin watched Melrose toss in red pompom balls, candy canes, and tiny jingle bells.

"Want the last one?" She held up a green shot glass filled with spiked Jell-O.

"Nah. Toss it."

Melrose threw it in. "Surprised there's any left, the way this lot was knocking 'em back."

"No kidding." Joaquin scooped up a few Hershey Kiss wrappers. "At least Dan was a good sport coming to pick up Bernie."

Melrose pointed to Luca, snoring on the couch. "What about him? You gonna drive him home?"

Joaquin cinched the bag. "Nah. Santa can sleep it off here. Are you good to drive, or . . ." He gestured to the other couch.

"Totally good. I only had one drink. The couch is all yours." She grabbed her purse as the opening notes of "Blue Christmas" played.

"Wait." Joaquin jogged to his office, returning with the ornament. "Before you go, I wanted to give you something."

Melrose eyed it. "What's this?"

"Just something small to remind you of home while you're here in Bluesummer, having a 'Blue Christmas.'" He nodded toward the speaker.

"Well, thank you. I love it. But nothing at all blue about this Christmas," she said, gaze flickering to the floor.

Joaquin stuffed his hands in his pockets. "Yeah, it was fun."

Silence stretched between them. Melrose shifted her weight. "I should go."

"Okay." Joaquin's eyes lingered on her lips. "Merry Christmas, Melrose."

"Merry Christmas, Joaquin." She gave a tentative smile and turned toward the door. Joaquin watched her taillights fade before locking up.

Searching for Luca's phone to turn off the music, his eyes landed on a single Hershey's Kiss on the empty couch. He must have missed it while cleaning, but a part of him hoped Melrose had left it there for him.

He powered off the portable speaker, but the music kept playing, albeit softer. Tracing the sound, he found Luca's phone under Bernie's desk. He tried to lower the volume, but the controls were unresponsive.

With the battery at three percent, Elvis wouldn't be crooning much longer. A notification caught Joaquin's eye—an email from Dr. Maya Whitmore, genetic genealogist at Dixon DNA Labs, sent six hours ago. Subject: Results Case 03241-082.

"Luca!" He nudged his friend's arm, but Luca's snoring only faltered before resuming. Joaquin grabbed Luca's hand and pressed his thumb to the side of the phone. The screen unlocked. The phone died before he finished reading, but he'd seen enough.

*Holy shit.* He shook Luca harder. "Get up! You're not gonna believe this."

# CHAPTER 40

reer struggled to focus on the Bible study lesson. Christmas was tomorrow, and she still had to wrap Si's gifts, make up the couch for Farren, and prep casseroles while Hayes picked up their daughter from the airport.

She wished she were at Zach's, where the schedule and meal were handled by her sister-in-law—something she'd ruined with an unfounded accusation.

Still, things weren't all bad, she reminded herself. Troy wouldn't complain about washing sheets or sliding a casserole into the oven. Greer thought about all the Christmases he'd missed—all the stockings he'd never filled, cookies for Santa he'd never eaten.

Hayes mouthed, "You okay?" at the sight of her tears.

She blinked them back and nodded.

"Jesus was conceived in Mary without the agency of a human father," Pastor Foster said. "A miracle. And we still serve the God of miracles."

Did they, though? If so, why wasn't her family speaking to her? Why was Caleb dead? Why was Troy on death row?

"Anyone here need a miracle?" the pastor asked.

For years, Greer sat silently in church events—never praying, never asking or answering questions. But today, she lifted her arm, feeling the weight of the room shifting toward her.

"Yes, Mrs. Sheridan?" The pastor's voice was almost too eager.

"Troy Terrell needs a miracle."

Chairs shuffled. A cough. A slight gasp.

"Thank you, Mrs. Sheridan." The pastor's tone softened. "The Bible tells us the Lord does not despise the captives. Whatever we do for the least, including prisoners, we do unto Him." He scanned the room. "Anyone else?"

After a few more requests, he announced he would lead them in prayer, asking everyone to place a hand on the shoulder of someone nearby and agree with them for their miracle. The elderly woman beside Greer placed a gentle hand on her shoulder. To her right, Hayes's hands remained clasped in his lap.

"What was that about this morning?" Hayes asked, standing by the oven.

"What do you mean?" Greer feigned ignorance.

Hayes slipped on an oven mitt. "The stunt about Troy."

"It wasn't a stunt. Troy needs a miracle."

Hayes crossed his arms, leaning against the counter. "Not the right place."

Greer huffed. "Since when is church the wrong place to ask for prayer?"

"Since Tilly's parents attend."

Greer rolled her eyes. "On Easter. Never Christmas Eve."

"A lot of their friends do. Maggie Donovan was there—Wendy Knott's great-aunt. Do you care about their feelings?"

Greer shrugged. "Not really. An innocent man's spent his life behind bars, and now they're going to kill him. Why should I care about a bunch of self-righteous people's feelings?"

Before Hayes could respond, the oven timer dinged.

"Put the rolls on a plate." Greer sprinkled more fried onions over the green bean casserole. "Let's eat."

"Come on, Si." Quinn positioned the booster seat between her and Red.

From across the room, Si rubbed his eyes. "No food, Mama."

"Yes, food." Quinn's tone sharpened. "You're eating."

"He's exhausted," Greer said. "Barely napped. His routine's off."

Quinn shoved her chair back. "Stop making excuses. If he doesn't eat now, he'll be hungry later."

"Then I'll get it back out. It's no trouble."

Hayes patted Greer's leg, a silent cue to let it go—to let their daughter parent.

The adults passed dishes, ignoring Quinn wrestling a screaming toddler into his seat. Red tore off a piece of his roll and handed it to Si.

"Sorry." Quinn pushed the hair from her face. "He's always worse when his dad's on shift."

"The boy just needed carbs." Red handed Si another piece.

Joanne clasped her hands, rings clanking. "Children always act worse with their moms. It's their safe place. I'm sure it was the same with you and your mother."

Greer kept her eyes on her plate. It wasn't the same for Quinn. The girls had always been more careful around her, more at ease with Hayes.

Across the table, Hayes must have felt the tension thickening. He reached for Greer's hand, his touch warm against her cold fingers.

"How about I say grace?" he said.

Greer realized she should do the dishes, but Si had fallen asleep in her lap, and she couldn't bear to move him.

"Grandpa looked worse than I thought," Farren whispered.

"He doesn't have long," Quinn said flatly. "I've been trying to tell you."

"We don't know that for sure," Hayes said, though they all did—the doctors, Joanne, and even Red.

"Will he come out later?" Farren asked. "Or Grandma?"

"No. Grandma said they want to be rested up for tomorrow," Hayes answered. "If you want to see friends, go ahead."

Farren and Quinn shared a look. Greer recognized that conspiratorial glance from their teenage years. They were hiding something.

"What's going on?" Hayes asked, catching it, too.

Quinn sighed. "We were thinking of heading to Dallas tonight."

Greer's stomach twisted. "Oh."

"Farren's only here for a few days," Quinn explained. "She wanted to see Grandma Linda."

"I have a gift for her," Farren added as if justifying the visit.

Greer shifted in her seat, careful not to wake Si. "You should go." She glanced out the window. "The roads are a little icy, but it's not a long drive."

"We'll be back by lunchtime tomorrow for Si's gifts," Quinn said.

"If that's okay?" Farren asked.

Greer's muscles tensed. No, it wasn't okay. Quinn and Rafael alternated Christmases, and this year was Greer's.

"But I have all Si's stocking stuffers here." She glanced at her sleeping grandson. "And the Santa gift," she whispered.

"You can still do Santa here," Quinn said.

"At noon?" Si's sweaty head made Greer suddenly hot. She fanned herself.

Quinn tapped her nails, adorned with red and gold Christmas designs, on the table. "Come on, Mom. He's four."

"But he knows Santa comes at night. He can't wake up at my brother's and think Santa skipped him." She looked at Hayes, silently pleading for backup.

"Maybe he could do Santa at both places?" Hayes suggested.

"Good idea," Quinn said quickly. "I'll make one of our gifts from Santa."

"But he asked Santa for the firetruck. If he doesn't get it, he'll be devastated," Greer argued.

Quinn blew out a dramatic breath, but Farren spoke instead. "We can just go tomorrow after we open here."

"No," Quinn said firmly. "I already told Uncle Zach we were doing gifts with them tonight."

Tears burned Greer's eyes, but she wouldn't let Quinn see. "Hayes, get the firetruck and put it in Quinn's trunk."

"Come on, Mom!" Quinn snapped. "You bought the damn truck. I know you want to see him get it. If you don't, you'll hold it over me forever."

Greer flinched. "What have I ever held over you?"

Quinn's nostrils flared. "How about that I'm not Caleb?"

Hayes stood. "Quinn, enough."

Quinn's voice wavered. "You never loved me like you loved him, and I felt it. Farren did, too."

Greer's hands shook. She glanced at Farren, who was staring at her shoes.

"You always kept us at arm's length," Quinn continued.

"I did my best," Greer whispered.

Quinn slammed her hand on the table, rattling the glasses. Si stirred in Greer's arms. "Well, your best wasn't enough."

Hayes's jaw tightened. "That's enough," he said, low and firm.

"You left us," Quinn pressed on, her voice rising. "For over a month, you disappeared. What were you thinking, leaving your ten-year-old daughters?"

"Get out!" Hayes shouted. Everyone in the room went still.

Quinn took a step back. "What?"

"Get out," Hayes repeated, his voice quieter but steady, tinged with authority. "You will *not* talk to your mother like that."

Quinn raised her hands in mock surrender. "Whatever. That makes Christmas planning easier. Grab my purse, Farren."

Farren hesitated, then obeyed. As Quinn yanked Si from Greer's arms, his eyes fluttered open, confused. Greer kissed his forehead. "Please take the firetruck," she whispered, but Quinn didn't look back.

The door closed behind them, and Greer buried her face in her hands. Hayes kneeled beside her. "Don't listen to her. You've always been a great mom," he said softly. "And we'll figure out the firetruck."

But Greer wasn't crying over the firetruck. She was crying because Quinn was right. She *hadn't* been the mother she had wanted to be. And now, it was too late. Children had only one childhood; once it was gone, no regret or effort could undo the damage.

She lifted her head to thank Hayes for standing up for her—but froze at the tears in his eyes.

"I'm sorry," she whispered. "I'm sure if you call Quinn—"

"No," Hayes interrupted. "I have to tell you something."

Pressure built in her chest. The weight of those words sent her back to another night, another confession at this table. She knew that whatever he was about to say had the potential to unravel everything, just as Ally Swanson had. She wanted him to spit it out, but also to keep it hidden forever.

"Remember when I said I had to go to the office late Saturday night?" Hayes's chin trembled.

Greer pulled her hands away. "Where did you *really* go?"

"I was meeting with Rick."

"Our attorney, Rick?"

He raked a hand through his hair. "I didn't want to ruin Christmas. I wanted to wait, but—"

Greer stood abruptly. "But *what*, Hayes?"

He exhaled. "They're saying the semen sample found on Wendy's clothing matches my DNA."

Greer's knees buckled. "What?"

"It's bullshit," he said, a single tear slipping down his cheek. "It can't be. Someone's setting me up."

Greer stumbled into the bathroom. Gasping. Vomiting.

"Are you okay?" Hayes tried to hand her a washcloth.

"Stay away from me."

"I didn't hurt Wendy."

Her head spun. "DNA doesn't lie, Hayes."

"It doesn't make any sense." His shoulders sagged. "We fooled around once. We were drunk, but—"

"Wait, you cheated on Tilly? Just like you cheated on me, you stupid son of a bitch." Greer forced herself to breathe. "When?"

Hayes winced. "A few days before Wendy went missing. But we didn't have sex. I mean, the night's a blur, but I'd remember if we had. And why would she be wearing the same underwear when she died?"

Greer sank onto the tub's edge, breathing hard. "You're lying."

"I'm not. Wendy left my house, and I never saw her again."

Greer's head was spinning. "They asked me to get your DNA, you know? And I didn't—because I trusted you." She shoved him hard. "I TRUSTED YOU."

"Keep your voice down," Hayes hissed, shutting the bathroom door. "My parents will hear."

"That's what you're worried about, really?"

"Listen," Hayes said. "Rick didn't test my DNA directly. They used an ancestry database. Farren did a test years ago. Her markers matched the crime scene. They're assuming it's me—but it could be a second cousin or something."

Greer gave a bitter laugh. "Any second cousins stalking Bluesummer in 1986?"

"I don't know. It's a complicated process, and I don't understand it, but Rick says familial DNA searches aren't exact. They misidentify cousins as siblings all the time."

The room felt smaller, the walls pressing in. Greer pushed past him into the bedroom and yanked her duffel bag from the closet.

"Greer, please." His voice cracked. "This is a mistake. Nothing makes sense."

She started throwing clothes into the bag. "No, it *finally* makes sense." She turned, eyes burning. "You were intimate with at least three of the victims."

"What?" His face went pale. "Three?"

"Nicole Garcia."

Hayes blinked rapidly. "What are you talking about?"

She zipped the bag with a sharp pull. "I saw the picture."

"What picture?"

"At church camp. She was sitting on your shoulders."

His brow furrowed. "On my—" Then his expression shifted, and a relieved look crossed his face. "We were playing chicken."

"You told the cops you didn't know her."

"I *barely* did! We barely spoke." He exhaled, his frustration rising. "Come on, Greer. You *know* me."

Her pulse pounded as she slung a jacket over her shoulder. "Did you set up Troy?"

"You can't be serious, Greer."

"You had Wendy's blood in your freezer," she said, tugging the bag strap tighter. "Why the hell were you keeping it?"

"From the experiment? I didn't know how to dispose of it," Hayes said.

"Well, you must have figured it out eventually. How did you get rid of it? When?"

Hayes looked flustered, his eyes darting. "I don't remember, Greer. It was a long time ago. Look . . . this will all get sorted. You'll regret doubting me."

Maybe he was right. Greer remembered suspecting Hayes of hurting Ally Swanson and hating herself for it.

Hayes took a cautious step toward her. "You know me, Greer. Better than anyone. You always have."

Did she? The Hayes she knew wouldn't have slept with Ally Swanson or fooled around with his lab partner. He wouldn't have lied about knowing a girl in a bikini whose thighs pressed against his neck.

"I'm not sure I do anymore," she said, grabbing the bag and storming out the door.

Greer drove down Bluesummer's slushy roads, her tears flowing.

It felt like July 4, 1986—Greer heartbroken, confused, and once again fleeing from Hayes Sheridan.

And, like that night, she was back in the driveway of her childhood home. She had a key, and her mom was in Dallas at Zach's house, where Greer's girls and Si would arrive any minute.

The porch light was off, so she used her phone as a flashlight. She had silenced it an hour ago, avoiding Hayes's calls and messages. But now, she saw two missed calls and several texts from him. *I'm sorry. Please believe me.* Then, more desperate: *Where are you? I'm worried.* Greer sighed, the familiar sting of guilt washing over her. He deserved to be the one worried for once, but she couldn't let him stew. The roads were slick.

*I'm okay*, she typed. *I'm not coming home, but I'm safe. I'll call tomorrow.*

It wouldn't be hard for Hayes to guess where she was—but at least he didn't have a key. She stepped into the dark house, the air calm and still. The hallway stretched before her. The boy's old room had become a craft room, while her own—now a guest room—remained as she left it when she went off to college, minus the Matt Dillon posters.

Her fingers hovered over her old doorknob. As she touched it, the heater kicked on, its sudden noise jarring. Why was she so jumpy? She turned the knob—but it wouldn't budge. It felt locked, which didn't make sense. Her mom wouldn't lock it with no one home. The resistance was different, though—deliberate, controlled—almost like someone was holding the door shut from the other side.

She yanked her hand back, stepping away. Something wasn't right.

Before she could react, the door burst open. Hands slammed her against the wall. Stars spun before her eyes.

"Don't move!" The voice was cold, sharp—familiar, but she couldn't place it.

As she tried to recover, a cold, hard metal pressed against her forehead—a gun. The realization hit like a punch to the gut, freezing her in place. The headlights of a passing vehicle cut through her bedroom curtains, briefly illuminating the hallway. Through the glow, she saw the figure holding the gun.

"Keaton?" she managed, the name slipping out before everything went black again.

# CHAPTER 41

"There's no way Hayes Sheridan killed anyone," Troy repeated.

Joaquin's phone beeped with a low battery warning. He powered it down, slipping it into his jacket. "The DNA says otherwise."

Troy paused. "Maybe he slept with her. I slept with Tilly. Doesn't make me a killer."

Joaquin unwrapped a Little Debbie Christmas Tree cake. "The police officially reopened the investigation."

Troy sat up straighter. "Does that mean they have to release me?"

Joaquin took a bite. "I wish it were that simple. Either the prosecution drops the charges, or the court rules in our favor. But it's a step forward."

Troy pressed his forehead against the plexiglass. "So why does it feel like you're replacing one innocent man with another?"

Frosting clung to Joaquin's mouth. He licked it away. "The Sheridans turned on you—Red and Hayes both. You were a pawn in Red's plan."

"I'd sooner believe I murdered five girls in my sleep than accept Hayes hurt anybody," Troy said. "He doesn't have it in him."

Joaquin took another bite of the cake. "Never thought I'd meet someone as stubborn as me until you became my client."

"Hey, I grew up around pigs," Troy said. "What's your excuse?"

Joaquin wiped his mouth with his sleeve. "Wait till you meet my parents."

"So this theory about Hayes," Troy said, his tone shifting. "Have you told Greer?"

"I haven't yet, but she'll find out soon one way or another. The cops will want to question Hayes. They may have already."

"Christmas Eve. What timing?" Troy raised an eyebrow. "Speaking of, why are you here eating vending machine snacks with me instead of dinner with your family?"

"I'm heading to Tyler soon, but I wanted to share the good news first and wish you a Merry Christmas."

"Not sure I'd call this good news," Troy said. "Not the part about Hayes being a suspect."

Joaquin crumpled the wrapper. "This is your last Christmas behind bars, Troy. If that's not good news, I don't know what is."

Greer's eyes fluttered open, disoriented. Was it Christmas morning? Had she forgotten to put Si's firetruck out?

*No*, she remembered. The girls had left, and . . .

Greer shot up from the couch, panic rushing in as everything came back in a flood. The room spun.

"Greer? Are you okay?"

Her vision blurred, but her brother's voice cut through. She remembered the gun. "Get away from me!" she cried.

She tried to stand, but her legs buckled. Keaton caught her before she fell. "You hit your head. You need to lie down."

"*You* hit my head! *You* pointed a gun at me!"

"I'm sorry. I didn't expect you," Keaton said, lowering her back onto the couch.

Greer blinked, the room sharpening into focus. "Well, ditto. What are you doing here?"

Keaton sat on the coffee table. "Samantha went to Arizona to see her folks. I was at Zach's, but the kids' noise was overwhelming."

Greer didn't trust him. "Why not go to your own house?"

"The heater's out. Mom said I should decompress here."

Greer paused. *If he had wanted to kill me, he would've*, she assured herself. "So your idea of decompressing is sleeping with Mom's gun?"

"It's not loaded," Keaton said, fidgeting with his smartwatch, avoiding her gaze.

She patted her pockets, frantic. "Where's my phone?" she demanded, tearing through the couch, tossing pillows, and digging between cushions.

Keaton shrugged. "Did you leave it in your car?"

"I need my phone! Hayes already knows I'm here," she lied. "He's probably on his way."

Keaton tapped his watch. "Okay. I'll call him and let him know what happened. You might need to go to the ER."

"What did you do with my phone?" Greer's vision blurred again. "And my purse?"

"I haven't touched your stuff," Keaton said, his voice tight. "Why do you always accuse me?"

A memory surfaced—her mom, before her first night shift, telling the boys and Greer that anything could be a weapon. *If someone tries to break in, start throwing things, then get away. Anything that creates an obstacle will buy you time.*

Good advice, but useless when your head felt like it was splitting open and you could barely stand.

Keaton stood and walked toward the door. Before Greer could ask, he returned with her purse.

"Thanks," she muttered, rifling through it. "My keys are in here, but not my phone. I had it in my pocket." She patted her jeans again.

"I'll call it," Keaton offered.

A familiar ring echoed faintly. "Sounds like it's coming from here," Greer said, pressing her hands between the cushions.

"Probably fell through." Keaton knelt and shone his phone's flashlight under the couch. "Yep, got it." He grabbed it and tossed it to her.

She checked her notifications. The only text was from Hayes, sent five minutes after she'd told him where she was: *OK. Merry Christmas.*

Before she could text him again, the screen went dark. She cursed under her breath. "It's dead."

Keaton extended his hand. "Give it here. My charger is in your old room."

She drew a quick breath, fingers tightening around her phone. Her eyes flicked to his, then back down. "Okay . . . but while you're back here, put Mom's gun away."

"No problem," he said, his glance unreadable, before taking her phone and heading toward the hallway.

Silence stretched. Something about Keaton was off—he was too quiet, too still. She thought of the gun. Was he planning to hurt himself? He'd tried before. Maybe that was the real reason he was here alone on Christmas.

"Want me to call Hayes to come get you?" Keaton asked, making his way back toward her.

Greer took a slow breath, trying to settle her nerves. She couldn't shake the fear that, alone, Keaton might make a decision he couldn't take back. And she didn't want to be around Hayes right now. "I don't want to go home. Would you mind company?"

Keaton smiled. "It would be kinda nice to have someone to talk to. I'll put some coffee on."

Greer gave a small, uncertain nod and settled back onto the couch.

But as Keaton turned away toward the kitchen, Greer's gaze wandered. Her eyes caught the slight bulge at the back of his jeans—the gun, still there, tucked out of sight.

"Are you shitting me?" Joaquin's brother-in-law asked as Joaquin scrubbed the last pan from Christmas Eve dinner.

"Nope. Familial DNA points straight to Hayes Sheridan. Think it's enough?" Joaquin handed him the pan.

"For a warrant? Sure. But Sheridan will claim it was consensual. Might've been."

Joaquin pulled the drain plug, watching the soapy water swirl away. "Right before she died? Come on, man."

"You'd better pray he doesn't have an alibi—and that you can tie him to the first victim." Favian dried the dish and opened the cabinet.

"I'm pretty sure he and Nicole had something going on." Joaquin rolled down his sleeves. "They were counselors at this church camp, and they got pretty close. Luca got a scrapbook from her parents with some camp photos. I borrowed it for the holiday, figured I'd look closer."

Favian placed the pan inside and closed the cabinet. "Let's take a look."

"Please, no talking about murder on Christ's birthday." Joaquin's mom appeared, wiping down the splashed counter.

"Just a few minutes, I promise." Joaquin kissed her forehead. "Then we'll watch *It's a Wonderful Life* or whatever."

"Be glad they're getting along, Isabel," his dad called from the table, watching his grandson move a chess piece.

Joaquin grabbed the scrapbook from his suitcase and sat next to Favian on the couch. "Nicole made this," he said, flipping through pages full of dorm room snapshots, friend photos, and academic awards.

"Beautiful, bright girl," Favian said. "Such a loss."

"You can just make out Hayes here." Joaquin pointed to the figure on the bus steps. Joaquin studied each subsequent photo, looking for Hayes, but only found him in the one Luca had—the one where Nicole sat on his shoulders.

"This could be something." Favian pointed at the picture. "See this kid doing the peace sign? He's not in any other pictures. Have you seen him before?"

Joaquin flipped back through the beach shots—mostly Nicole with other female counselors. "You're right."

Favian clasped his hands. "If she wasn't close to him and didn't take this photo herself, why include it? Maybe it's what's happening in the background she wanted to remember."

"Right, but why no other pictures of her and Hayes?"

"What if it was a secret relationship?" Favian asked. "Wasn't Hayes underage?"

"Nope. He was seventeen—the age of consent in Texas. But if he was cheating on Tilly, it makes sense he wouldn't want evidence."

Joaquin scanned the rest of the summer photos. Hayes Sheridan was nowhere to be found.

He set the scrapbook down, knocking over Favian's near-empty Fresca. He shoved the album aside before the liquid could reach it.

"I'll grab paper towels." Favian stood.

Joaquin collected some loose photos that had fallen out. He flipped through, trying to find where they belonged.

When he reached the camp section, he noticed the corner of a photo was loose from its adhesive mount. As he moved to fix it, the white backing of another Polaroid peeked from behind. Where had that come from? Carefully, he lifted the front photo.

"You're lucky your mom didn't see that spill," Favian said, blotting the table.

"Hey, there's another picture stuck behind this one." Joaquin pulled at it. "But if I yank too hard, it'll tear. I need to return this to Nicole's parents in one piece."

"Use steam," Favian suggested. "Or heat."

"Told you we should've loaded the dishwasher." Joaquin stood. "Come on. I've got another idea."

Joaquin rummaged through the bathroom drawers until he found his mom's blow-dryer. He plugged it in and handed it to Favian. "Low setting. Not too close."

Favian followed the instructions. After a few minutes, Joaquin freed the picture with minimal damage.

It took a second to register what he was seeing in the photo that had been hidden. His heart pounded. *Holy shit.*

Favian fumbled with the dryer, accidentally blasting it on high before shutting it off. It clattered to the floor. "Is that who I think it is?"

"What's going on in there?" Isabel called. "Who's drying their hair, and why are there wet paper towels on my table?"

Joaquin's legs felt unsteady. He took a step back, catching himself before stumbling into the toilet.

No wonder Nicole had hidden this photo. It was irrefutable proof of a love affair that had occurred that week at church camp.

A candid selfie, before selfies were a thing. When you had to hold a Polaroid camera at arm's length and hope for the best.

The picture was taken in a hotel room. Nicole wore a hot pink swimsuit, pressing her lips to the cheek of the man beside her. Only half of his face was visible. Maybe intentional, maybe not.

But Joaquin knew exactly who it was.

Not Hayes Sheridan.

Hayes Sheridan's father.

# CHAPTER 42

"Midnight laundry isn't how I pictured spending Christmas." Greer took a sip of coffee. Two hours had passed. Her headache had eased, her phone was fully charged, and her mom's gun was secured again. For maybe the first time ever, she felt safe around her brother. Still, she planned to figure out how to change the code to the gun safe before she left.

Keaton tipped back his Diet Coke. "Figured I've left enough messes for Mom. Might as well wash my own towels this time."

It was oddly peaceful out here. Wood smoke from their chimney drifted in through the slightly raised garage door, mingling with the sharp, clean scent of citrus detergent. The cold night air, tempered by the dryer's warmth, carried the sound of tumbling clothes, steady like a heartbeat.

"You remember that month I stayed with Mom?" Greer said, tracing the edge of the table. "When Hayes and I separated . . . we spent plenty of time out here talking about marriage while the dryer tumbled."

Keaton fiddled with the tab on his empty can. "Marriage is tough. One moment it's smooth sailing, and the next—a hurricane."

*Hurricane.* That perfectly described the chaos of the Ally Swanson era. But if that was a hurricane, what did you call your husband being suspected of serial murder? A tsunami? A nuclear fallout?

"Mom had the right idea after Dad left," Greer mused. "Stay single, enjoy your laundry and cigarettes in peace."

"Not that we made things easy for her. Especially me." Keaton crushed the empty can underfoot. "I've apologized to Mom—a byproduct of therapy. But I've never apologized to you."

A dry lump formed in Greer's throat. "You don't have to."

"Oh, I do. I wasn't a good brother. I'm sorry for the careless words, for stealing your stuff, and for that day in the kitchen. And I'm sorry I lied about it."

Greer's eyes widened. "You mean . . ."

"I remember what I did." His voice carried regret. "I can't blame the medication. I didn't confuse you with someone else. I was just angry."

Her mind raced, disbelief and unease knotting together. "About what?"

"About Dad."

"But Dad had been gone since . . ."

"Since you were born," Keaton finished.

Suddenly, everything clicked into place. "You blamed me."

"It wasn't your fault. But as a kid, all I saw was that one day you were there, and he wasn't."

Greer thought back to that day in the kitchen. "But he had been gone for years by then."

"After he left, he still sent Zach and me Valentines."

Jealousy stirred, though it made no sense to be bitter about never receiving a Valentine from a man she'd never known. "Did Mom stay in touch with him?"

"I wondered, but that year, I noticed the handwriting—it looked like Mom's."

"Mom was behind the Valentines? That doesn't sound like her. She always emphasized honesty."

Keaton shrugged. "Maybe she thought our happiness came first."

"Did you ever tell her you figured it out?"

"Yeah. If I hadn't, she'd probably still be sending them." Keaton rubbed his hands on his pajama pants. "A few days later, I saw you making Valentines. Amid the glitter and stickers, I spotted one with a big heart that said 'Dad.'"

Greer frowned. "I don't remember making that."

"When I turned it over, I saw it wasn't for *our* dad. It was for Red. That set me off. I'd learned Dad didn't send those cards, and in my mind, you were the reason he left. But there you were, making a Valentine for this new dad, a dad who was only yours. A dad who bought you clothes, took you to dinner, showed up for your school events. I snapped." His chin trembled. "I'm not making excuses. I'm sorry, Greer."

Greer scooted her chair closer. "It's okay. Those are confusing feelings for a kid."

"The feelings confused me well into adulthood. That's why I tried so hard to have a relationship with Red."

In hindsight, it made sense. Keaton had always sought Red's attention.

"When I came back from college, he finally noticed me," Keaton continued. "Hiring me for his accounting wasn't the same as buying you a prom dress or Troy's class ring, but it was something. Finally, it was something."

"Not to split hairs, but he didn't buy Troy's ring. I was at the Terrells' when Troy's dad filled out the paperwork and wrote the check. Frank was so proud to do it."

"Right, but Red bought him a replacement." Keaton tapped his foot against the concrete. "I overheard him talking to Jostens. Troy lost the original, and Red was surprising him with a new one."

Greer smiled. "That sounds like Red."

"He's a good man," Keaton said. "He helped me finish my degree, get my first job, helped me . . ." His face twisted—something unspoken caught in his throat.

"What?" Greer asked.

Keaton's hands trembled. "I went to him, Greer," he choked out. "The night Tilly died."

Greer recoiled, springing from her chair. "What?"

Keaton turned to her, eyes pleading. "I didn't kill her, but I had been with her right before she died. I was terrified they'd come after me."

Greer pressed her hands to her temples. "Wait, you told Red you'd been with Tilly that night?"

"He told me not to worry," Keaton said. "Said no one saw me, and as long as no one knew about Tilly and me, I'd be fine. But I mentioned the phone call . . ."

A cold gust swept through the garage. Greer shivered. If Red knew Keaton was with Tilly, he knew Troy couldn't have killed her.

"What did he say?"

"That he'd take care of it. Advised me not to talk to the cops. Later, when I told him about the call, he promised to handle it. But I never got questioned. I guess I got lucky."

"Excuse me? Lucky?" Greer's voice sharpened. "Your 'luck' cost an innocent man his life!"

Keaton stood. "Okay, that came out wrong. I regret what happened to Troy. I've thought about coming forward so many times. Keeping this secret has weighed on me and contributed to all my issues."

Greer paced, trying to process everything, but the noise in the garage drowned out her thoughts.

*Clunk. Clunk. Clunk.* The dryer tumbled.

*Rat-a-tat-tat.* Sleet pelted the garage door.

*Bang!* The furnace roared to life.

"Greer?" Keaton called out. "Are you okay?"

Greer tried to speak but couldn't. She only shook her head, the truth settling over her like the cold creeping in under the garage door.

# CHAPTER 43

Waking up in her childhood home on Christmas morning felt both foreign and strangely familiar to Greer. She'd slept on the couch the night before—despite everything, the colored lights brought comfort.

She powered on her phone. Only one message had come through—not from Hayes, but from Joaquin: *Call me.*

Greer rubbed her eyes, sitting up. It was 3:30 a.m. Too late to call back, so she texted instead: *What's up?*

The three dots appeared, vanished, then reappeared. She was surprised he was still awake. His reply was brief: *Look at this.*

Below the message, a photo of a photo appeared. She increased the screen's brightness and zoomed in on the faces.

The sick feeling from the garage crept back in. Greer had tried convincing herself that Keaton might've been lying about the kind of man Red Sheridan was. But this picture erased any doubt.

She grabbed her keys and drove through town, envious of the happy families inside the snow-dusted houses. This Christmas would be far from idyllic for Greer—no filled stockings, no children rushing downstairs, just a firetruck in the hall closet and three people she'd known her whole life but now seemed like strangers.

At the house, Greer pushed Red's door open and let the sliver of hallway light cut across the rumpled bed. Red blinked awake, and reached for his water glass. "Already five?" he mumbled, voice thick with sleep.

"I'm not here to give you medicine," she snapped.

Her sharp tone seemed to grab Red's attention. "What's going on?"

"The police think Hayes is the Strangler."

Red's fingers tightened around the glass. "Ridiculous. What evidence could—"

"Familial DNA," Greer interrupted. "The semen found in Wendy's underwear came from someone in our family."

Red barked a laugh that died too fast, too sharp. "Sounds like bullshit."

"Familial DNA isn't bullshit," Greer countered. "Bullshit is the story you've been selling all these years."

Red's face went still. He set the glass down with exaggerated care. "Let's not play games, Greer. How much do you know?"

Greer sank into the chair, blinking back angry tears and taking a slow, steadying breath.

She pulled her phone out and tapped. The recording icon blinked. She didn't hide it. "I know Troy didn't kill Tilly, and so do you. Keaton talked to Tilly that night and showed up at her house. You covered for him."

"I don't believe your brother killed Chantilly, if that's what you're worried about. But no one would've trusted him, given what a loony tune he was."

"So who did, Red? Who killed Tilly? Who are you actually covering for?"

Red locked eyes with hers, and in that moment, Greer saw nothing but a cold, empty void where she could have sworn kindness once existed.

"Hayes did it, didn't he?" She choked back tears.

Footsteps creaked—Joanne, probably heading to the bathroom. Red's eyes darted toward the door, hand rising instinctively. "Shhh," he whispered, low and urgent.

Greer froze. A faint flush echoed from the bathroom, followed by the gurgle of water. They waited, barely breathing, listening as the door clicked closed.

Red exhaled slowly, his shoulders sagging. The moment stretched, the room shrinking around them. Greer held out her phone, letting the recording light blink at them both as she spoke.

"You told the police Joanne had Hayes's keys, but last month, you let it slip that Hayes had them, and that's how you knew he was planning on sneaking out. You were having an affair with Nicole Garcia, and I'm guessing Hayes found out and took his rage out on her. Guilt over the affair spurred you to cover for him, but things escalated. Hayes killed another girl. And another."

Red's mouth opened; closed. He rubbed the side of his neck. "You're reaching. This is nonsense."

"Come on, Red, there's no way you'd set up Hayes's best friend for Keaton."

"Troy slept with Hayes's girlfriend—some best friend." Red scoffed.

"All while Hayes fooled around with Wendy Knott," Greer shot back.

Red's fingers found the hem of his blanket and fiddled with it like a child.

When he finally spoke, the words were defensive. "I helped him because—because he was your family. Keaton called frantic. Said she was alive when he left."

"You believed him and decided to frame Troy instead—someone who meant more to you than my brother ever did?"

Red froze, gaze flicking toward the window. "Troy was betraying Hayes."

"And so was Keaton," Greer pointed out.

"Keaton didn't pretend to be Hayes's best friend! Yeah, the kid was always a screw-up; no surprises there. But Troy knew better and still chose betrayal. That's why it had to be him. But I had to deal with that damn phone call Tilly made to Keaton."

"So you made up the theory about Troy strangling Tilly while she was trying to call me?"

Red nodded. "And those idiot detectives didn't notice the phone call lasted for several minutes. I worried Tilly's dad might, so I took care of that too."

"How?"

"Stole the phone bill from their mailbox after putting an anonymous credit on their account to cover the rest of the year. Told the phone company to notify Mr. Price about the credit. That way, he wouldn't question the missing bill."

"But you ordered a new class ring for Troy," Greer pressed. "To leave at the bower. That wasn't a last-minute decision. It had been in motion for a long time—probably since finding out Hayes was a killer."

Red smiled. "Nice digging. But the ring was a lucky break. I ordered it because Troy had lost his. The Terrells lacked the means to replace it, so I handled it."

"Listen to yourself. What started as a kind gesture ended up costing someone their life. This isn't you. There's no way you would do all this for Keaton or even me." Greer shrugged off her coat, the heat pressing in like a truth she couldn't ignore. "Hayes went to Tilly's that night, didn't he? Found out she'd been cheating and—"

"No!" Red's forceful denial triggered a coughing fit. He took a drink of water, then managed, "Hayes never left the house."

"Then how did you know Troy and Tilly had slept together?" Greer asked.

Red blinked; his eyes drifted to a crack in the plaster. "I think Keaton told me. Tilly must have fessed up when he saw her that night."

Greer recalled her conversation with Keaton in his office. He had no idea about Troy and Tilly. "You're lying, and we're done talking. Hayes will give his DNA, and it'll be a match. He'll crack and tell the cops the truth. He'll be 'convicted,'" she mimed with her fingers, "and you'll go down as an accomplice."

Red swallowed hard. "And his lawyer is letting him do that? Give his DNA?"

Greer shrugged. "If not, they'll get a warrant."

Red ran a thumb along his lip. "How accurate can DNA that old be? Can it distinguish Hayes from some distant cousin?"

Greer snatched her jacket. He sounded just like Hayes. "Come on, Red, it's not like Hayes had a distant cousin around here killing—"

Her voice died. Her hands trembled, and her coat fell into her lap. No distant Sheridan cousin had been around Bluesummer in 1986—but Red Sheridan had been.

She whispered, almost to herself, "It was you. Not Hayes. You."

His eyes darted to the floor, then flicked up at her, sharp and guarded. "It's not like you think," he said, voice brittle, tight. "I made mistakes. But I'm not a monster."

Greer collapsed into the chair. "All of them? Tilly?"

Red pinched the bridge of his nose, trembling. "I didn't plan to hurt her. It's . . . it's complicated." His words came slowly, like someone testing the waters before diving into the unknown.

Greer's stomach dropped, but her voice stayed firm. "Start talking. From the beginning."

Red's eyes darted away, hands clenching in his lap. Finally, he exhaled, voice low and raw. "I . . . I loved Nicole. She was studying criminal justice and reached out. We just clicked."

Greer's throat tightened. "So that's why you drove her to church camp?"

Red sighed. "It should've been a beautiful week, but it all went to hell when she started flirting with my son. I had no choice but to end things."

"Then why kill her? Almost a year later?"

"Nic and I stayed in touch. We slept together once when she came home for spring break, and then she lost it. She begged me to leave Joanne." Red's eyes locked with Greer's, his gaze hardening. "That wasn't ever going to happen. Nicole knew from the start that I'm a family man."

"Did she threaten to tell Jo?" Greer met his gaze.

Red nodded. "And I couldn't let that happen."

"So you strangled her?"

Red's voice turned matter-of-fact. "I enjoyed strangling her."

*Like Bundy*, Greer thought, bile rising in her throat. "Why did you take the body?"

"I wanted her to look like a runaway," Red said, almost clinical. "Buy myself some time to figure out what to do. Then, when I got her in the trunk, I saw the wind chimes—the ones I'd heard the night before when we made love. I guess I felt sentimental, so I took them."

Greer forced herself to stay calm. "And then what?"

"I took her body to a secluded spot. To what would soon be known as the bower."

"You were just going to leave her there?"

"That was the plan. But as I was taking off the earrings I'd given Nicole—real diamonds, I decided I'd clean them up for Jo—I had this epiphany: a story about a serial killer who made a nest of his victims' bones and mementos. A killer who stalked families with wind chimes. A killer the cops thought they'd never catch—until some old, washed-up crime writer solved the case."

Greer recoiled. "You killed five women for a book deal?"

Red applied ChapStick, unfazed. "Some of those gals brought it on themselves."

Greer's fists clenched. "Andrea Dalton was sixteen years old. She deserved to die?"

Red's voice softened, almost a whisper. "I'll admit . . . that one was my fault."

*That one was his fault?* The man she loved no longer existed, replaced by an impostor casually recounting horrific facts.

"I killed Andrea because I couldn't stop myself," Red continued. "I kept remembering what it was like with Nicole—how good it felt to have my hands around her neck. The urge . . . it kept coming back."

Greer's stomach lurched.

"This is hard to explain, Greer, but for the first time, I felt real power. Growing up, you're taught to obey. But nobody tells you what happens when you take control. It's intoxicating. I hate to use it as an excuse, but my mom left me—and that messed me up. I blamed Mom for everything my dad did to me. Fantasized about getting my revenge—"

"Enough," Greer cut in. "Why Andrea?"

Red didn't hesitate. "The Daltons had wind chimes. Her window was open. Opportunity."

"And you sexually assaulted her?"

Red shook his head. "The house was small. Her dad was in the living room. I had to move fast. Took her body, the wind chimes, and her hooker-red lipstick as a keepsake. Left only Nicole's picture behind." Red wrinkled his nose. "Nic's body was still at the bower. The decomposition was bad—drawing animals. That's when I got the idea to feed the bodies to the hogs." He raised a finger. "Not to set up Troy. The original plan was to let them rot at the bower, but the smell—you can't imagine. Plus, it was easier. I was already feeding the hogs, so I stopped for a few days and then let them take care of the evidence once they were good and hungry. I cleaned up the manure and scattered it in the woods, not the Terrells' fields. Didn't want anything tying back to Troy."

Greer thought about the distance between the bower and the Terrell farm. "How did you move the bodies?"

Red shifted in bed. "This is where it gets . . . messy. Literally. Had to use a hacksaw. I kept the bones I needed for the nest and carried the others in my backpack over the course of several days."

A cold shudder ran through Greer at the mental image of Red trudging through the woods, hauling a bag of bones. But she had to push forward. These families deserved answers. "Tell me about Erin."

"Erin was supposed to be the last. Three victims make a serial killer. Once people noticed the wind chimes, I figured it was game over. I'd never find another pair in this town."

"Why did you choose Erin?" she pressed.

"Her father and I went to school together. Arthur was insufferable— a real one-upper. The apple didn't fall far from the tree. Erin always had to outshine Hayes—every science fair, debate tournament, math competition. Whenever Hayes took second, she swiped first."

"So you were jealous she was smarter than your son?"

"Erin wasn't smarter! She had her dad's name. She loaded up on honors classes just to snatch scholarships and the chance to be valedictorian from Hayes."

Greer let out a sharp laugh. "Yet Hayes still wasn't valedictorian."

Red's voice rose. "It was close, dammit—a hundredth of a point difference."

"No wonder Hayes always expects to win. You always made sure he did whatever the cost."

Red's gaze darkened. "Hayes never asked me to do anything. Don't drag him into this."

The clock above the TV ticked. Hayes would wake up soon. "So you killed Erin, took a memento . . ."

"A Rubik's Cube." Red grinned. "Hayes started competing in seventh grade, but guess who always beat him?" He waved dismissively. "Doesn't matter. Everything was perfect. If I'd stopped, it would've stayed that way."

"So why didn't you? Why Wendy?"

"Wendy was a nice girl, but she was after my son. It was harmless flirting at first."

"Until what?" Greer asked.

"She hadn't been over since finishing the competition, but one night at the end of June, she showed up, apparently with a bottle of whiskey in her backpack," Red explained. "Hayes seemed surprised, like he didn't know what to do with her now that they weren't doing sciencey shit. He asked me if they could play Nintendo in the brig. About an hour later, I went outside and peeked through the open window. Let's just say what they were playing didn't look like Nintendo."

"They had sex?"

"Just about. They were both sloppy drunk, sloppy kissing. Hayes said he needed to sneak into his room to get a condom. She tried to stop him. Tell me, Greer—what smart, college-bound young lady wouldn't want her one-night stand to wear protection?"

"Maybe one who's drunk. Or on birth control. Or afraid Hayes might back out if she gave him time to think."

Red scoffed. "More like one trying to trap him."

Greer shook her head, appalled. He was delusional.

"So you broke it up?" Greer asked, needing to know if Hayes really wouldn't have remembered what went down that night as he claimed.

"Didn't have to. He came to his senses and told her he loved Tilly. Wendy was embarrassed, apologized, and left. She was drunk—I shouldn't have let her drive, but some girls are reckless. Not my problem. Not my son's problem."

"But you couldn't let it go?"

"That bitch tried to ruin my son's future," Red said coldly. "The problem was, Wendy fought like hell when I tried to give her what she'd been after from my son that night in the brig. It got messy—there was blood everywhere. I knew they'd follow it to the bower. I needed a scapegoat, and fast."

"Wait. Are you saying you hadn't planned who would take the fall from the start?" Greer asked.

"Ollie Ford was the plan, but I realized I killed Nicole right after your brother came back. Keaton idolized me, so I knew he'd be easy to manipulate."

Greer's hand flew to her mouth, rage and disbelief rising. "So, hiring my brother—"

"Allowed me to collect fingerprints, hair, handwriting samples, and belongings to plant at the bower. Plus, it made it believable that I solved the case, with the 'killer' sharing an office with me three days a week."

"You were going to frame my brother. Do you know what that would've done to my family? To me?"

"Oh, come on, you never gave two craps about him. Hayes told me how he treated you growing up, and well . . ." Red lifted his hands to his neck. "One story in particular pissed me off."

The irony wasn't lost on Greer. Red hated the idea of Keaton's hands around her throat—yet had strangled his victims.

"But Tilly and Troy ruined everything," Red muttered. "I had just killed a girl standing in the way of Hayes and Tilly's future, only to find out that she was in bed with the boy Hayes loved like a brother. The boy I loved like a son. Imagine my humiliation."

"How did you know they slept together?" Greer gripped her locket. "Keaton told me he didn't know until my interview, so there's no way he told you. Did you hear me yelling at Hayes when I left?"

"No, I don't remember you yelling anything. The first clue was how tense you kids were. Troy and Tilly didn't show up at the brig, and you left. Troy pulled up later—smelling like chlorine and Chantilly Price's perfume. Wouldn't look me in the eye. I just knew."

"So you went to kill her?"

"I went to *talk* to her. I told her I knew she cheated, but that Hayes had bought a ring and would be devastated. I promised to stay quiet—as long as she happily accepted my son's proposal."

Greer's phone rang: *Hayes*. She silenced it. He was awake. They had to hurry. "And what did Tilly say?"

"That she was breaking up with Hayes. That she didn't love him anymore. Apologized for cheating but said she loved Keaton and needed to fix things with him."

Greer had assumed Tilly and Keaton just had a fling. But now it seemed they might have really loved each other. She blinked, the room tilting for a second as the thought rewired itself.

"I told her she was drunk. That she was confusing Troy and Keaton. I turned to leave and told her we'd talk when she sobered up. But she followed me, saying sleeping with Troy that night was a mistake—what she had with Keaton wasn't." Red's voice tightened. "My son's girlfriend was about to leave him for some batshit crazy college dropout. I didn't just feel rage. I became it."

"She grabbed me." Red clutched his shoulder as if still feeling her grip.

Tears filled Greer's eyes. If only Tilly had let him leave. She heard the shower running in the master bathroom. Time was running out. "Then what?"

"Tilly begged me to listen, but when she saw the anger in my eyes, she backed into the hallway. She was talking, but I couldn't comprehend a word. I pulled the phone cord out of the wall and chased her into her room."

"Wait." Greer held up a trembling hand, tears streaming. She wasn't sure she could handle the details.

"It's not like you're thinking, Greer. I only strangled her, and it was over so quickly. She barely suffered."

"Then I showed up?" Greer asked, voice trembling.

"Not yet. Since I hadn't worn gloves, I went to wipe down everything I'd touched. That's when I found the positive pregnancy test in her trash. I knew the cops would assume her boyfriend had killed her—panicked over a baby."

"Wait." Greer's voice wavered. "She told my brother the test was negative."

Red shrugged. "I know what I saw."

"But the autopsy—"

"Missed it. Only me and Chantilly knew. I tied the trash bag just as I heard a car door slam outside."

Guilt suffocated Greer. If she'd only been a few minutes earlier.

"I grabbed the bag and Tilly's charm bracelet and left out the back," Red continued. "Didn't have my bones, but I had the test. I had enough to save my son."

Greer shivered. He'd left through the same door she'd entered. If their paths had crossed . . .

"I wrestled with whether I should go through with my original plan or have Troy take the fall," Red said, his voice low. "They'd both tried to ruin my son's future. If I'd known Keaton had been there that night, maybe he'd be the one awaiting the needle. But at the time, I thought Troy was the last to see Chantilly alive. They'd slept together, and in a town like Bluesummer, no one would've believed it was consensual. I decided that when I fed Wendy to his hogs this time, I wouldn't bother shaving her head or pulling her teeth first—and I wouldn't bother cleaning up the mess the hogs left in their manure. Then, when Troy's class ring showed up in the mail, I knew it was fate. Took it to the bower and planted Wendy's blood on it and inside his truck."

"And you had Wendy's blood from the science—"

"I had blood from *all* my victims," Red interrupted. "Dismembering is messy. I didn't get that far with Wendy since they found her body so quickly—but her scalp wounds bled a lot."

Greer stiffened as the shower turned off. "I have to go."

She stepped toward the door, then paused. "Did anyone else know? Jo, or . . ." Her throat tightened. "Hayes?"

"No." Red didn't hesitate. "They had no idea."

Some of the weight in Greer's chest loosened. "I want to believe you, but . . ."

"But what?" His voice sharpened. "I've told you everything. Why would I lie about this?"

A tear slipped down her cheek. "Why did you tell me? You can't think I'll let you go free."

"No, you'll turn me in. I want you to."

"But why?"

Red held her gaze. "What did I always tell you? The story is everything. This is a hell of a good one."

"Bullshit." She glared. "You wouldn't destroy your legacy for me."

"Look, I didn't plan to confess. But the DNA from Wendy's sample—when the cops see Hayes isn't a match, they'll figure it out. I'm giving you time to beat those sons of bitches to it."

"They'll come for you."

"Of course. They'll make a spectacle of it. But what are they going to do? Execute a dying man?" He picked up a small, bloody handkerchief as if it were a prop. "Doubt I'll make it to trial."

Greer's stomach twisted. "That's not what I'm worried about. I'm worried about Jo and Hayes. You need to tell them."

"Give me today with them. One last Christmas. I'll come clean tomorrow."

Her pulse hammered. Everything he'd done, everything he was—Hayes and Jo would never recover.

She stared at the floor, heart heavy. "Okay."

Red's voice softened. "I'm sorry for the pain I've caused you. For what this will do to them. But if anyone can understand why I did it—why I needed the story—it's you."

"I don't understand. I'll NEVER understand."

Red frowned. "Well, regardless, just know I love you. Always have."

She reached for the doorknob, then turned back for one last look at the man she thought she knew—the man who had shattered five families and was about to destroy his own.

There was nothing left to say.

With a steady breath, she twisted the knob, stepped into the dark, and shut the door behind her for good.

# CHAPTER 44

Keaton was awake when Greer returned, but didn't ask where she'd been, only what she wanted for breakfast. Sitting at her old desk, the one where she'd written countless high school newspaper articles, she began downloading her conversation with Red and started typing.

She wasn't focused on details yet—those would come later, and the police would request she withhold certain ones, anyway. Though not legally bound, she would . . . for now. This was about rawness: the shock of finding her best friend's body, the guilt of betraying Troy, and the horror of learning a monster lived under her roof. The reminder that some monsters wore badges, held gavels, and hid behind justice. Hardest of all, admitting that a monster lived inside her, ignoring the truth for all these years.

The past couldn't be undone—not by her, the state, or the public screaming for blood. But they had to try to be better, to mend the fractures that let this happen.

"Sure you don't want to talk about it?" Keaton set coffee on the desk.

"Not yet." Greer didn't look up from her screen. Talking sometimes helped, but writing *always* did.

Her phone lit up. There were a few missed calls and one message from Hayes: *Are you coming home? It's Christmas.*

She wouldn't be going home today, and there was no way to explain to Hayes that she was giving them one last quiet Christmas with Red. The girls might come after all, knowing their failure of a mother wouldn't be there. She turned her phone face down and kept typing until the doorbell rang.

*Hayes. Shit.* She stepped into the hallway as Keaton checked the peephole.

"Tell him I'm asleep," she whispered.

"It's not Hayes," Keaton said, turning from the door. "It's Quinn."

Her breath caught. "Okay. Answer it."

Quinn hugged her uncle quickly as she stepped inside. "Sorry to bother you, but Dad said Mom might be here." Her eyes met Greer's briefly before darting away.

"No bother at all." Keaton took her coat. "Coffee?"

"Black, thanks."

Once Keaton disappeared, Greer watched her daughter unwrap a wool scarf and drape it over the couch. She wore dark jeans, brown boots, and a silver top that caught the light—she looked so grown-up, so elegant.

"I tried calling."

"Oh. Sorry." Greer glanced outside. "Farren and Si still at Zach's?"

"No, we came back." Quinn took the coffee Keaton handed her. "Si's napping, but I know he'd love to see you when he wakes up. Maybe get his firetruck." Quinn sat on the couch, slow and deliberate.

Greer hesitated, then joined her. Quinn tucked her legs beneath her, fingers wrapped tightly around her coffee. A sudden ache hit Greer—this should've been familiar. These moments, these quiet talks between mother and daughter, should've filled a lifetime. But not a single one came to mind.

"I need to apologize," Quinn whispered.

Greer shook her head. "You have the right to feel however you want about your childhood. I wasn't the best mom. I did abandon you."

"But you didn't," Quinn said. "You took the time you needed." She sipped her coffee. "Dad called last night. Told me about his affair."

Greer's heart sank. She never imagined Hayes would step off the pedestal his daughters had placed him on.

"I feel awful, Mom. I can't believe we never knew."

"You didn't need to," Greer said. "What good would it have done?"

"A lot." Quinn's features softened. "I spent my whole life wondering why you left when I should've been wondering why you came back."

"I loved him, honey. Since we were kids, I have loved him. Tried to stop. I couldn't. Still can't."

Quinn shook her head. "I'm so pissed at him. Didn't sleep at all. I didn't want to come home, but Farren begged. I haven't told her about Dad yet."

"Don't." Greer touched her daughter's knee. "And don't transfer your anger to him. We both made mistakes. You'll make yours, too. You're a better mom than I was, but you'll still have regrets."

"But I missed out on a relationship with you because I focused on what you did wrong instead of what you did right," Quinn said, her shoulders hunched.

"And I missed out because I couldn't get past Caleb's death," Greer admitted, letting out a shaky breath. "I'm sorry."

Quinn wiped a tear away. "It's like we lived together for eighteen years and don't know each other."

"Well, it's not too late. We should meet every week for coffee. Dad's retiring next month. He can watch Si."

"I'd like that." Quinn smiled, then turned serious. "But for today, will you come home? It's Grandpa's last Christmas."

Greer squeezed her eyes shut. She could fake a lot, but not her way through today. "Earlier, you said you understood why I needed time after Dad cheated?"

"Yeah."

"Well, it's the same now. I mean, Dad didn't do anything wrong," she said, praying that was true. "But I need time again. Just today. Bring Farren by in the morning before taking her to the airport."

"But Si?" Quinn's voice tightened.

"Take lots of pictures. Dad can set up the firetruck. Tell Si I need to stay with Uncle Keat, but he can FaceTime me later if he wants."

Quinn crossed her arms. "Mom, I don't understand."

Greer wanted to say she'd understand tomorrow, but instead, she wrapped her arms around her daughter. After a day like today, it was exactly what she needed.

# CHAPTER 45

Red Sheridan was the Songbird Strangler. Joaquin couldn't wrap his head around it, even after seeing the picture the night before and learning Red had confessed. He'd planned to call Greer to discuss the picture that pointed to either Red or Hayes. Instead, he woke to her call. Red confessed. Greer recorded it. Would he go with her to the police station?

Would he ever. He'd said a quick goodbye to his parents and was on his way to Bluesummer.

Joaquin tapped the steering wheel, mapping out the day. He'd meet Greer, Luca, and Melrose at the police station and probably be there all morning. Then he'd go to the office to call DA Hench. A confession and familial DNA should be enough to vacate the conviction. Next, he'd call his parents, Bernie, and the Director of DPAP. Maybe he could squeeze in a visit to Troy in prison, possibly the last one. DPAP would push for release; the media would apply pressure. His blue Hugo Boss suit needed dry cleaning—he'd wear it the day he walked out of prison with his client. And he'd need to write a speech.

Bluesummer appeared ahead.

The roads were empty. Snow from yesterday's flurry piled along the streets. Holiday decorations clung to lampposts—wreaths, red bows, silver bells, and flickering lights. As the station neared, his breath fogged the window. Each turn felt like a countdown. This case was almost over. Really over.

The parking lot sat nearly empty when he arrived. Leaning back, he stared at the dashboard, thoughts consumed by all the sleepless nights, paperwork, close calls, and setbacks. The biggest case of his career had pushed him to the limit. An innocent man almost died, and he'd helped stop it. The enormity hit, and tears came, shoulders shaking as pent-up emotion broke free.

A soft knock on the passenger window jolted him. He blinked away tears. Melrose stood outside.

His face, ears, and neck grew warm. How long had she been standing there, witnessing this emotional meltdown?

"You okay?" Melrose asked, climbing into the passenger seat.

"Yeah, sorry." He focused on the dashboard.

"Nothing to be sorry for. This is a lot."

"Not sure what's wrong with me. Went from bubbling with excitement to blubbering like a baby."

Melrose placed a hand on his arm. "All normal. This case has pushed us all to the limit."

"More so for you," Joaquin noted, seeing the tiredness in her eyes and the rash spreading across her cheeks. "Time to focus on your health."

"So you're firing me?" Melrose grinned.

Joaquin sighed. Not seeing her every day would be the hardest part of this case ending. DPAP would stop paying her salary. His business needed to stabilize. "Yeah, I guess I have to, but—"

"Thank God!" she interrupted, grabbing his collar and pulling him into a kiss. Joaquin froze only for a moment. Shock quickly melted into certainty as he tangled his fingers in her hair, drawing her closer and deepening the kiss. Every second of waiting, every doubt, ended here.

Greer left the police station and headed to her mom's house to say goodbye to Keaton before he returned home. She hadn't told him what was coming later today if the judge signed the warrant as expected. She almost had last night, but decided to enjoy Christmas with her brother. They had cooked frozen pizzas, made sundaes, and watched movies until they fell asleep in the living room.

She'd have to call him tomorrow, along with a dozen others.

Had Red kept his promise to tell Hayes and Jo? Doubtful—Hayes hadn't texted all day. She dreaded breaking the news, but had prepared herself—no more hiding.

Just as Keaton drove off, her phone rang: *Hayes.*

"Hello?"

"Dad told us." Hayes's voice shook.

Greer gripped the phone tighter, wishing she could reach through it and comfort him. "I'm so sorry."

"Are you leaving me, Greer?"

"No," she blurted, then hesitated. "Unless you haven't been honest with me."

"I didn't know," he choked out. "I swear to God, Greer. Please come home."

She clicked her key fob. "On my way."

Joanne clutched her chest. "You already went to the police?"

"Yes, this morning," Greer replied, her gaze fixed on the kitchen table, noticing the crumbs scattered across it. Crumbs from the last normal breakfast Hayes and Joanne would ever have.

"You've ruined us!" Joanne shrieked.

Hayes stopped pacing and placed a hand on Greer's shoulder. "She had to, Mom. They were going to kill an innocent man."

"Maybe it's the drugs," Joanne muttered, dabbing her nose. "Sometimes he says the darndest things."

"It's not the medication, Mom." Hayes's voice hardened. "Dad lied to us. He's a killer."

"He's your father!" Joanne snapped. "The man who taught you multiplication, the value of hard work, how to be a good man."

"He's the man who killed five girls." Hayes turned and slammed a fist on the counter. "He killed my girlfriend."

"He's both," Greer said. "And that's what makes this so hard."

"What now?" Joanne whispered. "Will they arrest him or—"

"Today, most likely." Greer stood. "If you haven't called your lawyer, you should. He can arrange for Red to turn himself in."

Joanne gasped, clutching her collar.

Hayes pulled out his phone. "I'll call Rick."

"Don't bother!" Joanne stormed toward Red's room. "Let me handle it."

Hayes collapsed into a kitchen chair. "This is like a bad dream."

Greer stepped around the island, kneeling slightly to reach for his hand. "I'm sorry I wasn't here yesterday. I promised Red I'd give you all one last Christmas. I couldn't fake it."

"He explained." Hayes squeezed her hand. "He also mentioned your story."

Greer looked away. "It's going to come out, Hayes. We can't stop it."

"But this is personal. Our family."

"I'm writing it. I already have."

"Without talking to me?"

Greer sighed. "I don't expect you to understand, but I ask you to support me."

He snatched his hand away. "You're right. I don't understand you, Greer."

She stood. "And you never could. Not really."

Greer woke to her alarm. It was time for Red's medication. But that responsibility now lay with the medical staff at Bluesummer Jail. He'd been booked last night and would face a judge on Monday.

Her back ached from the couch, but it felt easier than sleeping next to Hayes. She'd stayed up late, working on final edits to her story. Today, she'd send it to her ex-boyfriend, Tate Adams, at the *Dallas Morning News*. Most people would expect her to give the scoop to her former employer, the *Tyler Tribune*, but Tate had been so good to her, and she'd hurt him when she left him for Hayes. She wondered how different her life might be if she hadn't gone to the Sheridans' 1989 New Year's party.

Greer paused at the back door, her gaze flicking toward the open storage unit door. She knew she hadn't left it that way. She went to investigate and was startled to find her mother-in-law rummaging through a box. "Jo? What are you doing?"

"Looking for my recipe box." Joanne moved a few items aside.

"At 5 a.m.?" Greer asked.

"I thought I'd make my granny's famous cinnamon rolls. I can't just sit in my room all day."

Sympathy washed over Greer. Poor Jo. She cupped her mother-in-law's shoulder. "Go on inside. I'll find it."

Joanne nodded, wiping away a tear. "It's brown with—"

"I've seen it," Greer reassured her.

Joanne broke into tears. "What am I going to do, Greer?"

Uncertain how to respond, Greer wrapped her arms around Joanne and let her cry.

Cinnamon rolls would have to wait. An hour had passed, and Greer still hadn't found the damn recipe box. *Just one more box*, she told herself, pulling down an unlabeled box from the top shelf. Dust rained down, making her sneeze.

Inside were trophies and medals from Hayes's glory days—first place, Academic Decathlon 1985; third place, Track and Field Long Jump 1982; second place, Art Fair 1980. Greer held the Science Olympiad first-place medal, staring at it as it spun in her fingers. Her thoughts drifted to Wendy Knott and the blood vials in Hayes's fridge. Red had claimed he had all the victims' blood, but why only plant Wendy's in Troy's truck and on the ring? DNA wasn't what it is now, but they'd know the girls' blood types. Planting all of it would've been smarter—and just as easy. She placed the medal back. Red must have run out of time. She'd probably never know.

Greer walked back into her office and stopped short, seeing Hayes sitting at her desk. "What are you doing?" she asked.

Hayes swiveled around. "Reading your article. Well, the section you are emailing *Tate*, anyway." He practically spat out her ex's name.

"Yeah, I need to click send," Greer said, stepping closer. "So, if you'll excuse me . . ."

Hayes didn't move but spun back to her computer. Greer tensed as he grabbed the mouse. What did he think he was going to do? Delete it? The article was backed up to Google Docs. Rewriting the email would only take a few minutes.

"It's good," he whispered. "Really good writing."

Greer tightened her grip on her robe. "Thank you. Look, I know you don't want—"

Before she could finish, Hayes clicked send. The black "Sending" box blinked on her screen.

"Not like we can keep it quiet," Hayes said. "You got the confession. It's your story to tell."

Greer placed her hands on his shoulders. Hayes slumped in the chair, his body trembling. She stayed, watching the screen until the "Undo sent message" option disappeared.

There was no turning back now.

# CHAPTER 46

Inmates cheered and banged on their cells as Joaquin waited for Troy. Even a guard clapped along.

Troy reached him and threw his arms around Joaquin. The sheer size and strength caught Joaquin off guard—something he hadn't fully grasped through the glass. He was not a hugger himself; he didn't pull away. This was Troy's first physical contact in decades.

Joaquin grabbed the clothes from the chair and handed them to Troy. "Brought you these."

Troy glanced at the door. "A lot of people out there?"

"Yes. The public and the media are behind a barrier. But Melrose, Luca, Greer, my assistant Bernie, and your cousin Vic are on the steps. I'll give a short statement, then it's up to you if you want to speak."

Joaquin exhaled. This was happening. Troy was free. The judge had granted the joint motion, apologizing on behalf of the State of Texas. It was not enough, but more than most innocent men got. The next step was securing an affidavit of innocence for a settlement.

When Troy reappeared in a charcoal suit, Joaquin clapped his back. "Ready to get the hell outta here?"

"Am I ever."

As Troy smoothed his suit jacket, the door cracked open. Greer slipped inside and took Troy's hand. "Told you I'd walk you out here." She smiled.

Joaquin nudged the door open, sunlight flooding in as the crowd cheered. Hand in hand, Troy and Greer stepped forward.

Joaquin doubted Red Sheridan would ever see justice. He'd lived out most of his days—days Troy could never reclaim. Red was dying, and justice moved slowly, but Joaquin didn't dwell on that. He'd done his job. Troy Terrell was officially free.

Joaquin approached the microphone and pulled a paper from his pocket. He had dreamed of this moment all his life—a major victory, a vast crowd, a rousing speech. But suddenly, the spotlight seemed unimportant. Folding the paper away, he said, "I had a speech prepared, but I just want to say thank you to everyone who supported Troy Terrell—not just those behind me, but those watching from home. If you want to help save others like him, contact DPAP and get involved."

The cheers seemed endless as Troy approached the mic. Joaquin knew some in this crowd had called for Troy's execution in 1986. He hoped they'd learned something along the way.

Troy began. "There are so many to thank for this blessing of fresh air. My late parents believed in my innocence and spent every cent proving it. The Death Penalty Abolition Project supplied the legal team behind me. Melrose Reed got them to take my case, and Joaquin Ramos promised he'd get me out. It's the first promise anyone's kept to me in a long time." He cleared his throat. "As grateful as I am, I'm angry too. Lawyers and nonprofits shouldn't have to solve cases"—he glanced at Greer—"nor should journalists. Detectives should. Make no mistake: the system didn't work in this case. My team did." He let the crowd cheer before continuing. "I'm looking forward to the rest of my life with my family"— he nodded at Vic—"and my friends, who are like family." He smiled at Greer. "Thank you."

Applause roared. Questions flew. "Troy will address inquiries later," Joaquin said. "For now, we kindly ask you to respect his privacy as he enjoys his first cheeseburger in thirty-eight years."

Troy wanted Whataburger for his first meal as a free man, but they didn't offer private space, and Joaquin worried the media might show up. So instead, he held Melrose's hand as they stepped into Grill and Chill Burgers, where a back room had been reserved. Eyes followed them as Joaquin pulled out Melrose's chair.

"Called it!" Bernie shook her head. "What've I been telling you about those two?"

"How Marcia Clark and Chris Darden of you," Luca murmured in Joaquin's ear.

Heat crept up Joaquin's cheeks. He needed to steer the conversation to safer ground. "So, which burger is it gonna be, Troy?" he asked.

"The Mega Melt." Troy pointed to the biggest burger on the menu. "In prison, I only dreamed of four things—freedom, a passport, Vanessa Williams, and a greasy cheeseburger."

"That sounds good," Luca said, closing his menu.

Bernie peered over her glasses. "So, what's next for Luca Moretti?"

"Already on to the next case," he said.

"And you, Melrose?" Bernie propped her chin on her elbow. "Should I be adding your name to the payroll? Or maybe next of kin on Joaquin's emergency contact sheet?"

Melrose laughed. "I actually got hired by a local immigration attorney."

Bernie raised an eyebrow. "Ought to be a busy four years for you."

"No doubt. But I hope to help DPAP with another case, too."

"Yep," Joaquin said with a small smile. "On to do important work while I get back to the usual cases."

"It's all important work," Troy's cousin said. "But does this mean you won't take another death penalty case?"

"Not for a while. A *long* while."

"Well, that's damn good news. Someone's gotta pay the bills," Bernie said.

"About that . . ." Joaquin exchanged a smile with Melrose. "If you see a big charge from Qantas on the company card, it's legit."

"He used all his airline points," Melrose cut in before Bernie could protest. "And the rest is a Christmas gift from my parents. They'll send a reimbursement check."

Bernie arched a brow. "Heading to Vegas?"

"Australia, mate," Joaquin said, his accent still rough around the edges. "We leave in two weeks."

"A nice way to beat the winter," Troy said.

"A nice way to get to know each other better," Luca added with a smirk.

Melrose sipped her water. "This trip isn't about that."

"Oh yeah? Two tickets to paradise aren't what they seem?" Luca asked.

"Three tickets." Melrose smiled at Joaquin. "Ollie Ford is finally going to see the beach."

Greer bit into a stale peanut butter sandwich and instantly regretted not joining Troy and his team for lunch. She'd thought it important to return home to Hayes, but when she found him passed out in bed, she decided not to wake him. He hadn't had real sleep in days, not since his father's confession.

She wiped crumbs off the counter with a damp towel. The house felt neglected; cleaning hadn't been a priority, and the rotting smell from the trash caught her attention. She tossed the rest of her sandwich into the bin. She needed to clean. She needed to find Jo's recipe box. She'd been asking about it daily. Maybe Greer would find it and surprise her with those cinnamon rolls she hadn't stopped talking about.

Greer pulled the cord inside the shed, and the light flickered on. The police had ransacked the room two days before. She didn't understand why they'd taken boxes from Red's office when they already had a confession, but Troy's lawyer said it was standard procedure to gather corroborating evidence.

Unsure if Joanne's recipes were still in one of those boxes or had been moved elsewhere, Greer moved to the far side of the shed and scanned the boxes. There were no more labeled "kitchen." Sighing, she grabbed the first box marked "linens." Expecting sheets, she found Joanne's kitchen curtains instead. Hope rose as she dug through tablecloths until a hard object caught her hand—the recipe box. Triumph filled her—one item off the ever-growing to-do list.

She carried the box inside and opened the weathered lid, revealing yellowed index cards, neatly organized. She could almost smell vanilla and cinnamon from past baking sessions. Flipping through the recipes, her fingers stopped on a folded piece of stationery. Puzzled, she unfolded it to find an old Polaroid photograph, its edges as yellowed as the cards around it.

Greer froze. Why would Joanne have a photo of blood vials? Leaning in closer, Greer saw names on them carefully typed with an old label maker—the same kind Red used to mark the titles of the movies he recorded off television.

Her breath caught as she read the names—names she had become horrifyingly familiar with: Nicole, Andrea, Erin, and Wendy.

Joanne slid on her glasses, glanced at the photo Greer held, then looked away. "I have no idea what this is. Red must have put it there."

"Don't lie to me!" Greer snapped.

Joanne set her glasses on the bedside table. "Honestly, Greer, that wasn't there the last time I used it."

"So you weren't desperate to find this box before the cops for a reason?"

Joanne's chin trembled. "I didn't know it was him."

"Until when?" Greer crossed her arms. "You didn't know Red was the Strangler until—"

Joanne's voice faltered. "I saw him leave the night Chantilly was killed. Thought I'd caught Hayes sneaking out. But it was Redman."

Greer's knees buckled. She sat on the edge of the bed. "And then?"

"I went to bed." Joanne's voice broke. "If I'd known where he was going, I would've called the police. But I just assumed he was having an affair."

"Did you confront him?"

"Didn't get the chance. We woke up to the news about Chantilly. Red was at the station with you kids. I was losing my mind alone in that house, so I just started cleaning. When I finished, I did something I never had—I cleaned the brig."

Greer's mind raced. "The blood was in Red's fridge?"

"The freezer." Joanne's voice dropped. "Inside an open bag of frozen vegetables that I was about to toss. I laid them out on the bar and waited all day for Red to come home."

"You weren't scared?" Greer asked.

"I was too angry to be afraid."

"He admitted it all?"

Joanne nodded. "It got heated. I shattered the vials on the floor."

"Then how did he plant Wendy's blood in Troy's truck and inside the ring?"

"I honestly don't know. I just assumed he'd gone back to the bower. Wendy's body was still there."

*Maybe*, Greer thought. Or maybe he had used the vial from Hayes's freezer. It would explain why he used only Wendy's blood to set up Troy. Thanks to Jo, it's all he had.

"Okay, so you obviously took this picture before you confronted him?" Greer asked.

Joanne swallowed. "In case I ever needed it."

"Then why didn't you go to the police?"

Joanne's gaze dropped. "I don't expect you to understand, but he did it for us."

Greer stood. "Come on, Jo. He did it for a book deal. Because he's a sick—"

"We were out of money!" Joanne cut in. "The house was on the line. Hayes's college fund was gone."

Greer took a step closer. "What?"

Tears streaked Joanne's face. "We'd burned through my parents' inheritance. Red hadn't sold a book in years. That advance saved our family."

Greer grabbed a fistful of hair. "So you were okay with all this because you needed money?"

Joanne leaned back against her pillows, clutching the quilt. "Of course not! But in his mind, those girls were a threat. They were trying to hurt Hayes—to tear our family apart."

"Enough." Greer's hand shot up. "There's no excuse. You not seeing that—well, that's terrifying."

"I told him I had proof and that I'd turn him in if he did it again," Joanne said.

"God, Jo, you're lucky he didn't kill *you*."

"He never looked for the photo," Joanne whispered. "Never touched another girl. Don't you see, Greer? I stopped him."

Greer turned toward the door. "I can't listen to this."

Joanne's voice cracked. "He might have killed more . . . if I hadn't stopped him."

Greer whipped around, pulse hammering. "Did Hayes know?"

"No." Joanne shook her head wildly. "I swear, he knew nothing. And because you love him, I trust you'll keep it that way."

"A little late for that."

"I mean about me," Joanne pleaded. "It would destroy him. Get rid of that picture. Let it go. I'm not a murderer. I'm a good person. I only ever wanted what was best for my boy. You understand, don't you?"

"No," Greer said coldly. "Not even a little."

Greer woke disoriented, cocooned in the fuzzy warmth of a blanket on the couch. Blinking, she took in her surroundings—the dimming light through the French doors, dusk stretching long shadows across the floor. The day's events sharpened: Troy's release, the unsettling photo, and Joanne's chilling confession. She had planned to wait for Hayes to wake, but somewhere along the way, she had drifted off too. She settled deeper under the blanket, fighting the pull of sleep. Just as she teetered on the edge of dreams, Hayes's frantic voice sliced through the quiet. "Greer! Come here, Greer. Something's wrong with Mom!"

# EPILOGUE

Packing tape frayed and tore as Greer sealed the box. In three weeks, they would hand over their keys to the new owners.

Leaving the home Hayes built—where their children grew up—was bittersweet. Cherished memories mixed with painful ones, like Joanne's overdose—the final straw for Hayes.

"We've gotta get out of here," he'd said, staring into his parents' empty rooms days after the funeral. Though Hayes resisted accepting it, Joanne's death was ruled a suicide.

She'd swallowed a handful of Red's morphine pills. Only Greer knew the full reason: Joanne couldn't bear her secret coming out. Concerned about appearances till the end.

"One final victim of Red Sheridan," Hayes said as they lowered Joanne's coffin.

*Yeah*, Greer had thought. *Something like that.*

Whenever sadness about the move crept in, she reminded herself of the fresh start ahead. Hayes was already excited about retirement, planning for chickens, goats, and a few dairy cows. He deserved the farm he'd always dreamed of. He deserved peace.

The detached apartment offered possibilities—a future home for Greer's mother or, for now, her new studio. Hayes designed graphics for her podcast, *The Justice Divide*, which would launch next month with an exclusive interview with Troy Terrell. The national media buzz made a strong debut virtually inevitable.

Troy was living in Carthage with his cousin, but he was coming over today. It would be his first time seeing Hayes since his arrest. Anticipation tightened Greer's chest, but the time felt right.

Besides grieving his parents, Hayes mourned the baby Tilly might have been carrying. Was that why she'd seemed distracted, he wondered, setting aside the fact she'd been cheating with Greer's brother. "I'd have married her," he'd said one night. "We could have figured it out."

Greer wondered if he realized that with that fantasy, he was wishing away the life he had made with her. But she understood there was something pure—untouchable—about the dream of what might have been.

Keaton clung to his own fantasy, insisting the baby was his. "The second line must've appeared after I left. I would've taken care of the bay, taken care of her."

They'd never know, and Greer figured that was for the best.

"Dad's pleading guilty," Hayes said, lifting the box Greer finished taping.

"I figured he'd want to avoid a trial," Greer said.

Hayes set the box with the others in the entryway and returned to Greer. "He wants to see me, but I'm not ready. I'm not sure I'll ever be."

"I'll support whatever you decide."

Hayes knelt and kissed Greer. "You're the best thing that ever happened to me."

A knock at the door interrupted the moment.

"Should I get it?" Hayes asked, rising to his feet.

Greer stood and brushed off her jeans. "If you're ready."

Greer stood behind Hayes as he opened the door. Troy stood there, with a case of beer tucked under his arm.

"Hey," Hayes said, extending his hand. Troy ignored it, pulling him into a hug instead.

"Damn, it's good to see you," Troy said, his voice full of genuine happiness.

"I'm sorry, Troy," Hayes said.

Troy stepped back. "For what? Not inviting me to dinner since Reagan was in the White House?"

Hayes exhaled. "Seriously, Troy."

"I'm serious too. The last time we sat down together properly was on your parents' back porch—G ruining our appetite talking about Ted Bundy."

Greer thought back to that night—four kids who thought they knew everything but had no idea what lay ahead—no idea who sat at the table with them.

"So, can I come in?" Troy asked, lifting the beer. "We've got some catching up to do."

After a long night of drinking and talking, Troy woke up on Sheridan's couch. Even after six weeks out, his body still ran on prison time— sleeping past four proved impossible. An early-morning drive was the only solution.

Though relieved to be free, facing the truth was a blow. He had to accept that the man he'd loved like a father not only falsely accused him but set him up. Worse yet, he killed Tilly. The same man who'd bought him cleats, helped with barn chores, and wrote a college recommendation letter turned out to be a monster.

But Troy couldn't dwell on that. He was free. He'd applied for a passport. Once the state compensated him for wrongful imprisonment, he'd visit all the places from his prison maps.

For now, there was somewhere he needed to go in Bluesummer.

A wave of nostalgia hit as he drove past his old school. He could almost hear the crowd cheering his name as he sprinted into the end zone, ball in hand.

He passed the cemetery. Later, he'd leave flowers on his parents' graves—Tilly's too. Then, he'd circle the lake, fire off some Roman candles, and hit the Whataburger drive-thru.

But first, the most important stop.

He slowed at the driveway of the only real home he'd ever known. The house was worse than he had imagined—weather-beaten and nearly swallowed by overgrown weeds. Every window was boarded, and the patched roof sagged. Greer had warned him that it was condemned and set to be demolished soon. The new owners of Red and Joanne's former house didn't want the eyesore distracting from their perfectly manicured lawn.

His mother's words echoed: *The grass ain't always greener.*

He hadn't understood then. Now he did. On that seemingly greener grass lived a man with two faces—a serial killer who left his writing shed to commit unspeakable acts.

It was all a facade: a house of cards, a nest of bones.

Tears stung as he trudged past rusted farm equipment, his knees throbbing with each step. At the woods' edge, the scent of damp earth and wet bark filled his lungs, and for a moment, he felt young again— renewed. The spongy ground sank beneath him as if the woods were a time machine.

He smiled and began to run.

# ACKNOWLEDGMENTS

To my family—especially Jaleigh, Aidan, and Asa. You inspire me every single day. Jaleigh and Aidan, I blinked, and you grew into such thoughtful, wonderful adults—more than my heart ever hoped for. Asa, special thanks for this book's title. I'll never forget that trip (one of many) to the public library when you were four. We were sitting outside reading *Bone Dog* together when you looked up and saw a nest in the tree above us. You turned to me and said, "*The Bone Nest* would be a good name for a book." I tucked it away and saved it for the perfect story. This is it.

To Josh—thank you for waiting three books until one finally had your name on the dedication page. The truth is, every single one of them belongs to you in some way. I couldn't do this without you, and I wouldn't want to.

To my parents, who filled my childhood with stories. You put me to bed with books on tape before I could read a word on my own. I can still hear the chime that told me to turn the page. That small ritual gave me a lifelong love of reading, and eventually, the courage to tell stories of my own. For that, I owe you everything.

To my friends—thank you for keeping me sane, talking me off ledges, distracting me when I needed a break, and cheering me on as though every milestone were your own. I'm so lucky to have you in my corner.

To Maryssa Gordon, my developmental editor—thank you for your big-picture vision, thoughtful guidance, and unwavering belief in this story; to Ana Joldesx and Sarah Anderson, my line editors and proofreaders— thank you for your sharp eyes, precision, and care on the page that strengthened every sentence; to my cover artist, Aleksandra Mandic— thank you for creating such a hauntingly beautiful cover that perfectly captures the spirit of the story; to Stuart Wahlin—thank you for the incredible book trailers that bring my books to life in a whole new way; and to the publishers who have brought my stories to readers in print, electronic, and audio formats—thank you for giving my books wings.

To Brian Stolarz, lawyer extraordinaire—thank you for *Grace and Justice on Death Row*, which guided me through a death row case and modeled what it looks like to fight for justice with integrity and care. I thought the legal research for this book would be easy, given my own legal background, but I learned that death penalty cases are an entirely different animal. Thank you also for answering every legal question I had along the way. Any mistakes are my own.

To the Innocence Project—for your tireless work on behalf of the wrongfully convicted. Your dedication inspires and humbles me, and gave shape to this story.

To my author friends—thank you for every piece of advice, pep talk, and shared victory and disappointment. You've made the writing life richer and less lonely. This is the best community to be part of (right next to Swifties). And to every author whose words light the path ahead—thank you you for inspiring me to keep going.

To the librarians across our country who stand on the front lines against book bans: your courage, dedication, and unwavering belief in the power of stories ensure that readers of every age can discover, question, and imagine. You fight not just for books, but for ideas, knowledge, and the freedom to explore the world through words.

To the readers—those who read, raved, reviewed, and reached out. You keep these stories alive. Knowing they matter to you makes every long night at the desk worthwhile.

To everyone who champions justice, truth, and the power of story—thank you for giving this book meaning, and for reminding us that even in the darkest places, hope and courage can prevail.

# ALSO BY SHANESSA GLUHM

*A River of Crows*

In 1988, Sloan Hadfield's brother Ridge went fishing with their father and never came home. Their father, a good-natured Vietnam veteran prone to violent outbursts, was arrested and charged with murder. Ridge's body was never recovered, and Sloan's mother—a brilliant ornithologist— slowly descended into madness, insisting her son was still alive.

Now, twenty years later, Sloan's life is unraveling. In the middle of a bitter divorce, she's forced to return to her rural Texas hometown when her mother is discharged from a mental health facility.

Overwhelmed by memories and unanswered questions, Sloan returns to the last place her brother was seen all those years ago: Crow's Nest Creek. There, she is shocked to hear a crow murmuring the same syllable over and over: *Ridge, Ridge, Ridge.*

When the body of another boy is found, Sloan begins to question what really happened to her brother all those years ago. What she discovers will shock her small community and turn her family upside down.

## Enemies of Doves

On a summer night in 1932, twelve-year-old Joel Fitchett wanders into an East Texas diner badly beaten and carrying his unconscious brother, Clancy. Though both boys claim they have no memory of what happened, the horrific details are etched into their minds as deep as the scar left across Joel's face. Thirteen years later, both men still struggle with the aftershocks of that long-ago night and the pact they made to hide the truth. When they find themselves at the center of a murder investigation, they make a decision that will change everything. A second lie, a second pact, and for a time, a second chance.

In 1991, college student Garrison Stark travels to Texas chasing a rumor that Clancy Fitchett is his biological grandfather. Clancy has been missing since 1946, and Garrison hopes to find him, and in doing so, find a family. What he doesn't expect to discover is a tangle of secrets spanning sixty years involving Clancy, Joel, and the woman they both loved, Lorraine.

# ABOUT THE AUTHOR

Shanessa Gluhm works as a librarian at an elementary school in New Mexico, where she lives with her husband and children. It was during her own elementary days that a teacher encouraged Shanessa to share a story she had written with the class. She hasn't stopped writing since.

Her debut novel, *Enemies of Doves*, was an IAN Book of the Year Finalist in the category of first novel, an NIEA Finalist for cross-genre fiction, and first place winner in the Chanticleer Clue Awards for mystery, suspense, and thriller fiction. Her second novel, *A River of Crows*, also won first place in the Chanticleer Clue Awards.

When Shanessa is not writing, she enjoys birdwatching, reading, and true crime podcasts.

*The Bone Nest* is her third novel.

9 798218 757670